Lost

M. Lathan

DEDICATION

To Mom
Sleep in peace as angels sing. My love, my everything.

CONTENTS

PROLOGUE

I understood why she wanted to kill me. I didn't belong here in the first place. The world would be better off without me in it. I closed my eyes, torn between wanting to escape and wanting it to be over. I should have been more prepared. I'd known for years what face I'd see in my final moments, but no power of mine could have predicted what would lead me here.

CHAPTER ONE

I woke up, pouring sweat, in Nathan's bed.

With his eyes closed and mouth open, he rolled away and yanked the blanket off of me, attending to my needs in his sleep. I shrugged off the creepy dream of me drowning. Over the last three months, I'd dreamed plenty of things that hadn't happened. Nate had held me underwater in the pool earlier. I was sure that moment had just followed me to sleep. The odds of it being a vision were low.

It had been almost two months since I stopped letting myself have them or use any of my powers. They were getting worse as I used them openly for little things. I would try to move something, and it wouldn't just lift. It would slam into the wall before I felt it moving. I didn't know mental powers could grow, develop even more than they already were. They were getting faster, stronger, and wilder, so I was back to suppressing them like I had at St. Catalina. Life was simpler that way, normal. Or as normal as living with three magical beings that should be extinct could get.

I closed my eyes to force myself back to sleep, and an angry snore rattled Nate's throat. I snatched my phone from the charger quickly. He wouldn't be able to deny this one. Another series of snores ripped through the silent pool house just as I pressed record. I laughed, and he opened his eyes.

"Smile, baby," I said. He groaned and reached for the phone.

"What are you doing?"

"Oh, nothing. Just collecting evidence."

He wrestled my new phone from my hands and held it out of my reach. "How do I stop the video?"

"Like I'd tell you."

He grunted and threw the phone to the foot of his bed. "That thing is too expensive to be so complicated," he said.

"It's not complicated. It's probably just made for humans and you're—"

He grabbed me and wedged his fingers under my arms before I could tease him about the side of him that barks. "I'm what? What am I, Chris?" I squealed, flopping around in his arms like a dying fish.

"Handsome!" I offered, to end the tickle attack.

"Liar."

"Smart. Kind. Loving. Sexy!" He relaxed his fingers and slid them from my armpits to my back. "Which one did it?" I asked.

"Sexy," he whispered and kissed me. And that was really all it ever took to kick things off between us. Steamy kisses, roaming hands.

That was how we'd spent most of our time during our three-month-old relationship— – in my bed, in his bed, in the common areas when we had the house to ourselves. I kept waiting for this to get old, his lips on mine, but every kiss felt like the first, and like I'd die if it were the last.

His lips slowed, and he rolled away. "Why are you all sweaty?" he asked.

"Weird dream about a pool. It's all your fault." I rolled on top of him and pouted. "Why did you stop kissing me?"

"Because it's four in the morning."

"Since when is that a problem?"

I could have answered my own question. It was a problem since now. Since tomorrow stopped being this distant day I'd feared. For a long minute, the only sound was the hum of his refrigerator, then the crackle of his ice maker. I grabbed my phone to stop the video and lay down with my back facing him. I was hoping if I pretended to sleep we wouldn't have to talk about him leaving me in a few hours.

We'd fallen asleep without mentioning that he, Emma, and Paul were starting a job tomorrow. And worse, in two weeks, that job would take them away from me for two whole months.

"I wish you would talk to me about it," he whispered.

"We've talked."

He wrapped his arms around to my stomach.

"*I've* talked," he said. "You've only said three words. 'Cool', when I told you about the job, 'Congrats', after my interview, and 'Oh', when I told you I'd accepted it."

And none of those times had he asked me if I approved of him leaving for two months. Like it didn't matter. Like he'd do it anyway, even if it were killing me. So I'd decided to ignore it altogether.

"What other words would you like me to say?" I asked.

"How about words like … St. Catalina, or try a phrase like … my boyfriend and my friends are leaving me alone again."

I shifted uncomfortably in his arms. Those were the exact words I didn't want to say, along with—*things are changing, the fun times are over, and you guys are moving on with your lives without me.*

Their new job was with The Peace Group, a charity that served

3

magical kind. They would be helping their people find food and shelter on a two-month long mission trip while I sat in the house alone. I'd offered to donate money in lieu of their time, but Sophia wouldn't allow it.

"I'm not talking about the job because it doesn't matter. People without trust funds go to work," I said, quoting Sophia like I usually did when I didn't know what to say, or rather, when I couldn't say what was on my mind. "I get it."

"Babe, it matters to you. Emma told me about the application that Sophia ripped up." I rolled my eyes. My second favorite witch in the world had tried to help me apply, even though it wasn't a job for humans. Especially not the kind of human I was—technically the enemy of the poor creatures they would be helping. Sophia had murdered that plan. And that was the end of my solutions that didn't involve bribery.

"So ... I tried to apply, but Sophia wouldn't let me. Whatever. It wasn't a big deal."

"She said you cried for an hour straight." I needed to remember to strangle Emma later. "I know you're upset. Just talk to me."

He forced me to turn in his arms and pulled my face to his, nose to nose, waiting for me to say what he already knew. His magic allowed him to smell my moods. At times, he knew me better than I knew myself. He just wanted me to be honest and open up to him, but I couldn't. Soon, he wouldn't be here to close me up.

"You're right," I said. He smiled with one corner of his mouth, celebrating too soon. "It's four in the morning. I should go to my room and let you rest." He sighed and pecked my nose. "And Sophia said she was coming to make breakfast. We don't know how early she'll get here. I shouldn't be in your bed when she does."

"Good idea. If she finds us together one more time, I think she's going to skin me alive. And she'll just kiss you and ask you if you need anything with my blood still on her hands."

I laughed, but it wouldn't shock me if that were to actually happen. I could do no wrong in the eyes of our pretend grandmother. Several mornings, she'd barged in on us knocked out in bed together, and somehow, it was always Nate's fault. His ear would probably be perpetually sore from her yanking it so much.

"Or she'll yell at you until she loses her voice again like she did on Cinco de Mayo," I said.

He threw a pillow over his head and groaned, probably remembering what he now called the worst day of his life.

On Cinco de Mayo, Emma and Paul had finally persuaded us to party with them by the pool. Nate had taken one sip of beer and exploded out of his clothes and into his fur. None of them knew of any other magical creature that couldn't stomach alcohol. Apparently, it was unique to my boyfriend, adding more mystery to the past he didn't want to explore.

After he'd shifted back, I took my first sip. It wasn't so bad. *Bad* was trying to keep up with Emma and taking four too many shots of tequila. I ended up hanging over his toilet for hours, and Sophia found me sick and drunk in his bed. She freaked out and gave him a week of hard labor re-shingling the roof. I pledged to never drink again, and he'd become hypersensitive to sounds mimicking the soft steps of sweet old ladies.

"Now she thinks I'm a predator trying to liquor up her angel to deflower her," he groaned.

"I'm sorry. I told her you're a perfect gentleman, but Sophia is weird about me and sex … because of my mom, I think."

I chuckled. Nate and I had nothing on CC. I'd avoided the sexual exploits she'd written about in her diary, but Sophia had told me an awful story of when she got to know my parents way better than she wanted to.

I knew it would gross me out, but I wanted to read the diary again without skipping anything. But Sophia was holding it hostage, fearing it would combat my progress out of depression. I still wanted to read it. Those words were all that was left of my parents.

Months ago, Sophia helped their trapped spirits pass on in a quick ceremony. I wasn't allowed to ask them anything, so the goodbye was not enough. The only way to contact them now was through a séance, and Sophia refused to do one with me. She wanted me to let them go, not care, but my heart wasn't as calloused as it was when I met her.

If hiding my mother's diary wasn't enough, she'd also banned me from my house in New Orleans. Apparently, Kamon visited there frequently, hoping to find me, lock me up, and control the powers I didn't use.

Wonderful.

I gave Nate a peck on the cheek and slid out of his bed. I looked around for my shoes then remembered I hadn't been wearing any.

"I'll walk you out," he said.

I shook my head. "Stay in bed. It's late."

He got up anyway. "That's exactly why I'm going to walk you." He patted around on his nightstand, his bed, then on the counter of his mini-kitchen. "I think my keys are in your room."

I groaned. "Mine, too. And I'm sure they've locked the doors by now."

"Sophia is going to wring my neck." He fell backwards onto his bed and clutched his throat.

"I'll just call Em," I said. "No, she also has to go somewhere in the morning."

"We could try to break in," he said. I didn't bother answering him. We both knew Sophia had enough magic swarming our house that no one could get in without a key or the right spell.

The only solution made my heart race.

"I guess I'll have to bypass the door," I said.

"You don't have to use your powers, babe. Let's just wake one of them up. I don't want you to hurt yourself."

I didn't want to have a nosebleed or seizure either. That was the biggest reason why I'd decided not to use them. But I'd moved myself from classrooms to my dorm room on accident for years without bleeding.

"It should be fine," I said. "Just this once."

He kissed me and stepped away. I pictured my room, how the carpet felt under my toes, how the fan made a constant whooshing sound, how it smelled like lemons more than any other room in the house.

I'd forgotten how fast it happened, yanking myself from one room and seamlessly landing in another. I couldn't deny how exhilarating it felt. Freeing. My blood soared through my veins, leaving me aching for more.

I had to stop myself and ignore how alive I felt. Even though I knew my powers had nothing to do with the devil now, they were still dangerous. I'd almost slit Emma's throat a few months ago while trying to butter toast from across the room.

Psychic powers definitely weren't meant to play with.

When I came to my senses and shoved the desire to be more than human back inside of me, I opened my eyes in front of my sofa. I scrambled to find the remote. The news flashed on the screen instead of the music videos I remembered being on when I'd turned the television off before dinner. Either way, the flashing colors soothed the panic the moment in darkness had caused. Even as a child, I wasn't particularly afraid of the dark, but now that a sick hunter wanted to capture me, I required either company or a light at all times.

My heart jumped for the girl who wasn't lucky enough to escape from Kamon like the rest of us. I thought about Remi constantly. A sickening feeling burned my chest each time someone said her name. I pictured her in Kamon's chapel, worshiping him like a god. I prayed every night that she hadn't been bred.

I'd discovered the heinous truth about the hunters who enforce the rules magical kind lived by from my mother's diary. Psychic powers took years of training the human brain to do extraordinary things. Some hunters don't like to wait. Some hunters like to breed copies—children with inherited powers and a desire to use them to harm. And they did so at the expense of female hunters.

Remi was psychotic, but she didn't deserve to be treated like an animal, which she wasn't anymore. She'd been changed from a shape shifting panther into one of Kamon's brainwashed followers. I hated him for what he was doing to those people. I hated him more for what his dead master, Julian, had done to my family.

He was the reason my mother's art studio felt like a bloody and terrible death. I'd sensed that my parents were brutally murdered in there. I wished he wasn't dead so I could watch the light leave his eyes as I…

"Ow!" I said. I unclenched my fists. My nails had left a line of red crescent moons across my palms. This was the kind of thing Sophia would want me to call her about, times when my anger boiled over. But the skin was barely broken and would probably be fine in the morning. No need to bother her at four a. m. for nothing.

I took a deep breath and counted to ten. I exhaled slowly and willed myself to put hunters and the hateful thoughts they spurred out of my mind.

I raised the remote to mute the television and caught a glimpse of the headline.

Death toll rises to 2,000 in Guatemala.

The monotone reporter said, "Experts are saying that a contagion may be the cause of the sudden deaths of so many in Sololá. The government is assuring that the problem is being contained and will not spread to—"

I muted the television, still needing the light, but not interested in hearing about contagious diseases. I crawled in bed and rolled my eyes. Soggy tissues covered my pillow and the occupied one next to it. I pulled out one of Emma's earbuds. "What are you doing in here?" I asked.

She blew her nose and flung the tissue too close to my face. "I fell asleep waiting for my so-called friend to answer my text," she whined. "Since you were so busy with your PG-13 kissing that you couldn't check on me, this is what you get, a mess in your bed, and I'm not leaving. I don't have enough energy to go to my room."

Dramatic. She lived literally three steps down the hall, assuming she wouldn't use magic to get there.

"You haven't texted me since seven when you spilled your drink on the table," I said. "I replied with the smiley that looks shocked."

She popped the other earbud out and checked her phone. "Oh. I didn't press SEND. You're forgiven."

"Merci." Her mascara had run under her eyes and onto my very white pillowcase. "What's wrong?"

"Paul ..." She flipped from her stomach to her back, freeing the mountain of tissues underneath her. This was her third *I love Paul but he doesn't love me back* breakdown this week. "When he asked me to go to his parents' house for dinner, I thought it was for something special. He made it seem that way." I would say she'd thought it was going to be a little more than special. She'd raided my closet for the perfect dress, like they were going to the altar, not someone's dining room. "It was a special night ... for him. He said he wanted the people who meant the most to him to meet-" She sucked in a broken breath and grabbed a fresh tissue. "... his new girlfriend," she whispered.

"Oh my God."

"Annabelle. Stupid Annabelle. What a dumb name. And she's hot with huge …" She took a moment to catch her breath again. "Boobs. She's some witch one of his friends set him up with. She was Miss Teen Nebraska a few years ago. I hate Nebraska!" I was pretty sure Em had never been to or known anyone from Nebraska. She was from Paris, and besides living with Sophia in Texas, she'd only explored America's party towns. "And she came in right when his mom was cleaning the tea I spilled. I could die."

She sobbed into her hands. I wanted to reach for her, hug her like a normal friend, but I couldn't. I usually waited for her to touch me if we were going to make contact.

I could hear human thoughts without doing a thing, but I was rarely around them now. I only had to worry about my powers stirring when I touched Paul and Emma. Nathan was immune for some reason, and Sophia knew how to block people like me. Paul and Em had learned to be careful. They usually didn't touch me or limited contact to quick encounters that didn't reveal too much of their minds.

Now, Emma stayed on her side of the bed, with a safe distance between us.

"Maybe he wouldn't date her if he knew how you felt," I said.

"He knows. He has to know."

I brushed two stray tissues from my pillow and lay down. "You've never told him. I think he thinks that you two only hook up when you're drunk. That's why you need to talk to him about it … without a drink in your hand."

She peeked at me through her fingers. I smiled, trying to show her that I wasn't judging. She'd gotten into a terrible pattern with Paul. She played the role of best friend all day, and as soon as she took a tiny sip of anything stronger than water, she used it as an excuse to be all over him. The worst part, she acted clueless the following day, blaming alcohol for her selective memory loss.

"What am I going to do?" she asked.

"Tell Paul you love him. Tell him you remember everything. Or I might just say it. I don't know how long I can keep this from Nate. He brings it up all the time."

"Christine Grant!" She popped up in bed and glared at me. "What will happen to you if you breathe a word of this to anyone?"

I groaned. "You will tell Sophia that we have Lydia Shaw's shoes."

I didn't want to find out what Sophia would do to me for stealing from the woman who saved the world from magical domination and was in charge of the hunters, all of them but Kamon.

The thievery had started as an accident, but it was my idea to keep the shoes for good. They were for Lydia *freaking* Shaw, and for some reason, having something that belonged to her excited me.

"Damn right, I will. As far as you know, I don't feel anything for Paul, and I can't handle my liquor. Are we clear, klepto?" she said, pointing a glittery finger in my face as she blackmailed me.

"You're nuts. And I should throw you out. You told Nathan about the application. I can't believe you did that."

"That's not the same kind of secret. You *have* to talk to him. Sophie told me not to let you hold things in. She said it's dangerous for you."

I rolled my eyes at Sophia's theory of why I got so angry at times. According to her, I didn't speak my mind enough. Problem was, what was on my mind wasn't always polite to say. And I had to be careful of what I said since I lived in a house full of creatures humans like me were typically made to destroy. I didn't want to scare them.

They accepted me and believed what Sophia and my mother's diary said, that I was naturally psychic but not bred like other copies. We talked about it, joked about it, but I knew they kept the idea that I could kill them in a moment somewhere in the back of their minds. They'd have to.

"Oh, Chris. I'm sorry. I didn't get a chance to ask Mrs. Ewing about the candles," she said, sniffing between each word. Since Sophia wouldn't help me contact my parents, I'd asked Emma. She'd gotten a list of magical ingredients needed to open a door to the spirit world. We were only missing red candles made with magical wax. No one she knew had them. They were used for magic that toed the line between light and dark, and apparently, it was classless to have them, or admit that you did.

"Don't worry about it," I said. "We'll find them. I'm sorry about your night. Maybe Paul's not that serious about her."

"I think he is. Their kiss was very passionate. Just like the ones … I don't remember having with him."

"Don't give up before you tell him," I said.

"I can't. It's *Paul*. Paul Harrison Ewing. Sophie used to bathe us together. He's supposed to be my brother." I laughed. The times I'd seen Emma and Paul make out, they'd looked nothing like siblings. "I don't want to get my feelings crushed."

I took one of the fresh peonies from my vase and brushed it under Emma's nose. "My love," I said, imitating Sophia. "They are already crushed."

She giggled, took the flower, and rolled over. I tucked her in as she jammed the earbuds back into her ears.

Emma snored as loud as Nathan. I never slept alone, so I'd learned to tune out the sound. In the morning, I smelled lemons before I heard Sophia whispering protection spells in the hall.

I would never admit it to anyone, but my first real thought of the day was always about Remi. Before I opened my eyes, I prayed for her, that she was safe, that Lydia Shaw would rescue her soon.

"Good morning, loves," Sophia said, her voice bright and happy.

She liked this bed guest better than my other. "I made breakfast for your first day of …"

She paused and cleared her throat, deleting the rest of her sentence.

"Just say it, Sophia," I said. "Work. Work. Work. The word isn't going to kill me." She picked up one of the tissues from the pile covering both of our pillows.

I couldn't say it wasn't mine.

Emma was more terrified of telling Sophia about her feelings than telling Paul. She didn't think she'd be accepted into the Ewing family outside of being a charity case. She was so delusional, but I was her friend. It was my job to listen to her cry and deny her feelings right along with her.

And I knew how to be a friend now. You don't sit and let them talk without replying for hours and stare at random specks on the wall. Sometimes, I wanted to go to New Haven and apologize to my old roommate, Whitney, for putting her through hell with me. But she'd dished out her own brand of hell after, torturing me with the queen of our orphanage, so I considered us even.

"I didn't say it wouldn't make me cry." I pulled the tissue from Sophia's hand to own it for Emma. "I said it wouldn't kill me."

"Don't worry, angel-pie. We'll be having so much fun, you won't even realize they're gone."

I stifled and eye roll and got out of bed.

Since my friends had decided to kill me with the mission trip, she'd been here most of the day, watching me closely with her sparkling blue eyes. Like she was waiting for me to spiral and act like my mother. I knew from her diary that she couldn't handle being alone and away from my dad. She loved him too much, which could be another reason why I didn't have parents.

Sophia didn't know if CC died with my dad or by her own hands after Julian killed her husband. Some days, I believe she did because of her diary. Others, something makes me sure that she was stronger than that and wouldn't have left me if she didn't have to. I wouldn't know for sure until Emma and I found those red candles.

I brushed my teeth as Sophia wrestled Emma out of bed. "My love, please. The boys are already up."

"She could stay," I said, my mouth full of minty toothpaste.

"I could," Emma said. "And continue to have twenty-three dollars in my checking account."

I rolled my eyes. Twenty-three dollars could go a long way when you never had to buy anything. Oddly, I was the only human in this house, and I was the least concerned about human currency.

When Emma left, Sophia joined me in the bathroom. She put her wrinkled hand on my shoulder and sighed.

"How are you?" she asked, searching my eyes for the truth.

"Fine." I dried my mouth and didn't fill the silence like I knew she wanted me to.

"Christine ..."

I tightened my ponytail in the mirror, even though I didn't really have a reason to comb my hair. Thanks to her, *I* wasn't going anywhere today.

She cleared her throat and the eye roll I'd held back earlier escaped me. She wanted me to say: *this job just shows how different I am from my friends—not the same species, not capable of the same things. I'll be alone. I don't want to lose them. They are all I have outside of you.* But she'd have to do more than bat her white eyelashes to get that much honesty out of me.

"I'm okay," I said. "Can we not make this a thing? Please?"

She pulled me to her chest, totally making it a thing, and held me until Nate knocked on my open door.

Sophia hugged him on her way out. This was my life: being passed from person to person, never having to be alone until now.

"Do I look like I'm ready to bring peace to a shattered kind?" he asked, pointing to his new, hideous work shirt that was the color of rotting peas. I stopped myself from commenting on the ridiculous motto he'd chanted.

Peace for a shattered kind.

According to my friends, the unemployment rate for magical kind was triple the human rate. Most had trouble keeping jobs and those of them who didn't appear human lived so deeply in the shadows that they couldn't work at all. It sounded like an awful life, but some would argue that the millions of humans killed during the war were a fair trade for the poverty many of them endured.

But I couldn't say that out loud. My shifter boyfriend and my witch and wizard best friends wouldn't like that very much. Plus, it would make me sound a lot like a copy—a real one.

"You didn't answer. I must look awful," he said, leaning in for a kiss.

We used all of our allotted five minutes before I could refute that.

Paul and Em were also in those awful pea-colored shirts at the dining table. Paul had on a green and white scarf over his, managing to look fashionable and slightly homeless for his first day of work.

"Nana, this is your last chance to let me stay with Chris," he said.

"Hush," Sophia said. "You should be happy to do something with your life."

"You act like I'm the only Ewing without a career. Dad's a freaking photographer for crying out loud. He makes no money! And I really don't need a job. I'm going to eventually marry Chris and become a millionaire."

Sophia pushed his head down as she passed him on the way to her seat, and Nate chucked a biscuit at him.

"Don't be silly. I'm going to draw up a wonderful prenuptial agreement before Christine marries anyone," Sophia said, eyeing Nate.

I rubbed his leg under the table. I knew it hurt him that Sophia treated him like a gold-digging pervert at times.

"Where did you disappear to last night, Em?" Paul asked.

She looked up from her plate and smiled. "With Chris. I slept in her bed. We talked about a boy I like." I held my breath, both proud and petrified. "This guy from home. He lives in L.A. now."

"What's his name?" Sophia asked, smiling, ready for girl talk.

"Uh … Louis. I call him Lou," Emma said. She glared at me, begging for support. I didn't want to participate in her lie, so I grabbed my glass to chug the grape juice I'd finally developed a taste for. I'd given up on getting oranges or orange juice in this house. Sophia just happened to miss it on the grocery list four weeks in a row. I didn't bother asking for it anymore.

Emma narrowed her eyes at me, and I continued to ignore her. "My favorite thing about Lou is that he has a connection to a shoe dealer. Chris and I love expensive shoes at low prices. It's practically stealing."

I choked on the grape juice, and Nate patted my back. Sophia ordered me to lift my arms. How that was supposed to help with choking, I didn't know.

"Yeah, Lou, he's perfect for her," I croaked.

She flashed me a sneaky smile, outlined in red lipstick. "When

Chris is less famous, I hope to introduce you all to him."

Sophia cleared her throat. "Maybe. I don't know how I feel about that," she said.

Emma knew Sophia wouldn't like that. It was probably why she'd mentioned it. Bringing more people into our lives would complicate our already complicated situation.

The world was still reeling from the rumored witch sighting. Even though most believed I'd staged the abduction to escape my bullies, my face still appeared on the news at least once a week.

My friends had to explain why they were in the media with a human to their new bosses, and Emma had the bright idea to tell them I wasn't one. So at home, I was sort of a copy. To Sophia, sort of an angel. To Paul and Em's parents and their stupid new job, I was a witch like I'd mistakenly thought I was for years.

It was hard to feel like one person with so many versions of me, of the Christine I'd fought so hard to become.

"Nana, please loosen the reins on Chris," Paul said. "I want to go on a triple date. Annabelle is dying to meet them, and I'm sure she'll love 'ole Lou."

"Maybe," Sophia said. I couldn't have been the only one to see Emma sink into her seat. Poor thing. "Is today an actual workday or training?"

"Training," Nate said.

"But with everything happening in Guatemala, I would assume The Peace Group would be there," she said.

I swallowed the eggs in my mouth and said, "With the contagion? I hope not. The news said 2,000 people died." Sophia narrowed her eyes at me. It felt like I'd given away how late I'd been up last night, like the death toll was specific to four a.m.. "And why would they go there anyway?" I asked, to distract her.

"Sololá, Guatemala is and has always been heavily populated with our kind," she said. "And the deaths were sudden, obviously from powers faster than magic or they would have protected themselves. Disease is the only thing humans have to explain it. We know differently."

The expressions on all of their faces told me they believed hunters attacked that city. I thought of Kamon's triplet copies then. How fast they were, as fast as I could be.

"They won't … get away with it, right?" I asked.

"Some people are above the law," Nate said.

Forks clinked against the glass plates as I felt even more different and threatening than I usually did. *I'm not like them*, I chanted in my head. *I'm not like the hunters.*

"Hello, hello," a man said in the living room. It took me a moment to place the voice as Paul's dad. I should've known immediately from the way he'd sung his greeting instead of speaking it, like someone raised by Sophia would do.

Both of his parents walked into the dining room.

At least once a week, they dropped in on their baby boy. I hadn't expected to see them this morning since Paul and Em had eaten with them last night, but by the looks on their faces and the camera in Mr. Ewing's hands, they were too excited and proud to let this morning go undocumented.

"Good morning, Richard," Sophia said, as Paul's dad kissed her on the cheek. "Vanessa, what a beautiful dress." I chuckled. Paul's mother dressed a lot like Sophia. Embroidered ladybugs covered her collar and sleeves, and she had matching ladybug studs in her ears.

"Thanks, Mom," she said.

Paul cringed as Mrs. Ewing straightened his hair.

"Smile, Paully," his dad said. He pointed his huge camera at his son's fake smile. "Now you, Em." Emma showed off her work shirt and a kissy face for the camera. "Your turn, Nate." My dorky boyfriend crossed his eyes and pointed to the Peace Group's logo.

"Christine, dear," Mrs. Ewing said. "We know you're not working, but do you want a picture?" All heads turned to Sophia for approval.

"Why not?" Sophia said. "Only family will see these, and she's family." I smiled, but my heart squeezed so hard that I thought they would see it move through my pajama top. I wanted to be considered family, to be the orphaned witch who Sophia loved for no reason like they thought, but as I stared at the way Mrs. Ewing adjusted Paul's scarf, loving on him so effortlessly that she probably didn't notice it, I wanted my own family. The one that was taken from me.

"Don't mouth off when you are asked to do something," Mr. Ewing instructed them. "Be polite. Be gracious. Be willing to get dirty." He ruffled Em's hair, aiming that at her specifically, and snapped a shot of it before she fixed it.

I wanted to throw my juice on him. This whole job thing was his fault. Some random wizard had recognized Paul as his son and offered him a job. Paul extended the invitation to Em and Nate, and now they were all working for a magical company that even Sophia wasn't sure about. But since the three of them had fallen in love with the boss and it was technically charitable work, she didn't object to the job.

That was the biggest difference between us—Sophia approved of or objected to their decisions. She made mine.

Mr. and Mrs. Ewing left after another wave of Sophia-like kisses on their youngest son, and the rest of breakfast passed too quickly. With each morsel of food disappearing from their plates, I felt them move away from me. I glanced around the table, not seeing my boyfriend, best friend, and make-believe cousin. I saw a shifter, a witch, and a wizard. Each with their own paths, and dreams, and futures. All different from mine.

Feeling this way, different from everyone around me, reminded me of those long days and even longer nights at St. Catalina. I was constantly numb and lonely. I'd let myself drown there, falsely believing that my death was certain and burning in hell was imminent. I was sad and sick and I'd give anything not to go back to the state where I hated myself and weighed almost nothing.

I wished I'd had time to heal without Nate, because now that I was forced to let him live his own life, I felt like I'd be Leah any moment now. And Leah wasn't just sad. She had a host of other problems. Terrible ones.

"Can I talk to you in the living room?" Nate whispered in my ear, probably sensing me slipping under. Since he could smell my moods, he always intervened and tried to cheer me up. That was what terrified me the most about him going on the trip. How would I smile without him? What would stop me from picking a point on the wall to stare at until he came back? What would distract me from missing my parents?

Over the past three months, I'd become obsessed with them— their lives, their love, the way they died. Since I'd actually talked to CC, my obsessed mind had made me delusional about our relationship, making up memories of her singing to me and holding me. In these contrived memories, I am seventeen and in my living room and blurry arms are wrapped around me.

I shivered, seeing it now, seeing those arms and hearing the song I'd sung to myself every night for years. The voice was warped and deep, like something was wrong with a tape. I wanted to hear that voice, hear her sing to me. I shivered harder, suddenly sure that the voice was hers, just tampered with somehow, forgotten. I pulled closer to it, as exhilarated as I had been this morning when I'd used my powers for the first time in months.

"Sweetheart!" Sophia yelled. She leaned my head back and pushed a napkin under my nose to catch the blood. "Can you hear me?"

I nodded and glanced around the table. I cringed at my friends' faces. Great. There wasn't a better way to look like a copy than having a spontaneous nosebleed.

Sophia cleaned my face. She had a hard time remembering I had hands at times.

"Good one, Chris," Paul said. "Psychic theatrics to get us to stay."

Emma smacked his arm.

"Dude, not funny," Nate said. He lifted me out of the chair. "Can we be excused?" Sophia nodded, and he carried me to the living room, squeezing me and apologizing softly in my ear. "Does that happen when you're mad? Baby, please don't be mad at me."

I shook my head and kissed his cheek. "It's not you. It doesn't happen when I'm mad. I don't know what I did. I was just thinking about CC. I'm fine about you leaving. It's no big deal."

"Look at me," he said, ignoring my lie. I did for a moment, before his eyes made my heart stammer. "I don't want to go. Work is just something I *have* to do. If I were rich, I would never leave your side, but I'm not. I have to make something of myself, and this is the best way."

He kissed me and finally let me stand on my own. It felt symbolic, like he'd carried me out of darkness and now he couldn't be here to carry me anymore.

"Don't get worked up about missing CC again. No nosebleeds; that's an order. Think about the happy stuff in her diary. And missing your mom is normal, babe. I didn't even meet her, and I miss her, too," he said. I laughed. It was the perfect thing to say. "We'll be back at four. Four-thirty at the latest. I swear." I allowed myself a few tears and brushed them away as he kissed me goodbye. "I'll text you if it turns out the no phone thing is a rumor. Love you."

"Love you more."

After a few more kisses and a few more tears, Emma and Paul

came into the living room to say goodbye. Then they vanished, moving on with their lives in a moment, in the world they were born to be in.

The quiet hum of the AC made me think of my dorm room at St. Catalina. How quiet it used to be. How quiet I used to be.

"I can be alone," I whispered.

"Of course you can, love," Sophia said, wrapping her arms around me. "You've been alone since school, remember?" I nodded. I'd spent a few days alone in Paris in Lydia Shaw's apartment after my dramatic breakup with Nate. I didn't remember much of it, but I didn't crumble. I was watching movies, distracting myself from heartache, and stealing her shoes. "You'll be just fine, dear." Her phone buzzed in her dress pocket. She sighed as she answered. "Does *day off* not mean anything to you? Why are you calling me?"

My heart sped. It was her boss—*the* Lydia Shaw. I waved my hands in Sophia's face. "Ask her. Ask her, please." She knew what I wanted to know. We talked about it every day. And she told me to mind my own business every day, too.

"Lydia, Christine would like to know if Remi is okay."

I crossed my fingers and closed my eyes, standard wish stance. *Please let her be okay.*

Sophia tapped my shoulder and passed me her phone. I breathed into the speaker for a few seconds before I worked up the courage to speak to her.

"Hi," I said.

"Hi. How are you?" she asked.

I couldn't answer for a moment. I got a starstruck feeling every time I thought about her, so hearing her voice was sending me into a state of frenzy. She was so famous that people bowed in her presence, and I was privileged to know her because she was Sophia's boss.

I once thought she would want to kill me, but having inherited powers didn't bother her at all. She was surprisingly understanding. She didn't care about what kind of creature I sort of was or that Nate and I were technically breaking the treaty by dating. She was only strict about one thing—me leaving the house. I had to ask her permission every time we wanted to go somewhere, and she'd arrange it to make sure Kamon or his hunters wouldn't meet us there.

I was virtually helpless on my own. I didn't use my powers, and even if I did, I didn't know how helpful they'd be in a fight against someone other than Remi. Lydia had offered me lessons I had yet to take her up on. I figured the time she would use to train the powers I didn't want would be better spent rescuing Remi and Kamon's other hostages.

Sadly, Lydia didn't know Catherine personally from her hunter days. She'd heard of her, but couldn't tell me any more about my parents than Sophia could.

"I'm doing okay," I finally said.

"Wonderful. But excuse my weak ears. I know I must be mistaken. I thought Sophia said you asked me something about Remi. That can't be true, right?"

"I'm worried."

"You promised."

I had. I'd promised her I'd be a normal teenager, but I felt anything but normal today. My friends were gone, leaving me here alone with my thoughts. Alone to let worry seep in.

"Christine, Sophia has taken off to spend the day with you. She must have something nice planned that warrants leaving me to fend for myself. Forget about Remi and have a good day."

"I'll try, but will you—" She cleared her throat, and all of my muscles froze at once. I'd forgotten how powerful and important she was and how I probably shouldn't question her. "Sorry, Lydia. Bye."

"Bye."

I sighed and passed Sophia her phone. "Hello?" She rolled her eyes and closed it. Lydia had hung up. "Come upstairs with me, dear."

She smiled and winked, probably up to something.

Upstairs, she walked me to the door of the empty room, the one that should belong to Nate if she didn't make him live outside. The one I wished could belong to Remi. She covered my eyes with her wrinkled hand. Her bracelets clinked against each other as she giggled.

"You're going to love this," she squealed.

She dropped her hand from my eyes, and I gasped. She'd filled the empty room with easels and stools, and she'd replaced the carpet with sand-colored wood. Magically, I was sure, since I hadn't heard any construction noises coming from across the hall.

I hadn't drawn much since I'd left St. Catalina. Chatting with Emma or making out with Nate was always more appealing.

I'd inherited my artistic skills from my mother.

Catherine was an artist, after she'd decided not to be a hunter. I imagined she spent her days painting and loving my father … until Julian ruined that.

Sophia pulled me into the room and wrapped an arm around my waist. She must have known I'd need help to stand when I saw the whole thing.

The paintings on the walls made my knees buckle. I'd seen them in my mother's studio the night I'd first talked to her. They were all here, the finished ones, the ones with pencil markings still visible, the watercolors, the abstracts, the one of a ballerina on pointe with unfinished legs.

"You went to New Orleans? Is it not dangerous anymore?" I whispered through my tear-clogged throat.

"It's still dangerous, dear. I used magic."

I'd asked for these paintings several times. And each time, she'd told me to be patient. She was right about there being a "right time" for me to have them.

"Thank you. I love it," I said. "What about the diary?"

She shook her head. "Maybe later … when you're stronger," she said. She pulled me to her chest before I could even start to complain. "Trust me on this. It's too soon for you to have that. You miss them too much right now. Give yourself time."

I took a deep breath and shook off the part of me that could be ungrateful and bratty in a moment like this. I'd see the diary eventually and find the candles for the séance, too.

I just needed to be patient and trust Sophia. She wanted the best for me, to protect me, and she knew I'd cried all night after reading it the last time and would probably do the same again.

Real life tragedies can't be revised and given better endings.

I crept around the room, gazing at my mother's work. Sophia stayed at my side, gazing, too, like we were in a gallery.

"You hate when I act like my mother, Sophia. Why would you do this?" She swatted my butt, telling me to hush and enjoy the surprise.

"It's something for you to do."

Oh … this was a pity gift. Something to occupy me while my friends moved on with their lives. I didn't have anywhere to go with mine. Sophia had arranged for me to take a battery of tests last month to expedite my diploma from St. Catalina. She wanted me to finish, and I'd told her I was tired of spending four hours a day working for a piece of paper that would collect dust in my closet. I'd banned the idea of college long ago. Never mind my GPA issues that would probably stop me; if I never sat in a classroom again, it would still be too soon.

She tapped a stool and sat on the one next to it. She stared at me for a moment, and I narrowed my eyes at her. "Why do you look so sneaky?" I asked.

She smiled. "I wanted to discuss something with you." She rested her hand on my knee. "There are so many colleges in the area that offer the Bachelor of Fine Arts degree." I rolled my eyes. "The next semester starts in August. There's still time to apply."

"I don't need to go to art school, Sophia," I moaned.

"I was born a witch, and yet I practiced it every day at your age."

"At Witch College?" After a quick stare off, we both laughed.

"Okay, smarty-pants. Just tell me you'll think about it."

"I'll think about it."

She smiled and snapped her fingers. My laptop popped into the room. She clicked on the internet radio and asked if I liked the station with lifted eyebrows.

"Cool," I said.

"I'll be in your room catching up on my soaps."

She walked to the door but turned around before leaving. I knew it wouldn't be that easy.

"Sweetie, can I say something?" I nodded, my eyes on the blank canvas in front of me, white space begging to be more. "You belong. It may not seem that way right now, but there is a place for you in this world. A perfect place."

I guessed it was time for our daily therapy session. Today's topic: my in-between-ness and how lonely it feels to be not quite human, not quite magical, and unlike anyone else on the planet.

"I didn't belong in a human school, I don't belong in the magical world with my friends, and you won't let me contact the spirit world to speak with my parents. I'd say you're wrong about this one, Sophia."

"I've only been wrong about one thing in my entire life," she said, looking down at her hands.

I was not willing to discuss her guilt about believing that I was CC's copy and letting me rot at St. Catalina, so I got up and scanned the fully stocked shelves. I grabbed a bottle of midnight blue paint and one of the wooden palettes on the bottom shelf. I turned up the volume on my laptop to end the conversation.

"Okay. How about I call Lydia and ask her if you all can go out for dinner?"

"Can we do it tomorrow night? For Nate's birthday?"

His gift would be delivered this afternoon. He was going to freak. We were watching TV two weeks ago and he *happened* to mention his eighteenth birthday while a BMW commercial was on. He'd never ask, not in a million years, but I'd ordered him a jet-black M3 Coupe the same day. I planned to make his birthday as wonderful as he'd made mine.

A car was a big gift, but it didn't match his effort. He'd given me everything he had on my birthday. With the money my parents left behind, I could give him the world, things he wouldn't have dreamed of as he slept behind stores and stole food from restaurants. And I planned to start with the car he'd hinted at.

"Where would you like to go?" she asked, because she had to get it approved first and planned to the tiniest detail. Neither Sophia nor Lydia wanted us to be bombarded by paparazzi again. Our first time out for pizza ended up on the cover of every magazine and newspaper, with headlines all slandering me—the runaway orphan.

"Somewhere with crazy kinds of burgers. He likes that."

"I'll arrange it," she said. "Have fun in here."

I slathered the blue across the canvas as she shut the door. A soothing violin floated from the laptop speakers. I matched my brushstrokes to it, painting the music. A woman with a beautiful, airy voice sang about the love she'd lost over the violins and a barely audible guitar. I pulled a bottle of white paint to me from the shelf before I felt myself using my powers. But with the paintbrush in my hand, I couldn't worry about losing control of them.

I swept it across the canvas, swirling white and blue. I shut my eyes and focused on the muscles in my wrist. The movement felt so automatic, and the palette felt so natural in my other hand. I was born, bred, to do this. Catherine must have known I'd pick this up from her. I imagined her speaking to the bump in her stomach, coaching me, the only art teacher I would ever need.

"This is what you wanted me to do," I whispered. "Paint and love." If I were in New Orleans and they hadn't passed on, she would've responded in her own way—freezing whatever part of me she touched and typing next to me on my laptop. "I miss you."

I'd never met her outside of her ghostly (nagging) form, but I missed her like I'd known her every day of my life. Missed her like she'd held me for longer than my records said she could have. Now that I had a name to call the ache in my chest, I knew that I'd felt this grief, the pain of their deaths, for as long as I could remember.

But again, as I painted and followed the path my mother intended for me, I wasn't allowed to dwell in that pain.

I opened my eyes and smiled. I'd painted a beautiful night sky. It was almost good enough to hang next to my mother's work.

I dipped a brush in black and set a gangly tree against the sky. I made the branches reach like enchanted claws into the air. I dipped a thinner brush in orange and dangled my favorite fruit from the tip of a branch. I titled the painting *A peaceful night*.

CHAPTER TWO

Sophia checked on me throughout the day, twice before lunch, twice after. On her fifth visit, she asked, "Am I going to have to put your bed in here?"

"No, I'll just sleep on the floor."

"And the brushes." She gasped. "You cleaned them yourself?" I nodded with pride. "And the bathroom isn't splattered with paint?"

"I can't promise that." I chuckled, and she kissed the top of my head.

"This is spectacular. You are amazing."

"She was amazing," I whispered. I turned around and stretched my teeth and lips in the widest grin my mouth would allow. She didn't like me to speak of my mother that way. Like I knew her. The smile was supposed to get us past that moment, and it did.

I was working on my second painting, an eerily good depiction of the pool house. It reminded me of the birthday boy.

"Hey, can you make me a huge red bow? Like ..." I threw my arms open so she could get an idea of how large it needed to be. "Huge."

"For?"

"Nathan's gift."

"What are you getting him?" I embellished the yard in front of Nathan's house instead of answering. I painted a magnolia in a garden we didn't have. In this painting, maybe the only place I had any real control, they could grow out of the ground. "Keeping secrets, are we?"

"It's a surprise that he's going to love. That's all you need to know."

She turned my shoulders and forced me to spin on the stool. She pointed a long and wrinkled finger in my face. "I'm not giving you a bow to put on yourself. I don't care that he's leaving for two months or that it's his birthday! You don't owe Nathan Reece anything. Especially not your body!"

I coughed, choking on air and the absurdity of her comment. "Oh my God! It's a real gift, Sophia. Not my ... *body*." She sighed, and I turned back to my painting, mortified. "Why would you even think that?"

"Well ... you won't tell me what it is. What else am I supposed to think?" I rolled my eyes. There were millions of things to think before deciding I was offering myself to my boyfriend for his birthday. She'd only caught us kissing a handful of times, fully clothed. I hadn't given her much of a reason to jump to that conclusion.

I hadn't, but CC probably had.

"Did my mother do that? The bow thing?" I finished the first magnolia and started another next to it. A whole minute passed before I turned to see if she intended to answer me. Her eyes were fixed on her sandals. "Let me guess ... you don't want to talk about her. Again."

"Sweetie, it's not healthy to dwell."

"Maybe I wouldn't have to dwell if I knew more than three things about her." Besides her powers, who she loved, and how she may have died, I knew nothing about CC. She seemed bratty from the few stories Sophia had told me, I gathered she wasn't a fan of magical kind from how she'd acted in New Orleans, but it still felt like I had nothing. Fistfuls of air.

Sophia was even vague with her description of my parents. *They were average looking people*, she'd said. *With eyes that changed colors in different lights, too many to pin down just one.* Then she'd suddenly needed to wash dishes like it would be a crime to let them sit for a second and talk to me about my parents.

"I've told you everything … I can. I'm sorry it's not enough."

"You told me she was mean and validated her promiscuous side with my father. You knew her for years. There has to be something else."

She tucked my hair behind my ears and leaned down to kiss my cheek. "We weren't anything like you and I. I cooked and cleaned for her and did my best to stay out of her way. Sweetie, you want to know the girl in the diary, but I didn't know her. Not that side. I'm sorry."

She pulled at my shirt to make me turn to face her. Painting seemed more appealing.

"It's fine. Case closed. They're dead and I'll never know them. I won't bring them up again." She groaned and wrapped her arms around me. I shrugged her off. "You've kept me busy all day and fed me several times. Are you waiting around to burp me, or will you be leaving soon?"

"Christine Cecilia Grant, you are not too old for a spanking." She tickled me until I let go of the desire to be an asshole. "I love you. See you in the morning."

"Love you, too." I let her kiss my cheek four times before I shooed her away.

The doorbell rang a minute after Sophia vanished. I knew not to answer it before putting on a hat.

We had a protocol for visitors, in case anyone recognized me in or near the house. Exposing my residence would lead Remi here. God, I wanted that, but she wouldn't come to stay. She'd come to haul us off to her master again.

I pulled my ponytail through the back of the cap and pulled the lid over my eyes.

"Delivery for Cecilia Neal."

"That's me," I said, to the guy. I signed my fake name on his clipboard as his partners unloaded Nate's car from the tow. It had taken several calls to a nearby dealership to get it shipped here. If I'd done things the typical way, I would have had to call Sophia, who would've called the famous woman, who would've called the dealership to clear it out before I got there.

So I'd skipped the hassle and hadn't even told Emma about the car. I wanted it to be a surprise. I couldn't wait to see Nathan lose his mind tomorrow.

"Keys," the guy said. He shook them in my face and dropped them into my hand. "Everything else is in the car, Ms. Neal."

"Thank you."

I waited until the truck pulled away to run out there like a giddy lunatic. Sophia hadn't left the bow, but it looked stellar without it. A toy car for a grown-up boy. It was perfect. He wouldn't see it out here until I showed him. They'd magically pop into the house when they got home; we rarely used the front door.

I bounced inside and all the way back to my studio. Ten minutes and one magnolia later, Nate sang my name as he ran up the stairs.

"In here," I whispered, knowing he'd hear me.

"Whoa! Look at this!"

I dropped my paintbrush and jumped into his arms. He smelled like what I could only guess to be a hard day's work.

"Sophia made me an art studio," I said. He winked like he'd known about the surprise. "So ... how was it?"

He smiled. Ordinarily, that smile would brighten my day, but I was hoping he would hate it. He reached in his pocket and pulled out a hundred dollar bill. "I loved it. We get paid one hundred dollars a day for the two weeks of training, in addition to the thousands we'll make on the trip. Isn't that great?"

"Yay," I said, failing to sound enthused. He smiled at his crumpled money and ignored me. "This isn't the first time you've had your own money, right?" I asked. He was staring at it like it was.

"No. John makes great money, and my mom—" He cleared his throat and shook his head. "*Theresa* made sure I got an allowance."

I wanted to press, but I was too shocked to. He never, *ever*, talked about his parents. And he'd called Theresa *mom* accidentally. It made me wonder if he called her that in his head, thought of her as more than the quiet woman in the house who took orders from her husband.

We'd been in Los Angeles for two days before I asked him if they lived nearby. He got quiet but eventually told me how close. Incredibly close. Get on the highway and go down two exits, close. That was the last time he'd ever mentioned them.

"When I left, I had a few thousand dollars. I never mentioned that?" I shook my head. "Yeah ... I spent it all in a few months on food and motels and stuff."

I leaned my head on his shoulder. I hated thinking of him on the streets, homeless and hungry.

"We agreed that I'd give you every penny I earned if I stayed with you, so here you go."

"That was in New Orleans. I don't want your money." He slid his hand from my hip to my butt. I jumped and giggled. "What are you doing?"

"Looking for a pocket to slip this money into." He didn't find one back there. I didn't think he'd expected to. He slid his hand to the obvious pocket on my hip. "What's this?" He yanked out his new keys I'd forgotten in there, and I grabbed at them.

"Nothing."

"Car keys?" I tried to wrestle them away. "You have a car?"

I sighed. "You're ruining it!"

"What?"

I wiggled out of his arms and led him to the front door. "Close your eyes."

"Why?"

"Just do it." He closed them, and I pulled him outside to his birthday present. "I was going to wait until tomorrow, but … Happy Birthday, baby!" He opened his eyes, then they bulged out of his head. "It's the same one you said you liked." His jaw dropped, but not in a good way. "Did you not want it in black? We can change it."

"No. It's fine. Thank you." He looked at his feet and let a long and unnecessarily loud breath out of his nose. Not quite the reaction I'd hoped for.

"What's wrong?" I asked.

"Nothing, Chris. I ... um ... have yard work to do. I'll see you in a little while."

I caught his arm as he stepped away. He stopped walking but didn't turn around. Nate was ten times worse than me when it came to talking about his feelings. Dismissing himself was code for *I don't want to talk right now*.

"You don't like it?" I asked.

"It's a beautiful car. What's not to like?" So we were in the sarcasm phase now, apparently. I sighed and tugged on his arm. He softened and pulled me to his chest. "I just don't think it's appropriate, babe. It's too much."

"Nothing is too much for you. Maybe you should see yourself like I see you. "

I thought that would work. Nate and I never disagreed for more than a few seconds. Other than starting the job, he hadn't done anything to upset me since running out in New Orleans. And I'd like to think it was the same for him, too.

"I see myself like I am," he said. "My birthday is not this big of a deal. I'm ... "He tensed against me and paused. I leaned back to see his face. He was staring at the car.

"Nate, you said you liked it then mentioned your birthday. I thought it was what you wanted. And I didn't do too much. I only got you this one thing."

He kissed my cheek and stepped away. "Baby, I love you, but if you don't see why this isn't okay, I really can't talk right now. I don't want to say the wrong thing, so I'm not going to say anything "

Embarrassment washed over me and mixed with the shock of him not loving the car. The emotions churned in my chest, then morphed into something entirely different. Anger. I would get a prize in one of Sophia's *name your feelings* exercises in her poorly camouflaged therapy sessions.

"I think it's awfully convenient that you never have to say how you feel while everyone in this house makes me spill my guts daily," I said. "It doesn't apply to you, right? Because you're not a copy, you get to walk away and keep it inside?"

"I don't want to fight. Let's drop it, Christine. Please." If my father were alive, I imagined that would be how he'd say my name when he disapproved.

"I don't want to drop it," I said. "I want you to say what you need to say so I don't have to spend the night guessing how you feel."

He groaned and whispered, "Fine. I'm wondering about how much the car cost you."

"Like seventy thousand ... ish." He threw his face in his hands.

"Oh my God, Christine." He tried to walk away, but I stopped him again. I tugged at the ends of his ugly work shirt to make him finish. "My boss doesn't even make seventy thousand dollars in a whole year." He looked up at the sky. His hands trembled like he was holding back, and his lips twitched like he was about to burst. "Do you know what we did today?" I shook my head. "Made food plates to deliver to the victims in Sololá. Hunters ripped through that city last night—killing, kidnapping, and destroying homes for no reason. For hours, I stood in a line packaging slices of meat and a freaking lump of potatoes, then I helped deliver them to people who looked a lot like I did a few months ago. This is so wasteful. I could feed so many people with what you spent on that car!"

"Don't think about it like that. It's a gift."

He opened his mouth but nothing came out of it for a minute. He pointed a finger at me and shook his head.

"You know what? I don't say anything about the ridiculously expensive clothes you wear, or worse, don't wear. I didn't say a peep when you bought a seven hundred dollar phone. Or when you tossed your diploma into your closet from a school that costs what most of my people make in a lifetime. But this is too far. You don't know the value of things. Real things. Important things." He caught his breath and stepped closer to me, still glaring at the car like it was an old enemy. He pressed his lips against my forehead. "I want you. Not cars. Not money. You. It's all I've wanted since I met you, but you can't make ..."

He sighed and walked into the house without finishing that sentence.

I didn't really know how to feel or if that classified as a fight or not. Nate hadn't raised his voice, and he'd ended it with a kiss, but before leaving me outside alone with the car.

Emma peeked through the window next to the door. I waved, and she ran out of the house. Her makeup had melted off and she'd slung her pretty hair into a messy ponytail. She'd had a hard day, too, it seemed.

She pointed over her shoulder with a curious look on her face. "Please tell me you did not buy that for him." I shrugged, feeling like an idiot for misreading his birthday wish.

Paul dashed out of the house and straight to the car with the keys in his hands. I guessed Nate had given them up freely, officially declining the car.

"Chris, why didn't you tell me about this?" she asked.

"I wanted it to be a surprise!" And to make my own decision for once. Apparently, I wasn't good at that.

Paul zoomed out of the driveway and sped down the street, yelling, "Woooo," out of the window.

Emma ordered me to follow her to our pillow room. She closed the door behind her and pointed to the floor.

"Sit," she said. I plopped down and crossed my arms. "A car?"

"What's wrong with that?"

"Are you kidding me? Were you dropped on your head as a baby?"

"I don't know. I'll go ask the nuns at St. Catalina, or we'll find out if my parents were clumsy when you get the candles."

She frowned, and I looked away as I realized I'd taken sarcasm too far, too deep into my painful past. She sat next to me, as close as she could get without touching.

"Sorry for saying that. I wasn't thinking. Forgive me?" I nodded as I toyed with the tassels on one of her pink pillows. "What did he say?" she asked.

"A lot of stuff about money, the job, and my phone. Which isn't fair. He threw me into the pool with my old one in my pocket. What was I supposed to do?"

It stung even more when I realized he'd been keeping things to himself for three months and compiling a list of things that annoyed him about me. What else wasn't he saying?

"He's overreacting about the phone, but he has a reason to be upset about the car." I almost walked out on her. I was always on her side with Paul, right there listening to her cry after she'd put herself in the same compromising and uncomfortable position time and time again, but when it came down to it, she didn't extend me the same courtesy. "Don't get mad when I say this, but when I let myself think about it, being your friend feels weird and … wrong."

Her words plowed into my chest. I looked at her slowly, praying that my face wasn't showing how much that had burned.

"You think I'm going to do something to you?"

She reached her hand to my shoulder, nearly touching me, then yanked it away. That burned even more.

"No, Chris. Of course I don't think that. It's not your powers that makes us feel awkward. It's your money. Sophie has always been the richest person in the world to me, and you … make her seem poor." She sighed and picked at her nails that were not so grungy and chipped this morning. "And we're living here and haven't been able to pay you a dime until now. That's not right. Sometimes, it feels weird being friends with someone who has so much. I have one hundred and twenty three dollars. You have millions. I have to work. You'll never have to. If a hunter captures me, I would be priced at eight thousand dollars like I always am. If you were …"

She paused, approaching highly uncomfortable territory—what I would be worth to hunters and what they would do to me.

"It would be millions," I said. "My mother was worth three million."

That was why CC had run away from Julian. In her diary, I'd read that he'd tried to auction her off, and her highest bid was three million dollars.

I was starting to see the real things Nathan said I didn't value. Important things like how much a person could cost. Witches and wizards around our age went for a few thousand. Shifters, a few hundred. I had a price, too. I prayed I'd never know exactly what it was. Because I wouldn't sit in a cage until someone came for me. Girls with powers were sold like well-bred animals, to make more well-bred animals.

"I don't know why I assumed you'd do something simple and sweet for him," she said.

"Is a car not sweet?" She chuckled and shook her head. "I just wanted to make him happy, Em."

She snapped and a white rose appeared in her hand. "Christine, my love," she said, in a better imitation of Sophia's voice. "He was already happy." I took the rose, chuckling, and her phone rang. "It's my parents. I'll be talking about the job they're so surprised I have for the next few millennia. Goodnight, hun."

She answered her phone, speaking in full speed French. She managed to sound bored despite the beauty of the language. In addition to the one with Paul, she also had an awkward relationship with her parents. They were waiting for her to turn into her sister, an evil witch who was killed for the crimes she'd committed. I'd bet feeding the homeless would help with that.

I searched downstairs for Nate so I could apologize for giving him the worst gift ever. When I didn't find him, I checked the pool house. Not there either.

I found him in my room, curled up at the foot of my bed with his paws under his snout. He'd left a note on my pillow.

I need a minute to calm down, but you're what calms me. Put me out if you're too mad.

I dropped the note on my bed and petted his head. I couldn't apologize now. He'd remember it, but it wouldn't have the same effect. In this form, I was just a girl he liked to follow around and play fetch with, not his girlfriend. I should apologize after he shifted back.

I went into the closet to dig up my diploma. It was in the corner under a pile of shoes that never seemed to make their way back to the shelf if Sophia didn't put them there.

I rubbed my fingers across the embossed words.

Christine "Leah" Grant

A graduate of St. Catalina Preparatory Academy and Boarding School.

He was right. I didn't value this. I'd toiled day and night in that place. And that name, Leah, on this insignificant piece of paper had the power to bring tears to my eyes. My mother had left me there in preparation for her death—that Julian either caused directly or … indirectly. I hadn't known how expensive it was until Nate found the invoice in the package with the diploma. Twenty thousand a year, for eighteen years, was paid on the day she left me there.

I guessed I could buy a lot of Nathans with this. I propped it up on my desk, my eyes still wet with the tears I wouldn't let fall. But if it meant making Nate see that I wasn't a brat, I'd cringe at Leah's name in secret every time I passed it.

I went back into the closet, picked up my expensive shoes, and put them in their place. I wrangled up the clothes I hadn't worn to give to Emma. Wearing a sign that said: *Look, Nate, I'm charitable. Don't be mad at me*, would've been less obvious.

After my shower, I slipped on a tank top and a pair of Emma's little shorts that had gotten mixed in with my laundry. The white dog was missing from my room.

I went out on my balcony and leaned over the rail. I stared at my horrible gift, wishing I'd never bought it.

A BMW. A freaking BMW. What was I thinking? He didn't even have a license. He knew how to drive, but he didn't have the proper IDs to get one. He needed his birth certificate and a social security card and didn't want to go to John and Theresa to get them.

I heard him come in, but I didn't turn around. The door slammed, so he had hands now.

He wrapped his arms around my waist, and we stared at the M3 in silence. I could feel his bare chest against my back. Nate rarely wore shirts. He hated the feel of them and had put his foot down on the matter, even with Sophia.

"You were so happy when you got home," I said. "I ruined your first day of work."

He kissed my ear. "You didn't ruin anything, babe."

"I wasn't thinking. I didn't mean to make you feel … less fortunate. I just love you and wanted to do something nice. And you tried to walk away, but I kept pushing you to talk about something really uncomfortable. You never push me like that. I'm sorry."

He turned me around in his arms, leaning us into the rail. "I should've said thank you and meant it. I was rude and ungrateful, and I just tried to walk away after pissing you off like you weren't going to react to that. *I'm* sorry." I pressed my face against his chest to avoid his eyes. "I still can't accept the car. Do you forgive me?"

"Yeah. Do you forgive me for buying it?" He raised my chin and kissed me, so passionately that I might have fallen over the rail if his hands weren't digging into my sides.

"It's over and done with," he said. We held each other in the steamy summer night, mending from the tiff that had disturbed the usually calm waters of our relationship. "You didn't have to display the diploma. That was an insensitive thing for me to say. I know you hated it there."

"I'll keep it out. My mom bought it."

We walked into the room, and I locked the balcony doors behind us. I hugged him from behind and rested my head on his so-called birthmarks, four long scratches that covered most of his back. They looked more like ancient injuries to me, but he was sure that they weren't.

I was still holding him as he reheated the leftovers from last night, and we ate standing up, still pressed against each other, like letting go was not an option.

After dinner, he carried me to my bed. At first, we just held hands and stared at each other. Then his leg brushed mine, my hand gravitated to his chest, and we stopped pretending we could cuddle in bed and not kiss.

"Where did you get these shorts?" he asked, his hand on the back of my thigh where the tiny shorts ended.

"Emma."

"Keep them."

I hooked one of my legs around his waist, cranking up the heat in the bed.

He wanted more. I wanted more. But I had to stop us. I'd missed many typical parental moments with Raymond and CC. Walking, talking, riding a bike. At the séance, I planned to speak with Raymond first and ask him more about his life. Then, I planned to summon CC and give her the only parental moment she could ever have with me—*the talk*.

She wrote about her sex life for pages upon pages. My mother was the perfect person to talk to about sex, and I wanted to do that before I experienced it. I would ask uncomfortable questions and probably defend Nate for not being human. I fantasized about what she'd say all the time. But I couldn't have the talk until we pulled off the séance, so that part of our relationship was on hold.

Nate sniffed loudly and his lips slowed, like blades of a ceiling fan coasting to a gentle stop. My mood had flipped his switch. His amazing senses always detected when I wanted to stop. I never had to push him away. "Sorry, baby," he said, as he rolled to the other side of the bed. He landed face down in the pillows.

"Don't be sorry," I said. He chuckled through a groan, still not looking at me. "*I* am. I know this can't be easy for you."

"We have forever. No rush."

I wasn't sure if he realized he said those same five words at least once a week. They flowed out of his mouth now, automatic, rehearsed.

After a minute, he rolled back to me and moved us to a much cooler position. He patted around the bed and found the remote. The television was awkwardly far away, and if we were in bed, it really only served as background noise.

"Nate," I said. "Do you think it's hard to be around me? Like you don't belong here? Or I don't belong around you guys?"

"Do you?"

"Sort of," I admitted.

He linked or fingers and kissed my hair. "I can see why you would think that. It's hard being different. I remember feeling that way before I left my house. Like no one understood me, like an alien." I nodded. It was exactly how I felt. Foreign in my own home, around people who loved me but couldn't fully relate. "You're more powerful than any of us could imagine being. Your brain can literally tell this bed to move out of this house and it would. I won't lie. Sometimes, it's strange being with someone who can have anything she wants. Whether by buying it or speaking it into existence. It makes me wonder what the hell she is doing with me."

I reached a hand to his cheek. The tiniest hairs pricked my

fingers, signs of Nathan, the man, replacing the boy.

"I am with you because you are the best person on this planet. And I would do anything to stay here. Right here." I rubbed his side from his armpit to his waist. His nook, a place where I couldn't deny how well I fit. "I already don't use my powers. If I had to, I'd give away all of my money to fit—"

"That's nuts. You don't have to do that. Nothing can break us up. Not money. Not magic. Not even deadly brains." He took a deep breath and let it out with a chuckle. "And I'd stalk you if you ever left me, so don't even try."

"You're such a creep."

We laughed, and I burrowed deeper into his nook.

"I'm kidding about the stalking. But I know we won't ever break up. I think you're my soul mate. I'd bet I would've found you eventually, even without Sophia's help. I always wanted to go to New Haven."

"What? You've never told me that."

"Yeah. It sounded like a peaceful place. I bet that's why your parents left you there. *New Haven*. Has a safe ring to it."

I smiled and added that to the list of things to thank my parents for at the séance. I might have died in any other town during that time— the darkest year of the war against humans. After searching the Internet, we'd learned that New Haven had a fourth of the deaths as most places. It couldn't have been a coincidence that she'd left me there.

"Or I would've roamed in an orange field and found you, the creep who thought she could live in one, sleeping under a tree." I pinched his arm, and he laughed. "Seriously, I would've stayed there with you. Doesn't matter the place or circumstance, I think we would always be together." I wanted to do too many things at once—kiss him, undress him, cry. I loved the thought of us being soul mates. He sniffed the air and hummed. "I ... sort of like whatever you're feeling. Sort of love it, actually."

I threw one leg over both of his. He closed his eyes and smiled. I gradually pulled it back when I thought about CC and the talk we needed to have.

"You wouldn't believe the things I saw today, Chris." His handsome face sank, serious now. "Those people were starving, even before the attack. The shifters can't work, the witches and wizards do as best they can, and the assistance they are supposed to get from the agents never comes." He shook his head and sighed. "And there were so many kids. My boss put me in charge of them. I don't know why, but he did. Even though it was my first day."

"I know why. You're great with kids." I remembered how he'd treated little Kelsey in Kamon's prison. He was kind and gentle. I wasn't sure if it was because of the friendly dog in him or the goofy boy who still watched cartoons every day.

"When I grow up, which, incidentally, is in two hours ..." He chuckled. "I want to be as giving as my boss. Devin is awesome. He gives every penny he has and every second of his time. I want to help people like he does." I brought his hand to my lips and kissed the back of it, touched by how caring he was. "What will you be when you grow up?"

I hunched my shoulders. I'd never planned my future. Before Sophia came, my only goal was to stay alive. Then I wanted to be with Nathan, like that was a career or something.

"What about ... an artist?" he said, throwing out options to help.

"That would be nice, but it's selfish compared to your goal."

He gently grabbed my jaw and pulled my face to his. "You're not selfish. Frivolous, maybe, but not selfish." He chuckled. "But seriously, babe, even if you were selfish, you would deserve to be. You're waiting for a man I should've sank my teeth into in that chapel to give up on capturing you ... to possibly breed you. You have money, but your life is far from easy."

Nate went on about how he wished he would have killed Kamon that night, instead of writhing in pain from his broken spine. I tuned out his heroic delusions as Kamon's hypnotizing eyes flashed in my mind.

I'd thought I hated Sienna Martin. That was nothing, a childish grudge. I used to hate Remi until my heart started bleeding for her. That was nothing, too. Hate was what I felt for Kamon.

I'd give anything to know what he was up to, pull him out of the shadows and into the light. Was he getting close? Did he know who and what I was?

I welcomed the energy that rushed over my skin, and his name echoed in my head.

He was in New Orleans. I knew it for a fact.

I faintly heard when Nate turned off the TV. I didn't open my eyes, too wrapped up in the buzzing, in the power I pretended I didn't have.

Behind my eyelids, I saw a blurry picture of my New Orleans backyard.

Kamon chuckled, circling Lydia Shaw near the pool. *"Where is she?"* he asked.

"That's not your business, and stay away from this house."

"She is very much so my business. A girl with her potential does not come along every day. I noticed it the first time I saw her. I knew then."

Lydia laughed and stepped closer to his face. *"I can't wait for this to be over,"* she said.

My muscles quivered. Lydia and Kamon shook with me.

"Me, either. I have big plans. I've been working on my new title.

What do you think of Emperor Kamon? Too much?" He laughed.
"There's finally a date after your dash. I guess I'm lucky Leah's so unstable. I know you're terrified. It's getting so close. July 4ᵗʰ."

I shook even harder and heard a far away scream.

Lydia spun around, and Remi wiggled her fingers at her, a taunting wave. Her jet-black hair dangled to her waist now. *My Master, My Lord*, in a fancy, ancient script, was permanently inked on her stomach, right above her low-cutting leather pants.

"Remi is one of the best things to ever happen to me. Her first offering brought my nemesis barging through the doors. In time, she'll bring me Leah. I've seen July 4ᵗʰ, Lydia. It is your pet's destiny, and I'm going to help her fulfill it."

My backyard trembled like an earthquake was ravishing New Orleans, and someone screamed, "Emma, hold her head!"

Nate.

"Wake up, Chris," Emma said.

I opened my eyes. Nate and Em were shaking me and swatting at my cheeks. Blood was everywhere—on Nate's hands, his chest, my pillow.

I'd had another fit. Correction. I was still having a fit, shaking and bleeding and buzzing. Em's thoughts were frantic and in fluent French. But understandable. I had a feeling she could speak Chinese, and I would understand it right now.

She snapped and disappeared, leaving me alone with Nate. His face vibrated as I shook, and he braced me against his chest.

After a moment, his body tensed against mine, and he drew his arms away, no longer holding me. My nails were in his sides, and they didn't want to let go.

Embers blew around us, and found their way to his head, circling and sparkling, crowning him with fire. I coughed from the smoke tickling my throat. He didn't seem to see them at all.

A deep voice I'd never heard screamed, "*Dali!*" It echoed several times after. With each repeat, Nate clutched his head tighter, in pain.

All day I had been questioning where I belonged. Now I knew. I belonged in a cage, not allowed to roam freely around my enemies.

I didn't want to hurt him. Or myself. I needed to listen to my body. Someone had told me that. Someone …

A flash of light blinded me, and Sophia and Emma appeared when it cleared.

Sophia pried my clenched jaw open. Something warm filled my mouth and slithered down my throat.

Then there was nothing but darkness.

CHAPTER THREE

I woke up to sounds I'd only heard on TV shows and movies, hospital sounds—a constant beep over my head and hissing from a tube tickling the base of my nose.

I blinked a few times to get the room into focus. Blue walls, white curtains. Not my room. A television flickered an array of colors around the blue room. Cartoons were on, and Nate was knocked out and snoring in the recliner next to the bed.

"Babe," I said. His snore caught in his throat. He jumped up and scurried to me.

"You're up!"

"What happened?"

"You had a … well Sophia told us to call it a seizure. I don't know if it was. She stopped it, but Lydia wanted you to get a brain scan to make sure you hadn't hurt yourself."

I stretched in bed and pulled at the tube under my nose. "Lydia? She was here?"

He nodded. "She brought us here." I pouted, not because I was in a hospital bed. I'd missed a visit from the famous woman.

"How long have I been out?"

"About three hours." He leaned in to kiss me and left his face pressed against mine for a long minute. "Chris, please don't scare me like that again."

"I'm sorry. I guess … I can't help being a copy sometimes."

I jerked away, remembering that I'd hurt him in bed. He pulled my face back to his. "You're not a copy, baby. And I'm not afraid of you." He paused for a moment then chuckled. "Especially since I have your kryptonite now."

"What?"

"Sophia has a potion to turn your powers off. That's what she gave you."

I stirred in bed, my body heavy and tired. I stared at the blanket, trying to lift it without my hands. It didn't budge. "How long does the potion last?"

"You had a lot. Sophia said it would be a few more hours."

I crashed back onto the pillows, dazed and wondering how the potion worked. Did it shut my brain off? Make me weak? And because I wasn't currently psychic, those questions did nothing in my head. "Where are we?"

"New Zealand, in some swanky hospital Lydia brought us to. I think it's for the military. There are lots of people in uniform walking around. Sophia didn't come in just in case someone recognized you from the news, and Lydia left half an hour ago. Em and Paul stayed home because they said you were totally fine."

I looked over his shoulder to the window. The sun peeked through the bottom of the thick curtains. Lydia had brought me to a hospital on the other side of the world. Odd.

"I'm sorry you have to spend your birthday here." He pushed me over in bed and made room for himself under the blanket.

50

"Where else would I be? I'm your next-of-kin on your records now, by the way, in addition to being the keeper of the kryptonite."

I smiled. I shouldn't let myself get so worked up about missing my family. Family was right here in bed with me.

I sang him a terrible version of the birthday song as the monitors beeped and hissed in the background. A nurse with a friendly face walked in and fanned at Nathan, telling him to stay in bed.

I assumed she was human, I couldn't hear her thoughts to know for sure. Before, I'd ignored my powers and didn't ask too many questions so I didn't have to be psychic. It was a different feeling entirely not having them at all. I felt very human. Very vulnerable.

"You're finally awake, Cecilia," she said. I nodded. Apparently, I was Cecilia Neal today. Her accent was unfamiliar. If I hadn't known we were in New Zealand, I wouldn't have guessed it from that. "Want another blanket, Nate?" she asked, like they were old friends.

"No thanks, Wendy."

She peeked into my gown and unhooked me from the monitors and oxygen cord. She waved at us on her way out, the patient and her best friend.

"What's a date after a dash?" I asked, recalling what I'd heard Kamon say to Lydia before my fit.

"It sounds like a tombstone. Like date of birth to date of death."

For a moment, the world stopped spinning and everything made sense. First, the dream of the child singing "The Star-Spangled Banner" as I sank with another person. Then, seeing Kamon tell Lydia that it was my destiny to give her a date after her dash on July 4th. According to him, I would kill Lydia Shaw in less than a month. That was why he wanted to capture me. He wanted to help me kill her.

I'd thought of myself as unstable and murderous my whole life. But killing the woman who saved the world, the woman who saved me, would be beyond anything I ever thought I was capable of.

In the loudest voice I could manage, I told Nate about what I'd seen. He smacked his lips and chuckled. "You fell asleep when I was talking about work. Your eyes were closed. And he wouldn't really call himself an emperor in real life, no one would. It's silly. It was just a dream."

"It felt like more."

"It wasn't. You like Lydia. Why would you kill her or anyone? There's no Sienna or Whitney or anyone to bully you. You don't have a motive, so it must be just a dream, babe." He pressed his nose against my cheek. "Stop worrying. You're going to give yourself indigestion. And this room is too tiny to escape a gas attack from you."

I laughed and denied ever having gas a day in my life. It was just like Nathan to say something perfect to lighten the mood and make me forget about July 4th. He was probably right. I liked Lydia. The mere mention of her name could make me smile. My affection bordered on creepy—peeking at her stolen shoes once a week, creepy. I wouldn't kill Lydia. It had to be a dream. A really over stimulating, seizure causing dream.

"Does the name Dali mean anything to you?" I asked, because that part of the night was certainly not a dream. He shook his head. "I heard someone scream it when I was … hurting you. And I saw embers, kind of like we were around a campfire."

"Weird," he said, and nothing else. I dropped it. He obviously didn't want to discuss his past and the possibility of it involving crowns made of fire.

The phone on the nightstand rang as we watched an episode of Family Guy we'd seen before.

"Hello?" Nate said. "Yes, ma'am. She came in and unhooked her a while ago. She's up. Hold on." He gave me the phone and mouthed: *Lydia.*

My heart jumped to my throat. "Hi," I said.

"Hi. How are you feeling?"

"Fine." For a moment, I considered telling her about my dream, but I remembered she probably didn't have time to hear about my nightmares. She had a world to run.

"Sophia will be there to bring you two home in fifteen minutes. Meet her outside."

"Okay. Um … why did I have to go to a military hospital?"

After a long pause she said, "More privacy. People like us need that."

I smiled and twisted my lips to hide it. People like *us*. I was like Lydia Shaw. That thought warmed me and made me giddy inside. So giddy that I missed her goodbye and listened to the dial tone for a few seconds before I realized she'd hung up.

Nate slid out of bed and walked to a closet I hadn't noticed in the corner. As I sat up and placed the phone on the receiver, he unzipped a duffle bag and pitched me a pair of jeans and a thick sweater I'd never seen before. He pulled a fluffy white jacket from the bag and threw it on the bed. He smirked at whatever was left inside.

"What?" I asked.

He pulled out a pink knitted hat with a goofy pom-pom. "This is adorable," he said. "Sophia really thinks you're a toddler."

I rolled my eyes, and he turned his back as I changed.

I saw his reflection in the mirror on the wall. He was watching me through it with his mouth hanging open. Our eyes met, and he bowed his head.

"Sorry," he whispered.

I chuckled. "It's fine. You didn't have to turn away." He spun around in a blur as I pulled the sweater down the rest of the way. I thought the hospital room would catch fire as I pulled my jeans up. Nate's eyes glazed over at the sight of me in my underwear. He'd seen me in a bikini countless times, but somehow this was riskier, sexier.

I kept my distance. It was not the right moment to kiss him and tempt him more.

He finally recovered as we left the room and navigated the sterile hallways of the hospital. He pulled on a blue tweed jacket Sophia had packed for him and mumbled about how he hated the feel of it, even more than shirts.

"Goodbye, Wendy," Nate said, waving at her behind the nurse's station.

"Bye, Nate. Feel better, Cecilia."

"Thanks," I said.

The automatic door opened to a snowy wonderland, mounds of it as far as my eyes could see. There was nothing else but pure, untouched snow. The hospital was in the middle of nowhere. I tucked my hands into the furry pockets of my new jacket, freezing already. It felt like I was trapped in a snow globe, in the arms of the person I wouldn't mind being trapped with.

Nate exhaled loudly and shut his eyes. I didn't think he noticed himself smiling, like the snow and the cold had touched something in his heart. I imagined that was how I looked with an orange to my nose.

He slowed his steps, lingering on purpose, and leaned his head back. The snow fell on his face and rolled away like rain as it melted instantly on his warm skin. The black of his hair drained from the roots, sending stark white streaming to the tips. I snatched the hat from my head and threw it on his.

He opened his eyes and smiled.

"My hair?" he asked. I nodded, tugging the hat over his ears. I stretched it as far as it would go over his forehead, trying to cover his now white eyebrows. "This is probably the worst place to shift." He yanked his head toward the roof. An armed guard marched into view then headed back in the opposite direction, luckily not seeing anything strange. His gun looked powerful enough to strike us from up there, and seeing the magic in Nathan's hair would be enough for him to pull that trigger. "I'm fine. Don't worry."

He shivered and pulled off the cap, hair black and back to normal. Nate hated talking about his past, so I treaded lightly. "It seems like you like the cold," I said.

He hunched his shoulders, face still slightly angled more to the air than to me. "I guess. Winter is my favorite season. I also take a lot of cold showers." He chuckled and looked down at me. "But that one doesn't have anything to do with being a shifter."

I laughed and pecked his lips.

Sophia honked the horn as she slowly drove through the snow, the street barely visible under the tires. We drove for a while. Nate stared out of the window with a longing in his eyes that I was dying to ask about. But I didn't. I just rubbed his hand and pretended he wasn't looking at the snow like he belonged in it until Sophia brought us back to our side of the world.

At home, I immediately went from healthy to terminally ill. Sophia tucked me in bed like I'd had the flu and not a psychic seizure.

"I can call my boss and tell him I can't come. He said we couldn't miss training, but he's cool. He might understand," Nate said, dread weighing heavy in his tone.

"No, I'm fine." I pointed at Sophia as she mixed things with her back turned to us, smoke and magic wafting around her. "She'll be hovering all day, I'm sure."

"I sure will. Nathan, get in bed. I'll wake you in time to leave for work, dear."

He kissed me and left, and Sophia got to work on me, pouring potions down my throat and rubbing scented oils on my forehead.

"I told Lydia bringing you to the hospital would be a waste," she grumbled. "And I was right. They found nothing because the potion worked perfectly."

It seemed like Lydia had more authority over me than my pretend grandmother-slash-witch. Made sense; I was the hidden child of an ex-hunter. My mother would've answered to …

"Honey!" Sophia yelled. "Can you hear me?"

"Huh?" I checked my nose. I'd spaced out but hadn't had another nosebleed, thankfully.

"I said … don't think I didn't notice that Nathan was in your bed shirtless when I got here."

"We weren't doing anything, Sophia." I sat up to tell her about hurting Nathan and the dream, and she dipped her finger in a bowl of crushed flowers and oil she'd been stirring and drew a star on my forehead. The corners of my mouth curled up.

She chuckled.

"What are you doing to me?" I asked, beaming for no reason, no natural reason.

"Simple charm. Helps you relax." She guided my weak body to my pillows. "Pleasant dreams, my love."

My eyes closed on command. I dreamed of Nate running through the snow on four legs, happy and free. His eyes were the only part of him that didn't blend with the world around him.

Even as I slept, I could feel the difference between dreaming and having a vision. This was a dream, fantasy. It wasn't blurry, and I didn't have to strain to see it.

"No," I said, as soon as my eyes popped open. "Last night was just a dream."

I chanted that a few more times as I unfolded the note propped up on my nightstand.

My heart, something came up. I'll come back to see you all off to dinner. Your lunch is in the microwave.

Love, Sophia.

I'd slept most of the day away and missed two meals. I made another sandwich after devouring the one Sophia left. After stealing an oatmeal pie from a box clearly labeled with Paul's name, I made the huge mistake of looking out of the window.

"What am I going to do with that thing?" I said, rolling my eyes at the car. I sort of knew before I asked. Finding the keys for *my* new car and throwing on a hat, I went outside. I hopped in the driver's seat and stared at the key, wondering where the hell I was supposed to stick it. "Oooooh," I said, pressing the obvious START button, but nothing happened.

I opened the manual and read up on my new car. It didn't really instruct me on how to drive it ... but how hard could it be? I pressed the brake and started the engine. I fiddled with the shift, testing the different directions and pretending I was shifting gears in a race car. With the tips of my toes, I barely tapped the gas, and the car flew backwards out of my driveway and into the yard across the street. I banged into something and slammed on the brake.

"Hey!" I tugged my hat down over my eyes and pressed the window button. "You okay?" The older man squatted so that he was at eye level with me.

"Did I kill anyone?"

He laughed. "Yeah ... my trashcan." When I calmed down, I heard his thoughts, human and open to me with no effort. It felt odd hearing thoughts again; my house was silent and the bowling alleys and arcades we'd gone to had been mostly emptied out for my safety. Thankfully, he didn't recognize me from the news. In his thoughts, I heard that his daughter had done the same thing when she was my age. He wondered if poor driving was a curse of young girls in expensive cars.

"Let me guess. Your parents just got you this and you have no clue what you're doing." I nodded, lying. "Okay. I'll get you back across the street until they get home. I haven't met them. I'm always gone on business. I hope they don't think I'm antisocial."

"No. It's fine. They don't think that. They … uh … work too." I didn't know why I didn't just tell him they were dead. That wasn't a secret. It was public knowledge, actually. I guessed I just wanted to pretend they were alive for a while.

"Tell them you need driving lessons, okay?"

"Yes, sir."

I watched him pick up his dented trashcan through the side mirror.

"Okay, honey," he said, back at the window. "Put it in drive." It took me two tries and a few chuckles from him to get there. "Ease slowly off of the break."

"I don't know about that …"

"Trust me. Lift your foot slowly." I did, and the car rolled forward, less like an uncontrollable bull this time. "Good. Now give the gas a tiny, tiny tap." I squealed and nudged the gas. He walked with my slow-moving car until I made it safely to my driveway. "Now park it until you get driving lessons. My daughter said it is better to go with your dad than your mom. We tend to nag less."

"Thanks. I'll go with my dad." I waved, and he ran back to his house. "No, I won't."

I punched the steering wheel, suddenly pissed about hunters ruining my life and killing everyone who would've been important to me. Given how hard CC and Raymond loved each other, I would have grown up smothered with it. Sickeningly happy. Wonderfully normal. I'd bet Nate would have made his way to New Orleans, where I would've been raised, led there by his soul that was destined to find mine.

I wouldn't be hiding from Kamon or waking up in hospitals or planning séances to speak with my own parents.

I locked the car and went back into the house. My heart pounded hard enough to drown out the world. I didn't know if my vision was blurry from tears or the sudden rage fuming inside of me.

"I hate him," I said, slamming the front door behind me, like Kamon was my only problem. I guessed he was the only person I could be upset with. Julian was dead and Remi was brainwashed.

I headed for the stairs but landed in my studio, accidentally shifting my surroundings with a thought.

Trying to calm myself and get a grip on the powers I didn't want to use, I grabbed paintbrushes from the supply shelf that were cleaner than I'd left them yesterday.

I thought of things to paint—flowers, trees, anything calming—but Kamon's face wouldn't leave my mind. My chest went up in flames as I remembered his voice, from the chapel and from my dream last night. The hateful side of me wanted him dead.

Then it would be over, and I would be free to go where I wanted, be what I wanted, without fearing someone would capture me, copy me, or make me fulfill a destiny I didn't want.

I shivered and threw the paintbrushes to the floor, pissed at myself for wasting murderous energy on silly little girls. I would give anything for Kamon to meet Leah. His bones wouldn't be safe. His home wouldn't be safe. They'd all be ash if she had her way.

"Chris!" Nate yelled.

I opened my eyes, but I couldn't see a thing. Thick smoke poured into my lungs and clouded my vision. I coughed violently. My chest was heavy like I'd been breathing tainted air for a while.

I didn't remember sitting, but I was on the floor.

"Ouch," I said, as I scraped my hand on what felt like shattered glass.

Nate picked me up and carried me to my room. He sat on my bed with me in his lap.

"*What happened?*" he yelled.

"Why are you home?" I asked.

"It's 4:30. What happened?"

I hadn't felt those hours pass.

"We put the fire out," Paul said.

Fire? I ran across the hall to my studio. Smoke flooded out of the door and the new hole in the wall where three huge windows used to be. The sand-colored floorboards were charred, especially along the left wall. I held my breath as I brought my eyes up to my mother's paintings. They still hung on the walls, untouched but surrounded by the clearing smoke. I crept towards the opening and peered into our backyard. The shattered glass covering the bushes and grass gleaned in the light.

I turned back to my friends. The three of them were huddled in the corner, around a pool of red paint.

Red footprints led away from it and to the window where I stood. I lifted my foot. The bottom was covered in paint. So were my hands. I didn't remember touching paint today.

"Chris," Emma said. "What happened?" I hunched my shoulders. I really had no clue, but it was frighteningly obvious that I'd smashed the windows and started the fire. I had been thinking about hurting Kamon, breaking his bones and burning his chapel down, and had accidentally broken and burned things in my studio, painfully close to my mother's artwork. "You could've hurt yourself," Emma said. "What if we hadn't come home?"

I supposed I would've sat there in a trance while my house burned down.

"I thought we had a deal," Nate said. "I thought you weren't going to scare me anymore." He pulled me to his chest, and I whispered an apology into his shirt. "What's going on with your powers? You were fine until yesterday."

"I don't know. I was upset, but I don't remember doing this."

I took another glance at my mother's paintings, wondering how I'd managed to miss them. The marks on the floor looked like a fireball had started in the right corner of the room by the supply shelf and fanned out before smashing through the wall.

"I feel like scum for going on the trip now," Nate said. "First, the seizure. Now this."

"Me, too," Emma said.

"Me, three," Paul said.

And now *I* felt like scum. They were going to make thousands on the mission trip. It wasn't a lot of money to me, but to them, it was everything, and now I was complicating it for them.

"I'm fine. Don't worry," I said.

Nate carried me to my bathroom and started the shower. I passed the mirror and cringed at the red paint splattered all over my face and hair. I looked wild and unstable. I couldn't tune out my own intrusive thoughts. If I could smash three windows and set a fire without realizing it, could I also take a life and not remember a thing after? If I weren't cognizant of it, it didn't matter how much I liked Lydia. I wouldn't be in control of myself.

"Nate, the dream …"

"It was just a dream," he said. "You know you would smell weird to me if you were capable of killing Lydia Shaw or anyone. Please don't worry."

He was right. Even if I couldn't trust what I thought I knew about myself, I could trust his nose. He could detect the slightest change in my mood. He knew me. He'd know if there was a murderer lurking inside of me.

I heard Nate just outside of the door when I stepped out of the shower. It felt like he was afraid to leave me unsupervised. He'd put a pair of sweats and a t-shirt on the counter for me. I left them there, wrapped myself in a towel, and changed into real clothes in the closet.

"It's your birthday," I said. "We're going out for dinner."

"I'm not in the mood," he said.

"I'm not ruining this day more than I already have. Please. Get dressed."

Like I was two years old, he pulled me by my wrist, walked me to Emma's room, and left me with my next sitter. She was sifting through the pile of laundry on her bed.

"I called Sophie," she said.

"I figured you would."

"She's on her way."

"I figured she would be."

She threw on a navy blazer with her jeans and adorned it with a pink scarf. I must've looked plain, because she tossed me a yellow one to put on over my white shirt, then carefully clasped a silver bracelet around my wrist without touching my skin once.

My eyebrows yanked together when Emma passed in front of her television. She usually watched MTV or VH1, but her channel was set on CNN. Maybe working for the Peace Group was to blame. I guessed being in the middle of extreme poverty all day would force you to grow up. Or maybe it was because the boy she usually played mind games with had left the court and joined another team, leaving a more adult, news-watching Emma in the place of the old one.

She misted herself with fruity perfume and tossed it to me to do the same.

"That's so gross," she said, pointing to the screen I was still watching. The image was of a bloody mess in the ocean off of the Gulf coast of Florida. "It's been there for days. The fish have gone crazy. Your BFF news guy said they're killing each other."

She was referring to Ken, the primary reporter during my disappearance. I cringed at the close-up of the water. She was right … those fish were out of their minds. Their dismembered pieces floated and slushed in the waves. The headline had a different theory—that the contagion that swept through Sololá was now in the water.

"Good thing there's not really a virus, right?" I said. She chuckled and nodded. "And since when do you watch the news?"

"Since everyone at work is an expert on current events. I don't want to look like the idiot who can only discuss what happened on *The Real World*."

I chuckled, and Sophia announced herself in song, high-pitched and slightly off key. "My love?" She'd walked into the wrong room.

"In here," I said.

She smiled and came over to Emma's bed and gave me a silver cup, the size of a shot glass. Green liquid sloshed inside.

"Drink this. It'll turn your powers down. Not off like last night, but enough for you to enjoy yourself and not worry about anything happening." I tossed the warm potion back, wondering if I could drink it every day, all day, to stop myself from burning my house down or worse. "I put a license plate on your car and got you insurance, for when you learn." I hadn't even talked to her about the car. Maybe Emma had or … she'd used her powers to stay a step ahead of us as usual. "Paul has the keys. He'll drive tonight. The restaurant is in town."

"Yes!" he said at the door. "Slowly but surely, that car will be mine."

Sophia chuckled and kissed my forehead. "I'll clean up in there, okay? You are not to worry. Have fun with your friends." Nathan stepped into the room, and Sophia walked to him with open arms. "Happy Birthday, sweet boy. Don't stay out too late. You all have work tomorrow, and Christine …" She released Nate from her rocking hug and turned to me. "You have a meeting tomorrow morning."

"With?" I asked.

"Lydia."

My heart sank. Usually, hearing that name would thrilled me, but after the dream and losing my mind in my studio, I couldn't imagine anything more terrifying than Lydia wanting to meet with me.

"Why does she have to see her?" Nate asked, probably sensing my silent panic.

"She wants to talk about some things," Sophia said.

"What if she doesn't want to go?" he asked.

Sophia cleared her throat. "It isn't exactly voluntary." Not voluntary? So Lydia Shaw didn't *want* to talk to me. She was demanding to. That was much worse. "Now get going. I want everyone in bed by midnight." She shooed us out of Emma's room. "In your *own* beds by midnight," she added as we headed down the stairs.

During the drive to the restaurant, Emma texted me while she sat a foot away. Her new crisis, which she couldn't discuss in her room for fear of Paul overhearing, distracted me from my eventful evening. His new girlfriend, Annabelle, had joined the Peace Group today so she wouldn't have to spend two months away from him.

That sucks, I replied. *How was she?*

Nice, charming, excellent potato scooping skills.

She sounds like a skank! I'll hate her with you.

We laughed and the boys looked over their seats to us. The light moment seemed to give everyone a license to enjoy the night. I did my best to shake out of the fog, but I went in and out.

The restaurant was mostly empty, Lydia's doing. I finished half of my spicy buffalo burger and tried to keep up with the conversation that never seemed to move away from their boss, Devin, and how great he was.

I couldn't stop thinking about my involuntary meeting.

"Sophia will be there," Nate whispered to me. He took a bite out of his green olive burger as I stared at him, waiting for him to expound upon that. "Sophia will probably be at the meeting with you tomorrow. I'm sure it will be fine. You'll discuss whatever it is she wants to discuss and go home."

His tone was more hopeful than certain.

"What if she wants to talk about the fact that my powers are dangerous and unstable?" I asked.

He didn't answer. He just stared at me without blinking until our waitress brought out a cake that Sophia had obviously set up beforehand. We sang to him, and he blew out his eighteen candles with a huge smile on his face.

"I wished for you to come on the trip with me," Nate said.

"I could try, but I wouldn't get very far." I chuckled, imagining

Sophia catching up to the bus and dragging me off of it. "She treats me like a psychotic baby that might hurt itself or someone else."

I'd meant that as a joke, but it was too true to be funny. His body stiffened next to me, and he took another bite out of his burger like nothing was wrong. That was what stressed looked like for Nathan, too still, purposefully calm.

At home, I presented him with a better birthday gift—the two paintings I'd finished and managed to not ruin in my tirade. He leaned one against the wall by his little kitchen and the other by his bed. He walked away, then back to it, and adjusted it in its temporary spot like it mattered. I laughed. Over the past three months, I'd also noticed that Nate was a tiny bit OCD. He wasn't excessively clean, but he liked things to stay in a weird order and exactly where he put them.

He thanked me with a sweet kiss, and went into his kitchen. He came back with a tiny vial of green liquid and sat it on his nightstand.

"Just in case," he said.

We lay in each other's arms without uttering a word or mentioning the obvious—that I needed Sophia's version of kryptonite to sleep in the bed with my boyfriend, and that Lydia Shaw probably wanted to discuss that very thing in the morning.

CHAPTER FOUR

At 6:30, I crawled out of his arms and turned off the *Sophia* alarm—my signal to go to my room before she got here and freaked out about us being in bed together.

I was close to passing out as I stared into my closet. What do you wear to a meeting with a famous assassin?

I went with a light blue dress with a lace collar. I was going for innocent.

I couldn't imagine what the house smelled like to Nate over breakfast. Everyone was on edge. Paul didn't say a single joke, and Emma had nervously brought up her sister. She always blurted out something about Edith when she was in a panic.

"Technically, Lydia Shaw didn't kill my sister. She left the decision up to the magical council, and *they* killed my sister."

"Not that this situation has anything to do with that," Nate said, shaking his head at her. "It's just a meeting. My girlfriend is not a murderer."

I cleared my throat. "Just attempted," I said, thinking of my darkest moment in the first floor bathroom at St. Catalina. Their eyes looked like they could've fallen out and rolled onto the table. "That was supposed to be funny."

They all faked chuckles, which made the moment even tenser than it was before.

Sophia blew in like a fresh summer breeze, smiling and kissing everyone, twice on both cheeks.

"Have a wonderful day, loves," she said to them while pulling my chair away from the table. Nate stood and clutched me in a long hug.

"It'll be fine," he whispered into my ear before Sophia snapped us out of the room.

We landed in a hallway with shiny silver walls and black tile. In a way, it reminded me of Lydia's apartment—elegant and so neat that I'd be too afraid to spill something and cause the one strand of chaos in the rigid order.

"Nervous?" she asked, as calm, mundane music hummed in the hall.

"Extremely."

"Don't be, love."

She pressed her hand against a sensor on the wall. A green light flashed, and a door opened in front of us.

"Sophia, there's annoying construction outside. Will you do something about it, please?" Lydia said, over the speakers.

"Can she see us?" I asked.

"No. The scanner tells her who opened the door."

We walked into an empty waiting area decorated with the flags of different countries. I had assumed Lydia worked in Paris since she lived there. I looked out of the window and saw the unmistakable landscape of New York City.

"I'm going to go see what I can do about the noise that's bothering her. Go through that door. I'll be in in a minute."

Sophia took an elevator down, instead of using magic. The humans who believed witches were extinct would probably die if she popped in out of nowhere.

I knocked on Lydia's door, my heart thumping in my throat.

"Come in," she said. I pulled on the handle and stepped inside. She turned around in her chair with a phone to her ear. If her voice made me frantic, I didn't have a word for what seeing her in person did.

She looked up at me for a second then back to her desk. "Prime Minister, I am confident in our abilities to stop the attacks. What happened in Guatemala and Cuba will not happen again." Attacks? Cuba? "We are well on our way to ending this. I would love to chat more, but I apologize, something just came up. I will have to call you back. Thank you." She groaned, pressed a button on the phone on her desk, and leaned back in her chair. "Sophia, are you out there? If you can hear me, come in here. I need you."

"She went outside," I said. "I think she did, anyway." Lydia sighed and looked up, but not exactly at me. Through me, actually. "Something happened in Cuba?"

She didn't answer me.

"Door opened. Sophia Ewing," a feminine, robotic voice said.

"Sophia," Lydia said, on the speaker again. "I'm having a headache. A special one. Make me something for it."

Sophia flashed into the room and placed a bottle of water in front of Lydia. She stared at it like it wasn't what she wanted. "Christine, would you like some water before you two talk?" she asked.

I shook my head.

Lydia finally looked at me, and the delicate features of her face lifted. "Is today ... Thursday?" she asked.

"Wednesday. You asked me to bring her here today," Sophia

said.

"I'm sorry. I can come back tomorrow if you're busy," I said.

Lydia smiled. "No. I have time. I was just … confused for a moment. I told Sophia to bring you tomorrow, but she must have not realized it was Wednesday for me already when I said that."

"My apologies," Sophia said.

Lydia stood and brushed the creases sitting had caused on her figure-hugging, calf length, black dress. She towered over me in her pumps, forcing me to look up at her and idolize her even more.

"Reschedule my next three appointments for tomorrow morning starting at eight," she said, still smiling at me. I had to smile back. "Make sure you get the day right this time."

Sophia rolled her eyes and kissed my cheek. She walked to the door, and I panicked.

"You're leaving me?" I asked.

"Yes, dear. Just for a moment. I have friends coming in from Cuba to stay with me. I need to drop in to say hi. I will be back in a few minutes. I promise."

People Sophia knew, probably magical kind, were leaving Cuba. Something had obviously happened there, like Guatemala.

Lydia smiled harder when Sophia left, yanking my attention from the attacks to her beautiful teeth. I didn't think I was ever going to get used to seeing her this way. Not all stern and serious like she was portrayed in my history books. I hoped that smile would stay there throughout this meeting.

She walked over to a sitting area in the corner of her office. I took the chair across from her, nervous and slightly giddy.

"I invited you here months ago. Why haven't you taken me up

on my offer?"

"I thought you needed time to help Remi," I said. "How is she, by the way?"

She sighed, and I didn't dare look at her, fearing the sting of her disapproving expression.

"We had a deal. And I didn't ask you to come here to talk about a girl you only knew for a few days before she almost had you killed." I looked at my feet, hearing how stupid I sounded to care about Remi so much. "I want to talk about *you*. Something's going on with your powers, and I feel like it's my job to stop it."

My heart pounded in my throat, and I had to force myself to breathe. My lungs refused to move on their own.

A book flew from her shelf and hovered over her hand. It rotated on its spine, its pages fanning back and forth with the motion. "Do you understand how this works?" she asked, nodding to the twirling book.

I shook my head. I didn't know anything about psychic powers other than the horror stories Nate had told me.

"It's simple. There's nothing more powerful than the human brain. Not weapons. Not magic. It is capable of so much more than most humans use it for. Blue monkey."

"Huh?" I asked, wondering if I'd missed something she'd said.

"I said, 'blue monkey'. What are you thinking of?"

"A blue monkey, actually." It was hopping around in my head. I could even hear it shrieking.

"All humans can imagine things, like being at the beach when they are really at work. But imagination is only a fraction of what the brain can do. When you move yourself from one place to another, you are doing the same thing all humans do when they imagine themselves somewhere different. And it's the same with all of your powers. It starts with a thought, and your brain handles the rest." The book closed on its own and flew back to the shelf. She extended her arm and held her palm open in the space between us. "What do you see?"

At the risk of stating the obvious I said, "Your hand."

She chuckled. "No, it's the start of human powers. Palmistry. Or really, the curiosity that led to it. When people began to wonder about things outside of the present, the natural power to predict the future and read the past emerged. The brain is incredible. It is constantly organizing all of the things you are sensing and putting them in a logical order for you to understand. For example, it is how you are aware that I have blonde hair. It can also decode less obvious things about me … or anyone … if you pushed it to."

I remembered my old life at St. Catalina and how I could stare at any of the girls and just *know* things, both random and important.

"The most ambitious of the humans who had harnessed their natural powers tested the limits of them and discovered they could command things to move and manifest things from nothing but a thought. At first, the powers were used for trivial things, food and travel, then eventually to battle magical kind. Unfortunately, when the wrong people started to train, mental powers took on a more sinister purpose."

And I wasn't sure where I stood. On the trivial side or the sinister one. I wished I could blame last night's incident on the emotional issues I was striving to overcome, but it clearly had nothing to do with that kind of instability. It was a psychic thing, a copy thing. Given more time alone, I could've ruined much more. It was the kind of destruction a hunter might cause, like they'd done to those poor creatures in Sololá.

I stared at the store-bought paintings on her walls of putrid green seascapes with frothy waves, working overtime to push my next words out.

"How would someone know if they are sinister or not?" I asked.

"That someone would need to know who she is. And trust that."

I brought my eyes back to hers. "Sophia said you were doing better with this issue."

"I am. It's just that ... something feels wrong. Really wrong."

As soon as the words left my lips, my skin buzzed all over. It felt like someone had turned up the volume on it, like it had been there all along, just humming in the background. I closed my eyes and saw children running through dirty streets around toppled houses. I was overwhelmingly sure that I was seeing Sololá. I'd thought the eerie feeling in my chest was about me, about something being wrong with me, but my powers weren't interested in being selfish right now.

My vision switched to burning buildings. Cuba. I knew it without a doubt.

"Find my voice and open your eyes." Lydia's voice was an echo. "Open your eyes. Open your eyes."

I forced my eyelids to obey her.

"What's going on?" I asked. "These attacks. What are the hunters doing? Is it Kamon?"

"Yes, but that would classify as my business. Wouldn't it?"

I disagreed. Kamon felt like my business, my problem. I desperately wanted to stay with the buzzing and let it lead me to the answer.

I remembered the hooded people on their knees in Kamon's chapel. If he was attacking magical kind, he wasn't doing it alone. He'd built an army of desperate, brainwashed souls like Remi.

Lydia cleared her throat, and I let the power drain from my veins, thoroughly afraid of disobeying her in her face.

"Do you have questions about things that are your business?" she asked.

Actually, I had a question about questions.

"How can I know *some* things, but at other times, I can ask all of the questions I want, and nothing will happen?" I asked.

She smiled and nodded, approving of the topic change.

"Most humans recognize natural intuition. They call it a *feeling*. Pursuing that feeling can lead you to remarkable insights if you let the brain function like it is meant to. But with anything, there are limits. There are things that are far too complicated for the brain to decipher as quickly as you want it to."

I nodded. That made sense. I guessed Kamon and his entire sick operation was complicated. He experimented on magical kind—purging their powers scientifically. Then I guessed he turned them into hunters, only to attack more magical creatures. What was the point of that? What did he want? Of course, my brain couldn't answer that complicated question, especially as I sat in front of her.

"So does that mean Nathan is complicated?" I asked.

"Yes. Most magical beings have a shield … and some humans. Just knowing that someone can read your thoughts could prompt a natural one. But Nathan is different. His shield is too strong to be natural. I'm not really sure what to make of it."

Since we were talking about my boyfriend, I decided to use him to ease into a harder conversation.

"Nathan told me when powers are passed to babies, it messes them up. Like drugs. Is that true?" I asked, wincing. I was talking to Lydia Shaw about being a copy. I couldn't stop my heart from racing.

"Actually, it would be the exact opposite of that. Babies affected by drugs and alcohol are developmentally delayed and have learning and memory problems. If *they* are underdeveloped, you could say that babies affected by mental powers are overdeveloped. Well before they are born, they learn how to do things, most importantly, they learn what is possible and what is not. Like not having to touch something to move it, or walk everywhere. It becomes normal and natural to them."

I thought of CC using powers with me inside of her, teaching me what was normal and natural. My life wouldn't have been so dark and complicated if she hadn't made that mistake.

"Tell me about what happened in your art studio," she said.

"I don't remember it."

"Interesting. What about the night before that?"

I swallowed hard, my eyes in my lap. "I went to bed thinking about Kamon, and I had a dream about him, and you, and Remi. You were in New Orleans … talking about me."

"You didn't dream that," she said. "That actually happened."

All of the air expelled out of my lungs at once. It wasn't a dream. Kamon really thought I would kill her. And he was psychic, so it was more than a thought.

"So…," I said.

"So, what?"

"July 4th isn't that far away. What are you going to do?" I asked, tears welling in my eyes.

She scooted to the edge of her seat and leaned over to mine, slow and calm, but still managed to speed my heart to deathly rates.

"Nothing."

A tear dropped from my eye, so thick that it splashed across my arm on impact.

"What do you mean, nothing?" I said.

"I mean … I'm not going to do whatever you're thinking that has you crying. I've seen what he's seen, but I'm not worried. You are not a murderer. Your only problem is controlling your powers."

"That's exactly the problem. I lost it yesterday. I could lose it again. And if you're gone, no one will stop Kamon. He'll be an emperor just like he called himself in my vision. What if these attacks are just the beginning? A preview of how he'd rule? It could be the end of the world as we know it!"

She covered her mouth and laughed, leaning her head back and sighing happily after. Then the laughter took her again and didn't release her for a long minute. The light sound relaxed me a little, eased me down from panic.

"Christine, has anyone ever told you that you're dramatic?" I shook my head, and a smile slowly formed on my lips. "Kamon is like your classic villain from any superhero movie." She dabbed the corners of her eyes, catching what seemed like happy tears. "He plans to take over the world every week of his life and never succeeds. He's not getting any closer, even though he believes he is. He senses that you have an issue controlling your powers, mostly from what Remi has told him and the nosebleed you had in his chapel. He's hoping that means you will lose control and kill me."

"Could I? I mean, realistically, could I kill you if I tried? Wouldn't you just stop me?"

She hunched her shoulders. "Probably."

Probably wasn't good enough, not when it came to taking a life. Her life.

"How is it at all possible? Aren't you the best?"

She shook her head.

"You're younger, so your brain is probably faster than mine, but don't worry about any of that. It doesn't matter. I'm sure it won't be an issue. The attacks will stop like they always do. That's my job. And it's also my job to keep you away from Kamon, and I plan to do just that. I'd also like to help with the other things. Seizures, zoning out. I want you to start coming here every day to practice with me. Your powers need to be trained by someone experienced. At your level, it would have to be Kamon or me. I'm assuming you'd rather it be me."

I nodded slowly, agreeing. I hadn't expected to come here every day, but I didn't want to say no to her, and I needed the help.

"So ... you're saying there's no problem?" I asked. "The attacks? The prediction? Everything is fine?"

"More than fine, Christine. Do you trust me?"

I nodded, meaning it wholeheartedly, and she motioned me to follow her to a wall. She pressed 2160 into a keypad, and it opened like a sliding door to another silver hallway. She bumped me with her hip as we stepped through the wall, and I staggered to the side.

"Lesson one," she said. "Loosen up. I don't bite." I smiled, entirely too big, and she joined me. "And that even goes for people who take my shoes."

I nearly fell over. She stopped walking with me and laughed. I babbled an apology, and she tugged at my hand to make me walk again.

"They're just shoes. You can have them. It's hilarious that you thought I didn't know." Of course she knew. She actually used her powers, didn't lock them inside like I did. "Hopefully that helps you relax. You are too young to be so serious and stressed all the time. When you're here, be comfortable. Try to have fun."

I wanted to bump her back, but I never worked up the nerve. She typed the same code into another keypad, and the doors opened into a large gym. I hadn't dressed appropriately.

I'd never worked out a day in my life, but I had a feeling all of that was about to change by the array of exercise machines, weights scattered around the room, and the track painted around the edges.

"Lesson two. I will ask you questions. Say the first thing that comes to your mind," she said. "Kamon has triplet boys. What are they?"

"Copies?"

She nodded. "And you are?"

"Also a copy," I said. "Technically."

"One," the robotic voice said over the speakers.

"You sure?" Lydia asked. I hunched my shoulders. "Think about it. I just want you to answer honestly. Go with what you really feel."

I cleared my throat as we walked further into the gym.

"I have powers naturally. So, yes, I think I am a copy."

"Two," the robot lady said.

"What is that?" I asked.

Lydia smiled. "Don't mind her, she's just counting." She walked ahead of me and spun around, then continued walking backwards, smiling at me. "So if I told you I killed copies, hundreds of them, because they were dangerous, would you think you deserved that?"

"Um, maybe. I mean … I'm a copy, but technically, I haven't done anything you would probably consider worthy of death … hopefully. Just because I'm a copy, doesn't—uh—automatically make me a murderer. I mean, I've wanted to, but that probably had nothing to do with me being a copy. I was going through some things." I swallowed and ended my ramble.

"Five," the robot said.

"What is that thing counting?" I asked, getting frantic.

She chuckled and folded her arms over her chest.

"Didn't we just discuss how powerful the brain is? Especially yours? What you say and think has more impact than you realize. If you call yourself a copy enough, you could convince your brain to make you behave like one. My friend, the robot, will count every time you say it, and you will run a mile for every time she catches you."

I gasped. "You said to relax and have fun!"

"I did. And I hope you will have a wonderful time here today, but you have a few bad habits I'm dying to break. This is one."

"But … but … I'm in a dress. And you asked me to answer you honestly, and I did. I *am* a copy, but I'm not freaking out about it like I used to."

"Six," it counted.

Lydia laughed. "It looks like you have six miles to run. Get started."

I walked to the track slowly with my mouth hanging open.

"But…"

She raised her eyebrows, begging for my excuse. I decided not to finish that sentence. I pulled off my sandals slowly, frowning, hoping she would change her mind.

She didn't.

The robot counted my miles as they passed. At mile three, I thought about what would be said at my funeral, since I was obviously about to die. Instead of complaining, I closed my eyes and pushed myself, forgetting everything but pounding my feet against the track.

"Mile six," the robot said, and I collapsed. While nearly coughing up my lungs, I pledged to never call myself a copy again.

Lydia kneeled in her nice dress and heels. She gave me a towel and a bottle of water. "Lesson learned?" she asked. I nodded, coughing and chugging the water. "Good. Maybe tomorrow we'll program the robot to detect every time you worry about Kamon. Wouldn't that be fun?" I shook my head, and she smiled. "Didn't think so. There's a shower through that door. I'll be waiting out here."

I limped to the door. It opened into a nice sitting room with a television, two sofas, and a little kitchen. Sophia was sitting on the longest sofa with a change of clothes on her lap. She held them out to me and pointed to a hallway. I rolled my eyes and snatched the clothes.

She laughed.

"Not funny," I panted. "You could've warned me about the robot."

I found the bathroom and started the shower. "I could have warned you, but you wouldn't have learned anything. She wanted to put one in your house. I stopped her, you should thank me."

"Thank you," I said, shedding my sweaty clothes without waiting for her to turn away. Naked did not mean *leave* to Sophia.

After my shower, I stood in front of the mirror over the sink. I smiled at myself but wondered if my mother would be upset about me being here, training in the world she ran away from.

"I'm just getting help to deal with the powers you left me," I whispered.

I didn't know why I always expected her to answer back, like she was always around, watching me, alive and near.

Sophia walked me out to Lydia who was now sitting in front of a chessboard. I sat across from her, fighting a smile. She was so pretty, in a really difficult to stare at kind of way.

"What's your favorite power?" she asked. I hunched my shoulders. "You have to have one. Mine is hearing thoughts. What people really think amuses me. What about you?"

I shrugged again. I didn't have many happy memories with my

powers. I'd always hidden them, and when I didn't have to hide them anymore, I started to worry about nosebleeds and seizures.

"Fire has to be fun to create, right?" she said.

"It's mostly scary," I said.

She chuckled, made a fist, and reached it across the table. She opened her hand near my nose and a fiery bird flew out of it. It flapped around the gym, a living ball of fire and work of art.

"It's all in how you look at it. The key is not to suppress your powers, Christine. That's why the last few days have been so eventful. When you open the door for them, intentionally or not, they will rush out, fierce and wild, because of the pressure you've put on them. You need to find balance and control."

The fire-bird flew back to the table and hovered over the chessboard. I reached my hand out to touch it, but Sophia grabbed my arm and stopped me.

"It's real fire, love," she said.

"Can I try one?" I asked.

"After we practice," Lydia said. "I'm not in the mood to have my eyebrows singed off." Sophia snapped and extinguished the bird. Smoke in the form of its shape lingered a few seconds after.

She scooted closer to the board and sat up in her chair. I mirrored her posture, not wanting to be a slouch across from a Nobel Peace Prize winner.

"Today, we're going to play chess my way. You will guess my move before I do it, and *nothing else*. Don't use any other power, and let go as soon as you see. Our friend will know if you don't." She pointed to the ceiling, and I rolled my eyes at my new enemy, the robot. "Breathe, relax, and simply tell me what I will do in thirty seconds without getting lost in your thoughts or the thrill of using your powers."

How could I relax with Lydia Shaw across from me, ordering me to peer into her future and control the urge to do anything else?

"Times up," the robot said.

I grunted.

"Let's try that again," Lydia said. "Turn the powers on and off. Make them obey you. It's the key to a normal life."

"I'm sitting across from *you*. This is nothing close to normal," I said.

They laughed, and I joined them for a moment before Lydia nodded to me, wordlessly telling me to focus.

It was as easy as it had always been when I relaxed. I saw Lydia in my head, moving the piece I vaguely knew to call a pawn. Curiosity tugged at me, the lure of what lied inside the famous woman's head. But I didn't want the robot to catch me and have to run again. Which was probably why she'd made me do that in the first place—more incentive to control myself.

I shook out of the vision and touched the piece she was going to move.

"Good," she said. "You will move this one, because you don't know what you're doing. You would have chosen it because it was closest to your hand. Your turn."

During our game of psychic chess, she taught me the proper way to breathe to ward off nosebleeds, and she stopped me every time I moved too quickly or pushed my powers too far. With her help, I started to feel the slight change in my muscles as the first tremors swept through me. Those were the warning signs, and listening to them would stop me from hurting myself, or Nate, or anyone who touched me when my powers were out of control.

"Am I the only person who's faster than you?" I asked.

She shook her head and said, "I'm getting old." I chuckled. She looked too young to complain about her age. "I'm sure there are tons of people stronger and faster, better." Something about her tone made that seem like a lie, or like she wasn't telling me everything. She cleared her throat and continued in her normal voice. "And there are things out of my range. I don't see Kamon clearly or some magical beings, like your boyfriend. I have to use technology and Sophia to keep the upper hand."

"Am I in your range?" I asked.

"At times. You have a strong shield, so it's difficult. We need to keep tabs on your future for your safety, so we try every day to break through it. I can see long-range things like what you might be doing when you're thirty, and Sophia is better at the day to day of your life. Which makes her a little more useful right now."

"You can make predictions about my day?" I asked, turning around in my chair to see Sophia. She nodded. "How do you do it?"

"I guess I could show you," Sophia said. "I haven't done it today."

Lydia tapped my hand. It was my turn. I guessed her move and looked back to Sophia. She closed her eyes, and her hands filled with yellow roses.

"Magic is so dramatic," Lydia mumbled. I chuckled at her tone.

"Stop complaining and help me," Sophia said.

Fire, from Lydia, I guessed, swirled around the roses and slowly caught the ends of the petals. The gentle burning sent whiffs of smoke into the air. Sophia stared at the forming cloud, like she could see something inside of it. She hummed and blew into the smoke. It swirled faster, and she leaned her face into the cloud.

"You're not in danger tonight, but something will happen. I don't know what it is." She blew over the roses and scattered embers into the smoke. "It involves Nathan." She gasped and snapped. The roses and the smoke vanished, and she pointed her finger at me. "You better not be planning on sleeping with him tonight!"

I felt myself melting out of the chair, but I hadn't moved. I was too embarrassed to do anything. It was one thing for Sophia to freak out about sex when we were alone. But in front of Lydia Shaw! I could've died.

"Oh my God!" I said. "Is that really what you see in there?"

"No. I see something changing about your relationship, and I just assumed it would be that." She gasped like something else had occurred to her. "Christine, I forbid it. If you accidentally have a child, I will lose my mind. I'd have to watch you around the clock so you don't give them powers."

"Enough, Sophia," Lydia said. "Go in the other room and relax. Put your head between your legs or something. You are going nuts for no reason. Isn't she, Christine?"

I babbled for a moment, looking guilty and confused and unsure of how Sophia had jumped to the topic of psychic children. "Nate and I haven't …"

Lydia held up her hand, cutting off what was sure to be an awkward declaration of my virginity.

"You having children is not something we need to worry about. She's jumping to conclusions as usual. Especially since I know you understand why you two need to be careful."

She nodded her head slowly, instructing me to do the same.

A hunter was after me, and my children could have powers *and* magic. I more than understood why we needed to be careful. It would be seventeen years ago all over again, with Kamon playing the role of Julian and me playing the role of my mother.

"I haven't seen much of your future, but I do know one thing. One part of your life is set because you're sure of it. It seems like Nathan

Reece will always be in your life. And I have seen that you will have children with names that begin with the letter N."

I screamed and covered my mouth to muffle the rest of my celebration. It was exactly the future I wanted. I hadn't thought about kids much, but I wanted to be with Nate forever and a family would come with that.

"I'm glad you're happy, but remember there is a time for everything. And now is the time to be …what?"

"Careful," I said.

And just like that, I'd had an impromptu sex talk with Lydia Shaw. It felt strangely appropriate for her to be the one to warn me. I guessed my kids would be her problem too if I gave them powers, needing to be watched and shown the way, and maybe even bound by her treaty.

It took a while for Sophia to relax, but when she did, she apologized for yelling at me. I thought my mother had caused her preoccupation with my nonexistent sex life, but now that I knew she was worried about me having shifting copies, I could forgive her for being a lunatic. I assured them again, as our chess game continued, that Nate and I would be careful … when we had a reason to be.

My lip shot out as I predicted what had to be Lydia's final move. I saw her smirking in my head as she trapped my king. "Aw! I lose?"

She nodded and motioned me to move her winning piece. "Good. You're a surprisingly fast learner. That should've taken us much longer." I hunched my shoulders. We both knew why I was such a fast learner, but I wouldn't dare call myself a copy again. "I guess it's time for a pop quiz. Try the bird."

I hopped to my feet, and her eyes told me to simmer down. I found my seat slowly.

"Make a fist," she said. I did and held it out to her. "You need a firm thought and a vivid picture."

I imagined the fire-bird in my hand, how hot it would be, the colors that would compose it.

I opened my hand and the bird fluttered out of it.

"Wonderful," Lydia said. "Enlarge it. Remember to breathe, four seconds in, five seconds out. If I see a single drop of blood come out of your nose, you will run. Understand?"

I pouted, and she chuckled. I wanted to pout again so I could make *the* Lydia Shaw laugh again.

I inhaled slowly like she'd taught me. I imagined the flaming bird expanding. It obeyed me in a moment, stretching its wings over my head and changing from a humming bird to an eagle in the blink of an eye.

Sophia applauded, and Lydia told me to stand. She took my wrist and raised my right arm. "Pointing helps with control," she said. She guided my hand in a circle, and we moved the bird around the gym. It soared faster and faster, a continuous streak of fire over our heads. Then slower, calmer, beautiful and controlled. Like my powers could be if I let them. If I listened to her.

"We'll do more of this tomorrow. And chess, too," Lydia said, still holding my wrist. For the oddest moment, I didn't want her to let go.

Sophia pulled me into a hug and away from Lydia. She snapped and turned my eagle into smoke.

"Do you guys think … never mind," I said.

"What?" Lydia said. I shook my head. I'd gotten too comfortable. I almost embarrassed myself. "Say what's on your mind. I can't read it and I'm curious."

Interesting. I was faster than her, out of her range, *and* she couldn't hear my thoughts. It made me wonder about my mother, what she would have become if she hadn't quit or died. If I was born with her powers, it seemed like she would've been stronger than Lydia.

The thought of that curled my stomach and burned my chest. It didn't sit well; it felt … off and wrong and …

Lydia cleared her throat and pointed at the track. "Lost in our thoughts, are we?"

I shook my head frantically, desperate not to have to run again, and brought my attention back to my statement.

I bit my lip and eased my words out. "I was just wondering if … people who are dead could be proud of you," I said.

"Without a doubt," Lydia said, like she believed it with all of her heart, like she had a reason to.

CHAPTER FIVE

I couldn't stop rambling about Lydia at dinner. And I wasn't finished, even after our plates were empty.

"So she just sat there, staring at me, waiting for me to make her next move," I said.

"And you guessed it right every time?" Nate asked, humoring me.

"Yes, she did. And Lydia won," Paul said.

I laughed. I'd come to that part of the story three times already.

"I'm glad you had a great day, Chris," Emma said. She yawned and Paul's head bobbed for the fifth time. "Sounds way better than cleaning a ballroom by hand. There were humans nearby and Devin wanted to be cautious." That explained the pungent smell of bleach in the dining room.

"Our job is throwing a ball to kick off our trip. It's in New York the night before we leave," Nate said. "We sort of have to go. Devin asked if you wanted to come with us, but I said no. I'm sure Sophia and Lydia wouldn't like that."

"Of course not," I said. "But it was nice to be invited."

I smiled, trying to show him that I was fine with him going to the ball without me. I'd be alone that night and sixty more after it … and that would be okay. It had to be. I would do my best not to lose myself and start any fires or kill any famous women.

"Em, did you get my mom's message?" Paul asked. Pain flashed across her face, and she nodded slowly.

"The one about the hairpin I borrowed for my sixteenth birthday that she's never asked about until now? Yes, I got that message." Her voice was barely above a whisper.

"Sorry. Annabelle saw a picture of it and really wants to wear it to the ball. If you don't mind."

"Why would I mind? Tell her I'll send it to her as soon as I find it."

Em looked like she wanted to die.

"Thanks," Paul said. "Are you bringing Louis?" She shook her head.

"He's busy. Chris, can I borrow Nate?"

"Of course. Don't kiss him too much." She chuckled and winked at me. "Did I tell you guys about the birds?"

"Twice," Paul said.

They laughed, and Nate put his arm around me. "You can tell me about the fire-eagle or whatever it was again, baby. Take a walk with me."

We left Emma and Paul, and I hid under one of my hats as he opened the door. The setting sun turned the world a soothing orange. In perfect harmony with the beautiful sky, Nate grabbed my hand and held my palm to his mouth.

"Is it safe to assume you'll be using your powers now?" he

asked, when we made it to the sidewalk.

"Yeah. She thinks I should. She wants me to come back every day to practice with her to make sure I don't zone out anymore. And I think ... I think we'll be friends."

He hummed like that had impressed him.

"If you tell me that I shouldn't worry, then I won't. I guess this is best ... since we're ... you know."

I nodded.

"Less than two weeks," I said.

We walked past our neighbor's home, the farthest I'd ever been down our street. I finished telling him about Lydia for maybe the fourth time as we circled the cul-de-sac, including informing him about our two future children who I'd named Naomi and Noah already.

"Is that it, Mrs. Reece? Sure you don't want to tell me again?" he asked. I shook my head and laughed. "If you're done, I want to talk about something. Devin needs me to get IDs for the trip. He said it's safer if we get stopped by hunters."

"We know Lydia. You'll be fine."

He hunched his shoulders and stopped walking. "I don't know about that," he said. "The hunters have never been this vicious before. Devin said ten thousand of our kind died today in Cuba. I don't want to give them a reason to take me anywhere for questioning. They do that when you don't have IDs. I might not make it back."

I frowned and hugged him. I didn't know if I should apologize on behalf of humans like me who made him and his people live in fear, especially in the last few days.

"Lydia said she's going to stop it. It's Kamon. She said not to worry."

He shivered, but not in fear. His jaw tightened and anger flashed in his deep green eyes. This was not the Nate I knew. "I didn't know it was Kamon." And I didn't know if that was privileged information or not. "I'm glad. If I see him on this trip, I'm going to—"

"Nate! No!" I pulled him closer by his collar. "You can't fight Kamon. Last time…"

"Last time, I was weak. This time, I'd kill him. You'd be safe. My people would be safe."

"Please," I begged. It wasn't that I didn't think Nathan was strong. He was the strongest person in the world to me. But it was a different kind of strength. The strength it takes to pull a shattered girl together and teach her how to live and love, not the kind of strength to end Kamon. "I can't let you go on this trip if you don't promise me you'll stay away from him if you see him." He twisted his mouth and cut his eyes away from mine. "I'm not kidding, Nate!"

The moment grew too serious for us, like we were standing in uncharted lands without a map. Like I knew he would, he smiled and made a joke to bring us back to the familiar comfort of our lighthearted relationship.

"Sheesh, one day with Lydia Shaw and all of a sudden you're bossy as hell!" I smiled and playfully punched his arm. "Okay. No fighting. I promise," he whispered.

"Thanks."

"One more heavy thing," he said. I groaned. I'd had enough heavy for today. "The IDs. You know I hate asking for things, but since you're going to be using powers now, I thought I'd ask for a favor."

"Anything," I said, looking down at our tangled hands, loving the look of them together.

He paused and traced circles on my palm, observing the moment with me. It was crazy how he always knew what to do and exactly when to do it.

He pecked my lips and continued.

"I want to visit John and Theresa. I could ask them for the truth and get my birth certificate. Anyway … I wanted to know if you would ask Sophia and Lydia if you could go with me. For support and because they wouldn't be able to lie to you. Maybe not tonight, but some time before I leave."

I squeezed his hand. He must've really needed this if he'd asked. He never asked me for anything. And he wanted to visit the parents he never mentioned. Hell was probably frozen solid underneath us.

"Of course," I said. I pulled my phone from my back pocket and called Sophia right then. As per usual, she answered before the first ring ended.

"Yes, dear?"

"Sophia, can you ask Lydia if—"

"Hold on, love. She's right here."

Apparently, I knew her well enough to ask her things for myself now.

"Hi, Christine," Lydia said.

"Hi. Um … can I meet Nathan's parents? Tonight or … tomorrow?"

She hummed and clicked her tongue in the speaker, audibly thinking.

"Sure. I guess this is what Sophia saw in the smoke. Go tonight. Don't call first. It will give them time to call the media if they wanted to. Just show up, and go straight there and back," she said. "Remember what you learned today. If you use your powers, don't strain. I'm not in the mood to go to the hospital tonight." We both chuckled, and I heard

Sophia's phlegmy laugh in the background. "Call if you need me," she said.

"I will. Bye." Nate winced like he hadn't expected the call to go that well. "Ready?" I asked him.

He groaned. "Taking my girl to meet the people who can't be my real parents?" He sighed. "I'm as ready as I'll ever be."

He distracted himself with talk of horsepower and fuel efficiency during the ten minute drive to his old house. It was about half the size of ours, but quaint, like a nice family lived inside. A black truck was parked in the front behind a white fence surrounding the neat lawn. The only odd thing was the three *KEEP OFF THE GRASS* signs. One seemed like enough to get the point across.

Nate pulled up behind the truck. We sat in the car in silence for a while.

"Babe," he finally said. "I should warn you. Theresa is kind of nuts."

"Crazier than me?" I chuckled. He kept his eyes on the steering wheel and nodded. Not in the mood to joke.

I took my hat off and straightened my hair in the mirror, ready to greet his painful past. I held his trembling hand on the way to the door. He rang the bell, and the curtain pulled back in the window.

John opened the door, and I glued my arms to my side. I hated him instantly. It grew stronger as he looked Nate over and cleared his throat. "What do you want?" he asked. It was exactly what he was thinking, no filter used like most people.

He was about my height, a baby compared to Nate, with cold, dark eyes and gray hair. He was in no way the father of the love of my life. "I need to talk to you and Theresa," Nate said.

If he thinks he's moving back in, he has another thought coming, John thought.

He sighed and opened the door to let us in. A chill crept over me as we stepped into their living room. Not a ghost. An eerie feeling of unease. Fear, maybe. Theresa walked into the room with an apron clinging to her bones, and my heart stopped.

She was frighteningly thin. Her collarbone jutted out of the neckline of her blue dress. She was barely there, barely living.

"Nathan? Hi." She smiled, a genuine one, at both of us.

My God. He's home, she thought. *John's not going to like this.*

"This is my girlfriend Christine," Nate said.

"The one from TV. We know," John said, plopping down in a leather chair. "Theresa made me watch you on the news. You're a hotshot now, driving up in that fancy car."

Again, he said the first thought that came to his mind.

Theresa held her emaciated hand out for me to shake. I took a deep breath, praying that I would control my powers, not the other way around.

He looks nice. Handsome and happy, she thought. *She's beautiful. I bet they live a nice life.*

Her thoughts were happy, but that feeling hovering in the air, that fear, was from her. I had the urge to stand up straight, enunciate my words, and be on my very best behavior.

"Nice to meet you," I said. I dropped Theresa's hand before her gloom pulled me under. I slouched my shoulders just because I could. It didn't feel like she had the same luxury.

"I have some questions for you two," Nate said.

Theresa tucked her thinning, dark hair behind her ear.

I gazed around the room. The pictures on the walls and shelves were of John. Just John. John with a huge fish in his hands. John at the

Grand Canyon. John reading in the same leather chair he was sitting in now.

Theresa offered us a seat on their yellow and brown plaid sofa. She sat on the small floral chair next to her husband who my powers revealed to be sixty-three, an accountant, from Maryland, the oldest of three siblings he never speaks to, and although he wasn't much of a looker, he had two other women besides Theresa—Harriet and Veronica.

I moved my eyes to his wife to read her. She was the youngest of seven children and wasn't allowed to speak to any of her family members. It had been two decades since her family had given up on her ever leaving John and coming around.

Most importantly, the biggest pain in her heart was that she was never able to have children.

"I'll just get right to it," Nate said. "Are you my biological parents?"

Nope, I could have answered that already.

John opened the newspaper on his lap, ignoring us. Theresa toyed with the apron she hadn't taken off.

"Why would you question that?" she asked, in her frail voice.

"Oh … could it be that I left a year ago and you have never reported me missing?"

"Oh, Mr. Hotshot has come to yell at us," John said, without dropping his newspaper. I wedged my hand behind Nate's back, trying to calm him down. "He's here, Theresa, you might as well tell him what you did so he can get out of my house for good."

She looked over to her husband. It felt like she'd do anything to change his tone. Like she'd been trying to for years. I closed my eyes, letting myself float where my powers wanted to take me.

I saw Theresa in a different time. A healthier one.

She stood at a kitchen counter wearing spiky heels with straps pressing painfully into her skin, meticulously cutting carrots. After each slice, she held it up to the light to inspect it. She threw away a few that didn't measure up. John walked in and leaned over her shoulder. She froze, and he inspected her work.

"*I think you're finally learning how to be a wife. Three years to train you, not bad,*" he said, laughing, but it didn't sound like a joke. She smiled and finally took a breath.

"*So, dear?*" she whispered. He stopped at the door and looked over his shoulder. "*Have you given any thought to what I asked? About us trying to have a baby?*"

"*Yeah. Sure. I want a boy, though.*"

Theresa smiled like it was Christmas, and Nate nudged my arm in their living room.

"Did he offend you?" Nate asked through his teeth.

I surveyed the room. Theresa's eyes were bulging, Nate's fists were clenched, and John had lowered the paper, eyeing me smugly. I'd zoned out; I had no idea how long I'd been wrapped up in Theresa's memories. I wiped under my nose. No blood.

At least I'd managed to keep that under control.

"Are you going to answer my question or not? What are you?" John said. "An Indian? Black? A mutt?"

Nate jumped up from the sofa, and I caught the back of his shirt. "Baby, relax."

My phone buzzed in my pocket. I reached for it with my other hand as Nate came back to his seat, boiling.

I opened the text from Sophia.

Get out of there. John might not live if you don't.

Oh, God. Sophia was watching. Maybe she meant Nate was close to losing it. Or maybe she was offended enough to come out of her sweetness and hurt him herself.

"Theresa, you were saying?" Nate said, rushing us along. I decided to stay and gamble with John's life, hoping to get more answers for my boyfriend.

"I ... uh ... adopted you, Nathan. I mean ... we did," she said. John huffed at her lie. I let my mind float into hers again, slower this time, more controlled.

By adopted she meant she'd bought him for six thousand dollars from a witch named Nicola. She couldn't have kids and wanted to give John a son. Nathan was a year old when she brought him here.

"From where?" Nate asked.

"Close by. This agency downtown. It was a crazy time. Lots of people were dying. It was easy to adopt," she said.

Lies. She'd met Nicola at a supermarket as she strolled down the baby aisle full of products she wished she needed. A week later, the witch brought her a baby as promised, wrapped in a fur blanket that she always suspected to be real and possibly from a bear. She was only told that the child was from Oregon and that the scars on his back were birthmarks. She didn't care. She handed over six thousand dollars of John's money, and named the baby Nathan Thomas Reece. She took the bus home and surprised John, seventeen years ago yesterday. He wasn't amused. And like the penny pincher he was, he let Nathan stay because Theresa couldn't find Nicola to get a refund. To him, Nate was his wife's pet that he had no obligation to feed or walk.

I strained myself to the seat and prayed he wouldn't speak his dog reference out loud. I'd let go of Nate's shirt if he did.

"Do you two want anything to eat? We have leftover chicken. We can all sit down for a nice dinner," Theresa said.

"Don't you think you've had enough?" John asked. She smiled and looked down at her hands. I wondered how many times he'd commented on her nonexistent weight problem. When the answer came to me, I wanted to get up and slap him.

She dealt with it all day, every day.

"He's right, and the rest we'll need for tomorrow. I can offer you a glass of water or something."

"Don't go through any trouble, Theresa," Nate said, shaking his head. "Do you have a birth certificate or a social for me?"

"The agency never sent it. That's why I homeschooled you. We never found one on you."

More lies. She'd never looked for any IDs. She suspected he might be a wizard but never saw Nate do any magic. And when she didn't, she'd thought she would be arrested for kidnapping someone's human baby and kept Nate in the house.

"Are you ready?" Nate asked me, looking like he'd had enough. I nodded. "We're going to get out of your way. Goodnight."

Theresa walked us to the door. John didn't look up from his newspaper. "Goodbye, Nathan," she said.

"Take care of yourself," he whispered.

"I will. Come visit any time, but um … call first. He goes out more these days. Or come when he's at work. You know the times. I'd love to see you again." Nate walked away without looking back. I waved at the sick woman and ran to the door Nate was holding open for me.

Two houses down, I took a deep breath and prepared to crush him with the truth. I'd hold him all night if he needed me to.

"She bought you from a witch. You're from Oregon. At least that's what she was told. You were one and you already had the scars. Yesterday … yesterday might not be your birthday. It's when she brought you home to surprise John. She doesn't know who your parents are. She doesn't know you're a shifter. She couldn't have children and John wanted a son. He's a horrible man, and she ..."

"Has no life outside of him."

He revved the engine, and the car raced down the quiet street. I buckled my seatbelt and he tightened his grip on the steering wheel. "Whatever. At least I know now." I rubbed his hand. "I'm so glad I left. It smells like something died in there, and she's been five pounds since I was ten. And I saw how you looked at her. Don't let her fool you, she's a piece of work, too. She's not a victim. Do *not* feel sorry for her."

How could I not? She weighed about half of what I did when I left St. Catalina. And I was sick then. They'd have to find a different word for her. One that captured the severity of her problem.

I let it go. It didn't seem like the right time to bring up that Theresa truly cared for him—in her own, warped way.

My phone buzzed in my hand. The number wasn't saved.

John Reece is a fool. Are you okay? –L. S.

Lydia freaking Shaw was texting me. I smiled but twisted it away. I shouldn't be smiling right now after all of that.

I'm totally fine, I replied.

"Do you want to go to Oregon?" I asked him. "We can find out more about your life. I'll help."

"If you don't mind, I'd like it to be over. My parents are probably dead or, worse, they sold me in the first place." My phone buzzed again. Lydia again. Nate looked over to my screen. "Who's that?"

"Lydia Shaw."

"Whoa. She's really your friend, huh?"

"Guess so."

Her text was about him, so it didn't feel rude to read it. "She was watching. She wants to know if you want your IDs to say Nathan Reece or … some other name."

He was quiet for a long moment, staring at the road, and slowed the car to a normal speed.

"Maybe if I hadn't met you I would change it. But you say my name so much and I love to hear it. That's who I am. I've never felt a part of that family, so nothing is different. I'm still Nathan Reece. Or Thomas when you're feeling frisky."

We laughed. "Frisky? Really?" I said.

I texted Lydia and told her he wanted to keep his name. She promised to have his records ready in a week.

Sophia said to tell you to have sweet dreams, she replied.

I pretended that had really come from her as I replied with a smiley face. Nate sniffed me and turned his head back to the road. "Do you have a girl-crush on the famous assassin? You sure smell like it."

"What? No."

He chuckled. "I'm not judging you. I like my boss, too. I wouldn't take him on a date or anything, but I think he's awesome."

"Boy-crush?"

"Not ashamed of it." We laughed like we hadn't just sat with his fake parents, one with an obvious eating disorder and the other crazy and controlling. "I like driving you around," he said, shutting off the engine in the garage. "It feels normal. Like what typical teenaged couples do."

"Good. My new trainer wants me to be normal. You may have heard of her. Lydia Shaw?"

He laughed. "Name-dropping, are we? Come on, Chris. You're

better than that. I don't go around saying I hang out with Devin St. Jermaine, do I?"

I narrowed my eyes and stopped myself from cackling. "That's because no one knows who that is."

"That's fair." He lifted up and pulled his phone from his back pocket. He pressed one button and held the phone to his ear, maybe returning a missed call. "We're back." He sighed. "I know. I know. Sorry, we had to do something sort of important. Where are you? Oh. Okay. Did you do it? Thanks. Sure, I'll tell her. Au revoir. Oui, oui. Croissant." I laughed. Nate knew French well. He just liked to string random words together to form awful French sentences for the fun of it.

"Why did you call Emma?" I asked.

"It's a surprise. She said goodnight, by the way. She's staying with her parents tonight. I can't help but wonder if that has something to do with the fact that Paul is out with Annabelle. You wouldn't know anything about that, right?"

I shook my head and glanced out of the window so I didn't have to lie to his face. Lydia knew about the shoes, so Em didn't have anything to hold over my head anymore. But I wanted to keep her secret anyway. She was my friend, and I didn't want to betray her, even though she was being completely ridiculous about this Paul thing.

Nate jumped out of the car and ran with magical speed to my door. He held it open and bowed to me.

"If we can put all of the parental craziness behind us, I'd like to get on with our plans."

"Plans?" I asked.

He locked the car and gave me the keys. Confused, I followed him out of the garage door, away from the house.

"I thought you were going to have a stressful day, so I planned something for you with Emma's help. Even though you had a good time with Lydia and we sort of just sat in my own version of hell, I still want to go through with it."

He led me to the gate to the backyard we never used. The pool was a far better hangout. We didn't even have lawn furniture out here, just grass that was usually brown and dried from the L. A. sun.

He held his hand over my eyes, and I smiled. The gate whined, and he gently nudged me to walk forward.

"I was thinking about what to do for a person who had a mandatory meeting with a terrifying woman," he said. "I came up with a few things, and Emma supplied the magic. Of course I couldn't have predicted that you'd have the best day ever, so now it seems like overkill."

He lowered his hand slowly, revealing the beautiful world he'd created back here. Green fog hovered over the grass and yellow balls of light, small like fireflies, zipped in and out of it. Most of them congregated in the middle of the yard, circling a blanket.

"Wow," was all I could say.

He smiled and led me there. I laughed at the bowl of popcorn and the two cans of soda waiting for us.

"Like our first date," he said. "That seemed to cheer you up. I thought it would work again." He sat down and pulled me into his lap. I grabbed a handful of popcorn and fed him one. "You can tell me if this is completely cheesy."

I chuckled and shook my head, a sweet lie.

He and Emma had made the backyard gorgeous and romantic, but I didn't need all of this. Nate could calm me with only his smile. Instead of saying that and ruining the moment, I popped open the sodas and inhaled another handful of popcorn.

"Thanks, baby," I said.

"It's nothing. Em did most of the work."

"No, not this. I'm talking about John and Theresa. Thanks for including me. I feel like I know you a little better now."

He lifted me out of his lap and stretched out next to me. He pressed his face into the blanket, masking his features in the fog. I loved the shy parts of him. He was vulnerable and adorable and finally open.

"I'm sorry I don't talk about them much," he said. "I just like to pretend they don't exist. It's how I deal with the whole thing."

"Someone wise once told me that the past didn't matter. That it was just the past." He peeked up at me, his gorgeous lips in a subtle smirk. I suddenly needed to be a little closer, touch him a little more.

I lay back on the blanket and scooted in next to him. He eased an arm across my stomach and nestled his head in the crook of my neck.

"That sounds strange coming from you," he said.

"Why?"

"Because the past *does* matter to you now. Your parents, their story. You smell like you love them, but your scent darkens when you talk about them. You get really sad. I'm scared you'll let that pull you back … where you were."

"I won't. Don't worry. It's just unfair that they lived this dream love story and no one will ever know. It's like it never happened."

He tightened his arm around me and tugged me closer. I didn't think we had any space between us to close, especially since John and Theresa and his reluctance to talk about himself weren't clogging the air anymore.

"We will know their love story happened because you're here," he said. "It's what you come from, passion and sweet sacrifice. That's exactly what you smell like. That's the story of your past and it made you who you are."

Fighting a stubborn tear, I asked, "And who are you?"

"A guy who is obsessed with the scent of passion and sweet sacrifice."

I pecked his lips and shook my head. He wasn't getting off that easy.

"What do you smell like to yourself?" I asked, surprised that I'd never thought to ask that before.

"I don't really have a scent." He bit his lip and gave away his lie. I glared at him, forcing the issue. "Okay … fine. I smell like snow."

I grinned, not expecting that, but it made perfect sense. "What do you think that means?" I asked. He hunched his shoulders. "Oh, come on, Nate. It means something. I smell like spice and something sweet, and you think that's my past. Sophia smells like sugar, and that's her sweet personality. You smell like snow … so …"

"I'm cold?" He laughed, and I pinched him. I wasn't going to let him joke his way out of this.

"Snow is beautiful, magical, and pure," I said. "You are obviously these things, a hundred times over. Of course you smell like snow. I should've guessed that."

He kissed me softly then trapped my lip in his teeth. A growl rumbled in his throat.

"Snow can also be dangerous … provided the right conditions. It's not always friendly and calm," he said. He held me with his eyes and my heart raced. "I … don't want you to think of me as a little timid snow flurry, Chris." He seized my lips and took my breath away. "I'm far from it."

He pulled me on top of him and showed me what he'd meant by that. His lips attacked me in wonderful ways, fiercer than they'd ever been. He didn't stop my hands from crawling under his shirt nor did I stop his from slipping under mine.

We kissed and kissed, and he sniffed every few minutes to gage if I wanted him to stop. He never got the signal because I couldn't force my brain to produce it.

The reason why I'd wanted to wait wasn't enough right now. I didn't know how long it would take to find the red candles and talk to CC, but I knew I loved him enough that my future with him was sealed. We would always be together, chase shifting children with *N* names around our home, escape Kamon for good and live the happily-ever-after my parents couldn't.

And technically, I'd had the talk with Lydia. The moments I'd fantasized about with CC didn't actually compare to the real thing.

"Nate, I trust you."

"Good to know," he said and kissed my neck softly and carefully like it was fragile glass.

"No, I mean, I *trust* you. You said we should wait until I trust my boyfriend that much. And I do. I trust you completely, and that's all that should matter."

His lips froze on my neck, but his hands worked their way to my hips.

"You think we're ready for that?" I nodded, and we stared at each other for several tense seconds, fireflies and fog swirling around us, then we crashed into each other and knocked a can of soda into the popcorn. It sounded like what my skin felt like, alive and buzzing and ready for more.

He rolled us over so that he hovered over me, breathing like a madman, then he rolled several feet away from the blanket.

"What are you doing?" I asked.

"I … um … need to go to my room."

Good point. We probably shouldn't make love in the backyard.

"Okay. Let's go."

He shook his head and rose to his knees.

"No … we should sleep separately tonight." I laughed at his joke. He didn't join me. "Seriously. I won't be able to control myself."

I crawled closer and lifted the ends of his t-shirt. He caught my hands. "Nate, that's sort of the point."

"Not tonight. I've fantasized about you saying what you just said since I met you." He looked away, his gorgeous face embarrassed. I chuckled and tried to reach a kiss to his lips. He jerked away. "I have our first time planned to the tiniest detail. And … if I let myself sleep in the same bed with you tonight, none of what I have planned to make it a special night we'll never forget will happen."

I forced his face back to mine and kissed him softly.

"You planned it?" I asked. He nodded and smiled. "Tell me. What happens?"

"I'll surprise you now that I know you're ready." He kissed my cheek and groaned. "I'll clean up out here. Goodnight, Chris."

A short laugh escaped my chest. Not only had he stopped us, he'd also ended the date. It took me a moment to appreciate the abrupt extinguishing of our beautiful fire. I wanted our first time to be special, not rushed and outside, and especially not on a day Sophia predicted it could happen.

I waved goodbye before walking to the house slowly, reflecting on my amazing day.

I wasn't going to kill Lydia Shaw, Nate had finally opened up about his past, and my future with the most romantic and wonderful boy in the world seemed brighter than ever.

Nearly seventeen years in a Catholic orphanage forced me to bow my head when I thought of the unsettled part of my life. I didn't have a candle to light, so I willed fire to simmer in my hand for her.

"Please watch over Remi," I whispered. "Keep her safe. Please don't let him hurt her. Please, God, don't let him breed her."

My skin buzzed when I realized I could do more than pray now. I took in a slow breath that Lydia would be proud of and pushed my brain to think of something she would be pissed about. Images flickered through my head until I saw Remi, brushing her hair in an ornate mirror. She slicked on dark purple lipstick and smiled at her reflection.

She was practically naked. Her top was sheer except for in the necessary places, and her leather shorts were more like underwear. She ran into a closet and laced up black boots that came to her knees. She closed the door, and I gasped.

An old newspaper clipping of my face was there, trapped against the door by a knife piercing my forehead.

CHAPTER SIX

In the morning, Nate gasped as I walked into the kitchen dressed in all black. "Oh boy, I'm in love with a hunter. This presents a problem."

"I'm not a hunter. It just seems like … appropriate attire for training." I kissed him and hooked my thumbs into the belt loops on the back of his jeans. It felt like we'd erased our boundaries last night and there was no place my hands couldn't go. And, for some reason, that was where they wanted to be. "How did you sleep?" I asked.

"I didn't. That was torture. I caved and walked halfway to your room … maybe a hundred times after you called me. I was trying to convince myself that I was coming to check on you after the vision about Remi, but I knew I wasn't coming to talk about that creep. I wasn't coming to talk at all, actually, so I stayed in my room."

I chuckled.

"Then I guess this romantic night you have planned is going to happen tonight?" He bit his lip and shook his head. "You're not sleeping over again?"

He leaned us into the counter. "I didn't say that. We'll just have to behave until I leave." He chuckled and pecked my lips. "Experiencing that and leaving for two months seems like a recipe for suicide."

"Agreed," I said.

He smiled and pressed his nose against my neck, enjoying my scent, I guessed.

Sophia cleared her throat, and we jerked away from each other.

She narrowed her eyes at Nathan and whipped up my breakfast with a snap. Oatmeal and a glass of grape juice. When she turned her back for a moment, our hands found each other again. Two of his fingers walked up my spine. I giggled and gave us away.

She swatted at Nathan with a newspaper and snatched me into white light before I had a chance to say goodbye.

When it cleared, we were standing in a small living room. Lydia's back was turned to us. She was staring at the photographs on the ledge of a fireplace.

"Good morning," she said, without turning around.

"Hi."

Sophia kissed my cheek. "I'll see you after your lesson, dear. What would you like for lunch?" she asked, like we weren't standing in a strange place with toys scattered around the floor, obviously someone's home.

"Anything is fine."

She winked and left me alone with Lydia who still hadn't turned to me.

"What kind of people do you think live here?" she asked. I glanced around the room and gave her an honest answer. "Messy people." I thought about it for a second, and a less judgmental answer came to mind. "Or busy people. Busy people without a maid."

"And?"

She finally turned around and clasped her hands in front of her.

"And ... they have kids. I assume they play a lot. Maybe that means they're happy."

She smiled and nodded. "Exactly. A happy family lives here. Money is tight but not scarce. Both of the parents work. There are six children. Four girls, two boys. They have everything they need and most of what they want. They only have one problem. One of the daughters has been missing for a year."

For a moment, I thought finding their daughter was my lesson, but my eyes found a photo on the wall of this dark-haired, blue-eyed family. All pale. All stunning. One frowning and sticking out like a sore thumb.

"I told you I intended to break your bad habits," Lydia said. "The sympathy you have for Remi Vaughn is one of them."

I wanted to cry as I stared at Remi's school pictures, especially at the ones with her smiling with missing teeth. She looked happy. Not at all what I expected of her past. I thought she would have lived alone and unloved in some heartbreaking place that made living with Kamon appealing.

"Why is wanting to help someone a bad habit?" I asked.

"Because that someone doesn't want to be helped. And because Kamon plans to use your weakness for her to capture you. He's right about her having that power. You'd run *to* her, not away, and get yourself hurt. I can't let that happen."

I followed her through Remi's former home, staring at the pictures of her happy family and the artwork of sleek black panthers in every room. They were obviously proud of what they were.

Lydia stopped in a room with two sets of bunked beds and dolls covering the floor.

"At one point in her life, she lived in this room and played with those toys until she outgrew them. I met with her parents a few months ago to tell them where she was. They weren't surprised. They invited me here and told me everything I needed to know about Remi. They described her as a fun child with a wonderful sense of humor. She loved spending time with her siblings and taking care of the younger ones when they came … until she shifted on her thirteenth birthday."

She pointed to the bottom of the door, at claw marks I hadn't noticed.

"She didn't handle it well. She'd known her entire life it would happen. They even celebrate each child's first shift with a party. But for some reason, she cried during hers. And didn't stop until a week after. She never returned to the fun child they knew."

If this was supposed to make me pity her less, it wasn't working. I could feel my heart breaking even more.

Lydia led me down a short staircase to a dark basement. She clicked on a light next to a twin-sized bed. It glowed red and cast an even darker shadow around the room. Remi must've lived in this drafty space. There were traces of her everywhere—the red light, black curtains, and Emo band posters on the walls.

"When she was fifteen, her parents noticed that she'd stay in her animal form longer than their other children. Sometimes for days. After she made seventeen, she would stay a panther for weeks at a time. They told her why it was happening. They told her to accept that she would always be a shifter or it would get worse, but she never did." Lydia sat on Remi's bed and opened the drawer of her nightstand. "Sit down," she said.

She pulled out magazine clippings and placed them on my lap. They were all of Kamon. Not the hunter I knew. The articles celebrated Dr. Kamon Yates.

"He's a doctor," I said. I'd meant it as a question, but I became sure of it before I'd asked it.

"Yes. Magical kind all know of him. Most know to stay away

from him. But some, the ones who want to be human, they flock to him. There are clippings here from three years ago. She was sixteen and dreaming of the exact life she is living now."

I shook my head as I flipped through the articles of Kamon and his miracle drugs. There were pictures of him cutting ribbons at hospital openings and kissing bald and incredibly cute children. He was two entirely different people.

"Just because she thinks she wants this, doesn't make it okay. We—*you* still have to help her. She's trapped with him."

"She's not trapped," Lydia said. "She wants to be there. I know what you fear for her. But you don't have to fear that. In a hunter's eyes, Remi is not good enough to breed. She's trying hard and has mastered teleporting already, but it will take her a decade to be up to standard in that sense. And even if he were to copy her, it wouldn't happen the way you think. He wouldn't sleep with her or have someone else to. He's surprisingly civilized when it comes to that. Does that make you feel better?"

I shook my head. It didn't matter if it happened tonight or ten years from now, in a bed or in a lab, I couldn't stomach the idea of Remi or anyone being bred.

"Un-brainwash her," I said. "Or let me try. She's in a trance or something."

"She's not brainwashed. She's in love." I turned my head to her slowly. My mouth hung open. "She fell in love with the idea of being human. Then she fell in love with him."

"He's old!"

"He's forty and she's almost twenty, but that doesn't matter. He doesn't feel anything for her. He uses that to keep her around so she can bring you to him."

The basement grew cold and quiet as I stared at the clippings in a new way, noticing the tiny stars drawn around his head and the scribbled hearts on the backs of the articles.

"She is not a victim," Lydia said. "She wants him. She believes she will have him. And she will sacrifice anything or anyone to get what she wants." She scooted closer to me and grabbed my hands. I felt fragile and young, but not in the way Nate and Sophia made me feel. It wasn't annoying when she did it. "The past is the past, Christine. You can't hope to save Remi to make up for your parents."

My breath caught as she jabbed at the wounded part of my heart. I squeezed her hands; it was all I could manage to do as I shattered next to her.

"She just got involved with the wrong type of people," I said, unsure if I was talking about Remi or CC. "She could've had a normal life."

She released my hands and caught the tears on my cheek. The most famous woman in the world was consoling me. It was unbelievable and wonderful and made me cry even more.

"You won't give them the normal lives you think they deserve. There's nothing you can do. Trust me, I know how frustrating it is to be powerful and powerless at the same time. But when the heart wants something that is impossible, you have to come to terms with the fact that it will never be."

I tried to say something about life being unfair but it came out blurred and broken.

"You will be in danger as long as your heart is open to Remi. I would have to keep you boarded up in a house forever for her not to find you, and I don't want that. Eventually, you will see her and you will have to choose between helping her and saving yourself. I've seen it. And right now, you choose wrong. You want her safe, and she wants you dead. You are all that Kamon talks about right now and she's livid. She will only need a moment, and you will give her several as you plead with her. I'm begging you to let this go. Let her go."

I was crying too hard for this to just be about Remi. All those mornings I'd prayed for her and the secret tears I'd cried had more to do with CC. I'd only known Remi for a few days, and even then, I'd hated her. This was about being powerless as a baby when my family died and being even more powerless now as I waited for candles for a séance or for Sophia to mention them. This was about the things I couldn't change, the things Raymond and CC would never have, and that I'd never have them.

Remi was happy, living her dream life. My parents were in the spirit world, likely still together as their souls were bound in life and death. I was the only one crying.

I felt it when the hook Remi had in my heart yanked out. I felt when I decided to choose correctly when I would see her, to not confuse her with CC and put her life over my own.

I felt lighter, freer. More settled than before.

A door slammed upstairs. Remi's younger siblings added life to the house, screaming playfully and growling, like one was chasing the others.

"Bren, I told you to pick up these toys!" a woman yelled. Her mother, I guessed.

"Ready to go get your butt kicked at chess?" Lydia whispered as the sounds of the normal life Remi had left behind rustled above us.

I smiled and nodded, and we left my second bad habit in the gloomy red room.

CHAPTER SEVEN

Training with Lydia and playing with fire was still exciting after doing it every day for a week.

Learning control hurt, physically and mentally. I'd lost count of how many miles I'd run, both for exercise and punishment. But Lydia always found a way to make my time with her fun.

I'd been having such a good time with her that I hadn't allowed myself to be sad about my friends leaving in the morning.

Today, she was tired of playing chess and wanted to do something different. Maybe she'd sensed her winning streak ending and wanted to stop before she started losing to me. I was getting the hang of chess, the strategy of it. A few more games, and I would probably beat her.

Instead, to test my focus, she had her robot inundate me with whispers and told me to follow one in an English accent. It told a story about angels walking around on Earth like normal people, while other voices hummed about traffic, taxes, and weather forecasts in China.

Sophia couldn't handle it, and had left to pack Em, Paul, and Nathan's bags for the trip. Right when the main character was about to kiss the wrong type of angel, she popped back into the lounge with us and waved her hand in the air to silence the story.

"Lydia, your dress choices for the ball are ready," she said.

"The ... Peace Group thing?" I asked. She nodded. "I didn't know you were going."

She stacked the papers in her lap and smiled at me. "They invited me as a special guest. It's supposed to show their cooperation with the treaty or some other bull—"

"Lydia," Sophia scolded.

"Bull-stuff. I was going to say bull-stuff."

"They are stealing my friends from me, so I also think the Peace Group is bull-stuff," I said, making my two favorite adults giggle.

Sophia and I followed Lydia into her office. She scanned the dresses hanging on the rack and picked a long green one.

"You're going to look lovely," Lydia said, holding the dress out to me.

"*What?*"

"Your friends are going to the ball, and it's your last night with them for a while. I don't want you home alone missing out."

Sudden euphoria shot through me, and I wrapped my arms around her. It took me a moment to realize I'd crossed the line by hugging her. I stepped away slowly as embarrassment crushed me.

"I'm sorry," I said. "That was weird."

She looked like she was going to say something but didn't. Eventually, she cleared her throat and walked away from the tense moment.

"We'll see you later," Sophia said. "She has a few meetings before the ball."

I gathered my things to leave in awkward silence. It was the weirdest three minutes of my life. Sophia was staring at her feet, and Lydia was staring at New York City with her arms crossed tightly over her chest.

Neither of them said goodbye.

Emma tortured me for two whole hours after I'd told her the good news, burning me countless times with the flatiron I couldn't talk her out of using.

"All done," she said. "You can turn around now."

I spun towards the mirror. My reflection startled me. I looked different with straight hair. Different and interesting. I twisted my face in different angles to inspect it, letting the light find new parts of me I hadn't noticed. The girl in the mirror captivated me, and in a way, reminded me of someone.

"Promise me you'll be okay," she said, luring my attention away from my face.

"I promise. When you get back, I will be in one piece … without a murder record."

"I can't promise the same. Two months on the road with Paul and Anna-skank with no technology? I might snap."

I rolled my eyes, more at their boss than Emma. He was being ridiculous and not letting anyone bring phones or laptops. Nate had stashed his phone and charger in his suitcase already. He liked his boss and didn't want to break his rules, but two months without talking to me didn't sit well with either of us.

A camera flashed as Emma and I walked down the stairs. Paul's dad didn't let any special moments go undocumented, apparently.

"Look at my two little angels," Sophia said, with her arm around Paul's mother. Mrs. Ewing smiled, especially at Em.

Nate winked at me from the bottom of the stairs, gorgeous in his tuxedo, with a bouquet of white roses in his hand. I could've died right then and wouldn't have complained.

"You look amazing," he said. I hid my smile behind my roses as Mr. Ewing snapped more pictures of us.

A bright blue light flashed in the room, and I jumped. "Did I miss it?" Emma's mother asked, as the light cleared around her and her husband. It was my fourth or fifth time seeing them, but I still wasn't used to how much they looked like Emma. Her mother's lips were bright red like her daughter's usually were, and her father's dark hair dangled down his back as far as Emma's. More than anyone in the house, he looked like a wizard. Paul's parents could pass for normal humans, but Mr. Arnaud looked like someone who chanted over candles.

"Miss what?" Emma said.

Paul strolled into the living room, carrying a bouquet of pink roses. He reached around Emma's back and held them in her face.

She turned around slowly, her eyes on the flowers.

"Did Annabelle not want them?" she asked.

"Shut up, Em," he said, and kissed her. Sophia and I gasped, and Mr. Ewing snapped pictures like the moment had been staged. "I don't have a girlfriend. I met Annabelle at my interview and asked her and my parents to help me out."

"With?" she asked.

"You! I thought if I made you jealous, you would finally stop playing games with me, but I'm tired of it. You're obviously never going to admit that you love me, so I give. You win."

I couldn't contain myself. A strange concoction of joy, relief, and the smug need to say *I told you so* bubbled inside of me.

"Why didn't anyone tell me about this?" Sophia said, holding Emma's mother's face between her hands like she did with us.

"Sophie, he just called this morning. I haven't had time to tell you."

Sophia looked massively offended. "You've had hours!"

118

"We've been in defense meetings all day," Emma's dad said. "The hunters have—"

Sophia cleared her throat and shook her head, shielding us from whatever he was about to reveal. Or maybe she was just shielding it from me. I was, of course, the only human in the room.

I grinned at Em when our eyes met. Nate didn't look shocked at all, obviously in on Paul's plan.

"So ... you're my what?" Emma asked Paul hesitantly.

"Your boyfriend. Duh. I guess you'll have to break up with Lou." I laughed first, then Em joined me. "By the way, that is the worst fake boyfriend name of all time. I can't believe you expected me to buy that."

We stayed in the living room for so long, celebrating their new relationship, that I thought we'd skip the ball altogether.

I fought the jealousy biting my heart as I watched them say goodbye to their parents for two months. Both of their moms were crying. Paul even got a little choked up while hugging his dad. I couldn't even picture what it would be like to say goodbye to my parents like this. I didn't even know what they looked like.

Sophia snapped and flashed us out of the house and into a ballroom. White lights twinkled on the ceiling, suspended there on their own. Gold dust swirled around the room, making enchanting designs in the air. The tables were covered in light blue linens with floating candles as centerpieces. Beautiful magic.

Paul and Em attacked each other as we weaved through the crowd. I didn't think Nate and I had that much skill. One of us would've fallen over by now, but not Paul and Em. Their lips didn't part until we made it to a table where a blonde girl was seated. Annabelle, I guessed. She looked as perfect as Emma had described her. Big smile, big hair, even bigger boobs. Nate pulled out a seat for me. Paul didn't have a chance to be a gentleman. Emma grabbed her own seat and started kissing him again.

Annabelle didn't seem bothered by it at all.

"Hi, Chris," she said and winced. "Sorry, I should've said Christine. It feels like I know you. You're kind of famous and they talk about you all day. That's a beautiful dress. You look gorgeous."

Darn, she was nice. Now I felt bad for calling her Anna-skank for two weeks.

"Thanks. You too. Nice to meet you," I said.

Emma and Paul came up for air as the other guests settled at their tables. Most of them looked normal, witches and wizards and shifters in human form. A few were slightly more obvious, like the man with far too much facial hair and the woman with strange proportions—long legs and a short torso.

"Oh my God! Look. Look. Look!" Annabelle said, startling me back into the ballroom. She pointed to the door and at the woman coming through it. "I thought they were kidding when they said she'd be here."

Lydia looked beautiful in her satin dress, black like everything else she wore. The long sleeves and neckline were sheer and elegant. The keyhole opening in the back put the dress over the top. A hush fell over the ballroom, and everyone stood and bowed.

She looked like royalty, a queen, and the colorful man greeting her looked like the court jester. He had on burgundy pants, a green jacket, and a Hawaiian shirt underneath it to pull it all together. And, *God*, his hair. The mixture of blonde and red fell around his shoulders in a mess of curls and dreads. He desperately needed a comb. No ... a razor to start over.

"Look, Chris," Nate said. "Our crushes are together. That's Devin." I didn't know what I was expecting of him, but this surely wasn't it. Nate talked about Devin like he was the coolest, most interesting person alive. He'd been so many places, seen so many things, according to my boyfriend. He was smart and cultured, but apparently he couldn't even find matching clothes for this formal event. And he was a wizard. Finding matching clothes should be as simple as a snap.

Devin escorted Lydia to her table and pulled out her chair.

She sat, and he bowed slightly before walking away from her.

"Great. Here he comes," Nate said. "I'll introduce you to him. Devin! Hey, Devin!" His flip-flops smacked against the marble floor as he jogged to our table.

"Hey, gang," he said, his voice low and relaxed like a surfer. "Thanks for all of your help with this place. I really appreciate it."

Each of them offered their own version of *no problem*.

"Dev," Nate said. They were on a pet name basis, apparently. "This is—"

"Christine," he finished, smiling. "Of course, man. You talk about her so much, who else would it be?" The table laughed, but I couldn't force it. For some reason, I didn't like Devin. He seemed too ... something I couldn't quite put my finger on. "Nice to meet you, Chris. Glad you could make it. Nate said you couldn't come." Apparently, we were also on a pet name basis.

"Last minute change of plans," I said.

"Awesome. You know ... I think it's badass that you almost exposed magic to humans." He laughed hard, finding joy in my terrifying ordeal. "Eventually, someone will have to be bold enough to do it if we're ever going to live in peace." He held up both of his hands, palms facing us. "Not me. But someone." Everyone at the table mirrored his hand gesture, like it was a thing they did at work, and inside joke I was on the outside of. "Have fun, guys. I'll come back to chat."

Nate leaned into my ear as his disheveled boss walked away and said, "You smell like you hate him."

"I don't even know him," I said and rolled my eyes.

"Be honest," he urged.

I sighed. "He's just … I don't know. I guess I just don't get your fascination with him."

"Just like I don't understand why you idolize a certain assassin." I felt my face flip up, cursing him out without opening my mouth.

"That was rude. I'm sorry," he said, half of his face wincing, the other half obviously lost in my scent. He loved how I smelled when I was angry.

He lifted my chin and kissed me. It felt like our lips needed to close on each other's to prevent our first screaming match.

A relationship between a shifter and the kind of human who hunted them had failure written all over it, even if we lived in a bubble and had no allegiances to either side. Nathan was what kept the broken pieces of me together. The parents I wouldn't know, the lonely life I used to live, the dangerous hunter searching for me. He made life sweet despite it all. But even at that, for some odd reason, the idea of him speaking against Lydia Shaw made me want to scratch his eyes out.

"I don't want to fight about Lydia and Devin," he said. "I spend my day with him and you spend your day with her, but whatever is happening between the hunters and magical kind is not our problem. It's me and you and no one else."

I nodded without moving my lips from his, feeling the last of our moments together speeding away. I didn't want to waste time being angry.

The lights dimmed and soft music hummed around us. We finally dragged our lips apart, and Paul stood and bowed in front of Emma.

"I would like to dance with my girlfriend," he said. She jumped up, ecstatic, and he escorted her to the dance floor. Other couples followed.

A bulky guy, maybe in his twenties, with muscles bulging out of his suit danced over to our table and tousled Nate's hair like he was his younger brother.

"Knock it off," Nate said. "Christine, this is one of our supervisors. Shane. And by supervisor … I mean he's annoying but happens to have a little authority."

Nate and Annabelle laughed, and I waved at Shane. "Nice to finally meet you," he said, then shook Nate's shoulder. "Dude, Dev just got shot down by Her Honor. He asked her to dance." They cackled. "Dev's cool and all, but what was he thinking? I'm sure he smells like a foot as usual. Or like he took a dip in that fish carnage they can't seem to stop in Florida."

Nate laughed so hard that no sound came out. I'd never seen him so amused. I hadn't realized the disgusting fish massacre was still going on. It had been over a week and was still a problem? Odd.

"That's actually disturbing when you put it that way," Nate said. "Lydia would gag. I asked him if he planned to bathe on the trip and he said … *maybe*." I faked a chuckle so I wouldn't seem odd, sitting silently as they poked fun at their boss.

"See … *I* have a reason to smell," Shane said. "I live in the woods most of the time. Dev has an apartment. It's ridiculous."

"You don't smell, Shane," Annabelle said, in her sweet drawl.

Nate cleared his throat like he disagreed. Shane trapped him in a playful chokehold with one arm and forced his face into his free armpit.

When they finished wrestling, Shane held his hand out to Annabelle. "How about a dance?" he asked. She took his hand and left Nate and I alone at the table.

Against my better judgment, knowing that I couldn't stay in tune with music without a paintbrush in my hand, I said, "Let's dance."

"Really?" he said.

"It's a ball. You're leaving. It's sort of mandatory."

I trailed behind him to the dance floor. My eyes caught Lydia's. She winked at me, and my heart squeezed, feeding my girl-crush. I watched her as she stood from her seat and excused herself. She put her phone to her ear when she neared the door.

She never stopped working, I guessed.

I hooked my arms around Nate's neck and focused on our dance. He stepped back, then up, then back again, forcing my body to move with his. He danced, and I swayed in the air like a doll amidst the gold dust.

He pulled me to his chest and pressed his lips to my ear. "I love you, Chris," he said.

"I love you more."

It was a perfect moment. Beautiful, romantic, enough to keep me dreaming of him for the two months he would be gone … and interrupted by a bloodcurdling scream.

There was a pause after, like everyone had stood still to assess the sound. Then havoc broke out. Nate lifted me into his arms and ran through the crowd of magical beings, some running, screaming, some bracing for a fight.

Shane burst out of his suit and landed on four furry legs as a large gray wolf. Like they were following his lead, other men shed their skin and raced towards the ballroom doors.

There was a series of snaps and cracks and bursts of light, magic shooting all around us.

"Stay right here," he said, sitting me in a chair in the corner of the ballroom.

"Nate!" I screamed.

"Don't move!"

Through the chaotic jumble of well-dressed creatures, I saw what had them scrambling for their lives.

My kind.

Kamon's triplet copies stormed through the crowd, snatching them, throwing them to the ground. And laughing. Shane, in wolf form, tackled the copy in the middle, and Nate, in his normal body, tackled the one to the right of him.

Were they crazy? They couldn't fight them. With a thought, their lives could be over.

"Nate!" I screamed.

He was too busy punching a copy that wasn't fighting him back. Not with his hands, anyway. Their brother that hadn't been taken down walked calmly to Devin. As I waited for their fight, someone's arm wrapped around my neck.

"Hey, Leah," Remi whispered in my ear. "I knew your friends would be here. I'm glad you decided to come. It's been hell trying to catch up with you. I missed you, friend."

I tried to wrestle her off of me, but I couldn't. She was different. Crazy strong.

"I would tell you to stay away from Kamon, but you're still living with the last boy I told you to stay away from."

"I don't want him!"

"And now he won't want you."

She punched me three times in the chest. It burned slightly before it numbed. Then I felt nothing. Not even her arm around my neck.

I spun around. She was gone. She'd started a fight and had abandoned it. I didn't even get a chance to choose like Lydia said I would need to. I couldn't see my protector through the commotion. I didn't know if she'd left or not while Nate and I were dancing.

I couldn't stay in my corner. I had to find him, and I hadn't seen Paul and Em since the music stopped. I jumped over groaning bodies. None of them were dead but had bones twisting in the wrong direction. One of those bodies was naked. Shane. He'd shifted back, probably when the fight with the copy went sour.

I expected my heart to race as I worried about Nate, but I didn't feel anything. I was numb. Numb and lost in the crowd of panicking creatures.

I dodged a wolf as it leapt over the bodies, still no sight of Nate or my friends.

"Calm down!" Devin yelled. "They're gone."

Time stood still as the magic settled and everyone froze. Groans of the injured replaced the sounds of terror and panic. The dance floor where couples had been laughing just minutes before was covered in broken creatures. Considering what the copies could have done, they were barely injured. I didn't know if this was another attack on magical kind or if it was about finding me. Either way, Lydia obviously hadn't stopped them yet.

"Chris," Paul said as he yanked my hand. "Nate is look…" His voice trailed off as his eyes moved to my chest. "Nate! Nate!"

Emma ran to us and gasped, and I looked down to see what was shocking them. I couldn't see anything but blood. Slimy, fresh, warm blood flowing out of me. I rubbed my hand across my chest. I felt one opening. Then another. Then a third.

Emma pulled out her phone and screamed to Sophia just as Nate sped to us.

"Oh, God!" he screamed. He yanked off his jacket and pressed it against the wounds I couldn't feel. I wasn't in pain. I felt nothing.

Remi had obviously hit me with more than her fist, but a slight punch was all I'd felt. I looked back to the corner where the quick fight had transpired.

Lydia was leaning against the wall next to the chair Nate had sat me in, falling slowly to her knees. Her coughs were suddenly the only sounds in the room. Nate's mouth was moving like he was yelling. I didn't hear it.

Sophia popped in. Her face was contorted like she was screaming. I couldn't hear that either. She pressed her hand against my chest. In the corner, Lydia groaned like Sophia had pressed a wound on her.

"I can't feel it," I said.

I rubbed my finger across one of the slits near my heart. I pressed my nail into the opening. Lydia squirmed on the wall, chasing after a breath she couldn't seem to catch.

And she wasn't bleeding.

She wasn't injured.

I was.

I wondered how I could be standing here without pain as she kneeled in agony, and my skin buzzed as my powers reached for an answer. A buried answer, deep in the shadows of my mind.

A sweet soprano voice whispered in my ear, a memory of my mother singing: *My heart is yours. My life is, too.*

CHAPTER EIGHT

I remembered the first time I'd heard her name.

"*Turn your books to page ten,*" Sister Constantine had said. My little fingers picked at the edge of the smooth page of the new *big girl* history book we'd gotten that year. "*Today we're learning about Lydia Shaw.*"

I used my whole hand to move from page nine to ten, being careful with the book full of words that were hard to sound out. Her picture was there. Her lips were in a straight and unfriendly line. Her hair was pulled back in a severe bun.

I remembered feeling strange, somewhere between fearful and sad.

"*Give me your attention, girls,*" Sister Constantine had said. "*We have to show some respect. This is the woman who killed the monsters.*"

That was before I thought I was one of them. Long before I knew I was her child.

CHAPTER NINE

I remembered it all—who she was, why she'd left me, and that she loved me more than life itself.

"We need to get her home!" Nate screamed.

"No. I have to, I mean, it has to be here," Sophia said. "We shouldn't move her. Nathan, I need you to hold her. Sit and hold her." He pulled me down to the floor. I stretched my neck over the broken bodies to see my mom. Sophia chanted something I couldn't even hope to understand, her tears falling onto my bloody chest.

Nate gasped and reached his hand to my cuts. Sophia smacked it away before he touched me.

She started chanting again, low and fast, drawing breaths in shallow gasps and releasing them in sobs.

She froze, panting like she'd been running for hours, and swept her hand back and forth over my chest.

I looked back at my mother. She braced her hands against the wall, panting like Sophia.

"Honey, breathe," Nate said. "It's going to be okay."

I *was* breathing. I *was* okay. But my mother wasn't. She'd pressed her face against the wall, gritting her teeth painfully. For a while her agony was all I could watch or hear, until the pool of blood on my chest changed direction and flowed back into the cuts.

"Sophie, how can I help?" Emma asked.

Sophia dried her eyes and shook her head. "It's done," she whispered.

Slowly, my mother stood and straightened her dress, declining help from the first person that had bothered or dared to go to her.

"I'm fine," she said. "Something knocked the wind out of me. That's all."

If I hadn't remembered who she was and that Sophia kept her secrets, I wouldn't have noticed her nod slightly in our direction.

Then she vanished.

Nate, Paul, and Em didn't notice. They were all still gawking at my chest.

"Bring your bags and meet us at the main shelter," Devin announced. "Our kind needs us now more than ever. The hunters will not ruin this trip. If anything, they have affirmed every reason we have to provide the help we do. I know it's just a few hours, but I can't wait. We are leaving now."

"Dev," a pale man said, standing to his feet and pulling a woman up with him. "We're sanctioned to leave tomorrow."

"I know. I'll talk to Her Honor. She can be understanding at times. She'll probably just fine us. I'll pay whatever it is. I just can't wait. Hunters have destroyed too many of our homes. They barge in, take parents, take incomes. Our people need us, and we are leaving right now."

Nate jumped up and sprinted to Devin. He held his bloody hands to his boss' face, then pointed at me. "I'm sorry, Dev. I can't go. Not tonight."

Devin frowned and rested his hand on Nate's shoulder. He shook his head and said, "I'm sorry, man, but you have to go. I don't want to be this strict, but in this situation I have to be. You're not just any worker. You've changed our entire atmosphere by working with those kids while we help their parents. We can't do this without you. She's fine, right?" Nate nodded. I wanted to run over there and smack Devin. I wasn't fine enough for him to still leave. "Go with the option I told you about yesterday, or we'll talk compensation on the bus. Okay?"

He nodded and slunk back to us, head low and defeated. "You don't look like you're staying," I said.

"I—I can't, babe. I've signed a contract, and I've taken their money for training. I have to go. And … this is important to me. The trip is *important*, babe."

"Then what am I?" Silly me for thinking *I* was important to him.

"The reason why I have to work. You're my future." I wished I were also his present. He rubbed his hand over my chest, as if to check if the cuts were healed. "The future I want for us is not one where I have to depend on you for everything. It's one where I take care of you, keep you safe and happy."

"How are you going to do that when you're not even here?" He looked away; he didn't have an answer, I guessed. I grabbed Sophia's hand to beg her to stop this. "Please. Make them stay."

"Honey, I can't do that. It's their decision."

Apparently, everyone had the right to decide things but me. I grabbed a handful of Nate's shirt and forced him to look at me. "I was just stabbed! By Remi! You would leave me for months after that? What if I'm not here when you get back?"

A tear dropped from his eye like he feared that, too.

"S-S-Sophia," he stuttered. "Dev offered her a spot on the trip yesterday. I didn't mention it because I knew you wouldn't say yes. But please. I'll watch her. I won't let her out of my sight. And Dev said we're not going to the attack zones on the trip. The stops were planned before all this happened. She'll be safe with me. Please."

She shook her head slowly, like she regretted crushing him. And me. Em and Paul, too. We were all crying now. "Nathan, she doesn't belong there. I'm sorry." Disregarding the bloody mess on my dress, Emma threw herself on top of me and kissed my cheek.

"I love you," she said. "I have to go. My parents would be upset if I quit. I'm sorry."

Paul had to pull her off of me. "Bye, Chris," he said. "We'll be back before you know it." My throat was too thick to speak. "I'll take care of her. And him. And you don't leave Nana's side. Swear it."

"Swear," I croaked. Nate was a blubbering mess. I'd never seen him so unraveled. He only got worse when I said, "Please."

He didn't bother saying he couldn't. He didn't bother saying anything, just clutched me and rocked and cried until Sophia took us from the ballroom to our house. There, our goodbye continued, tears, kisses, and finally words when we were able to speak.

I stood outside of the bathroom as he showered my blood off of his skin. He had to change his shirt twice after; he couldn't stop grabbing me. My hand was still in his as he held Emma's with his other. He kissed my palm and said, "I love you."

He dropped my hand, and they left me, really left me … after all of that.

I sat on his bed in silence for an eternity while Sophia hovered at the door of the pool house.

"He picked his job over me," I finally said.

"You didn't give him an ultimatum."

"It was unspoken."

She walked to the bed and tugged at my arm to get me to stand. "The unspoken usually goes unnoticed. He isn't psychic like you, dear."

She mentioned my powers, and the mind-numbing fog Nate's departure had caused lifted. I remembered how I'd gotten them. Who I'd gotten them from. I remembered the night in her dining room when her secret spilled from her lips. I remembered crying and hurting. And I remembered healing after she'd rescued me from Kamon.

Sophia and I took the long way to my room. I told her about Remi, but left out the part about my memories coming back. I knew I'd have to tell her eventually, but I wanted to talk to my mother first. I didn't want to risk powder being blown into my face, knocking me out, and waking up with my memory erased.

She hummed as she ran my bathwater. She snapped and a lavender bottle appeared in her hand. "What's more relaxing than bubbles?" she said.

"Not getting stabbed and having the people who are supposed to love you leave you," I said.

Her eyes fixed on my chest, then she smiled and started humming again.

I'd had a lot of practice being naked around Sophia. She would practically clean a shower with me in it, but this time, it was weird. My healed wounds had spilled enough blood to cover my chest and stream down my legs. She wiped me off before I got into the water, spending a lot of time on my back that must have been covered, too.

And she was singing softly, creepily, under her breath … the whole time. It was a lullaby, but not in English. I didn't need to understand the words to know she was doing a spell, just in song, to calm me.

"Get in, love. Let me know if it's too hot."

She busied herself in the bathroom as I soaked in lavender bubbles, remembering the woman who loved me and had to leave me, the woman living with the pain of giving away the impossible thing her heart wanted.

I wrung the towel over my red and swollen wounds. I was probably going to be scarred for life, but I had a feeling something far worse was supposed to happen.

Out of the tub, after fighting for the right to hook my own damn bra strap, Sophia slathered a minty cream over my heart. It tingled on the stab wounds. She held the collar of a t-shirt open for me. She was seriously about to pull it over my head.

"I'm seventeen, Sophia. I think I can handle putting on a shirt." Silently, she handed it to me. Somehow, pulling it over my own head felt liberating, like I'd made a step to stop coasting in the life she and my mother made for me after St. Catalina.

Most of what Sophia said to me was a lie. Lydia Shaw was not just concerned with taming my powers. My mother was not this vague memory of a person in her mind. She was alive and still bossing her around.

The former ghost I'd wanted to contact poked her head through my bedroom door. Until then, I wasn't sure what I'd say to her or if I'd have an attitude about the way she allowed my life to be. But when I saw her, my heart melted. I was goo, even more thrilled by her presence than I had been when she was just Lydia.

She'd changed into an all black outfit, like she'd done hunter business since the ball. I stood from the chair and walked to her slowly, trying to plan what I'd say on the way there.

The words never came, so I just wrapped my arms around her and dared her to move. She didn't, and eventually participated in the hug with me.

"Are you okay?" she asked.

I was more than okay.

"Yeah."

"I'm sorry. I didn't see what was going to happen until it was too late. Remi was not supposed to hurt you. Kamon is livid."

Her words weren't registering. Maybe because I couldn't care about anything other than my mother being alive. Or maybe it was because the most wonderful scent in the world was wafting from her hair—her orange scented shampoo that had been burned into my memory.

"Hi," I said. I pulled away and smiled. She looked confused. "Maybe I should say ... hi, Mom."

She gasped and glared at Sophia.

"I didn't," Sophia said.

"I saw you in the ballroom. You two can't cover that up. You were hurting, exactly where I pressed my nail. How is that?"

She bowed her head, like I'd touched on a bit of truth she couldn't bear to discuss, and tears poured out of her eyes.

"Don't worry about that. Let me fix this."

She brought her hands to the back of my head, and I jerked away. "Wait. Please," I said. "What if ... what if I want to remember you?"

She cried without speaking for a while. Sophia sniffled behind us, crying, too. I closed my eyes, waiting for her to remind me of all the reasons she couldn't be my mother.

She had several. She'd hidden me to protect me from hunters, and Kamon already wanted to capture me, so badly that his pet was jealous enough to stab me three times in the chest. He'd probably crave my head if he knew I was her daughter.

But I'd been longing for my mother since Sophia had helped my grandparents pass on, believing I'd suddenly fallen in love with ghosts.

But I loved *her*. She'd held me and kissed me and showed me how deep love could go.

Impressions like that were probably impossible to erase.

She cupped my chin in her hand. "That would be a dream come true. But … honey, it's not possible. My life is too dangerous for you, and I can't promise that I'll ever be what you need. I can never quit my job. I know too much to leave without any issues. And if anyone finds out who you are to me, I …"

She broke as I kissed her cheek. I cried, too, because I just wanted her to hug me and kiss me and be my mom, but our lives weren't that simple.

"Then can I just have some time with you as … you?" I asked.

She raised my hands to her lips and held them there. Very softly she said, "I don't deserve to be treated like this. You should hate me." I shook my head and leaned into her. "Look at the things I've done to you. You have years of reasons to hate my guts. Three deep reasons from tonight alone."

She pulled my collar down to spy on the cuts. It looked like I'd been in a knife fight last week. It was still swollen and had formed crust since Sophia had applied the cream.

"Gross," I said.

"It won't scar, baby. Right, Sophia?"

"Right. I'll pack her things. After you two say goodbye, I'll bring her to my place."

Mom laced her fingers through mine and snatched us out of the room.

We landed in high grass beside a sparkling pond. I spun around in the most beautiful place I'd ever been—trees as far as my eyes could see, impossibly green, with flowers of every kind shooting up out of the grass.

I stared at the sky while I waited for her to say something. Streaks of purple and orange circled above us, too beautiful to be natural.

"Magic?" I asked.

"Yeah. We're in the Congo, in a stretch of land that is protected by it. The people who live around here never come here. They think it's disrespectful to the land to walk on it." I stopped walking. I didn't want to be disrespectful. She chuckled. "You're not doing anything. They have the legend wrong. Decades ago, a coven of witches cast several spells over this place so humans wouldn't destroy it. It is literally protected, not *to be* protected like they think. Here, try to pick a flower."

I yanked on the nearest blood red flower, brilliant against the green, too beautiful to pick. Apparently, it thought so too because it didn't budge.

"Wow," I said. "How'd you find this place?"

"Your grandfather used to bring me here when I was upset. Which was a lot since I was born a … something that rhymes with pitch." I laughed and dropped her hand, walking ahead of her around the pond. "You've been here before," she said.

I glanced back at her for a brief moment. If she hadn't told me the powers she'd passed me expanded my memory, I would have thought I was fabricating the ones flittering through my head—the colors, the sounds, her rocking me and showing me the outside world.

"You said, 'You're always inside', right?" I asked. She nodded. The memory was faint and blurry but still tucked away in my head. "You're always inside, but not today. This is the sun. This is the world. And you're the—"

"Best thing about it," she finished with me.

I slowed my steps so she could catch up with me. I leaned my head to her shoulder, and she led us away from the pond and into a field of flowers that didn't seem like they could grow together naturally, in the same place and climate.

"Did we live here?" I asked.

"No. It would have been nice because it's so secluded. And there are many prophecies that this continent would be the last standing if something were to happen to the world. But it would've taken me years to finish a shelter sturdy enough for this weather. The magic throws it off. It can be storming one minute, perfect in the next, and snowing in the third. No place for a new baby."

We ducked as she led me under low branches interlocking over our heads. A stunning, flowery canopy. She sat in the middle, and I followed her lead, plopping down at her side.

I stared at the yellow flowers dangling over our heads, remembering them, too. But I remembered them being much bigger and closer to my face. She must have held me up to them.

"I was stabbed three times in the chest and didn't feel a thing," I said. "Are you going to tell me why?"

She tucked her head between her knees. It took a whole minute of suspenseful silence for her to continue.

"I know you saw that I was spoiled and awful in the memories I let Sophia show you." I nodded. "I changed when I met your dad."

The word closed my throat in a moment and rattled every piece of me. My dad, Christopher Gavin, was every bit as alive as she was. She'd met him when she was fifteen years old and had loved him every day since, even right now as she stared at my face, *his* face. I hadn't thought about him until then.

"I went from being this bratty kid obsessed with mental powers to loving someone like a maniac." She chuckled and shook her head. "It was overwhelming. I loved my parents, but not like that. Not in the way that makes you think you couldn't live without a person. Gavin and I would tell each other that all the time. *If you die, I will die with you.*"

"Like the poems in your diary."

"Yeah. And he was worse than me." She sighed and leaned back to the wall of vines enclosing us. "But when I found out about you, I changed. I went from thinking love was dying without the one you love, to knowing that it's about dying *for* them. In all of the futures I predicted, you died and that wasn't fair. You were innocent and perfect. You deserved life."

Our eyes met for a quick moment, then I looked away. The enchanted forest was easier to stare at.

"For six months of my pregnancy, I tried to convince myself that you would live despite every future I forecasted saying the opposite. Your dad's future cleared up as soon as I left. But not yours. I never saw you older than a few weeks old. Julian always found us."

She shrugged her shoulder across her cheek to catch a tear.

"I knew what I had to do, go to Julian before he came to me. I needed to do something to put my mind at ease about leaving you in New Haven, something that would protect you when I wasn't around. You learn a lot of magic by hunting creatures, and humans can do some of their spells, especially the ones involving spirits. One night before I had you, I summoned my mother. I didn't know if she would remember me, they'd died thinking they had no children, but I guess the truth came back in death. So ... she pops in and the first thing she said was ... 'God, your hair is greasy!' Never mind that my stomach was *huge*."

"Of course, she did."

We laughed, and I cleared my cheek when I felt the tears there.

"Like always, we didn't talk much. She didn't find it important to tell me she and Dad were trapped in the house. I didn't find it important to tell her everything that had happened with me either. After I told her you were a girl and what I wanted to do, she helped me do a spell I'd seen a witch do with her son in Julian's prison. He'd purged her, so she didn't have magic. You just need a spirit. They serve as a guide for your soul … when you … transfer it."

She peeked at me through the curtain of hair that had fallen over her face.

"Transfer your soul?" I asked. She nodded. "To me?"

"Yes. If you are fatally wounded, my soul will be taken before your own. You've had the ability to cheat death once for your entire life. The soul is yours whether I am alive or not, but if I *am* alive when it is taken, I will have to die in your place. I will feel the pain of it, too, and your wounds will heal once my soul is taken. Tonight, I would've died if Sophia hadn't intervened."

My breath caught and she cupped my face in her hands. "That's why Kamon sees me killing you?" I asked.

She nodded.

"Kamon sees a connection between our lives and is assuming that it means that you will murder me. He's assuming wrong. Our lives are connected but not in that way." I made a sound that was part groan, part sigh, and part *Oh my God*. Kamon or anyone could hurt me and kill my mother. Remi had almost succeeded tonight.

"It's going to happen on July 4th, isn't it?" I said.

She shrugged her shoulders slightly, more of a nervous twitch than a response. "Kamon and I have seen the same vision, this five second clip of the future. It's dark, you are upset, and somehow, I die. I know you're not going to kill me, even though you may be justified in doing so."

I pouted and shook my head. She may have left me when I was

two months old and stayed away from me for my entire life, but that wasn't a reason to murder her, even if I were capable of it or remotely upset with her. And I wasn't. I didn't feel an ounce of anger or betrayal. Just love.

"Since it's not murder, I'm assuming you will need my soul when someone hurts you. Then I'll be gone and out of Kamon's way. When I laughed at you in my office that day, it was more out of nervousness. You hit the nail right on the head. These attacks on magical kind are Kamon's previews. He's trying to show them that they should fear him even more than they already do. That's all. He's bragged to me about it a few times." She sighed heavily and massaged her throat like it had closed. "I believe in his attempt to make you murder me, someone else will take your life on the 4th. It's not Kamon. I've tried to figure out who it is and what they will do, but I can't see them. Sophia has tried and failed as well."

"It's obviously Remi," I said. She shook her head. "Then it's one of the triplets."

"No. Not them. They may be involved, but it won't be them. It's someone with a strong shield."

My mind flittered through what I knew about shields. Emma and Paul could protect their thoughts from me unless I touched them, and Sophia was shielded from it all. My boyfriend, too. I'd had to use excessive force, during my seizure, and had only heard a name, one he didn't recognize.

"I don't want you to worry about anything. Even Remi. I saw her hurting you in a different setting. You two were alone and you were begging her to leave Kamon's chapel. I highly doubt that will ever happen now. You'll probably never see her again. Kamon knows you are the key to ending my life. To him, he almost lost that key. I can't imagine the kind of punishment he's giving her." She grabbed my chin and lifted my face up, glaring into my eyes. "That's not for you to run off and try to save her."

I huffed. "That crazy bitch almost killed my mother. I think it's safe to say I won't be trying to help her anymore."

I covered my mouth, realizing I'd just sworn without meaning to, in front of my mom. She chuckled.

"Your *mother*," she said. "That's like music to my ears."

She stood and walked to the other end of the canopy, brushing the yellow flowers over her head.

I wanted to plead with her to take her soul back, but I knew it was pointless. I wouldn't remember anything about her or her soul after this.

My heart throbbed, missing her already, and I jumped to my feet. I didn't want to waste a second of my time with her. Tomorrow, we'd play chess and practice psychic powers. I wouldn't know the reason why I felt so calm around her, and happy.

I rested my head on her shoulder and let our problems blow away for a minute—Remi, her soul, and July 4th.

We walked into a field of blue and purple flowers. I couldn't deny the urge to run through them. She laughed, and I raced around in a circle, enjoying the magical world with my mother, ignoring the now throbbing wounds on my chest.

I ducked under low branches and hopped over streams that raced to larger water. I followed the sound, trying and failing to pick flowers on my way to a waterfall.

The sight of it literally took my breath away. This place was amazing, this woman was too, and it broke my heart that I wouldn't remember either one.

Mom and I sat on the ledge of a cliff overlooking the waterfall. I chuckled as she tugged be back, looking a little worried about me falling.

"I love you," I said, because I wouldn't be able to say it soon.

"I don't deserve your love."

"But you have it."

I spun on my butt and rested my head in her lap. She pressed her hand against both of my cheeks, like she was trying to memorize the feel and shape of them. I was torn between wanting to close my eyes to savor the moment and not wanting to even blink for too long, petrified of missing this.

She leaned down and kissed my forehead. A tear dropped from her chin and splashed on my cheek. Waterfalls all around me. "How the hell did you turn out so perfect?" she asked.

I chuckled. "I think Sophia would take credit for some of it."

"Trust me, she does. She thinks you're *her* daughter."

"But I'm yours," I whispered, mostly to myself, slow and quiet, like that statement was sacred. The waterfall roared as I fought with my chest, it was trembling and constricting under the weight of a cry I refused to let out. I didn't want to say goodbye to her again.

"I'm sorry, you know?" she said. "About everything I allowed you to deal with."

"It wasn't just you. It was the girls. The nuns, especially."

"The nuns loved you," she said. I bucked my eyes. "They did. They called my office every five minutes during your disappearance."

"They hated me. They named me after an unloved woman in the Bible."

She shrugged her shoulders. "I'm sure there's more to that story than that. I always thought the name meant that they saw you as strong and content, the same way I saw you." I rolled my eyes; they were all wrong. I was anything but strong and content. Currently, I was hanging on by a thread, about to lose it and scream about not having a mother.

"Nate thinks I have a crush on you," I said, reaching for something light and funny, the opposite of how I felt.

"Why?"

"Because I ... love you as Lydia ... in a totally appropriate way." She laughed and I joined her, the shaking movement freed a few of my tears. Soon, I was full out crying and couldn't stop. "I don't want you to die," I said. "It seems like you think you will."

"Technically, your mother is already dead."

"Technically, she's sitting right here." I tried to catch my breath, but my chest was heaving too hard. "Why is something always taking you away from me?"

She pulled me into her arms. I wanted to pull away, to sit next to her and talk about this like an adult, but I couldn't. I was losing my mother all over again, while knowing I would lose the memory of her in a few minutes. It was too much to handle, too much being taken from me at once.

"You're going to be fine," she said, sniffing and rocking me. "I'm sorry that this is your life, honey. I wish things were different. It's why I never wanted you to be a part of this world, magic and powers. It makes it impossible to live the life you want."

I suddenly couldn't live without that life, the one we were supposed to have. The thought of saying goodbye to her, now as well as on the 4th, felt like hell. Pure, biblical, agonizing hell. So was knowing that she was about to erase my memory so that I wouldn't feel the worst of it.

I was tired of living this way, having Sophia and my mother lie to me and orchestrate my life. She'd planned eighteen years of it before she left me. Now, she and Sophia made my decisions, and she was about to make yet another one. I cleared my throat and found my own voice.

"I want to keep you," I said. "I want you to work things out. Stop whoever you need to stop. Kamon or Remi or whoever it is. Do what Lydia Shaw does and make the monsters in my life go away. And you … stay."

It sounded like she was crumbling, like my words had shattered her tough façade and left the girl from the diary in its place.

"Sweetie." Her voice cracked, more fragile than it was a minute ago. "There are so many reasons why—"

"Make it work," I said, interrupting whatever excuse she was about to feed me. Logical or not, I didn't want to hear it. "I want you to fix my scarf." She narrowed her soaked eyes. "Like Paul's mother does. Or get too involved in my life. Or tell me I'm partying too much."

She chuckled at the jumbled examples of a normal parent that I'd gotten from Emma and Paul.

"You don't party too much," she said. "You've only been drunk once. You really pissed Sophia off that day."

I smiled, but it faded as my lips pushed into a pout. "I want to piss *you* off."

She laughed and wiped my cheeks. "That's not possible," she said. Those words felt like what I assumed getting stabbed in the chest would feel like, if I didn't have an extra soul. I was hoping that would work, demanding her to stay with me. "It's not possible because I don't think I could ever be pissed with you." I looked at her slowly. "I'll work it out if that's really what you want."

"It is!" I nodded hard enough to break my neck, still waiting for the other shoe to drop, the inevitable *but*.

"But," she said. I held my breath. "If, at any time, you come to your senses and hate me like you should … tell me. Tell me and I'll leave you alone. Okay?"

I could deal with that *but*.

I clutched her and stayed in her arms for a minute, until I felt the need to reclaim my age.

"So what do we do now?" I asked.

She smiled. "We go home before it starts raining." She pointed up to the heavy clouds. It looked like it was about to storm at any moment. She reached for my hand, and I gave it to her gladly. I was done crying. I'd escaped the hell that saying goodbye to her would be. I would get to keep her for longer than a few minutes. She'd be a hero and work out our problems. I would have a mother. In my opinion, despite the decisions she'd made, I had the best one in the world.

Instead of going to Sophia's, she took me to Paris with her.

After showers, we crawled in bed, and I finally asked the hard question I'd been tossing around in my head since we'd left the Congo.

"Will I get to meet him? Gavin? My dad?"

"Anything you want, baby," she whispered. "I'll work on his memories. Maybe Sophia can help. I made his brain believe a large portion of his life didn't happen. It's hard to undo that. It's dangerous."

"Dangerous how?" I asked, trying not to bury my nose in her pillow.

"Reversing what I did can cause him seizures, strokes, or brain damage. It's one of the biggest reasons why I never even considered telling him. But don't worry. I'll be careful."

"Let's watch him through your mirror!" I said, remembering the last time we'd spied on him through the magic mirror she'd changed the course of history for. In her memories, I'd seen her sign the treaty that allowed magical kind to live as they do for it.

For me.

She told me no and explained the dangers of spying on grown men in the middle of the night.

"Mom, I get it," I said. She hadn't stopped giving reasons why we couldn't watch my dad five minutes after she'd started. I thought I would vomit if she said the word *naked* as it applied to my father one more time. "What about Nate? Can I watch him? He won't be naked. At least he better not be."

She kissed my hair. "That kind of magic only works on the unsuspecting. Emma and Paul grew up knowing it exists, and Nathan has been schooled since joining the Peace Group. We wouldn't be able to see them, and, besides, it would be a violation of my part of the treaty. They have the right to not be under surveillance."

"That sucks."

"I know. Sorry." I yawned and tried to strike up a conversation about my first day in her office, how she'd thought she was hallucinating, but she shushed me. "You're fighting sleep, honey. You had a crazy night. Close your eyes," she said. I shook my heavy head. "I know you're scared. The last two times you've fallen asleep in my arms, I haven't been there when you woke up." I couldn't fight the tears or deny it. This whole thing was so unbelievable. Doubt hung in the air, thick and heavy, making me cling to this night in case I didn't get another. "Trust me, angel. I will be here."

She started the lullaby. My eyes fluttered closed before she started the second verse.

CHAPTER TEN

In the morning, I felt around in bed for her, my eyes still glued shut from sleep. My heart jumped a little when my hands only found soft, disheveled sheets.

"Over here, sleepyhead," she said. I rolled over and opened my eyes. Mom was standing in her doorway, dressed as Lydia Shaw. "Good morning."

"Morning, Mom."

I sat up and clutched my chest. It burned ten times worse than it had last night. "Be careful," she said. "As it heals, the pain becomes yours and not mine. It's no longer fatal. Sophia will give you something for it."

I ignored the ache and jumped out of bed. Like she knew where I was headed, she opened her arms. I debated on a few questions to ask her, how she'd slept, how long had she been up, but our long, wordless embrace said more than any frivolous conversation could.

"Lydia," Sophia said, from somewhere in the apartment. "I told you to hurry. I will tell Christine you said you're sorry for not being here when she wakes up. You don't have time for this." Mom squeezed me tighter as Sophia nagged her from another room in an unfamiliar voice. Not sweet or patient. Not a hint of love. "I'm already getting calls from friends in Mexico. It has started. You have to go." She made it to the door and paused. She cleared her throat and pulled me away from my mother. "Good morning, my heart," she said in her usual, overly sweet voice.

"Mexico? Another attack?" I asked.

She flailed her hand in the air, like what had her nagging Mom a second ago suddenly didn't matter.

"Get back in bed, honey," Mom said. "I'll be back in a few

hours. I just wanted to be here when you woke up."

She smiled and walked me back to bed. She kissed my cheek, and her thick curtains closed on their own, from her moving them without her hands, I guessed. It was night in the room again.

"Are we going to have a lesson today?" I asked.

"Not today. You need to heal."

"What about the … problem? Have you figured out anything else about how I will kill you? I mean … we have to figure it out before it's—"

She shushed me and shook her head. "You think about healing, and I'll think about everything else."

Sophia cleared her throat and rushed Mom off to work.

She served me a magic-laced breakfast in bed. She pointed to the eggs and said, "These are for the pain." She giggled as I lifted the fork to my mouth suspiciously. She pointed to her famous homemade biscuits and said, "This will help you sleep." She tapped the rim of the glass of orange juice. It wasn't banned anymore since the scent wouldn't remind me of Mom, I guessed. "This will close the wounds the rest of the way."

"I can't taste anything in it." She winked, and I scarfed down the rest of the delicious breakfast.

"You'll be all better when you wake up." She took my plate and kissed my cheek.

That was the last thing I remembered before Nate's ringtone woke me up hours later.

I brushed dried flower petals from my face that Sophia had obviously decorated me with. I dug through my duffle bag next to the bed, trying to get to the phone. It stopped ringing before I found it at the bottom.

I called him back, but it went straight to his friendly voicemail.

"Sorry, babe," I said, after the beep. "I was sleeping. I hope you're okay." I peeked into my shirt. "I don't even have a scar from last night. Sophia fixed me up. I miss you. I love you. Call me back when you can. You won't believe where I am right now."

I didn't want to drop the *Lydia Shaw is my mother* bomb over his voicemail. Nate didn't handle surprises well. I needed to break it to him slowly and just hope for the best.

I pulled the thick curtains back and smiled. Paris was beautiful at night. The city buzzed underneath me, and glowing lights lined the spectacular skyline. The moon was a tiny ball next to the Eiffel Tower, fighting for recognition in the beautiful sky.

I opened the doors to Mom's room and wandered around her apartment, looking for Sophia. I followed the odor of burning food, and I heard her and Mom bickering in the kitchen.

"What do you mean, you're done for the day?" Sophia said.

"I mean what I just said. I'm done. Everything else on my to-do list can wait until tomorrow. I have plans."

Sophia laughed. "Plans? Please. Do tell."

The smoke floating from the kitchen tickled my throat. I tiptoed closer and stayed out of view. Mom was standing over the stove, stirring something in the skillet that obviously didn't need to be in there anymore.

"I'm taking my daughter somewhere, if you must know."

"Have you lost your mind? You can't take her anywhere."

The smoke detectors wailed. Mom waved a towel in the air like that was going to do something. She still hadn't taken the skillet off of the stove. "Sophia, it is public knowledge that we know each other. To the world, I found her. It won't be odd if we're seen together. I've planned it all out."

"Planned!" Sophia said, sarcastically enthused. "Oh, I see. You planned it out. That makes me feel better. Does this plan occur before or after your meeting with the president? Or perhaps you'll squeeze it in between house visits with the hunters in Moscow today. Or after you find a way to dispose of the twenty thousand bodies you don't plan to report in the death toll for Cancun."

"I get it!" Mom shouted. "I'm busy, but she wants to spend time with me. Can you believe that? *My* baby wants to spend time with *me*. I have to make it happen."

"You have too much to do right now. Too many lives are hanging in the balance for you to take a day off!"

"They will wait until I come back from taking my daughter on a campus tour. I'm not even clearing out the school. I want her to have what any kid would have. She's going to love it, and I'll get to be there with her, doing something normal for once."

I couldn't stay silent after that. I couldn't imagine anything worse than having to go to school again. It was right up there with the thought of Kamon hitting another city, racking up even bigger numbers this time.

"Hi," I said.

They both turned around with huge grins. Mom reached for me first. Sophia snapped and silenced the smoke detectors. "Hi, baby. I popped in a few times throughout the day, but you were asleep." She held me for a while until I coughed on the smoke. "I'm making you a grilled cheese sandwich since it's technically lunch … your time."

Sophia laughed. "She's burning a grilled cheese sandwich." She snatched the skillet from the stove, like she'd been waiting for Mom to turn away to do so, and dumped the blackened bread into the trash.

"I thought you said not to worry about the attacks," I said.

"You shouldn't. It doesn't concern you," she said.

"My friends are out there and are not human. It concerns me."

Sophia laughed. "As if I would've let them go with less than a ton of magic coating their skin. Nothing can hurt them. Just like nothing can hurt you. I've taken drastic measures since last night."

She tossed a knife at me that I hadn't even seen her grab. The end never tilted to the ground. It sliced through the air, speeding towards my face. The sharp and threatening blade twinkled in the fluorescent lights of the kitchen before hitting the air in front of me. Pure white smoke engulfed the knife. The puff of protective magic drifted to the floor like a feather, cradling the blade and masking the clinking sound I expected it to make.

"Toss another knife at my child and I'm going to burn you alive!" Mom yelled.

I still hadn't caught my breath.

"Relax, Lydia. It was a simple demonstration."

"If magic was foolproof, your people would be ruling the world. Don't do it again."

"No, Mom! This is great! Thank you, Sophia. That means no one will kill me on the 4th, right?"

A deathly silence screamed in the kitchen, and both of them turned away from me. Apparently, this magic, as amazing as it looked, wouldn't be enough to keep my extra soul safe.

When Mom finally turned around, she flashed a smile so big and out of place that it looked painted on. "Today is a happy day. You are not allowed to worry."

"Not possible. Even if I play along and pretend I don't have your soul, I also heard you talking about college," I said, fanning the smoke out of my face. "I don't want to go."

"You'll change your mind. I have a fun day planned for us. I found a great school for you. It's called Trenton College of the Arts." I rolled my eyes at her. It even sounded awful. "It's a small college in Los Angeles. Close to your house. Very prestigious."

"She means expensive," Sophia said.

"How is it that you don't know how to cook?" I asked, purposefully changing the subject.

"Well … I had a mother, then maids, then …"

"My dad?" I said, because it seemed like she couldn't finish that sentence on her own. She nodded. "What about when it was just us? There was no one around to cook for you."

She smiled, a real one this time. "I just manifested whatever I wanted. I can't do that now. For one, it makes me tired, and two, I don't allow hunters and agents to manifest things they can buy. Food, homes, anything. It leads to greed and greed leads to something I really don't want to have to deal with again."

She must have meant the little thing she was famous for, killing Frederick Dreco and ending the magical apocalypse. "Do I have to follow that rule?" I asked.

"No, you can do whatever you want."

"Whatever you want within reason," Sophia amended. "Lydia, if you give any child an inch, regardless of how wonderful that child is, they will take ten miles." Mom rolled her eyes at the parenting advice, and Sophia handed me a plate of unburned food.

Mom pouted. "Well, my plan for lunch is ruined, but we can still go to Trenton."

"I was stabbed yesterday! I should definitely be in bed." I faked a groan. "How about we watch a movie or something instead. I need to heal."

She laughed and peered into my shirt. "You're fine."

I rolled my eyes at Sophia and her magic, and Mom's cellphone buzzed on the counter. She pressed the button on the side to silence the call. It buzzed again a second later. She sighed and answered this time.

"Shaw. Yes. I know. How many?" Her eyes slammed shut. "Okay. One minute." She hung up and frowned. "I'll call and push the tour back. We can go in a few hours."

"Mom," I whined, managing to fit three syllables into the word. "I don't want to go. I hate school."

"College is different. You'll like it."

"And she'll tour it on her own," Sophia said. "You don't have time, and besides, it's a horrible idea that you're too blind to see right now. Luckily, I'm here. I'll handle it. Don't worry."

Mom looked like she was about to argue, but her phone rang again. She answered and promised the caller she'd be there right away.

"I'm sorry," she said. "I know mothers typically are able to spend more than five minutes with their kids. I'm going t—"

I hugged her and interrupted her unnecessary apology. It would be more than easy to feel betrayed, cast aside and forgotten, from today and every day of my life, but some indescribable connection to her wouldn't allow it.

"Bye, Mom," I said.

"Bye, honey."

I blew her a kiss. She caught it, pressed it into her heart, and went back to being a hero.

Hoping I could butter Sophia up and get out of the campus tour, I helped wash the dishes. After, obviously desperate, I got on my knees and scrubbed Mom's tub with her.

"This is nice," I said. "I wouldn't mind doing this with you every day. Mom can go to work and I can hang out with you. Think of the things you could teach me to cook. It'll be fun."

"You're not getting out of the tour, Christine. It's important. Your friends will always need to work, and you need to have something to do that does not include pretending to want to clean with me. Lydia and I agree on very few things. This is one."

I dropped the sponge, done helping, and crawled back into Mom's bed to pout.

The handle of the magic mirror stuck out from under her pillow.

Sophia passed the door, singing a song I thought was too recent for her to know, something Emma would blast in her room while rifling through her closet. I frowned, missing her now.

"Emma Arnaud," I whispered into the mirror. Nothing happened. Just like Mom said it wouldn't. "Paul Ewing." Still nothing. "Nathan Reece." My reflection stared back at me as the magic failed once again.

I tiptoed into the hall. Sophia was in Mom's room-sized closet, humming and hanging up clothes.

It was the perfect time to be sneaky.

I shut the door to her bedroom and whispered, "Christopher Gavin," into the mirror. The glass rippled like gently disturbed water and showed him. He looked the same as he did in Mom's memories, low cut curly hair, same eyes as me. He'd gotten a few faint age lines, but other than that, he was the same boy that stole her heart in a coffee shop.

He propped his feet up on the rail of a patio overlooking a beautiful lake. The neighboring homes all circled the water, suggesting that it was manmade. He hummed to himself as he stared at the sky. He folded his arms behind his head. On one of them, not a piece of his brown skin was left without inked musical notes, stars, and other symbols I didn't understand.

His phone broke his concentration on the sky. "Yeah?" He chuckled. "I'm sorry, man. You know I'm the worst liar of all time. Why would you trust me with the details of your anniversary?" He laughed harder and caught his breath. "Well now she sort of suspects something. I told her I—uh—was just having a show at Murphy's." He smiled, listening to his friend who obviously had him helping with a surprise for his wife. Adorable. "I guess I'll have to sing now." He laughed. "Three songs max. See you at seven."

"Are you getting dressed?" Sophia yelled, her footsteps grew louder as she neared the door.

I scrambled to hide the mirror, and Dad started humming loudly. "Turn off, turn off. Um … presto!" I said, snapping uselessly, trying to find a command to shut off the magic. "Mirror, off."

I didn't know if the last command had done it or if shaking it was the key. Either way, my reflection replaced my father, and I tucked the mirror under a pillow.

"Are you?" she asked.

"I'm about to, Sophia!" My nerves made me yell.

She opened the door and glared at me.

"I don't want an attitude. Don't let Lydia rub off on you. I want you to stay my sweet Christine. Now, get dressed before I spank you."

She left the door open, and I peeled myself away from the bed.

Either Mom or Sophia had packed some of my fancier clothes from my closet, to make a good impression, I guessed.

I groaned when Sophia came in to get me. She handed me a purse, as if I didn't look dressed up enough, and took my hand. We landed in a single carport, in the front seat of the typical SUV Mom usually made me travel in. The windows were as dark as the interior, cloaked from the outside world.

She backed out slowly, causing a languid stream of sunlight to fall through the windshield.

"Buckle up, dear, " she said as she merged onto the busy street in front of a fancy condo.

"Does my mom live here, too? " I asked.

"Uh, not really. Your mother doesn't really live anywhere. She spends the most time in Paris but rarely sleeps there. "

I thought about asking where she slept if she didn't generally sleep in Paris, but I didn't. I had a feeling the answer would bother me, make me sad about her not having a typical home and a typical life.

"I'll be back for you at four. There's water in your bag with the potion inside, in case you have any issues controlling your powers." So I wouldn't beg her not to make me go to school, I kept my mouth closed on the ride over. In front of the stuffy brick buildings of Trenton College of the Arts, she said, "Try to enjoy yourself."

"As if," I mumbled.

I took a deep breath as I pushed out of the SUV and into the sweltering L. A. air. Sophia honked the horn and drove away. My memories of school were sad and painful. Lonely meals, lonelier nights. I was mute and missing my mother without knowing it. It made me friendless, strange, and deadly.

A skinny guy sped by me on a skateboard and snapped me out of the St. Catalina fog. He hopped up on a rail and crashed to the pavement a second later. No one laughed.

Actually, no one even saw it. Everyone outside seemed to be in their own worlds. The closest person to the crash, a girl with dark braids and a cool nose ring, didn't raise her eyes from her book.

I thought I would spend more time being lost in a new place, but the tour group was obvious. Parents and kids my age huddled around a short, very fashionable blonde.

"Hi, everyone. I'm Elizabeth. I'll be your guide today. We're just waiting on one more to get started," she said, in her squeaky voice. She spotted me walking up and smiled. She checked my name off of a clipboard, knowing who I was without asking. Her unprotected human mind whispered that she recognized me from the news.

Great.

I looked around to size up my future classmates while Elizabeth welcomed us and explained the history of the tall monument behind her. About half of them looked like me, disconnected from the group and completely disinterested in her speech.

The tour dragged painfully from building to building until she brought us to the student art gallery.

I tried to fight the smile, but it was no use. The different styles and types of art excited me and made me want to spend hours in this room. I circled an interesting sculpture, trying to find the end and beginning and make sense of the beautiful lines. But they only kept leading me around and around.

"Tree of Life," my tour guide said. She pointed at the sculpture. "One of my friends did it. He's super into philosophy and deep thought. It's supposed to make you do that." She snaked her neck, imitating what I was doing a moment ago.

"Oh. Like … life keeps going?" I asked.

"Yeah. You get it." I smiled with no teeth and walked to the next piece—a giant ball of yarn. "Your tour reservation says Christine." I looked over my shoulder. I guessed she wasn't done talking. "Not Leah. You go by that name now?"

Murderous urges aside, I wouldn't consider myself to be a rude person. But as I listened to Elizabeth's thoughts about how she wanted a picture with the runaway that caused an international panic attack, I wanted to pretend like she hadn't spoken and walk very far away.

And the rest of their thoughts were getting louder, annoying me even more.

"No, that's just my name. My real one."

A ship made of toothpicks sat in the middle of the huge ball of yarn. It wasn't as cool or clever as the Tree of Life. Unless I just wasn't philosophical enough to get the point behind it.

"So ... I heard you got an offer for a reality TV show. Is that true?" she asked.

"No."

She chuckled. "Good. I was hoping it wasn't. They're lame." Liar. She was looking forward to the make-believe show. "So ... there's this thing on campus tonight. The Summer Display. Everyone brings a piece and sets it out. There's music and food. It would be cool if you came."

She gave me a hot pink flyer with information about the event she wanted to lure me to ... for pictures and more badgering.

"Thanks," I said.

I tucked the flyer in my bag as she motioned for the group to assemble again. She glanced over to me and smiled. I heard her think: *I should get her to introduce herself. That would be so cool!*

No, it wouldn't. It would be the worst thing ever, actually. For some reason, I couldn't look away, and she hadn't stopped staring at me either. I did not want to introduce myself. I wanted to stand in the back and follow the natural urge to enjoy this place that breathed creativity.

I should let her stand in the back and follow the natural urge to enjoy this place that breathes creativity, she thought, repeating my unspoken words. Her eyes dulled for a moment, seemingly in a trance. My trance.

My heart pounded, and I looked away.

"Okay, guys. Let's get going," she said, her voice gaining speed as I released her, I guessed.

The group pushed out of the doors and I downed the water Sophia had packed for this very reason—because my powers were dangerous and unpredictable and I had no idea how much I could actually do.

The effect was immediate. My hands stopped trembling, my muscles relaxed, and the thoughts in the air reduced to soft whispers.

I stayed as far away from Elizabeth and the rest of the vulnerable humans as she showed us the dance studios.

We took turns peeking through the door of the class that was in session. The students, mostly girls with buns and unnecessary layers of clothing, extended and retracted their legs to muffled classical music.

"Okay, guys," Elizabeth said. "The next stop on our tour is Housing. Let's go check out where you will be living."

That was where I drew the line. I'd rather die than live in another dorm. I checked the time. Forty-five minutes until Sophia would be here. It could be forty-five minutes of torture and ignoring the awful memories a dorm could cause, or forty-five minutes of possibly controlling someone else's thoughts.

I'd rather not.

I intentionally wandered left as the rest of them went right, escaping the rest of the tour.

I walked and walked until I stumbled upon a bookstore. The scent of fresh coffee engulfed me as soon as I opened the door, along with new minds that were just loud enough to hear, but thankfully soft enough to ignore.

I roamed the aisles, reading the backs of books I knew I didn't want. My aimless stroll led me to the historical section. Even history was more exciting at art school. I opened a book titled *The Art the War Gave*

Us and flipped through the pictures of dark paintings of beasts and sculptures of screaming figures.

Someone cleared their throat on the other side of the aisle. I didn't look up … at first. Then, it happened again. The person poked a hand through the shelf and tapped the book I was holding. His hand was dark and smooth, almost airbrushed to perfection. He was wearing a gold ring with the initials T. R. engraved into it on his index finger.

"Don't be afraid," he whispered. I immediately disobeyed that order. I dropped the book, but my feet refused to move. I couldn't see the person on the other side, but I recognized his deep and terrifying voice from Kamon's chapel. He'd led the sick greeting, praising that twisted man. His voice sounded like crackling fire. If I had to imagine what the devil sounded like, it would be like him. "I was sent to express my master's deepest apologies."

"How did you find me?"

"This generation feels the need to tell everyone about every detail of their day. Especially meeting the famous Leah Grant. You're all over the Internet right now. I mean you no harm."

"Yeah, right."

He chuckled. The bass in his voice made it as terrifying as a scream.

"My master is offering you an opportunity. A home." I had a home. "A family." I had a family. "A chance to punish Remi Vaughn for the pain she inflicted on you last night." That … I didn't have, but I wasn't stupid enough to fall for that.

"I'm not interested."

"Is that so?" he asked.

I didn't stick around to answer. I took off running, too panicked to remember where the door was. I turned down an aisle, only to race in the other direction when I came to a dead end. He chuckled in the distance, a terrifying phantom. I felt like a small child, frightened by the boogieman or some other unseen thing. But he wasn't a monster in a closet, and I wasn't a helpless child.

I stopped running.

I had my mother's powers. Lydia freaking Shaw. He should be the one running.

I marched towards his laughter, ready to face a hunter dead on. When I made it to the spot I knew I'd heard his menacing laugh floating from, he wasn't there.

A white envelope sat in the middle of the aisle, alone and purposefully there for me. I looked around for a moment, then inched closer to pick it up.

I cracked the wax seal and pulled out a square of paper, thick like a postcard, fancy like it was from someone who sat on a throne.

Leah, I hope this letter finds you well and healed from the mistake my former pet made. I do not wish you any harm. I have seen the extent of your powers, and I am impressed. I am in awe of what you could become. Unstoppable. Powerful. Feared. Oh ... the lives you will take, the blood you will spill. My heart rejoices at the thought of it. The 4th will only be the beginning of your destiny if you join us. There is a place for you here, right next to my throne. We are waiting.

–Kamon.

And now I was afraid again, a child again. So I ran again, right out of the bookstore and into a group of boys playing hacky sack in front of the door, oblivious of the dangerous world we lived in. I stepped out of their way and caught my breath. At least the hunter had left without a fight.

This time.

Sophia called a few minutes later, I was still trying to ease myself down from panic over the letter, and I met her in the front of the school. I opened the back door like she'd instructed me to do over the phone. My heart jumped when I saw the passenger. I hadn't expected to see her.

"How was it?" Mom asked.

I crawled in, gave her a quick hug, and showed her Kamon's letter.

She slammed her head on her seat as she read it. "Sophia, here is good. We're not being followed." Sophia pulled over to the side of the road, a few blocks away from Trenton. I blinked, and we were standing in my dining room. "What happened?" Mom asked.

I told her everything, from stepping out of the SUV to running out of the bookstore, including controlling Elizabeth's thoughts. She inspected me several times, even though I'd told her the hunter hadn't touched me.

"This is when you lock me in the house, right?" I asked.

She shook her head. "No. You will live your life without fear. The hunters are my business, remember? " She kissed my nose, and I nodded. "And I'll show you how to stop yourself from influencing thoughts. You'll be fine. "

Fine? What did she mean, fine? I'd controlled someone's thoughts today, gotten a deadly pen pal, and there was still the horrible prediction that I'd kill her. Things were *not* fine. I wanted to tell her that I was no longer the infant she'd left or the shell of a girl they'd brought to New Orleans, and I didn't need her to sugarcoat the truth. My accidental and wild powers were right in the middle of whatever Kamon was planning.

Sophia led us to the table for an early dinner. I took the chair across from Mom.

"The blood I will spill?" I asked, quoting Kamon's letter, hoping that would make her be more honest with me.

"You know who you are," she said. "Don't allow this letter to shake that. You're not capable of anything evil. He's an idiot, sweetie. He has no idea what he's talking about. He's still trying to figure out if you were born human or not."

She chuckled as she gracefully placed her napkin in her lap. She scooped the potato soup from the far end of her bowl then neatly sipped from the spoon. It seemed like she didn't notice how formal and calm she was being in this serious moment. I didn't know who to blame for her ill placed table manners, her job or her mother.

"Well, that *idiot* sent someone to talk to me. T. R.," I said. "He had those initials in his ring ... if it helps." She nodded and took another formal sip. Her posture was perfect as I lurched over my bowl. At least one of us was too worried to care about etiquette. "He found me easily, Mom. And you don't plan to keep me in the house. He could find me again. Maybe he's the mysterious person who will kill me. Kill *you*, actually."

"He's not. I know Travis. He wouldn't be so hard to see."

"Then who else could it be?" If Kamon wasn't going to kill me, or Remi, or the triplets, I didn't know who else to question.

She hunched her shoulders. "Sophia and I can't see who it is, honey."

"If you can't see them and Sophia's magic can't protect me, how are you going to stop them?" I asked.

She didn't answer. Sophia tilted a pitcher of water over her glass. It was the only sound for a while, making it as loud as the waterfall from the Congo.

"I don't know, but it doesn't matter. If something gets past the charm, you still won't feel a thing. A bullet could go right through your head and you'll be fine."

I averted my eyes from hers. It sounded like she'd given up, accepted that she wouldn't find this person and would die. I hid my fists under my thighs. Giving up and accepting terrible fates was a habit of hers.

The emotions that flared in my chest were at war with each other, too different to share the space inside of me. Her blasé attitude made me want to flip the table but the fact that she was here made me want to crawl into her arms, and the girl I had always been wanted to run in fear but the girl I was becoming wanted to fight to change our lives. No more wanting things out of our reach—a family, a mother, a daughter, a normal life. We were strong, powerful. We shouldn't have to live like this. Like strangers and hidden cowards. This phantom person who Sophia's magic or Mom's mental powers couldn't find had to be stopped.

We'd been through this, the whole *she's going to die* thing, and I didn't want to do it again. The girl I was becoming and the things she wanted rose inside of me and trumped everything else.

If they weren't strong enough, or willing to fight hard enough, my powers could be our only hope. I thought about Kamon's letter. I didn't want to be feared, but I wouldn't mind being unstoppable and powerful right now if it would help her stay alive.

I didn't know if Mom was using her powers or if something about me had changed on the outside to show how much I'd just changed on the inside, but she narrowed her eyes at me and shook her head.

"Let us handle this, okay?" she said. "I know it's important to you, and it is technically your life that is in danger, but I don't want you getting involved and using your powers. It's not a good idea. Promise me you'll stay out if it."

"I promise," I said.

I'd never lied with that straight of a face in my entire life. I didn't plan to stay out of it. I wasn't going to sit around idly while my potential murderer roamed free, whoever he or she was.

And I wasn't afraid, at least not now. My heart was racing for another reason, at the thought and thrill of getting what I wanted. The family that Julian stole from me.

"How do you bring memories back? I asked, to change the subject. Apparently I hadn't chosen the right one. Mom cleared her throat and stared into her soup like something interesting was in it.

"They have to be triggered," Sophia said. "I'm already devising a plan for your father, dear. Lydia has put me in charge of that."

That burned, because it seemed like she'd willed her that responsibility so it would happen even in the event of her death.

"Enough negativity," Mom said. "Tell me about Trenton."

I relaxed in my chair and sighed, forcing myself to focus on this moment. I was having dinner with my mother. I should be grateful and cherish it and wait to plot on Kamon and the mystery person later.

I smiled at her, and her face that carried only a few of my features lit up.

"I liked it, actually," I said. "There was a nice art gallery, and it was nothing like St. Catalina. The girl I told you about, Elizabeth, she actually talked to me. I got invited to an art show on campus tonight."

They both applauded like I'd accomplished something major.

"You should go," Mom said. "Otherwise, you'll be here alone or collecting dust at Sophia's house." She closed her eyes. "It's at six on campus, too public for Kamon's style," she said. "I could send for a car and ride over with you. At six, I'll ..." Mom opened her eyes and glanced over to Sophia.

"You'll still be in court. I'll bring her and pick her up after I eat dinner with Greg," Sophia said. "And my house is *not* dusty."

Mom rolled her eyes.

I was about to tell them to save themselves the hassle of getting me to and from the show, I didn't really want to go, but the mischievous wheels in my head spun.

The art show and the anniversary party I'd heard my dad talking about were around the same time. I'd only miss an hour of it if I went to Trenton at six, eight his time, and snuck off to the party. There would be no harm in going to watch him sing those songs he'd promised his friend. I'd stay hidden in a corner. I'd see him. He wouldn't see me. The art show was the perfect alibi.

"Mom, I have a question. Um … the hunter, how did he get to Trenton? I always need to see a place in my head before I go there. Had he been there before?" I stifled a smile, impressed with how good my cover was, as I baited her to tell me everything I needed to know to get to Chicago.

"Probably not. He could have used a picture, maybe from the school's website once they got word of your location. Tonight, I'll make sure that's not an issue."

"Thanks. So … he used a picture, you said?"

She nodded. "Most likely. You only need a guide, and you can *feel* when it's safe to go there, when you won't be spotted. These days, it's easy because of the Internet. There are pictures of everything accessible at your fingertips. In my day, it was much more complicated."

I chuckled. "Mom, you were nineteen when you had me. That would only make you thirty-six, right?" She nodded, and I grinned. "When's your birthday?"

"You tell me. It'll be your lesson for the day."

I closed my eyes and wondered about it. It wasn't as easy as sifting through the buzzing in the air at St. Catalina, but when I focused, the date, July 23rd, whispered in my ear.

"It's coming up. We should have a party!" I said.

She smiled slightly and sipped out of her water. "Thirty-seven," she said, to herself mostly. "God, time flies."

Sophia changed the subject to Trenton and the classes I would take. No one mentioned that I'd foolishly proposed to throw a party for Lydia Shaw's 37th birthday, weeks after she was predicted to die. Even if I found this person they couldn't see and stopped them, who would go to the party other than me, and maybe Sophia? The most famous woman in the world didn't have enough people in her life to celebrate anything with.

I let it go. I didn't want to think about anything sad right now. I wanted to enjoy my mother, spy on my father, live a semblance of the normal life that Julian stole from me.

"Enjoy yourself tonight, baby. Be cautious of anyone you meet, but Sophia and I will have that place covered. Are you going to bring one of your pieces?"

I shook my head fast, suddenly nervous about showing my work, even though I wasn't really planning to go to the show.

"Where will you be?" I asked.

"Rome. Court is in session in exactly two minutes. And it can't start without the judge." My eyebrows pushed together. "Did you think they were calling me *Your Honor* for fun?"

I laughed and shook my head. A mother. A judge. A fabulous dresser. She was so many things, amazing things, a goddess in my mind.

I couldn't lose her.

"Bye, Super-Mom."

She chuckled and came over to my chair. Her lips barely reached my cheek before Sophia pulled at her arm and shooed her away.

Not long after she left, Paul's mother called with a baking crisis. Sophia whispered protection charms around the house and left to go calm her down. I'd declined the offer to tag along.

As soon as she vanished, I searched the web for Murphy's where the anniversary party was. It was in Chicago like I'd thought it would be. Luckily, there were several pictures of the red brick building on their website.

I hopped in the tub after, for no other reason than to soak and calm my nerves. Lying to Mom was my biggest worry. I didn't want to upset her, but I hoped to be in and out, see my dad, hear a song or two, and be on my way.

At the exact moment that my muscles relaxed, my phone rang on the floor next to the tub.

"You really are perfect, you know?" I said. Nate chuckled. "I miss you."

"Miss you more. Paul and I are sharing a room on this big boat. Which means Paul and Em and I are sharing a room on this big boat." We laughed, and I cranked on the hot water with my toe. "Please tell me you're not in the tub."

"I'm not in the tub." I splashed around loudly on purpose, and he groaned.

"*Subject change*," he begged. "I got your message. I'm glad you're feeling better. I didn't stop shaking until I heard that. Sorry I couldn't call. Where were you earlier that I wouldn't believe?"

I paused to think for a moment. I didn't want to hide something as huge as having living parents from Nate, but I felt the need to clam up. Worse than I had in New Orleans when I found out I was human. It didn't feel like the right time to tell him about how much my life had changed since last night.

"Oh, I was at Trenton College of the Arts," I said. "I'll probably be going to school there in August."

He hummed. "Wow. You're right. I wouldn't have believed that, but that's great. I'm so happy for you."

"Thanks."

I swept my hand over the water, making ripples that reminded me of the magic mirror.

"So ... did you see any cute guys there?" he asked.

"*So* many. I couldn't keep count." He whined, sounding like a wounded puppy, and I chuckled. "I didn't notice any guys, babe. I went on the tour like Sophia and ... Lydia told me to," I said.

"Good. I don't want to be replaced. I know how messed up it was to leave you ... all bloody and scared, but Noah, Naomi, Nicholas, Nia, and Noel need me to have this job." I laughed. "You can't buy them everything. I have to help."

"We're not having that many kids. Just the first two."

"Fine. Just thought I'd slip them in. I'm hiding in the pantry, by the way. I found an outlet in here."

"Baby, I don't want you to get in trouble. Go back to your room."

"No, I want to talk to you." I cranked the faucet off and lay back in the tub. He groaned like he'd heard me move. "Focus, Nate, and pretend your girlfriend is not naked right now." I giggled. "We fed thousands of people today, Chris. It was incredible. Of course, I missed you, but it was so unreal. These people come out of their little homes crying when we get there. It's amazing."

"You're staying away from the attack zones, right?" It took him too long to answer. "Nate!"

"We are, babe," he whispered. "I thought I heard something. Sorry."

A door slammed and the phone ruffled against something.

"I'm just hungry, man. I love … peanuts. I really really love peanuts."

He hung up.

"I love you, too," I said.

Nate hated peanuts.

CHAPTER ELEVEN

I rubbed my fingers across the smooth glass and cringed. The tiny vial of potion seemed so heavy in my hand.

Sophia hadn't mixed it with anything this time. She left the green slime in its pure form, unsure of how much I would need if necessary or how long I would be out.

"You have your phone?" she asked as the SUV rolled to a stop in front of Trenton.

"Yes."

"You will be careful?"

"Yes."

"If you encounter Kamon or any of his hunters, you will run and not fight." That was less of a question, more of an order. The answer stuck in my throat. I couldn't reply with another dry *yes* after she reminded me that I didn't have a dry life. "Promise me."

"I promise."

I waved at her through the tinted window, knowing she would see me even though I couldn't see her. We really hadn't needed the decoy vehicle. The front of the school was deserted and quiet. I half expected a tumbleweed to blow by.

I walked to the sign that said: *Summer Display, Main Gallery*. A tiny voice in my head told me to just follow the arrow and go to the art show like I'd promised. I would like it there. I would be surrounded by art and beautiful colors. But I'd rather be surrounded by my father's music.

I closed my eyes and pictured Murphy's, suddenly nervous that I'd searched the wrong bar or had misinterpreted Dad's words. What if Murphy was just a friend of his and the party was at his house? I felt like an idiot for assuming where he would be tonight.

"Will my dad be at Murphy's, *the bar*, tonight?" I asked. A moment later, I was undoubtedly sure that he would be.

Mom was right. I felt exactly when it was safe to go to the party. Like a gate had opened before me. I could almost hear it squeaking on its hinges.

I landed in front of the red bricks near the door, alone on a dark street. A couple rounded the corner a few seconds later. Perfect timing. They'd just missed an impossible sight.

I pulled my hood over my head and brushed my curls in my face to shield it. I opened the door and laughter and smoke poured out of the cramped room.

The thoughts in the air competed with the music. I heard hundreds of conversations at once—real voices, the unsaid things, the secret things, and the feelings behind them, too. I wrapped my arms around my stomach and slid into an empty booth.

The tremors Mom had taught me to recognize swept through me. I knew to stop listening, but I couldn't. The buzzing was too loud, too powerful. I couldn't pull away.

Worry felt different here. Not pimples and boyfriends. Their burdens were heavy. Cheating husbands, foreclosures, and all sorts of awful things crushed me into my seat.

I felt myself slipping away, growing less and less aware of the people in the bar, entranced by the buzzing, the power.

At this rate, I wouldn't hear my dad play and this sneak out would've been wasted. Not to mention that I would expose human powers if I lost control of mine.

My hand trembled as it wrapped around the potion in my bag. I needed something to discreetly dump it into. Tilting a glass of glowing, lime green liquid into my mouth would probably cause as much trouble as my kidnapping did.

I waved over a waiter. The red skullcap on his head fell to the ground. I froze. I knew I'd knocked it off, but he didn't notice. He picked it up and jogged over to my booth.

His name was the first thing that came to me. Drake Fisher. He was eighteen, despite what the thick beard on his face suggested. His thoughts screamed so loudly in my ears that I couldn't understand them, too blurred and mixed with the other clatter in the room.

"What can I get you?" Drake asked.

"I need a drink." My voice came out as desperate as I felt.

"Got some ID?"

"I meant a soda. Coke."

"Oh, right away."

Every minute it took for him to return with my drink, I sank a little deeper, drowning in screaming thoughts and adult anxiety.

"Coke, hold the Jack," Drake said, chuckling and handing me a straw.

"Thanks."

As soon as he stepped away, I opened a menu and shielded my cup. I dumped half of the vial into my drink and sucked it down as fast as I could.

The screams turned to whispers, and the emotions of the people around me drained from my chest. If I would've been with Mom right then, I would have asked her why the hell anyone would ever train to deliberately feel that way. Moving things without having to get up was one thing, convenient, but feeling the pain of others was another. It wasn't worth being psychic in my book.

When I felt like myself again, I searched the foggy, blue-lit room for my father. I was severely out of place here. Everyone looked to be in their thirties or forties. They were dressed in business-casual like they'd all come from work. Or maybe it was how adults dressed for parties, all of them except the man in the white t-shirt and black jeans sitting on the bar. His tattooed arm was around the neck of a very drunk man, and they were singing about some guy named Benny and his jets to the top of their lungs.

The woman I'd seen my father singing with through the mirror three months ago climbed up on the bar next to the drunk guy. She kissed my father's friend, and I smiled. She wasn't his girlfriend. Maybe he was still single and available to fall back in love with Mom … *if* his memories came back without harming him and *if* I didn't kill her.

"Happy 10th anniversary, Ken and Meg!" Dad shouted.

The crowd joined him and cheered for the couple. Ken and Meg hadn't stopped kissing. Dad hopped down and ran to the little stage in the front of the bar, and I sat on my feet so I could see him. He started tuning a guitar, getting ready to play and make my night.

Ken stumbled on stage and grabbed the microphone. The speakers screeched, turning all heads to him.

"Thanks for coming to our party," he slurred. "Meg? Where's Meg?" A huddle of women pointed at Meg dancing on the bar to no music. "I met Meg eleven years ago. Gavin said, 'Hey, she looks like your type.' Remember, Gav?" My father nodded in the corner, still tuning his guitar. "Anyway, my buddy introduced me to her and we've been together ever since." The crowd applauded, and Ken stumbled back before catching his balance. "And now, ladies and gentlemen, my buddy is going to sing the song he sang at our wedding."

"No, I'm not," Dad said.

"Yes, you are."

"I'm not."

"He is," Ken said to the crowd. "And I'm going to dance with my smokin' hot wife before you old geezers go home before ten. Gav, you remember when we used to rock this place to five in the morning? The good ole' days when…" My dad pulled the microphone from his friend's hands, laughing like he was about to say something inappropriate.

Ken stumbled back to the bar and, rather clumsily, helped his wife down and pulled her to the middle of the floor.

"Thanks for coming out—uh—everyone. I'm only going to do one more song since the happy couple is already *three sheets to the wind*," Dad said. "You guys know I'm not good at speeches and such. But—uh—" He ruffled his short curls as he paused. "I forgot what I was going to say, but … buddy, we've had some good times and even better times, and I'm happy for you. And—uh—to show it, I'll sing the song you two love so much."

He pulled up a stool and sat with his guitar in his lap. I braced my hand against my heart so it wouldn't explode out of my chest and land on the table. The song was slow and beautiful, about love being all he needed to live. The dancing couple sang along like they'd heard it a million times. Other couples joined them on the small dance floor and swayed to Dad's amazing tenor voice.

I wanted to run to him and tell him who I was, but I knew I had to wait. I closed my eyes as he sang his friends a love song. I pretended he was singing about Mom and she was right here next to me, listening to him too. I pretended that our lives were normal and we knew Meg and Ken, not that a dangerous man had forced Mom to make all three of us live separate lives.

"A fan?" Drake asked.

I opened my eyes and lowered my hand from my heart.

"Of music?" I asked.

"Of Gavin. Most people who come here come to hear him play. He used to be some famous backup guitarist if there is such a thing. I've never heard of him, myself, but these people have."

My dad was a famous backup. I could believe it. He was talented enough to have his own records, be on the radio, but he seemed happy up there on the little stage. Comfortable.

"I've never heard his music. I'm just here to hang out."

He took that as an invitation to sit.

"I'm Drake," he said. I knew that already. I craned my neck to the stage. He was blocking my view of my dad. He moved his ton-sized, mildly attractive, head back in my way. "And you are…"

"Christine."

"I thought you were going to say Leah." I squinted my eyes at him, and he laughed. I hadn't felt my hood bundled on my neck until then, no longer covering my head. "Come on. Everyone knows who you are."

"Great."

"I mean, you're famous. You were trending earlier, some girl said she saw you. Do you have a private jet or something? How'd you get here so fast?" I wanted to smack myself for not thinking about how odd it looked to suddenly be in Chicago when I had been spotted in L. A.

a few hours ago. "I have to ask. Why did you do it? I was picked on in high school, too, but I didn't stage a kidnapping. Don't you think that was a little dramatic?" I sighed, and he laughed. "Unless you didn't make it up."

"I didn't. You got me, Drake. The witch is my friend. She cooks for me every day and tucks me in, so if you'll just..." I motioned for him to leave my booth so I could catch the rest of the song.

"You're funny. Even if there were living witches, one wouldn't cook for you. Maybe she'd cook *you*." He shivered, an ingrained human response to magic.

The crowd applauded and Dad took a bow. Stupid Drake had made me miss the rest of the song. I sat on my hands, straining against the urge to make his body fly to the other end of the bar.

In an attempt to get to know me better, Drake told me all about his band, The Whispering Willows, who mostly screamed their lyrics. I smirked at the irony. The conversation reminded me of the countless ones I'd had with Whitney without saying a word or giving any inclination that I wanted it to continue. I'd resorted to staring at the bubbles in my Coke and stirring my straw to upset them again when they settled.

"Young Drake, you have to learn to notice when a lady is not interested in you." I snapped my head up and smiled. My father was standing at the end of my booth, holding a tray out to Drake. "Murphy said to tell you to get back to work."

Drake groaned and scooted out of the booth. "I wasn't hitting on her. I figured if I told a famous girl about my band, I'd be famous, too."

"Famous?" Dad asked.

"She's Leah Grant," Drake said. "You know ... the girl who lied and said a witch took her from school."

"I never said that. Everyone assumed that."

Dad leaned into the table and tilted his head slightly, taking in my face. "You know what I think?" I shook my head, trying to push myself into a shadowy corner. He was staring too hard and too long. I wondered how long it would take for him to see his face in mine. The potion made that just a question. My dulled powers didn't rev. "I think a witch *did* take you, and the government covered it up."

My heart pounded as he theorized too close to the truth. Drake tapped my dad on the shoulder. "Gavin, your friend just face planted on the dance floor."

"Oh, God." He ran to his friend who looked dead in the middle of the floor, and I scrambled out of the booth. It was time to go. I knew that. I felt it. Nothing good could come of staying any longer. I shouldn't have talked to him. Now, when Mom recovered his memories, he'd remember I was here tonight.

I threw a few ones on the table for the drink and ran out of the door. On the lonely street, I shut my eyes and tried to move myself to Trenton.

My body wouldn't go. Wouldn't move.

I grunted. The kryptonite had stranded me in Chicago. I could've called Sophia, but I preferred to wait for my powers to return. I didn't think she or Mom would seriously yell at me, but they'd probably keep a closer eye on me. And as soon as I was able to bring myself home, I was going to start searching for the mysterious murderer they couldn't see. I didn't need more attention from them.

The street in front of the club was dead and windy. Both directions looked haunted, crowded with ghostly shadows. I went left, towards the sound of squealing breaks and rumbling engines, hopefully the promise of a livelier street.

I obviously hadn't thought the night through, but at least I'd heard my father sing and the added bonus of talking to him. It was overwhelming how much I suddenly wanted more. It was as though years of my life were falling away as I walked down the quiet street. My lips quivered and my eyes watered like I was seven, not seventeen. Leaving my daddy, not a man I didn't know. I desperately wanted to run in the opposite direction to him. I wanted to know him as badly as I'd ever wanted anything in my life—staying alive at St. Catalina, for Nate to look past my faults, for Mom to be herself and not Lydia to me.

Something rattled behind me, and I jumped. An aluminum can scurried down the street, pushed by the gusting wind. My hair whipped around me, and I pulled my thin jacket tighter around my chest.

A few steps later, I heard another noise but didn't turn around.

"It's the can, Christine," I told myself.

The can rattled again, followed by a different sound. A softer one. Not a can. It sounded like feet. I wondered if Drake had tweeted or made a status about me that Kamon had seen again.

I sped my steps. Panic eventually made me run towards the streetlight. When the steps behind me sped too, I scrambled to find my phone to call Mom.

My touchscreen was too sensitive to my nervous fingers.

"Don't be afraid," the voice said, like the hunter had in the bookstore. "Leah or … Christine. Whatever name you're going by." This voice was not threatening. It was gentle, familiar. "I-I-I don't want to hurt you. I just want to talk." I stopped running, my shoes splashing in a puddle of water. I panted as he came closer. My dad held both of his hands up. "I don't have any weapons. And I'm not stalking you. Okay?"

"Okay."

"W-w-which name is it?" he asked, still creeping towards me.

"Christine."

He was breathing harder than I was, and his thoughts were a distant jumble, like faint white noise. "I watched you on the news. I've been thinking about you since then." He smacked his forehead. "That made me s-s-sound like a stalker, but I'm not. I swear."

If he weren't *the* Gavin from Mom's memories, this had all the makings of being my death scene, or hers—alone with a tattooed stranger on a dark street in an unfamiliar city. But he was *the* Gavin, so I said, "I'm not afraid of you."

"Good. I have a few questions for you. Is that okay?" I nodded. "My car is … right there." He pointed at a deep green truck parked at the end of the street, too nice to be an off-road vehicle but shaped like one. "That's not—uh—very safe, but I have a feeling you live a … sort of secret life. Am I right?"

I didn't really know how to answer, so I shrugged my shoulders.

We walked to the busier street where the city lights drove away the haunting shadows. I tried to push my brain to decipher why he wanted to talk to me, but nothing happened. It felt sluggish, weighed down by the potion like a soggy towel.

He opened the door for me and ran back to the other side. He slammed his door and locked us in. His eyes were on his dashboard, his thoughts still a jumble of soft words. He reached over me and opened the glove compartment. My heart jumped at the sight of a pistol amidst scattered papers and napkins. "There's my gun. That's yours to use if you feel unsafe. Okay?"

"Okay."

I took the car in as I waited for him to speak. Hints of tobacco clung to the seats without any visible evidence of actual cigarettes or ashes. I had the feeling that it only smelled like smoke because he spent his time singing in bars and clubs.

"The first time I watched the news report about you, they were calling you Leah."

"Yeah."

"Then … the next time I watched, they were calling you

Christine."

"It's … my real name."

"Wh—" He huffed and paused, like he was struggling through a stutter. "What—um—brings you h-h-here tonight?" I hunched my shoulders. I didn't want to lie to my dad, and I couldn't tell him the truth. "When I saw you in that booth, I almost … f-f-fainted."

"I didn't know I was *that* famous."

"It's not that … it's…"

He paused again and I stared out of the windshield. The glow on the slick asphalt reflected the changing colors of the streetlight. It went from green to yellow as he struggled to find his words. The whispers around him halted, too. They cranked on and off again in a moment, like a radio with a short. Like something was wrong with him.

The street glowed red, and my brain slowed with the cars passing us. Everything seemed to move in slow motion as it dawned on me that something could be wrong with him. That he said *uh* a lot, and paused a lot, and stuttered.

"Uh…," he continued to struggle.

"Are you okay?" I asked.

"Yeah. I just—uh—get a little lost sometimes. Especially when I'm nervous."

"Why are you nervous?"

He hunched his shoulders. A bus rumbled down the street and stopped a few feet away from us. Passengers shuffled out and dispersed into the windy night.

"B-b-because it's just weird that you're here. In Chicago. In this bar of all p-p-places … when I've wanted to ask you something for months. I even looked you up, but you don't have a page on anything like most kids do." His thoughts muted again and he gripped the steering wheel, his shoulders curling so violently I would've thought he was about to shift if I didn't know he was human. He took a deep breath. "I wanted to ask you if you knew the woman who was looking for you."

His question was all there was to the world for a moment. There were no lights, or sounds. No words. My silence seemed to answer for me. The moisture in his eyes said all there was to say about him, too. It explained why he stuttered and frequently lost his words.

He'd hurt himself, likely to recover memories of her.

"I was watching the news and thought ..." He coughed and took a moment to catch his breath after. "I thought ... if I had a kid, I'd bet she'd look like that. Then ... they f-f-f-flashed your picture, then her, then you again. I was drinking, so I thought I was just fabricating the resemblance. I thought it was the beer. A few days later, they said it was your birthday. And I counted nine months from that day. It's possible. But ... *impossible*. I didn't think she had a reason to hate me enough to do this, so ... I let it go. But you came here tonight. The odds of it b-b-being nothing now are slim."

He sighed loudly and leaned his head back on the seat, trembling now. Thick tears dropped from his eyes, and he paused. I wasn't sure if he'd lost his words again or if he just couldn't speak through the tears.

"How do you remember her?" I asked.

"I found pictures of a random girl in my house when I was moving out. This feeling of knowing her kept bothering me. It took years, a stroke, and permanent damage, but I finally remembered." He took my face in his hands and rubbed his thumbs under the eyes we shared. "Humor me. Who am I to you?"

His eyes were burning despite the tears cascading from them. There was no sense in lying. He already knew. "You're my father." He closed his eyes and nodded, yanking his head up and down several times, answering a question I hadn't asked. "She doesn't know that you know her," I said.

"She knows everything before most people know anything. If she wanted to talk to me, she would have. I've stayed out of her way to give her what she wanted, but she's been hiding my kid!"

"I know. I'm sorry, Dad. She is, too." Something broke him then. My apology, or hers, or calling him *dad*. He pulled me out of my seat and trapped me against his chest. "I'm sorry. I didn't mean to make you cry. I didn't mean to do any of this. I just wanted to hear you play."

He whispered things too teary to understand for a minute, soaking my hair and squeezing the life out of me. The first comprehensible thing he said was, "Call her. Right now, please."

I pulled out my phone, my heart close to giving out.

"Is everything okay?" Mom said after the first ring.

"Sort of. *Okay* ... not really."

"What's wrong?"

It took me a few seconds to get it out, but I finally forced the words, "I'm in Chicago," to my lips. Then I said, "Dad knows." She didn't say anything for a minute. "I'm sorry."

"Don't apologize, baby. I'm not mad. I'm just confused. What do you mean, he knows?"

I tried to work through the story—the bar, the pictures, the news. It must've frustrated Dad because he snatched my phone out of my hand.

"I'm not in the mood for you to play dumb. I'm taking her to my house. I assume you know where it is and can get there faster than I can."

He stepped out of the truck and stormed away with the phone. No amount of distance would've silenced the filthy words coming out of his mouth. He spat hateful names I didn't think Kamon would call her. Some of the insults baffled me, too foreign and adult for me to comprehend, but I knew they were killing her to hear. And it was apparently killing him to say. He ripped the phone from his ear and

184

screamed at the wind after their call ended.

After he'd stopped, he stood outside by his door for a minute before getting in, probably trying to calm down from his rage.

He cried the entire drive to his house, apologizing and calling himself a dead-beat-dad. It didn't seem to matter how many times I told him I wasn't upset. Especially when he asked me to tell him about my life before today—that I really was an orphan, that I met Mom three months ago for the first time, and that she'd tampered with my memories, too.

He gripped his steering wheel hard enough to rip it off.

It was silent until he pulled into his driveway and came around to open my door.

Mom was sitting on the deck that overlooked the dark lake. A gentle breeze caught her hair, making her look enchanted and gorgeous under the stars. She was sobbing.

"Gavin, I'm sorry," she said.

"Don't call me that. You don't know me, remember?"

"Okay … *Christopher*. I'm sorry. But it's more complicated than you probably think it is."

Dad clenched his jaw, and with a strange calm, unlocked his door and walked inside. The patio opened into a kitchen. The stainless steel appliances gave it a masculine feel. It was clean but lived in. Opened envelopes and newspapers littered the counters, and there were pots on the stove. If I had to make a more than educated guess, I'd say he'd made beef stew earlier today.

Mom pulled me to her side, covering my face with kisses and apologies, as we followed closely behind Dad. He obviously loved the guitar. They crowded his living room. A few glistening ones were mounted on the wall, looking down on the peasant guitars on the floor. Apparently, this was his idea of home décor. He didn't have art or photographs, just guitars and scattered sheet music on the sofa and coffee table.

"Christine, make yourself at home. We'll be back," he said.

He clicked on the television, cranked the volume as loud as it would go, and stormed past Mom down a dark hall. "I'm so sorry," I said. She shook her head, rejecting my apology, and followed Dad.

The TV wasn't loud enough to muffle the slamming door.

Of course I wasn't about to let them have a private conversation. I wasn't a baby.

I stayed as close to the door as I could to hear their fight. Mom tried to tell him about Julian. He didn't care. She tried to tell him about Kamon. He cared even less. She told him about her soul and the danger we were currently in. He didn't reply. He was silent while she cried and told him she wouldn't have left him if she'd had a choice. He waited until she ran out of words and screamed at her nonstop for half an hour, stuttering through curse words. That seemed to piss him off more.

"I should have you arrested for kidnapping. I can't believe you have the nerve to play this victim role, crying and all this bullshit. I hate you," was the last thing I heard Dad say.

So much for a sweet reunion for the crazy couple from the diary.

Someone touched the doorknob, and I ran back to the sofa. Mom came out first, face red and puffy.

She kneeled in front of me, grabbed my hands, and rested her head against my leg. "Should I even bother saying ... *I didn't know*? It's such a lame excuse, especially for me."

"I get it, Mom. You don't watch him. It's probably too hard to."

"Stop! Stop excusing all the bad things I do to you. Your powers, the orphanage, giving you enemies, now this."

I wasn't excusing those things; I was well aware of them. I'd decided to forgive her for the bad decisions she'd made and the things she'd missed, including the monumental oversight of not knowing her husband remembered her. I'd lumped everything together and wrapped them up in one wave of forgiveness. If I analyzed her mistakes one by one, I was afraid I wouldn't feel the same way about her. I knew I couldn't do it, kill her, but I didn't want to give myself a reason to be angry with her. Because my anger tended to fester and swell into something poisonous I couldn't control. And July 4th was far too close for that.

"We can get through this, Mom. I think we've been through worse."

She huffed. "I'm having a hard time imagining something worse than this, sweetie." Her lips twitched, nearly smiling, before her face turned to stone. "I bet you want to hang out here for a while." I nodded. "I'll come back for you later … if you still want me around."

"Mom, of course I do." She stood and straightened her dress. "I'm worried about you. Are you sure you can go back to work right now?"

She wiped her face and blew me a kiss. "I don't really have a choice."

She waved and vanished, and my heart broke for her. Nothing could be worse than having to leave your husband, except if he'd let you stay away.

My new father peeked into the room, looking nervous. I waved at him, not exactly sure of how to comfort him. I'd just changed his life in a minute. I thought about apologizing, but I heard that he wasn't upset with me in the whispers in the air. His thoughts were easier to decipher now that I felt less soggy. He was happy, beyond happy. He couldn't find a word to describe how he felt.

I tinkered with the guitar on the sofa as I listened to him compose a melody in his mind, trying to capture the feeling with music since his words had failed him. The notes were light and happy, like something you would hum while running through a field of flowers.

"Christine," he said. "I know it's weird being here with a stranger."

"You're not a stranger," I said. "I know a lot about you." He lifted his chin, challenging me. "You play the guitar. You're in a band. With … Meg, the redhead. And some other guy I didn't see tonight who plays the piano. And you like to cook."

"Are you reading me right now? Being psychic?"

"Nope." I plucked at his guitar again. "Mom told me you used to cook for her, and we watched you play a few months ago through this mirror she has."

"You call her *Mom*?" I nodded. "Why? She abandoned you. She kidnapped you from me. She's a criminal, baby, not a mother."

"She *is* my mother. I know it's not a perfect situation, but that's who she is to me."

We sat there in silence for so long that I almost expected the hairs on my arm to gray and my skin to wrinkle. I was beginning to think that Dad didn't address things that made him uncomfortable. It seemed like he let things be. Maybe things he couldn't control like Mom leaving him.

He finally lifted his eyes from the floor. "Okay, kid. What do you want to do?" he asked. I shrugged my shoulders.

"Anything with you. Something that makes me know you better, I guess."

"Everything I know about myself, I stash in my attic. I could show you if you aren't afraid, like a strange man is bringing you to your doom or something."

I laughed and followed him into a hallway. He pulled a string dangling from the ceiling and unfolded a little staircase. He went up first and I followed, holding his hand the whole way, trying to ignore his thoughts about how much he hated Mom.

He gestured over to the boxes in the corner. "I'll start with what I didn't have to work to remember. I woke up in a hospital in Miami. I wasn't injured, but I'd been knocked out for a week, they'd said."

With one arm around me, he walked us over to the dusty boxes. I was far too interested in his past, the part that happened after she'd slammed him into a tree, to let go of the connection I had to his mind.

I saw a blurry vision of him waking up disoriented in a hospital room, surrounded by nurses.

"They told me my name was Christopher Gavin," he said. "And I was driving a Mercedes, lost control of the car, and slammed into a tree. I had no—no—uh..." He grunted, frustrated with losing his words, it seemed. "I had no clue what they were talking about," he finished, speaking much slower.

In the vision I couldn't pull away from, I saw him staring at himself like a stranger in a mirror. Then at his wallet and license like foreign objects.

"After a day, they let me out. I took a cab to the address listed on my license. I spent a few months like that, not recognizing anything or anyone, waiting for it to come back to me like the doctor said it would."

He pulled a box from the middle of the stack. He plopped it down and dust swirled around us. We sat around the box of forgotten things, his shoes touching mine.

"I went to a doctor for months and didn't remember a thing until one random day. I was going to the hospital for a checkup, and I remembered being in a hospital when I was a little boy. Then I remembered my mother, Rohina."

He opened the box and pulled out an 8x10 canvas painting of a woman that was obviously related to me.

"This was in my house on the wall. I figured it was my mother, but I didn't remember her until that day. She was—uh—sick when I was a kid. Uh—she died when I was nine. But before she died, she got too sick to take care of me. She used to visit the home I lived in every day and ... bring me things. I-I remember her being very nice."

My father was an orphan. No wonder he'd yelled for thirty minutes straight, screaming obscenities, when he'd learned his child had lived as one, too.

"Why is she in a box?" I whispered, answering the multitude of questions I had about her with my powers as the rest of the potion wore off. She died of pancreatic cancer. She didn't know his father well. She was part Native American, part African American. I smiled, John was right, if that was what he'd meant by Indian.

"She wasn't in a box until I remembered who painted her for me."

He tossed my grandmother into the pile and closed his eyes. Curiosity made me stay with his thoughts. He was remembering when Mom gave him the painting on his 19th birthday. She'd used her powers to catch a glimpse of his mother and painted her. She had on an oversized shirt that was obviously his, and maybe no shorts on underneath it ... so I pulled out of his mind, vowing to never return.

"I'll paint you a new one," I said. "Would you like that?"

He opened his eyes, tears falling from them. "You paint?" I nodded. "I'd like that very much, thank you." He sniffed and scooted the final box closer with his leg. "So after I remembered my mom, I pieced my life together pretty quickly. I remembered the foster home, my high school, and the coffee shop. I went to visit and ... things got better. I decided to move here, and in the process of cleaning out my house, I found these."

He showed me three photos – all of Mom asleep in a hammock

wearing a blue bikini. "She's gorgeous," I said.

"She's the devil," he said.

We listened to the hum of his air conditioner for a minute.

Before I could defend her, he pulled out old magazine clippings of Mom: the hero. I'd seen the first picture several times over the years. It was always in her chapter in my history books. The twenty-year-old Nobel Peace Prize winner.

"I asked my old coworkers if I had a girlfriend, but they didn't know of anyone special. I finally matched the bikini girl to the magazines and wrote it off as a fling before she saved the world. But I couldn't shake the feeling that it was more than that, at least for me. I couldn't let it go. I *didn't* let it go. After years of trying, having crazy nosebleeds and blacking out, I remembered everything. A few times, I thought to say something to her, but …"

He hunched his shoulders and packed the Mom box up. He never finished that sentence.

"Dad," I said, as he led me down the shaky stairs from the attic.

"I'm never going to get tired of hearing that, but … what is it, baby?"

"Did you ever tell anyone about her or that you were married to a celebrity?" He shook his head. I kept waiting for him to expound upon that, but he didn't. He just let my question drift and drift until I forgot I'd ever asked it.

I kept waiting to feel odd snuggled up in his arms on the sofa. It never happened. I loved him instantly, and besides constantly having to tune his thoughts out, it was comfortable and natural.

"So … your last name. Is it Shaw? Grant?" he asked, sniffing hard. I hadn't noticed he was crying again.

"It's Gavin," I said, proud to share his name.

"Well, Ms. Gavin, who's the joker in the pictures with you in the tabloids? The tall, bulky one."

"He's not bulky!" He laughed. "And he's my boyfriend. His name is Nathan. He's away for work right now." I cleared my throat. "He's sort of a dog."

"The bastard *cheats* on you?"

"No. I meant that literally. Magical kind still exist. Witches, wizards, everything." He nodded, like he'd known that all along. "Nathan is a shifter. Canine." He groaned and said *no* about sixty times. "He's great, Dad. You're going to love him."

"I'm not. I hate him already," he said.

"So ... what about you?" I asked. "Is there some lady I should hate?"

He chuckled. "Not currently."

"Really?" He nodded, and I smiled. "You're a good-looking guy. Why are you single?" I asked, brows raised and waiting for him to say that he couldn't love anyone but Mom.

He sighed. "I'm single because most women my age don't like to be girlfriends. They want to be wives and ..." He shivered. "It's not my thing." Not exactly the answer I wanted, but I could work with that. I had a new ludicrous wish to add to the list of things I prayed for. Right under letting Mom keep her soul, I added: *Let my parents get back together.*

"You like music?" he asked. "I have tons of it."

He fished around for the remote and turned on his complicated-looking CD player. He clicked through his favorite album, and I booed every track.

"So you hate jazz," he assessed.

"I think it's safe to assume that. I like soft guitars and violins. I can't hear them in jazz. The other instruments are too loud."

He sprung to the wall, scanning the shelves and humming. "Guitars and violins, huh?" He popped in a new CD and met me back on the sofa.

This music was perfect to paint to, to get lost in—soft singing and strumming with barely audible violins in the background. "I love this," I said.

"It's yours then. I probably have a few more like it."

We listened to each song, not rushing through the disk like before. He bobbed his head and wiggled his fingers as if he were playing along. I thought of all the things I could paint as I lay there. Mom, Dad, my new grandmother like I'd promised.

"Christine," he whispered. I rolled my head and eyes back to see him, staying pinned to his chest. "I'm sorry."

"For what?"

"You would have been six years old when I remembered her. I missed your life because I hated her for leaving like she did." I looked away because he was crying again. It made me want to join him. "You're an adult. You have your own house and a boyfriend. I-I-I let her do this to you. I let it happen."

"You didn't do anything, Dad. You didn't know."

"I knew *her*. I should've made sure she hadn't done something this awful. Lydia ..." He paused to cry and started again, first with a stutter, then slowly pushing his words out. "I'm shocked, but I'm not. This is so like her. Everything always has to be her way and on her terms."

"She didn't do any of this on purpose. She thought she was going to die. She thought she was helping us. Well, she did. We're both living."

"Are we? I've been going to speech therapy for years, you were in an orphanage believing you were a witch, and *she* … rules the world. How is that fair?"

It grew quiet enough to hear every note of the song in the background, every breath he took between his cries, and every crack Mom put on his heart. I never answered his question. I had a feeling nothing I would say would be enough.

CHAPTER TWELVE

I tried to tidy up the lounge when I noticed my clothes thrown over both of the sofas and crumpled sketches covering the floor. I'd managed to turn it into a pigsty after three days of sleeping here, even with Sophia picking up after me in the mornings.

So I was running around picking up today's trash, really tonight's trash. Since meeting my father three days ago, I'd spent most of the day with him—either at his house or mine, but mostly in the car he was teaching me to drive. At night, since there was no way to see Mom otherwise, I slept in the lounge attached to her gym. She worked through the night, meeting with dignitaries and stopping acts of terrorism no one would ever know to thank her for. Even though she was only able to pop in every few hours, I liked being under the same roof, pretending I lived with her.

Never mind that the roof technically belonged to the U. N.; at least I had my fantasies.

I found my phone under a bundle of blankets that Sophia would tame in the morning far better than I ever could. I'd been looking for it since my phone-date with Nate. They'd finally made it to dry land and were staying the night in a motel. He'd planned for us to watch the same show, pretending we were together, but Em had snatched the phone and turned it into *her* date instead of his.

"Still awake?" Mom asked. I jumped. I hadn't heard her come in. I wasn't done cleaning up, not even close.

"Yeah. It's only eleven."

She plopped down on the sofa and winced. She wedged my hairbrush from under her butt.

"I can't believe I'm doing this to you. You're living in a gym … just to spend time with me. I'm beginning to doubt your sanity."

I laughed and pulled the brush from her hands.

"I'm fine, Mom. And I'm sorry it's so messy in here. I was talking to Dad, then Nate, then Em. I was sort of busy. Too busy to clean up, apparently." I gathered my clothes in my arms and tried to make them look neat in a pile on the floor. She rolled her eyes and threw her feet up on the sofa, on top of the mess of papers I'd left there. "I guess it's good that you've been so busy tonight. Are you—I don't know— interrogating people about the 4th?"

"No, sweetie. I've been busy with other things. Of course I hope to find this person, but …" She shrugged her shoulders. "You're safe. That's really all that matters. After the 4th, Sophia will make sure whoever it is will never come after you again."

I nearly screamed. Was she freaking kidding me? Why didn't she see that life wouldn't go on as usual if she died? I would lose my mother again. After the first time, I'd mourned her for seventeen years. I would never get over it, and *she* was shrugging her shoulders.

She yawned, and I forced myself to keep quiet and not mention how angry she'd made me.

I turned down the volume on the music videos Em had decided to watch and threw her a pillow. "I haven't seen you sleep much," I said. I grabbed my sketchbook and flipped to a blank page, deep in the back. "I can entertain myself so I won't distract you. Go to sleep."

She chuckled. "I wish," she said. "My night has barely started."

Her cellphone droned a mournful melody, and we laughed. I'd changed the setting to capture how I felt every time her phone rang. It usually meant we had to say goodbye for a few hours at least.

"Shaw. Yes." She rolled her eyes. "There's no need for that. I'm here. In the gym. I'll be right out." She faked a sob when she hung up, and I chuckled. "Back to work, I go. You'll be asleep the next time I'm able to step away."

"Wake me up. Please."

She nodded and unrolled a bag of Doritos that was stuffed between the seat cushions. She tipped the bag over and scattered crumbs on the carpet.

"I've been too busy to fight with Sophia lately. Tell her that's from me. I don't want her to think I'm getting soft."

I laughed and waved before she vanished, then I swept up the crumbs. I didn't want to add more work for Sophia than she'd already have.

I wasn't remotely close to being tired, and my back was killing me from sleeping on the hard sofa. But if I said that to Mom or Sophia, I would have to move in with the Ewings or sleep alone in California. I could sleep over at my dad's, he'd offered me a room and everything, but Mom wasn't allowed to even *think* of stepping foot in his house again, to quote him. I would never see her if I moved in with him.

I flipped through my sketchbook, past pictures of my loved ones—Sophia, my parents, my friends, my heart. My decoy drawings.

Mom usually popped in when my face was buried in my sketchbook. She always assumed I was drawing frivolous things, exactly what I wanted her to think, and I'd flip to another page before she came over to see my work. The decoy drawings of the happy parts of my life masked my investigation into the dark, depressing event that was only weeks away.

Since the night I'd met my dad, I'd been using my powers to search for the person Mom sensed but couldn't see, intent on finding them so either she or I could stop them. Doing the obvious, trying to see July 4th in the future, was impossible. I'd tried and it had made my muscles quake worse than they ever had. I knew I'd end up in the hospital for sure if I took that approach. So instead, I'd focused my thoughts on finding my enemies, outside of catty orphans, and had come up with one name. Not even Kamon. Remi Vaughn. Shocker.

After that, I'd aimed my powers at uncovering anyone who knew who I was to my mother. It was the only thing that made sense. Why else would someone try to kill me? I didn't know very many people, so there was no way I'd upset someone enough to drive them to murder. Other than Remi, and Mom was sure it wouldn't be her. It had to be someone trying to hurt Mom through me.

I'd come up with three people who knew the truth about our relationship.

Sophia Ewing

Gregory Ewing Sr.

Christopher Gavin

Not helpful at all. Sophia would never hurt me, my father wouldn't either, and Sophia's husband was just as harmless as she was.

I'd resorted to sitting with my eyes closed with my pencil in hand, scribbling down any whisper that floated my way. I rolled my eyes at my other useless notes under the names of the three people who would never hurt me.

July 4th.

Mom.

Me.

Death.

Chris, you have nothing.

At least I was being honest with myself.

I closed my sketchbook and went into Mom's mini-kitchen. I pulled out the to-go plate Dad had made for me, the rest of the feast that I couldn't bear to swallow down at dinner. As it warmed, I pretended my parents were in their room just down the hall, and I'd crept into the kitchen for a midnight snack. And of course, my boyfriend had snuck into the house and was waiting for me in my bed.

I opened my eyes and snapped out of the fantasy. I was in my mother's gym, in her office where she controlled international security. My life was so far from what I wanted it to be. My father was a perpetual bachelor who didn't believe in marriage anymore, my boyfriend was out there somewhere saving magical creatures, and my mother … God only knew where my mother was right now.

That made July 4th even more terrifying. This phantom person was threatening to take away a huge piece of my fractured family. I couldn't even hope for the three of us to reunite while she wasn't promised to live beyond the next two weeks. And because of me.

I finished the rest of my leftovers and sat in the middle of the floor, ready for another session of psychic spying.

"Who will kill me," I whispered. "Who will kill me and take Mom's soul?"

I closed my eyes and pressed my pencil against the paper. And I waited. And waited. Until my butt numbed from sitting so long.

There was no buzzing to search through. It was dead air, like there was no one to find. But there *was* something, an entire person none of us could see.

Even wondering about threats to my life turned up nothing. To say I was predicted to need my get-out-of-death-free card in two weeks, my future was clean and danger free from what my powers could sense.

It seemed like the worst that could happen to me would be if

Sophia spanked me for sending pictures to Nathan that she thought were too racy. In my defense, a tank top is not a bra, even though she swore I was in my underwear.

I hid my detective work, frustrated with not learning anything new tonight, and curled up on the backbreaking sofa. The pain was worth it. Mom woke me around three in the morning. She only had an hour until her next commitment, but it was just enough time to watch an old movie.

Just enough time for me to pray this never had to end.

For the next two weeks, I saw her less and less. Two minutes here, three minutes there. Because of the attacks, she hadn't even had time to do lessons with me, too many fires to put out with enraged and frightened magical beings. Her visits were so infrequent that Sophia made me move back into my house.

And I'd failed miserably in my search to find my murderer. So much for being unstoppable and powerful. I was forced to use my sketchbook for the proper thing, drawing, since my powers hadn't revealed anything. I mostly drew Mom and Dad, together and laughing like a normal couple. I was still praying I'd see that happen one day. I owed my existence to their love. I was having a hard time accepting that it was spoiled now, like fruit that had been left out for seventeen years.

And with July 4th close enough to breathe on my neck, my hands were constantly shaking.

Currently, they were shaking on my steering wheel. "Maybe I should buy you a slower car," Dad proposed.

"Why?"

He tapped my tensed knuckles. "You seem terrified, and we're only going five miles an hour … on your own street." He pointed to my house. It seemed hilariously close for me to be so tense. "A Volvo, maybe. Aren't they safe?"

"It's not the car. I have a lot on my mind."

"Talk to me. Is it the boyfriend?"

I smiled and eased on the brake at the stop sign. "He has a name, and you know what it is."

"Fine. Is *Nathan* bothering you?"

"No. It's this thing with Mom."

The M-word ended that short conversation. I almost followed up with something like, *I thought you said I could talk to you*, but I knew it was useless. When it came to her, Dad never wanted to talk.

I parked the car in the garage, so crooked it was almost sideways.

I figured he'd decided to pretend I hadn't said anything, so I silently slid my keys on the hook he'd mounted on the wall for me. I was still shaking and frustrated with feeling so powerless. Like a sitting duck waiting to be shot, or stabbed, or whatever the mystery person had planned.

"So my band always does this 4th of July thing," he said. "A barbecue. There's gonna be food, fireworks, and games. I-I- ... I ..." He paused for a moment to stop his stutter. It still broke my heart each time I saw him struggle with his speech. "I—uh—normally go alone or with a date. This year I was hoping to bring my kid, like everyone else does."

There were several problems with that. His friends shouldn't know about me, Lydia Shaw's secret child should not be out on the town with her secret ex-husband, and there was a prediction that I would kill her that day.

"You know what's supposed to happen that day, Dad."

"No one will know that you're there. They won't be twittering or whatever it's called. And you'll be safer with me. You barely see *what's her name*." I rolled my eyes. He wasn't even using her name now. "I'll bring my gun and dare someone to touch you."

I sighed. The kind of people who would be coming after me would be faster than bullets.

"It sounds fun, Dad, but…"

He frowned. "Please? I told my friends that I am the proud father of the most beautiful girl in the world, Christine Cecilia Gavin, and I want you to meet them. They know to keep it hush."

"Dad! You know how dangerous that is! We have enough problems without the world knowing that Lydia Shaw is my mother!"

"Relax. They don't know anything about her, and I—uh—ran it by Sophia first. She checked their futures or something. They won't tell. I've worked out a s-s-story and everything." I arched my eyebrows, anxious to hear what lie he'd concocted. "They think you ran away from school like the rest of the world, so I—uh—went with that. But I told them your … *mother* left you there to go to rehab."

I gasped. "Rehab? For what?"

"Heroin. What else would explain this?" he said. I batted my eyes in disbelief, too stunned to speak. "I said she was a road groupie from my touring days."

"So, I'm your long lost kid from a heroin using groupie, not your ex-wife?"

"Same thing," he mumbled. I just shook my head. I didn't think Dad knew how much it hurt that he had no plans to forgive Mom. Even though she could die this weekend, he didn't seem to care at all or want to make peace with her just in case.

"She's going to say no," I said.

"I was hoping you wouldn't ask her permission. I'm your parent, too. I don't need her to approve where you go with me."

Sophia casually strolled into the kitchen with her nose tucked in a book. She didn't speak, just walked through and headed down the hall that led to nothing but the laundry room. She'd already done laundry today. She just wanted Dad to know she was here and had heard him.

"Great. Now *what's her face* will know and you won't come," he groaned. "Perfect."

"Sorry, Dad."

He shrugged his shoulders and opened the fridge. As he pulled out the ingredients for the BLTs he had planned for lunch, I slouched at the island. A part of me wanted to enjoy this moment. The father I'd thought was dead was cooking for me, but the rest of me, the bigger parts of my heart, were too frazzled to enjoy anything.

I was out of prayers at this point. Every being in heaven knew what I wanted—for July 4th to come and go and leave my family unscathed, for us to rebuild from the bomb that had shattered us seventeen years ago, and for my mother not to die. I'd tried everything I knew to do—lighting candles and willing my powers to uncover the unknown. But it wasn't enough. I had a sketchbook full of nothing, a mother who accepted her fate, and a father who didn't care either way.

Since I was out of prayers and options and time, I closed my eyes to try the impossible thing—seeing a vision of July 4th. I promised myself to remember to breathe like Mom had taught me as the blurry image flashed in my head.

I shook and gripped the edge of my seat, sucking in a deep and controlled breath. I stayed with the vision, stayed focused, intent on figuring this out for us.

I saw exactly what Mom had described. It was dark, and I was upset—crying, huffing—as "The Star-Spangled Banner" hummed in the background. The vacant look in my eyes reminded me of the photo that had gone out to the world during my disappearance. I looked like Leah. When five seconds passed, I knew it was the end of the vision Mom and Kamon had seen. But my vision continued.

Fireworks exploded in the air. Red, then white, then blue.

"*No!*" Mom yelled. Her voice echoed in my ears.

"*Chris!*" Nate yelled. I spun around to see him in the vision, and my heart pounded in my kitchen.

God, no, please don't let it be Nate. He had a shield. A strong one. I felt everything in my stomach trying to come up at once.

In the vision he said, "*Baby, I don't know what's going on, but I'm on my way,*" as he sprinted towards us. Paul and Emma were inches behind him. Devin raced past them all, his red and yellow dreads gusting as he cut through the rain.

Kamon, Remi, and the triplets sped to us from the other direction, dressed in black, their faces twisted in anger like furious demons. Three separate worlds were about to collide. The magical world my friends had joined, Kamon's hunters, and my secret life with my mother.

As they ran, an image of the ruined city of Sololá flashed in my head. Then the burning buildings I'd seen in Cuba while sitting in Mom's office. Bloody streets replaced the buildings. My powers told me I was viewing the attack in Mexico. The final flash was of the slaughtered fish floating off the coast of Florida.

"*Leah, you are the one,*" Kamon yelled to me.

Nate ran faster, trying to get to me, but Devin pushed him back. I spun around to Mom. She smiled at me and vanished, leaving a gaping hole in my heart and tears in my eyes.

And blood on my hands.

My eyes drifted to the ground slowly. Water pooled around my feet. Red water, bloody water. She floated on top of it and bumped my leg. She ricocheted like a thing, a dead thing.

I shivered and pushed my powers harder, begging the future to show me something different, begging Karma, begging all of the candles I'd lit over my lifetime, all of the unanswered prayers to work for me now.

The fingers prying at my jaw forced me to open my eyes. Dad held me down as Sophia poured the potion into my mouth. I hadn't realized I was shaking. I hadn't realized I'd lost myself in my powers again. Dad's blood-smeared shirt was the last thing I saw before the world went black and cold.

CHAPTER THIRTEEN

My heavy eyelids opened slowly, and yellow flower petals tickled my nose. Dim light peeked through unfamiliar lace curtains. I followed the stream shining on the pink carpet until it hit sheet music scattered around bare feet.

"Dad?" I said.

He stood from the rocking chair and joined me on the bed. There wasn't much room for him. It was twin-sized, made for a kid. A young girl.

"Hey, pumpkin. How are you feeling?"

"I'm okay. Where are we?"

"Sophia's house." I rolled over and glanced around the room. It had Emma written all over it. Literally. She'd drawn her name in fancy letters and tacked them to the walls. My duffle bag was sitting on the pink dresser next to a bejeweled plastic wand. "I wanted to bring you to my house, but she insisted. She said it would be easier to care for you here. You know … it would be sort of …uh … weird if I bathed you."

He laughed, and I sat up in bed.

"Bathe me? Why?"

"You've been out for a few days, pumpkin. It's the 4th."

"*What?*" I screamed.

The door creaked open, and Sophia flipped on the lights. "Angel, you're awake!" She smiled, and I hopped out of bed, remembering the vision.

"I need to talk to Mom. I think it's Devin. He's connected to Kamon and the attacks." I yanked my duffle bag open to get real clothes and took my jeans and white t-shirt into the closet to change. Sophia followed me there and tried to pull me out.

"Honey, you're probably a little lightheaded from sleeping so much. Devin has nothing to do with Kamon. You need to eat. Come sit."

I didn't listen. I wasn't lightheaded. I'd solved the mystery. Devin was the person we couldn't see. Why else would he be racing towards Mom and I, opposite of Kamon, in my vision?

"Guatemala, Cuba, Mexico, the fish in Florida. I saw them, Sophia! It's not random killings. It can't be." I threw on the clothes, trying to breathe slowly and calm myself from panic. "What time is it?"

"Around five p. m.," Dad said. I gasped. "Come sit, honey. We have a problem."

I walked to the bed slowly, dreading him saying something that would kill me. Something like … I was too late and Mom was already gone.

"I don't like Nathan." That was the last thing I'd expected him to say. "He's been calling like a maniac, so I – uh – finally answered the phone. He went nuts. He thinks you're seeing s-s-someone. He's coming home to fight me, according to the text I read from him an hour ago."

He gave me my phone, and I scrolled through the sea of panicking texts from Nate. I groaned. He hadn't heard from me in days, then a random man had answered my phone. I was sure he was freaking out.

I listened to one of the ten voicemails he'd left.

"Baby, I don't know what's going on, but I'm on my way," his

recording said, just like he'd said in the vision. I threw the phone to the foot of the bed, shaking now.

"Sophia, bring me to Mom. This is serious."

"I can't," she said. "She's busy."

"W-w-what else is new?" Dad said, managing to sound smug through his stutter. "She stayed with her daughter for all of ten minutes while she was unconscious."

If she was busy, I had to do this on my own. It was up to me to figure out what Kamon and Devin had in common.

"Sololá, Cuba, Florida, Mexico," I said. "Why these places? What do they have in common other than magical kind?"

I felt my powers working, kicking into gear slowly after being dormant for a few days. Before I arrived at an answer a man said, "Location." Sophia's husband leaned into the doorway. I'd never met him before, but I knew it had to be Gregory. His eyes were a light, icy gray, and some of his hair still clung to its original dark color, unlike Sophia's. But he had the same happy smile as every Ewing I'd met. "They make a moon around the Gulf of Mexico. We've plotted it."

"Greg, please," Sophia said. "Leave her out of this."

"No, Mr. Ewing. Please tell me. Paul could be in danger. I had a vision of his boss and Kamon Yates. I think they're connected."

He motioned me to follow him, not needing to hear anything more. His feet shuffled on the carpet on the way to a small library. Ancient books lined the walls, ages of magical secrets, it seemed.

Sophia and my dad followed us in.

Her husband led me to the globe on his desk and pointed to a line connecting the three attack zones. "Lacy had a laughable theory about magic being involved. She drew these lines. But it doesn't make sense. The moon isn't connected to anything like this, and Kamon hates magic."

"I think a hunter would resort to magic if they were desperate enough," I said, thinking of Mom passing me her soul. I rubbed my fingers across the line Emma's mother had drawn. Something was here, the answer was here. I could feel it. "Or maybe he doesn't need to. Maybe that's what Devin is for."

"Devin is feeding the homeless," Sophia said. "I have their trip itinerary. He's nowhere near Kamon. They're in Kansas today."

"Are you sure?" I asked. She didn't answer. Frustrated, I closed my eyes to find out on my own. Wondering about Nate's location did nothing. Dead air. His shield was too strong. But wondering about Emma's told me what I needed to know.

"They're in New Orleans," I said.

I slid my finger from Sololá to Louisiana. With that added point, the shape changed. I grabbed a pen from the cup on his desk and filled in the line, then another from New Orleans to Cuba. And Cuba to Mexico. Then Mexico to the coast of Florida where the fish massacre was. They hadn't marked that point, but my vision led me to believe it was also involved.

The new lines formed a five-point star.

"Oh, sweet child, you are brilliant," Gregory said. "It's a star, Sophia. A star changes things. That is old magic."

"Old and dark when you add the blood," she said.

Mr. Ewing opened a dusty book on his desk and flipped through the pages frantically. He stopped abruptly and slid his wrinkled finger down the center. I leaned closer to the book but couldn't read a word of it.

"What language is that?" I asked.

My powers answered me slightly before he did. "Greek." He

gasped slowly. "The time that has passed can come again," he read. "Does anyone know of a reason why Kamon and Devin would want to travel back in time together?"

"Oh, my God," Sophia said, as she pulled out her phone. "Davis, Her Honor needs you to track a cellphone." She called out Nathan's phone number to whoever Davis was; she was shaking all over. She walked to the globe with her eyes closed and slowly pulled the pen from my hands. She began to mark *Xs* along the line I'd drawn. The Peace Group's trip followed it perfectly without ever hitting the actual attack zones. I guessed Nate hadn't technically lied to me about not going there.

"He must be dropping something on the ground," Gregory said. "Salt or some kind of herb. They are ... opening a portal."

"The trip is a cover," I whispered.

Sophia hung up and tugged at my arm. "Go get in bed, dear. Christopher, will you look after her while we..."

"No! I'm not a baby! Let me help!"

"I agree," Gregory said. "We've been looking at this for weeks and haven't seen this. We need her." I scooted closer to my ally as he peered over the book. "Roughly translated, this spell needs blood and work. Work as in ... legwork. I suppose that's Devin."

"And Kamon is supplying the blood," I said.

He nodded and turned the page. "It also says the spell needs a window. By window, they mean a view of the past. In their day, before video and even pictures, they used memories. It seems like ..." He shook his head, trying to decode the words. Impatience almost made me yell at him. I bit it back as he turned the page. A star, with its points dotted in red, sat right in the middle of the jumbled Greek words. "It seems like the portal is ... particular. It only works in the moment you send it to."

"Why would they want to go back in time?" Dad asked, joining us over the book. He sounded intrigued. "To relive something?"

"Or to change something," Sophia said. She leaned into the desk, gripping the end of it like she was about to fall over. "I've heard of this. It's never worked because you only have the slightest moment to cause a change that would be felt in the future."

"What would Kamon change?" Gregory asked.

Sophia and I said, "Julian," at the same time.

"And Devin," Gregory said. "If he's a radical in disguise, he'd want Dreco alive."

"Mom killed them both," I said.

"On the same night," Sophia said. "They're going back and changing Lydia's past."

Gregory tapped the page and sighed heavily. "This says, 'The host must bleed'. The host is the person supplying the memory." My breath caught. Mom was the host and her memories of killing Dreco and Julian were the windows. She must bleed for this spell to work, for them to open a portal to the past. "It says, 'Join the bleeding host inside the place where magic dwells. There, if the window is open, so shall the past be undone.'"

"Oh, dear," Sophia said, rubbing my back. "That's why he wanted you. He thinks you can kill her because of the connection between your lives. He must need her wounded. He thought you would do it." She covered her mouth. "We were wrong. Lydia and I assumed since you were involved, you would need her soul. That's not it. They are ending her life. This life. Life as we know it!"

That explained why none of us could see my murderer. There was no one to see.

There wasn't a bullet or knife coming for me. I wasn't going to die and take her soul. Devin wanted to bring peace to a shattered kind like those ugly pea green shirts said. He'd un-shatter them. They'd fallen apart when Mom torched their leaders and made them follow the treaty.

And Kamon and his followers chanted to his former master. He'd go back and save him. Set things right in his mind.

Today could be Independence Day for them both.

"I'm not going to hurt her," I said. "It won't work."

"Maybe he gave up on getting you. I'm sure he has a backup plan," Sophia said. "I need to warn her."

She pulled her phone from her dress pocket and dialed the number from memory. I could hear it ringing from where I stood. Each passing ring felt like a dagger to my heart, and I lost my balance when it reached a generic voicemail.

"Call her back," I said.

She did, a few times, but she never answered.

I closed my eyes and said, "Where is my mother? Where is my mother?"

My hands shook, and Sophia grabbed me. I pushed away from her. I needed to focus. "Let us handle this," she said.

I ignored her as my powers found my mother. I saw her golden hair shimmer in the dying light of the sun. Her limp body lay by a familiar pool, one with a mosaic of a magnolia at the bottom.

"She's in New Orleans!" I screamed.

"You're not going!" Sophia said, she yanked my arm and hauled me out of the study and back into Emma's room. "I'll go. She would want you to stay out of this."

I was overwhelmingly sure that she shouldn't go. Psychic powers were faster than magic, and Kamon was involved.

"You'll get hurt," I said. "I need to do this. I have to help her." My stomach twisted at the thought of her lying on that ground, quite possibly beyond my help.

But I still had to try.

I found a pair of shoes in my duffle bag, flimsy yellow flats that wouldn't do me any good in a fight. I closed my eyes and thought of the black boots in my closet. They appeared in my hands. Since I was preparing for a fight, I thought of a knife with a deadly blade and a short handle that fit securely in my palm. It, too, appeared at my will.

And now I was ready.

"Honey, please stop. Take the potion for me. You need to calm down," Sophia begged.

No way was I taking the kryptonite. I needed my powers more than I'd ever needed them before.

I threw on the boots in a panic and twirled the knife around my fingers, ready to jab it into whoever had hurt my mother.

"Wait," she said, and grabbed my face. "I have a bad feeling about this. About you doing this." She closed her eyes and tears seeped out of the corners. "I can't stop you," she whispered, mostly to herself. She sucked in a shaky breath, patted her neck, and took off the necklace she'd found there.

A bright yellow jewel in the center of silver rays sparkled in her hand. She pulled the necklace over my head and tucked the pendant inside my shirt.

"Tempting fruit usually bears poison," she said. Thicker tears poured out of her eyes. "Listen to me, Christine. You must remember who you are."

"I know who I am. I'm going to save her," I said, confused and annoyed that she was holding me up.

She kissed my cheek, crying harder, and dragged her lips to my ear. "If you get lost, as long as you can remember who gave this necklace to you, with a sacrifice of blood, under the sun when it is highest in the sky, one wish can be granted to you. But I so hope you won't need to use it."

She leaned away, and I stared at her like she'd lost her mind until my heart quaked, thinking of my mother on the ground by the pool.

I didn't have time to figure out why she was being so creepy.

I yanked myself from Sophia's house to my old one in New Orleans. They'd left the needle in Mom's neck. I yanked it out and checked her pulse. Her heart was still beating. I finally took a breath.

"Leah," Kamon said. "So nice of you to join us."

His voice sent a shiver up my spine. He and his triplets walked out of my old house, dressed in black, like I'd seen in my vision.

Only Remi was missing.

The knife in my hand suddenly felt vulnerable. Like one of them could take it and use it against me. I slipped it into the side of one of my boots.

Just as the handle thumped against my ankle, Devin appeared in a puff of smoke, without my friends. He reached in his pocket and tossed a handful of blue powder into the pool. It sounded like grains of sand as it scattered across the surface, and it made the water sparkle and churn.

It was the place where magic dwelled.

"You got her!" he said, to Kamon, smiling and pointing at me, not Mom. "I'm glad. I tried, but her boyfriend and friends couldn't get her to come with me, and your hunter ruined your chance at the ball."

Oh my God. Devin had recruited my friends to help Kamon capture me. And he'd invited me to the ball to trap me, the same ball I was stabbed at.

"Now are you finally going to tell me what you want with this witch?" he asked.

Witch? He didn't know I was human?

Kamon laughed hard and sighed after. "C-13," he said. "Please get rid of this fool for me. Thanks for doing so much of the work, Devin, but I'm afraid our partnership has reached its end."

"I knew you'd try to pull something like this," Devin said. He raised his palms to the sky and closed his eyes. Before he could do whatever dramatic spell he was attempting, he started choking.

One of the copies approached him, and he begged for freedom in squeals and coughs.

"I plead for mercy, Master," the copy killing Devin said. "I've seen that his life is needed."

"Kill him," Kamon said, like he was bored with the conversation. "Life is beginning again in a few short minutes."

"I've seen it, too," one of the brothers said.

Kamon sighed loudly and waved his hand, allowing them to spare Devin. "Fine. Let him go, but if he messes something up, you will pay."

The copy released Devin. He panted for a moment, then vanished with a snap.

Kamon grinned at me as he walked closer. The copies trailed a few inches behind him, pressing in.

Mom squirmed on the ground. Her eyes were open and panicking inside of her lifeless body. In her state, she wouldn't be able to fight.

Luckily, she'd passed me her powers. I could fight on her behalf.

I threw the first blow, not interested in waiting for them to finish their dramatically slow walk.

I imagined one copy flying to the other end of the yard, and his body obeyed me, darting through the darkening air as the sun left us.

That started and all out brawl. The four of them against me.

I blocked fists, dodged legs, and tossed more bodies as they got too close to Mom and me. They kept coming, reappearing in my face within the blink of an eye. And I kept fighting, tossing with my mind and eventually my hands when they dared to come closer.

The triplets distracted me from Kamon. He grabbed Mom and rammed his fist into her face, spewing blood from her mouth.

The boys laughed like they were having a good time watching me fight and watching her squirm.

I'd show them a good time.

I knew what power would end this. I was one hundred percent sure.

I remembered the first time I'd seen fire shoot seemingly out of nowhere. I was afraid then and every day after that for years. I remembered when Mom showed me how to control the flame, how small it could be. How it could fly if I wanted it to.

Or slither.

I commanded fire in the form of a snake to wrap around one of the triplets.

"No," Mom said, just like she had in my vision.

The unlit copies rushed to their brother's aid, fanning him and trying to control the fire I'd created. It wouldn't obey them. I uncoiled the snake and made it strike in their direction. They stumbled back.

"You cowards," Kamon spat. "Go home! Now!"

The trembling boys vanished, and I turned the snake on Kamon.

"Leave," Mom whimpered. "Right now."

I didn't listen. I wasn't a copy; she'd made sure I didn't think of

216

myself as one. She was my mother, not my master, and daughters disobey mothers all the time.

Kamon reached his hand to the snake, just over the fire, and pretended to pet it. He grinned, completely unafraid. Luckily, fire was not my only power.

With the lightest wave of my hand, he flew backwards into the side of the house. He crashed into the white bricks and slid to the ground. He struggled to get up, trying to look calm, and brushed dirt from his arms.

I slammed him again, drove his beautiful face into the home my grandparents would still live in if not for the man he was trying to save.

"Go home," Mom whispered, weak, desperate. "Go home, right now."

Kamon chuckled and stood. "This is perfect, Leah. It's happening just like I saw it." He tucked one hand in the pocket of his perfectly tailored pants and flung the other in the air. Mom flew back like a single feather in howling wind and crashed into the pool. The blood from her lip stretched across the water, multiplying in a moment into thousands of bloody vines.

A red burst of light crackled across the sky. Kamon smiled. White fireworks followed, the sounds seemed to linger longer than necessary as a gust of wind caught his hair. My heart was pounding too loudly to hear the blue firework burst into the sky.

"You are the one," Kamon said.

"And you are an idiot," I said.

He threw his head back and laughed. I raised my hand, ready to slam him again. "I'm not as dumb as you think, Christine," he said. He smiled and blew me a kiss. "See you soon."

He vanished, and I ran to the pool, ignoring what he'd said. My mother was sinking inside of a magical portal. I didn't have time to decode the cryptic message of an evil hunter.

I dove into the pool and pulled her to the surface.

She coughed water out of her lungs and smiled at me slightly. "I told you to stay out of this," she said.

"I'm here to save you. They opened a portal. They were trying to change your past."

The magic tingled my skin and swept the hair up on my arms.

"What?" she said.

"This is a portal to the past. It's what they've been up to. They needed a memory. And blood. They were going to go back and save Julian and Dreco. I stopped them."

She looked around at the churning water, like she'd just seen it for the first time.

"Let's get out of here. I don't have a good feeling ... right now. Let's go."

Her tone was like Sophia's had been when she'd mentioned poisonous fruit.

It took me a moment to see the temptation in all of this. I was in a magical portal, with a host who had a past I wanted to change.

And I knew several of her memories, one from the exact day I believed she'd changed our lives for the worse. The day she'd left dad.

I tried to force myself to think of the last time I'd been in this pool, with Nate, someone I could lose if I let temptation take me.

But ... there were countless things that had to come together in order for Nate and I to meet. St. Catalina, Sophia, him being in the right place to be captured by the same hunter that captured Emma. It was too intricate to be coincidental. He was my soul mate. I was sure of it. And in any life, under any circumstances, soul mates should be able to find each other. We shouldn't be bound by time. By anything.

If I used the portal, I would get what I was always supposed to have, two parents who adored me and wanted me. A family. There would be no need to pray for my mother's life. No guessing if I'd get to keep her forever. No awkward silence between her and the man she loved.

I was supposed to grow up with sickeningly happy parents. That was ruined, and now it could be fixed. Rewritten.

"Sweetie, get us out of here. Come on."

She looked worried. She must've figured out what had just dawned on me—that Kamon had been right about my destiny. I was meant to kill Lydia Shaw on July 4th, end the need for her to pretend to be that woman and be away from her husband and child.

More fireworks bombed in the air and the neighbors I'd never met cranked on their speakers, making me completely sure.

The Star-Spangled Banner hummed in the air, and Mom began to cry.

"Honey, please. Let's go."

"If you could have one thing, what would it be?" I asked.

"Don't do this," she said. "I can't move. Take us home." Her mouth ducked under the water, and I pulled her up again. "Let's just go home. We can make this life work. I'll talk to your friends and Nathan. I'll deal with Kamon. Just trust me."

I pulled her rigid body closer.

"You've been dealing with him for years. Maybe I should try."

"Sweetie, hang on to yourself. You are smart. You are logical. Please see what you are doing," she begged. "Take us home. My place. Your place. Anywhere."

"I don't want to go home. Or to Paris. I want to go to your house in Miami," I said, thinking of the memory that would serve as my window. "The one Dad was making eggs in that morning. He had on a suit and he was dancing." She pleaded with me, begging with tears and moans. "We need this portal. All of these years, you have been miserable. So has Dad. So have I."

"You have to stop. Right now."

I ignored her. I wanted this, I needed this, and it felt like I didn't have a choice now.

I touched her stomach.

"I was there with you two in the house that day. I think this is the day you fell in love with me. The day I made you ruin your life." I pressed my forehead against hers as she cried harder.

"Baby, please. It won't work. It won't work!"

"If it doesn't, we'll go home. But why not try, Mom? You don't try enough! You give up too easily. On Dad. On our family. Please, think about it with me. He was going to work. You were in the kitchen. So was I."

She fought it, but I saw exactly when the memory of him chasing her around overtook her. The pool roared as the water defied gravity and leapt into the air, glowing with red streams of light. Then it crashed down on us, sending us whirling underwater together.

I held my breath and felt myself floating, moving somewhere else.

To their kitchen.

I squinted my eyes against the bright yellow light streaming through the curtains. Mom raced past the window, her hair messy from sleep. Dad laughed and pinned her against the cabinets, but she wedged herself out and raced right through me.

"Mom," I yelled. She didn't respond. Right, I was a bundle of almost nothing inside of her. I couldn't speak. I couldn't do anything … except make her sick. If she vomited before he left, she'd notice she was pregnant and would have to tell him.

"I am powerful and unstoppable. I am powerful and unstoppable," I chanted. "Sick. Sick. Nauseous. Gag, Mom. Gag! Please!"

"You okay?" Dad asked. My eyes flew open. Mom had covered her mouth.

"Yeah. I'm fine."

She gagged again and ran to the sink. She hurled, and he held her hair. "I have never seen you puke without being wasted," Dad said, laughing.

"I'm fine. Go to work, baby."

He wiped her mouth with a napkin and shook his head. He picked her up and carried her to their bedroom. "I can't leave my sick wife. I'll start tomorrow." She begged him to leave, but he crawled in bed next to her with his suit on. "We ate the same thing last night. What could have made you sick?"

"I'm not sick. I'm never sick," she said. He adjusted a pillow behind her head. Her eyes slid from his to open space. "Gavin, how long ago did my parents … you know?"

"Four weeks ago, I guess."

"No way. That long?" she asked. He nodded and kicked off his shoes. Her hands moved to her stomach. I'd done it. She'd have no choice but to tell him now. He was home. "Gav, I haven't had my period since before that."

"So what?" She glared at him. "Oh! No way. It's not possible. We're careful."

She hummed, her eyes moving around like she was counting.

"Not always," she whispered. "Not that time when ..." She gasped. "That was almost six weeks ago."

They stared at each other for a moment. Dad smiled first. She squealed and looked down like she expected to see me there. He raised her shirt and kissed her stomach.

"A baby! A *girl*," Mom said. "She'll have your eyes."

"Stop, Lydia. You're going to make her psychic. We had a deal about the kids."

"It's not an exact thing, Gav. They'd have to be trained after. Without it, it's hit or miss."

"It would be our luck to have a *hit*. No powers, honey. You promised."

"Fine. Sorry. Sorry." The first was to him. The second to me.

He fluffed her pillow then stuffed more behind her head. "Hey, little baby. It's Daddy. Can you hear me?" he said to her belly.

"Yes," I whispered.

"Mama's going to be very careful and not move an inch for nine months. Oh, well, eight." They laughed and Mom tried to get up. He wasn't joking. "Seriously. I want you to be careful with my little bitty baby. I'm so happy. I'm going to have a family. I mean ...you're obviously my family, Lyd. But ... a baby! I thought it would be years from now."

Mom's face blanked and she touched me again. "No! Gavin! Julian!" she screamed, like I'd made her forget about her problems for a second before they came rushing back. Mom flapped around in bed, and Dad pinned her to the pillows. "She's going to die. You, too! Oh, God! He's not going to stop until he takes everything I love from me. I have to ... go back. I have to ... stop this."

Dad shook all over, trying to speak several times with no

success.

"You wouldn't do that to me," he said. "You wouldn't leave me. No, no, no, you can't…" Mom grabbed his face and kissed his trembling lips. "Swear you won't. I'll die. I'll die if you leave. And what about my baby?"

The mention of their new child made her frantic, like worry had passed from him to her like a virus. And now it was his turn to calm *her* again.

"Relax," he said. "You're not breathing. Please. She needs you to breathe." She took a loud breath, like I'd suddenly become the only reason for her to do that. "Everything will be fine, Lyd. As long as we're together."

He kissed her, and pressure crashed into my chest.

Water streamed down my arms out of nowhere, a little more than a trickle at first, then a pour. Soon, it gushed from my hands and hair, making a puddle on their floor. I heard the rest of the water before I felt it rush around my ankles. They didn't seem to notice their house going under, too busy easing down from panic and plotting their next move.

The water flooded the house and rose to my chest in seconds. "Mom!" I screamed. She still couldn't hear me. Another wave rushed into the room and submerged me completely. I gasped, stupidly, for air that wasn't there. The world turned to nothing but blue, deep blue, and white lights.

CHAPTER FOURTEEN

I was drowning.

Probably by Julian's hands, and it was my own fault. I saw a shadow over the water as I sank deeper, closer to the light. I watched my last breath bubble to the surface and let myself sink. I grabbed Sophia's necklace but dropped it. The sun wasn't highest in the sky to make a wish.

It was over.

"Christine," Mom said, sounding very far away. "Get out of the pool, baby. I don't want to have to tell you again." The figure above the water, a blurry Mom, pointed a finger at me.

I guessed I hadn't opened the portal. I hoped she would think of a humane way to punish me for trying.

My feet reached the bottom of the pool. I pushed up and gasped for air. "Out. Now," she ordered.

"I'm sorry."

I wiped the excess water from my face and blew my nose to unclog it. I opened my eyes. We were not in New Orleans. Not outside. She stormed away from what had to be our indoor pool in jeans and a yellow tank top. Normal clothes. The mom I knew never wore normal clothes and colors other than black.

"Mom!" I said. I hopped out of the pool. She didn't turn around.

"This is not negotiable. Pool time is officially over." I grabbed the towel sitting on one of the three lounge chairs. "Dad made his usual July 4th meal. I'll bring you a plate."

I covered my mouth to muffle the scream. I'd changed the past and caught up with time.

I pulled off my boots so I wouldn't track footprints through the house and wrapped myself in the towel. I didn't know my way around our home, so I scurried out of the room to catch her.

"Mom!"

"Christine, I'm too tired to fight about this. You know I hate when you disappear and I find you in the pool. And you were doing the floating thing again. I know you're mad, but that's not an excuse to give me a heart attack."

I followed Mom up a winding staircase. The next floor clued me in to how huge our house was. A palace really. The halls were endless and the ceilings were impossibly high. I dripped on the marble floor as Mom continued to ignore me.

"Mom."

"No whining."

A painful sigh pushed from my chest. Did the new Mom not love me like the old one did?

She glanced over her shoulder, and her eyebrows drew together. "Why do you look so sad? It's just the pool."

"I just wanted to say hi. Maybe hug you," I whispered carefully, realizing I didn't really know the woman in the hall with me.

"Hi, baby," she said and opened her arms. I ran and tackled her, dripping all over her normal clothes. "Did you hit your head in there?"

She pulled back, looking at me like I'd lost my mind. "Oh," I said, realizing my error. I wasn't the baby she had to watch and love from afar anymore. Seeing each other would be nothing special now. "No. I didn't hit my head. I'm fine."

"Good. Go dry off before you catch a cold."

"Okay."

She turned and walked away, and I caught up with her again, following her because I had no idea where I was going. "Was 'okay' code for *piss off, Mom, I'll do what I want?*"

"No."

"Then why are you walking away from your room?" She threw her hands up like she'd given up on figuring me out and turned down yet another hall in the huge house. I headed in the opposite direction.

I really needed a map.

I strolled down the hall aimlessly and saw the most beautiful thing in the world. A family picture on the wall. Mom was holding me and Dad was behind her. I was only dressed in a diaper. We looked so happy. So normal.

There was a picture mounted on the wall every few feet. My baby pictures, mostly. Tears streamed from my eyes. I had baby pictures!

One was too precious not to take off of the wall and kiss.

Mom and Dad were smiling at the camera with a little ghost between them. They'd cut holes in a sheet. I could see the smile in my deep brown eyes through them.

"I went trick-or-treating. This is crazy," I said.

I wept as I found pictures of Mom and Dad alone. They were mostly kissing and staring at each other. Being the Lydia and Gavin from the diary.

I roamed, crying and in awe, until I came to a door. I opened it and walked into the room. There was a crib in the center.

"Do I have a sister?"

I turned on the light. There were pictures everywhere. Of Mom and me as a baby. Dad kissing my little toes. Unless my sister looked exactly like the baby in Mom's memories, this was my nursery from a long time ago. Just preserved.

The next room was for an older child. An older me, I guessed. Dolls lined the shelves, neat and probably untouched for a decade. They'd preserved my childhood room, too. "Okay … this is more like the Mom I know," I said. "A little obsessed with me." I sighed, very relieved.

The next door had a handmade KEEP OUT sign taped to it. I guessed it was my current room. I creaked it open with my eyes closed. I expected to see pictures of Nate and my friends—I had my fingers crossed for Emma and Paul. It wasn't so farfetched. Nate was my soul mate and we should always find each other, and if Mom knew Sophia, we'd probably know Paul and Emma.

I opened my eyes and felt around for a light. I flipped it on. There were no pictures, and Sophia obviously wasn't our maid. Clothes and trash covered every inch of the floor. And the walls were covered in scribbles. It looked like I'd taken a black marker and tattooed swirls and stars everywhere.

"I guess that's cool."

I took off my wet clothes and threw them on the floor, with everything else I discarded apparently. I assumed my clean clothes were the pile on the bed. I sniffed a shirt. It had a sour, corn chip smell to it. I didn't dare sniff anything from the pile on the floor.

"Gross."

I took off Sophia's necklace and slushed through my room to the bathroom. I gagged. It was worse than the bedroom. Moldy towels hung from the shower curtain and about ten one-piece swimsuits were draped on the side of the dingy tub. And I'd doodled on the walls in here, too.

I reached to turn the shower on, but there were no knobs.

That made me feel a little better. I didn't actually use this bathroom.

I found a clean one at the end of the hall. I showered and tugged on a shirt and a pair of pants I'd found on my bed. Apparently, I was into fashion design or something in this life. My sweatpants looked purposefully ruined with bleach, and I'd cut the shirt so that it hung from my shoulders. The bottom was fringed.

"I guess this is trendy," I said, frowning at myself in the mirror.

I ran around our huge home, looking at our family photos on the wall and listening for my parents. I followed the smell of grilled burgers and found them in the kitchen.

My heart burst open. It was official. It was worth it. Maybe I didn't have pictures of my friends—and I hadn't given up hope—but as I stared at Dad feeding Mom, laughing and kissing, I knew I'd done the right thing. Dad looked mostly the same, minus the arm of tattoos he had in our old life. He only had a few scattered on his forearm and one peeking out of the sleeve of his shirt.

"Hey," I said.

Dad put up his hands like he was surrendering, and Mom moved away from his lap. "Sorry, pumpkin. Thought you were in for the night. Mom was going to bring your plate up in a minute."

"That's okay. I'll eat with you guys if I'm not intruding." They both gawked at me like I'd sprouted a third eye. "If I'm interrupting, I guess I'll go back to my room. Or trash pit," I said, wanting to gag at the thought of eating in there.

"You're not going to yell at us for ruining your dinner?" Dad asked. I shook my head slowly. "No ... *oh, my God, guys, go to your room or I'll kill myself?*" he said, in a whiny voice, without one stutter.

"That's not funny, Gavin. Don't tease her like that," Mom said. Gavin? She could call him that again. I could die happy now.

"Thanks, Mom." I grabbed a plate from the counter and sat at the table. They just stared at me. "What?"

"What's with you?" Mom asked. "First the hug. Now this." Dad gasped. "Yes, baby. There was a hug, a real one." She held her hand to my forehead and checked for a fever.

"Mom, I'm not sick. I'm just happy today." Apparently, I was never like this. I thought about the teenagers from my movies. They weren't all that happy at home. They were bratty. And we lived in a mansion. I was probably spoiled and used to getting my way. "Get used to it," I said. "I'm going to be happier, so don't think it's weird."

Mom kneeled next to my chair, her eyes glossy and her lip out. "Really?" she whispered. I nodded. "So the talk with your Dad went well last night?"

I had no memory of the last night she meant, but if I'd had a talk with my dad last night, I was sure it had gone well.

"Yeah."

"I thought you were ignoring me, kid," he said.

"Never." I blew him a kiss. "I would never ignore you. I mean ... I won't anymore."

"So you understand now?" Mom asked. I nodded, playing along. "I know you think everyone your age is going, but rules are rules."

It sounded like all of my friends were going somewhere for the 4th of July, and I wasn't allowed to. Maybe I was grounded. Maybe my filthy room was the reason.

"It's okay. I get it. I'll just stay here and enjoy my family." Her face turned up, in a shocked and appalled kind of way. "I mean it."

"Oh, honey. That's wonderful. You are making my day. You know I hate upsetting you, and you and I seem to fight every time I open my mouth these days. I'm so glad your Dad got through to you."

I swallowed a mouthful of baked beans then leaned down to kiss her cheek. She broke down. "I'm sorry for fighting with you. I'm sure it was no big deal. I love you." Dad joined her on his knees in front of me, equally as shocked. I kissed him, too. "Love you, Dad."

He pulled me out of the chair and they attacked me with hugs and teary kisses on the floor. Yep ... totally worth changing our lives for. If I didn't know Nate in this life, I'd hire an investigator to find him. This was perfection.

"I don't want to push it," Dad said. "But how about you join us tonight for movies? Like old times."

My heart jumped. We had old times. "Of course," I said.

Dad pulled me up and they joined me for dinner at the table.

After the initial allure of seeing them as a couple faded, it was sort of gross how much they touched. I didn't think they noticed that I could see them pawing at each other on the other side of the table.

I took my dish to the sink and turned on the water. "Oh my God!" Mom said. "Is this really happening? Christine Cecilia Gavin, washing a dish?"

Dad picked me up at the sink and spun me around. He carried me to our living room, kissing my cheek the whole way.

"Pick the movie, pumpkin," Dad said.

I turned around in his arms and stifled a laugh. Our TV was extremely dated. Big, but bulky, and we had a VCR and about a million tapes stacked on the wall.

"Um … I guess I'll pick a classic," I said. They were all classic. Apparently, we didn't believe in DVDs, let alone Blu-ray.

"Classic comedy, classic drama, or classic Christine?" he asked.

"I vote classic Christine," Mom said. Dad carried me over to another bookshelf.

"We have Christine: the early years," he said, waving his hand around the first few shelves. "Then Christine: the comic. And Christine's funny dances." I laughed. They were both obsessed with me. Wonderful. "The last few are the *Daddy stop following me around with the stupid camera* years."

"Sorry about those," I said.

He smiled, and I chose a tape from the early years shelf. We settled on the sofa. Mom crawled into Dad's arms before I could grab one of them. It looked like she'd done so out of habit.

The ancient movie flickered on the screen then took another moment to focus in on me blowing spit bubbles. Dad cooed at me from behind the camera. Mom was stretched out on the floor at my side.

It overwhelmed me. I tucked my face in my ripped up shirt, trying to hide the tears.

They'd filmed many different days on one tape. The first two that we watched were mostly my spit bubble performances. The rest of the early years were just as cute. I was a weird baby, and nothing like the nuns had described me at St. Catalina. I was loud, I laughed a lot, and I liked to play.

And just like I'd hoped, they obviously loved me on unconscionable levels, filming every second that I was awake and sometimes sleeping.

In the next video, Mom cooed at me as she hovered over my crib with the camera. I noticed construction sounds in the background.

"What's that?" I asked as Dad kissed Mom's ear. Equal parts adorable and disgusting.

"It sounds like Daddy," Mom said. "You know he worked on the house for ... Jesus, babe, how long?"

"Ten or so years to get it like this. We both did, my little helper." She giggled as he tickled her. I ignored their PDA. Apparently, this dad worked in construction instead of touring as a backup guitarist.

"She's about to walk!" Mom said. "This is my favorite one. Turn it up."

Dad cranked up the volume, and, in the video, Mom clapped and cooed at me. *"Come on, baby. Come to Mama,"* she said. I looked around skeptically and wobbled over to her.

We all cheered on the sofa, and I caught my new tears without them noticing. Dad chose one of his favorites next. I was five. I had to admit, I was very cute.

"Do you remember what to say?" Dad asked from behind the camera. I nodded, smiling big, then bolted up the stairs. Dad caught up with me as I knocked on a door. *"Come in,"* Mom said. I struggled with the doorknob, juggling a red heart made of construction paper in my hands. Dad opened it for me. *"Aww. Hey, cutie."*

I jumped on her bed then looked back at the camera, then back to Mom. *"Daddy wants to know if you will be his balentine."*

"Vvvvalentine," Dad corrected, at the door.

Mom chuckled. *"Tell him I already have one."* She tickled me and planted a million kisses on my face.

"Mama, is Daddy your boyfriend?" I asked.

We laughed on the sofa. I was the loudest. Mom looked over to me and held her arms open. I crawled to her and joined their snuggle. "I missed you," she whispered against my hair.

"Missed you, too."

We focused on the incredibly cute question I'd asked in the video. "*Yes, I am,*" Dad said.

"*Will I have a boyfriend?*" I asked.

They stopped laughing, on the sofa and in the movie, as I waited for an answer. "*Nope. I won't allow it,*" Dad said, bringing the camera closer. Mom chuckled lightly and pretended that the heart I'd scribbled on was a masterpiece.

On the sofa in the present, she tightened her arms around me. "Still okay?" she whispered.

"Yeah," I said, not understanding why I wouldn't be.

This life was amazing.

I wished I had the memories, but watching them was almost as good. It felt real. I'd been completely right in using the portal. I'd put them back together and erased St. Catalina completely. I was never Leah. Never depressed. Never alone. There was no Kamon here. No July 4th I'd kill her on.

It was a normal night. I'd bet there was a barbecue and fireworks show that my friends were at that I'd been banned from. I cringed a little. When summer was over, I'd probably have to go to high school. I doubted I had skipped my last year like I'd done in my old life.

Around ten, they started yawning excessively and stretching. It seemed like that was parent for: *we're about to go be disgusting.*

"Goodnight, baby," Mom said. "Don't stay up with Snowflake too long."

"Who?" I asked.

They turned to me slowly, brows tight and mouths open. "Snowflake, your bestest friend on the planet, the big white horse in the stable," Mom said. "Remember her?"

I laughed, trying to cover that up. "Of course. Snowflake. Sure. I won't stay up too late."

Figuring good 'ole Snowflake was outside, I looked around for a door. I didn't see one in the living room. I ran to the kitchen. There wasn't one in there either.

"What are you doing, kid?" Dad asked.

"Um … playing around before going outside?" I suggested.

Mom screamed, a screech that stalled my heart and nearly shattered my eardrums.

"Stop!" She ran through the living room towards me, and Dad caught her by her waist. "Why are you trying to go outside?"

"Uh … to see Snowflake?" I said, clueless and frightened.

"Lydia, breathe. Come on, honey. Just relax." Dad held Mom as she squirmed in his arms, crying and glaring at me. "Christine, that wasn't funny. Apologize to your mother."

"I'm … sorry?"

Dad shook his head at me, disappointment seeping from his eyes. He picked Mom up like a baby and carried her out of the room.

Maybe Mom had a weird thing about doors. Or maybe I'd freaked her out by not knowing where to find Snowflake. But that scream alluded to there being more behind it. Much more.

Instead of finding Snowflake, I ran upstairs, listening for them so I could apologize for upsetting her.

The door I'd gone into on the Valentine video was cracked open.

"I'll talk to her," Dad said. I could hear her sniffling from out here.

"She hates me. She's been pretending all night just to do this. Just to hurt me. I didn't tell you what she did earlier. She was in the pool, *naked*, doing the dead body thing. I did what you said. I didn't react. But she yanked a reaction out of me this time. I guess that's what she wanted."

This version of Mom was a liar. I wasn't naked in the pool. The wet clothes I'd taken off were still on the floor in my room. Dad sighed, and I walked in slowly.

"Mom," I said, crawling in bed next to her. "I'm sorry. The Snowflake thing, whatever I did. I'm really sorry."

I lifted her arm and forced myself to her side.

"You know how I feel about it," she whispered, her voice breaking twice. "Please don't do that again."

I agreed, but I didn't know what I was agreeing to. How could looking for doors be off limits? Did I only use powers to get out of the house?

And I'd asked a hell of a lot of questions and hadn't been led to one single answer.

"Tell me what I need to do to make you happy," I said. "I know you've probably said it a lot, but tell me what I shouldn't do, and I'll listen."

She sat up in bed and grabbed my hands. "It would be nice if you cleaned your room." I smiled. That one made sense, a normal mother-daughter problem. "Don't go in the pool without asking." Okay, that one was stranger, but I understood. Safety first. "And please, baby, please stop trying to leave. Just stop with the escape plots. It kills me. Please."

CHAPTER FIFTEEN

I didn't know what to say. Why would a seventeen-year-old need to escape from the house? Why couldn't I leave?

She and Dad were crying so I knew it was bigger than being grounded and missing a 4th of July barbecue. I stayed in their room all night, waiting for the courage to ask for an explanation. When that courage didn't come, I slipped out of their bed. Dad pulled Mom closer in his sleep, an instinctual movement, both of them snoring.

I roamed around our quiet home, following the long and twisting hallways to new parts of the house. I started opening doors, unlocking the mysteries of this life. We had an art studio with my grandmother's paintings adorning the walls. Across the hall, a bowling alley with an arcade. We were loaded, richer than rich.

I opened the next door and stepped into a photographer's darkroom. Pictures dangled from strings around the room and trays of water covered the countertops. I walked towards light peeking under a door in the back. It led to a gallery.

This must have been Dad's hobby. Most of the pictures were of Mom. In the kitchen, clipping her toenails, and painfully dragging a comb through my hair as a child. All framed and on the wall like art.

He'd made a section just for me in the gallery. This time, I curbed my enthusiasm over my baby pictures and stared at them in a way I hadn't before.

Whether I was in Mom's arms or Dad's, we were always in the house. I unhooked a picture of me blowing out seven candles on a cake from the wall. My parents were the only guests at my party.

I found one of me on a white horse. Snowflake, I assumed. I was hugging her like she was my only companion. A death grip, but happy.

I gasped. Snowflake's stable was indoors, probably somewhere in this house.

That hall turned into another long one with scribbles on the walls and hopscotch boards painted on the floor. It obviously belonged to me. It had three large rooms—one full of my artwork, done with much less skill than I had in my old life. The next was a playroom with a climbable wall. I walked into the last room on the hall, and the air in my lungs rushed out.

Inside, I saw a fully decorated classroom with a chalkboard lined with hand drawn alphabets, foam planets hanging from the ceiling, and one, lonely desk in the middle of the floor.

I didn't go to school, not a normal one. They'd even hung my work around the room—math problems and stories I'd written about Queen Mommy and King Daddy. I had to leave the classroom to breathe again.

"We live in hiding," I finally admitted. That was why she'd screamed when I'd mentioned going outside. We probably didn't exist outside of this house, outside of each other. And from the look of things, I wasn't happy living this way. I stayed in my disgusting room, destroying clothes and trying to escape.

I went down to the living room and watched the videos they didn't care to see, the unhappy me.

"*Dad, stop being lame,*" I said when he zoomed in on me

marking on the walls in my room. I must've been fifteen or so. "*Get out.*" My tone was harsh. He lowered the camera and closed my door. I felt awful for hurting his feelings, but ... at that point, I'd been in the house with them for fifteen years. I was sure this had gotten old.

"*Pumpkin pie,*" Dad said on the next video. "*It's your 16th birthday. You can't be sad on your birthday.*" I picked up my cake and tossed it off the table, splattering icing everywhere. Mom shook her head and bent down to clean it.

"*Baby, you're one year older. Let's just celebrate,*" she said.

"*I'm one year closer to death. Let's not,*" I said. Pressing through the awful birthday party, Mom and Dad put a box in front of me. I knocked that off the table, too. "*I want to talk about college,*" I said. "*I want to go.*"

"*No, baby. I'm sorry. You can't,*" Mom said. I stormed away from the table and Dad turned off the video.

Wonderful.

My parents and I were fighting because I wanted to leave the house we were boarded up in. I wiped the tears from my face. I didn't deserve to cry. I'd done this. I just had to make it work. Being here with my parents would have to be enough.

I closed my eyes and tried to move myself to my room. I didn't budge.

Mom must have been more careful with the powers with Dad here to look after her. So I walked to my room and slaved in there for an eternity, scrubbing and unearthing years of clutter.

I found two pairs of jeans that I hadn't ruined and a few shirts that still looked like shirts. I piled the rest of the grungy clothes outside of the door. I wanted to take them to the trash, but something told me we didn't have a normal system for that.

I peeked under the bed and groaned. There was another

civilization under there to tackle. I pushed the bundle of more trash and tattered clothes to the middle of the now clear floor. I stacked ten dirty plates and a cabinet full of sticky cups.

Amidst the junk, I found a notebook, and I flipped through it.

"This must be a journal," I said.

I'd written in the tiniest script possible. I squinted and brought it closer to my eyes.

I don't know who Julian is, but Mom sure cries a lot about him. This is the third night I've listened outside of their door. Mom is not okay. She's always sad. I don't know how I have gone thirteen years without seeing this. I know she gets sick and Dad has to take care of her, but now I'm starting to think she's not really sick. Not physically sick, anyway. I just don't understand why we can't leave or when I'll get to meet other people and have fun like they do on the movies. And every time I ask, they get so quiet.

That was the happiest I was in any of the entries. I could feel my decline into desperation for another life as I read through the notebook, growing angrier by the day. I'd uncovered the Julian mystery by eavesdropping. Mistakenly, I thought Mom was being dramatic about him and the other name she'd mention in secret—Kamon.

I tucked the notebook under the mattress. I couldn't be this girl anymore. Mom was right about them, and if we'd been here for years, Julian could be out there, still obsessed with her.

I sorted through the rest of the pile and used an old shirt to free the colonies of dust around the room. It smelled better already. With everything neat and tidy, Sophia's necklace seemed to glow on my bed, wrong and out of place in this life. I tucked it under my pillow, not ready to throw it out, but knowing I had to be stronger than this. Stronger than giving up and breaking my parents up again.

It was my fault the first time, and if not for me now, they would probably be worry-free in this house. I sighed. I was an accidental complication in any life.

It felt like I'd only slept for a brief moment. Mom tapped my shoulder and sang my name.

"Good morning," I said. She gestured her disbelief about my clean room. "Do you like it?"

"I love it, baby." I pushed over in bed and made her a space. "I'm starting to think I'm dreaming." I fit so naturally and easily next to her. It made me want to trust my choice to change the past. And she smelled the same, like oranges, like calm. Like my mother.

"Why are you up so early?" I asked. My room was dark, only lit by the light glinting in from the hall.

"It's almost ten, baby." I craned my neck, looking for a window, for light. I didn't find one. I didn't have a window, because this wasn't a normal house.

It was always night in here.

Lying here with Mom would have to eclipse that. I loved that she wasn't in a rush to get anywhere. She wasn't famous. She wasn't Lydia Shaw; I'd killed her on the 4th.

I smiled at her hands, not accustomed to seeing a diamond there.

"I love your ring," I said, rubbing a finger across it. It had to be three carats or more. And because I wasn't psychic, that was only a guess.

"Thanks. I know it may not seem like it, but it does bother me that it won't be yours one day. Like an official ring from a man. I know we fight about it, and I'm really sorry. I can't imagine what that must feel like to know."

So Mom and I fought about guys. Or really, the fact that I would never meet one. I shivered. My parents never expected me to get married and leave.

But it was my life now.

"I'm fine," I whispered. "Did you eat breakfast?"

"Dad ran out of eggs so I had to think him up some. Now I'm exhausted. He's going to bring the food to us."

So Mom still had powers but hadn't taught me. It was how we ate. What would happen if we didn't have her? We'd starve to death?

Mom giggled and kissed my hand. "Do you remember that time when you spit out my food and said it didn't taste real?" I smiled, ready to pretend, but ... a memory formed—me at a table in my pajamas and Mom manifesting a plate of food.

I remembered jumping in my chair, surprised by her powers, and then shoveling eggs into my mouth. I let them dribble back out to the plate. My parents laughed, and Dad fired up the stove to make me a real breakfast, the typical way.

I remembered something from this life and it felt as real as any memory from St. Catalina or my life with Nate.

Dad brought our breakfast in and flipped on the lights in my room. "Whoa, kid. This is great." He sat on my bed. We ate there and talked about how my room had slowly turned into a dumpster. Strangely, those memories didn't feel foreign either.

"Poor Snowflake is not used to seeing you this late," Dad said as he disgustingly brushed his hand across Mom's thigh.

That seemed like it was code for: *Get lost, Christine.* I was suddenly upset and tired of them doing that to me, using Snowflake to occupy me when they wanted to be alone.

Wait ... I couldn't be upset with them. This was my first morning here. *I* wasn't really fighting with them. I shook off the unfounded anger and got out of bed. They followed me out of my room.

At the end of the hall, I made a sharp and deliberate left, like I knew my way around better than yesterday.

They went right.

"See you later, baby," Mom said.

"Okay," I said.

Drawings of a white horse and a stick figure with curly hair covered the walls down the rest of the hall. Paper snowflakes dangled from the ceiling, guiding me to her stable. I vaguely remembered Dad helping me hang them. When I came to a glass door, memories bombarded me. Strong ones. Happy ones.

I saw Mom holding my hand and walking me down the hall. I was only as tall as her waist. *"Remember when you asked why Daddy was making all that noise by your room?"* she'd asked, in front of the glass door I was standing in front of in the present. It had a big yellow bow on it. *"He went out into the dangerous world and brought you back something wonderful."*

"He went out there with the monsters?" I'd asked.

"Yep, just for you."

I remembered bursting through the doors when I heard the horse. Dad was inside with her, brushing her hair.

I snapped out of the memory and opened the door. The floor was covered in sand and hay. The majestic and stunning white horse was out of her stall, sitting gracefully in the corner. I had a feeling I always left her out.

"Her house is too cramped," I whispered, remembering when I'd told Mom that years ago.

Like an old friend welcoming me to her home, she rose to her legs and met me in the middle of the stable. I smiled, my heart fluttering. I was in love with this horse.

The memory of when I got her swept me up again.

"*Happy Birthday, pumpkin,*" Dad said. "*You've been asking for a pet for years. We think eight is old enough to take care of one.*"

I screamed and Mom shushed me. "*You have to be calm around her. If she hurts you, I can't be held responsible—*"

"*She won't hurt her, baby,*" Dad cut in. "*The guy said she had a gentle spirit.*" Completely unafraid I rubbed my new horse and kissed her nose. "*What's her name?*" he asked.

"*Snowflake!*" I yelled.

They laughed, and Dad taught me how to mount her and hold myself up. I was a natural and rode her until they made me get down.

Back in the present, Snowflake followed me into her stall, and I paused, realizing that the memories meant this life was becoming permanent. Sophia had said that I would need to remember who'd given me the necklace for the wish to work. I guessed my other memories would fade, and soon, the life I'd given up would be forgotten, as though it never happened.

"That's what I wanted," I said, trying to convince myself of it. I opened the cabinet, suddenly remembering where I stored her food. She mostly ate the feed Mom manifested for her, but I usually snuck her treats from the kitchen. Red apples were her favorite.

Snowflake liked to munch slowly all day. I only pretended to feed her on a schedule to disappear for a while without being questioned and followed.

I grabbed an apple from where I always hid them in the cabinet, behind her brushes and cleaning supplies. I also had blankets and pillows in there. Because I slept in here ... a lot.

I remembered trying to have a slumber party with her in my room once. She'd made a huge mess for Dad to clean up and got banned from the house.

Under her food and my blankets, I found another notebook. I'd written in a barely perceivable size again.

Dad says Snowflake and I are the same age. She's fifteen and so am I. If she's lucky, she will live to her thirties. If I am lucky, I will die with her so I won't have to stay here until I'm old. Or at least until Mom and Dad die. I assume he will die first from Mom wearing him down and making him take care of us. Then she'll go. She'll try to hold on for me, but they are more in love than the people in the movies we watch. It won't take her long to die without him. I'm scared to bury Snowflake. I'm terrified to bury my parents. But I know I will have to. Who else is there to do it? Then I'll escape finally and live in the world they think is full of monsters. I bet there is no such person as Julian. I bet people sing and dance in the streets like the movies. And go to college and cheer at football games.

I sank to the floor of the stall. I'd written about saying goodbye to my horse one day. And if we were living in this secluded life, I would at least have to bury one of my parents alone. And I thought that would be my mother.

Snowflake came in and lay next to me. I rested my head on her, like I'd done it a million times. "At least they're happy, right?" She grunted, and I chuckled. "They weren't happy in our old life, Snow. She worked too much, sacrificed everything. I can sacrifice for them now."

I fed her an apple as we lay there. I flipped through the notebook, fighting terror. In this life, I was preoccupied with how my parents would die. How I would find them. I assumed I'd bury them in the stable next to Snowflake. I'd written several pages about what life would be like after Dad died—cooking for Mom and taking care of her when the thought of Julian made her sick. I was worried about how I'd keep everything running. I didn't understand how the generator worked. I didn't know how to care for the pipes that flushed fresh water into the house and our waste out.

"I can do this, Snow. Everything is going to be fine."

I kissed Snowflake and left. I took a shower to wash the stable off of me. I found Mom and Dad in the kitchen, dancing to no music. It was the cutest thing ever. It took them a moment to notice me. When they did, they danced over and pulled me into the huddle.

I twirled around the kitchen with my parents, letting my head lull back. The racing cabinets made me dizzy as I basked in the sounds of their laughter. The sounds of a happy family. Round and around we went, cackling and squealing, finding joy in this terrible existence.

It overwhelmed Mom first. She stopped spinning and pulled me tight into a hug, crying and thanking God for giving them their baby back.

I hugged her back, cutting Dad out of the tearful celebration of our twisted life.

"I'll start lunch," he said. "It'll take me a while. I'm thinking we should have a mid-day feast." Mom yanked me behind her back.

"Be careful, Gavin." I stood on my toes to see what he needed to be careful with. He'd pulled out a knife and started chopping onions. "Sweetie, let's go in the other room. I'm too tired to worry about that knife slipping out of your Dad's hand or something."

She tugged me toward the doorway.

"Lyd, everything's fine. I have the knife." He shot her a reassuring glance, and she loosened her grip on my arm. The memories I'd gained from this life didn't help me understand. Common sense told me she didn't want me around knives. Maybe she was worried I'd do something to myself. Maybe I had before.

"I'll stay right here next to you, Mom. I'm okay." She put her arm around my shoulder, and we watched Dad chop. I could feel her shaking at my side. "I won't go anywhere near it."

I wanted to apologize for trying to hurt myself or whatever I'd done to frighten her, but it seemed like the wrong time to bring it up. Her face was soaked and scarlet now.

"Gavin, please. I told you I was tired. Why can't we cook later? Why does it have to be now?"

"Lydia, honey, please. Everything is completely fine. Just breathe and relax."

She pushed me behind her again. "How am I supposed to relax!" she screamed. "I've told you time after time, keep sharp things away from my baby. I won't let her get hurt. I love you, but … it applies to you too. Put the knife down!"

Dad dropped the knife and stepped back with his hands up. "Let's go upstairs, baby. You need to rest. You don't sound like you feel well."

Mom held out her hand, and the knife flew into it. "When is the last time you left the house, Gavin?" she whispered.

I stepped away, terrified of her. Of the knife. Of her tone.

"I went outside three weeks ago to check the water. To see if it was safe to drink. Remember?" He spoke slowly, like she was a mental patient. She sure looked like one.

"Did you talk to anyone? Did someone ask you to turn us in? I had a dream about it." I rubbed her back, trying to calm her down. Her chest was huffing like she couldn't get enough air. "I'm sorry, baby. But I can't let you hurt her."

She pointed the knife at him, and I screamed. I wrapped my arms around her waist, pulling her away from him, struggling to reach her hands to free the knife.

"Christine, honey, let her go," he said.

"No! Dad! What's wrong with her?"

He shushed me and smiled at Mom. "Okay. You're right, baby. I understand that you need to protect her."

246

"Dad!" He held a finger to his lip and stepped slowly to Mom who was still wielding a knife and bawling. "Please, Mom. Stop!"

"You have to do what you have to do, Lyd." Dad opened his arms. "Can I have a kiss first? One last kiss." She nodded and walked to him, dragging me with her. I screamed for either of them to stop. They didn't listen. I was about to have to bury him sooner than I'd thought if he was going to be a psycho and let her stab him. "Let go, Christine," he whispered and winked at me.

Wanting desperately to trust that our lives couldn't be this insane, I let go. Dad let Mom kiss him as she held the knife dangerously close to his neck. He reached behind him and pulled out a drawer. I gasped, praying that I was not about to witness the lovebirds having a knife fight.

He pulled out a needle and thrust it into her arm.

Neither of them answered my screams or pleas to help me understand what was happening. He drained the contents of the syringe into her arm, and she dropped the knife. Dad picked her up. She didn't look like she could stand on her own anymore, her muscles lax and flimsy.

"I'm going to put Mom to bed, honey. I'll be right back." He smiled and carried her out of the room. I stood there, stunned and confused, until I crept to the drawer he'd gotten the needle from, expecting to see something even more terrifying. Fear stalled my feet, but I forced them forward, like sloshing through mud. I peered into the drawer and gasped. It was full of needles. How often did she need to be sedated? How often did she freak out and try to stab him?

I ran up the stairs to either check on them or to see if I'd imagined the whole thing. I wasn't sure. He laid her on their bed and threw a blanket over her.

"I'm so sorry," she slurred. "I got confused."

"I know, baby. You're just tired."

"I should've killed Julian. If you'd let me find him, I wouldn't have to worry. I should've—"

He shushed her. "Rest, baby. I know you want to feel better for tonight. We're watching your favorite movie." He kissed her on her dead lips and turned off the lamp by their bed.

He looked at me with hiked eyebrows. "What's with you, kid? You're freaking me out."

I shook all over. "*I'm* freaking *you* out? What the hell?"

He pushed us out of the room and closed the door. "You haven't reacted to your mother taking her medicine like that since you were maybe ... ten. Why is it bothering you?" I couldn't answer. Mom needed sedatives to calm down and had needed them for years. Oh, God. "You usually laugh at her and go to your room."

"She almost stabbed you. That's not funny."

He wiped my face and put an arm around my shoulder. "Well do you want to go play the guitar like we used to do when Mom got sick?" He looked at me skeptically, like he was afraid I'd hurt his feelings.

"Sure," I said, even though I didn't know how to play the guitar.

Crooked and colorful musical notes covered his studio door. In the center, he'd posted my drawing of him playing the guitar next to a stick figure with yellow hair—Mom. In my old life, I'd skipped stick figures. I could draw full bodies and faces before I'd learned to read. A humorless chuckle jerked up to my throat. Using the portal had made me a normal child in the least normal life possible.

"How long has it been since you've been in my studio, pumpkin?" Still shaking from the terrifying moment he was apparently desensitized to, I hunched my shoulders. "I dust your guitar, so it doesn't seem so long to me."

He held me close to his side as we eased down the dark steps that I assumed, almost more than assumed, would lead to our basement. I remembered that most of it belonged to Dad and was where he spent his time when he wanted to be alone. But he never shunned visitors; we were always welcome to come listen to him play.

He flipped on a light at the end of the stairs, and I stopped myself from shaking my head in awe. His studio was as immaculate as the rest of the house, our well-equipped prison. My throat tightened. It felt like I hadn't been in here in years, not like it was my first time. My old life was floating further away as this one settled into my veins.

He motioned me over to the pink and white guitar I'd obviously outgrown years ago. I grabbed it tentatively, hoping he wouldn't ask me to play.

"I'll do your favorite," he said. He propped a guitar on his lap. Within seconds, I knew the song. It was my favorite because I would make up different words to it every time I heard it.

I'd made up one about my teddy bears, a few about Mom singing me to sleep, and countless ones about Snowflake. He jerked his head to a table at my side. I took the pick he wanted me to see. Like I'd played it a million times before, I found the chords I needed. Only three—A, D, and E—composed my favorite thing to hear and sing to. I knew how to play the guitar. And well. I wanted to fight these memories as tears streamed from my eyes, thinking of my mother lying sedated in her bed.

The song I'd make up today would be about regret, about ignoring that I had everything I needed, and in a moment of extreme selfishness and stupidity, gave it all away. My skin felt as though it wanted to fall from my bones, help me disappear into the nothing I felt like for leaving Nate in another world.

My best friend. My heart. He loved me, maybe not as much as Mom because it was impossible, but he loved me with all of him. With all that he had. And I didn't honor that. I didn't choose him.

And … poor Dad. He didn't have friends and a life outside of Mom in this world. My heart bled for him. He went along with anything she wanted in any life, hiding together or living apart. Like they shared a brain. A sick one, in this new world.

"Talk to me. What's going on with you?" he asked without skipping a note.

"Would you believe me if I told you none if this was real? That yesterday we were doing something very different?"

"Yes, I can. Yesterday, you wouldn't come out of your room. I hope this is real. I miss my daughter."

Dad changed the song to one of his favorites, a duet. I remembered when he wrote it for us to sing to Mom on her 27th birthday and their 10th anniversary. They'd laughed when I'd belted out an ad lib, getting far too carried away with a high note.

I snapped out of the memory, my heart twisting so painfully I thought it would stop.

"How are you letting this happen, Dad? She needs help."

He played for another minute without answering. "Mom feels guilty, and sometimes it scrambles her head. She feels responsible for your sadness and the state of the world. And because she chose us, I will be here every day to support her decisions, even the hard ones."

He didn't know hard decisions. The one Mom had made was gone now. I'd forced her to take the easy route. Hard was letting your husband and child live separately since the only other option was this.

"I love you, but you have to be more grateful for what you have," Dad said. "We are safe, alive, we love each other, and every day you choose to see only the bad."

That was truer than he knew. I'd been focusing on the bad my entire life. I lived in an upscale orphanage with nuns who let girls do whatever they wanted, and I chose to sulk for years. I never tried to make a friend to make it better. And I couldn't remember one instance of trying to find Leah's story in the Bible to see if there was something good about her, to see if the nuns cared for me, even a little. And worse, after Sophia rescued me from the hell I allowed myself to live in, I discovered I was human, like I always wanted to be, *and* a millionaire, and could only focus on keeping Nathan. When I kept him, I started obsessing over the parents I didn't have.

And when I got *them*, I still wasn't satisfied, still only saw the bad.

"I know I tell you this all the time, baby, but you have the wrong idea about what life is like outside of this house. The movies we have are old. People don't live that way anymore, and I doubt there is even such a thing as college now. I have to go out there three, four, times a year. It's horrible. Trust me."

I cried on my tiny guitar. It was 1:30 in the afternoon. I'd missed the sun at its highest point, but as I played in harmony with the father I thought I was fighting for, I decided that fight was far from over. I wouldn't let us die here.

Sophia knew I'd need her to save me again.

"Gavin?" Mom said, staggering through the door. He jumped up and ran to her.

"Sweetie, you could have hurt yourself on the stairs." She wrapped her arms around him, crying and apologizing. "You didn't even cut me today, baby. It's fine."

Today? Didn't cut him today? Oh, God. Their kiss quickly turned into something I didn't care to see. They weren't making out, but the tears and her loose limbs made it entirely too intense.

"I'm going to check on Snowflake," I said, walking past them with my eyes on the floor. "Feel better, Mom." She slurred a thank you.

It was up to me to make her better. Strong like she was before.

I walked around our house, memorizing our photos, kissing the ones that tugged at my heart the most. I had to say goodbye to this life, break out of this house, and find my way to the sun.

CHAPTER SIXTEEN

I heard Dad carrying Mom downstairs as I said goodbye to my family's photographs.

She was still apologizing and telling him how much she loved him. Until they went to bed, I wouldn't be able to search for a way out. I'd save that for later.

I closed my bedroom door and slipped the necklace from its hiding spot. I pulled it over my head and tucked it into my shirt. I searched my now neat room for shoes, not remembering seeing a single pair last night as I cleaned.

"You don't have shoes because you've never been outside, idiot."

I sat on my bed and tried to scheme. Nothing came to me. I got the feeling I'd think a lot better next to Snowflake, like she'd calm me down and inspire me with her beauty like she always did.

"No, she's not real. This life isn't real," I said, still running towards her stable.

She greeted me at the door. I pressed my cheek against hers. It felt like she understood my pain. She bent slightly, telling me to hop on. In one motion, I jumped onto her back with my legs at her sides. I wanted to cry again when I remembered how long it had taken me to learn how to get on without a saddle.

"Snow," I said, as she trotted around the stable. "Dad has to have tools or something somewhere. I could try to open a window. There's one in the basement, isn't there?" She grunted. "Right ... tried that. Silent alarm. Red flashing lights. I remember."

I remembered Mom bursting into the basement, screaming and crying as the lights flashed. She didn't come out of her room for days after that.

"I would only need a minute, Snow." She jerked forward and sped into a run. "Right, if I'm fast enough." She slowed again, and I chuckled. I loved having these conversations with her. "But Dad probably hid his tools since I did that." I sighed, remembering that I'd used a fork in my last attempt.

She sped towards the other end of the stable, fierce and fast, but gentle enough that I barely budged on her back. She was trying to cheer me up.

I gave in and closed my eyes, flying through the air on the back of my best friend. My only friend. The only one I'd ever have. My heart deflated as I rode. I felt time slipping away, taking the Christine I knew with it. The girl who lived here and rode this horse was stronger inside of me. Her pain was mine. Her hopelessness too.

I'd been caught every time I'd tried to leave. Why even bother? My only hope was their deaths. After I fragmented my already broken mind by burying them, I would break out of this house, with a head of gray hair, and find a human friend at college. According to all of my favorite movies, that was where friends were. And sororities and fraternities and parties and fun.

And nachos at games. Dad always made me nachos when we watched old football games. But now I knew the endings to them all, so it wasn't fun. With my gray hair, I'll watch one in person. With nachos in my lap. And I wouldn't know who would fumble the ball, or whose ankle would twist, or which team would leave with their heads hanging low, trying to be gracious while they shook hands with the winners.

At that point, I'd probably have to fall in love with an old professor instead of a frat boy. I'd seen a movie once where a student fell in love with her teacher. The guy went to jail, but ... I would be old, so it would be okay.

My eyes flew open. I'd seen more movies than the old ones set in high school or college or cartoons. I'd seen countless ones with Emma. And action movies with blood and gore with Nate. This was not my life.

It was getting harder to remember that.

"Baby," Mom said. Snowflake slowed and took me to the door. Well trained, she bowed and I hopped down. She trotted away and lay in a far away corner of the stable. "Dinner's ready."

"What time is it?"

"Seven. Dad came in to give you lunch, but he said you were in one of your zones with Snowflake." Wow. I did not feel all of those hours fly by. "Do you want to eat in here? Your Dad said you were really upset. I could bring you a plate so you can stay with her."

Feeling desperately out of time, I grabbed Mom's hands to plead with her. "Don't get mad, Mom, but I really need to go outside. Just for a second. Tomorrow at noon. Please?"

She sighed and her face twisted to a frown. "I can't handle this today. I'm tired. I'm sick. I just can't do it."

"No, Mom. See that's the problem. You're never sick like this. Not in our real life. You left Dad. You took me to a school and we just met a few months ago. None of this is real."

"This is a new low, Christine. I'll come back when you're not out of your mind."

She turned to leave and I grabbed her. "No! I'm not. Kamon and a wizard named Devin opened a portal and I went through it and changed one of your memories. I made you tell Dad you were pregnant with me.

In real life, you didn't. You left him and killed Fredrick Dreco and Julian."

Her eyes were wide and horrified. She tugged her arm from my grip. "How do you know about them? Have you been listening at our door again? We told you to stop."

"No. I know this because I lived it. Yesterday, we didn't live like this. Sophia knew I'd do this. She told me how to fix it, and I need to be outside with the sun and use this necklace."

I pulled it out of my shirt and held it to her eyes.

She grabbed my face. "Please stop, baby. You are scaring me."

"Look at it!"

"There's nothing there."

I dangled it closer to her eyes, and she looked right through it, not seeing it at all. That was why she'd thought I was naked in the pool. She couldn't see things from our past life.

"Well ... how else would I know that Sophia was your maid when you lived with an agent named Mona?" I asked, since she couldn't see my evidence.

She kissed my forehead. "Because we've talked about it thousands of times," she whispered. "I'm going to tell Daddy to bring your plate, baby. You know I can't deal with you like this."

She stormed out of the door, and I lay next to the only soul in this house that understood me, and she couldn't speak outside of her grunts and neighs.

Later, Dad lectured me about getting his beloved wife worked up while I ate. I apologized and kissed him goodnight. Hopefully goodbye. He turned out the lights in the stable on his way out, assuming I was sleeping in here. I stretched out next to Snowflake, holding the necklace. Of course Sophia wouldn't make it easy. Of course I'd need to pull off the impossible to fix this. I didn't even own shoes, and I needed to get outside at noon before my memories dissolved. Or else—

Shoes! I had shoes! And a knife tucked in one of my boots. I'd taken them off by the pool. Even though I wasn't any closer to getting out, somehow the boots gave me a little hope, a little more fight than I had before. I ran to the pool. They were still there with the knife inside. I threw them on and ran back to the stable, and straight into Mom.

It took all the energy I had not to jump and look guilty.

"Don't make me resort to listening to your thoughts. I don't want to do that. I want to trust you."

"You can trust me. I just thought I left something at the pool..." I glanced down at my feet and so did she. She didn't see the shoes. Thank God. "I was writing a poem before I got in."

She sighed. It took almost a minute, but she smiled and relaxed her grimace. "I'd love to hear it some time. What was it about?"

"Snowflake."

She smiled harder. "Of course it was."

She opened the stable door for me, and I went in.

"I love you, Mom," I said.

"I love you, too. I know after a day like today, you usually want your space, so when you're ready to see us, come find us, okay? We'll stay out of your way, but if I hear you in the halls ..." She closed her eyes and paused, straining like she didn't want to continue. "You know we don't want to lock you in. We really don't. So don't make us."

"I won't," I whispered.

My heart didn't stop pounding until well after she'd walked away from the stable doors.

I lay down in the corner Snowflake seemed to want to be in. It was colder than the rest of the stable. Chilled air floated in from behind her.

"Snow, what is that?" I wedged my hand between her side and the wall, feeling the wind brush against my fingers. "A vent?"

The Christine who lived here knew that she'd trained Snowflake to sit here. To hide something.

"Up, girl," I said. She obeyed and strutted to her stall. The sand was thinner beneath her. I brushed a layer away and found a pink and yellow school bag. I remembered crying for it. I'd wanted a bag to take to my school down the hall like the normal kids had on the movies. Mom had manifested it for me. And I'd hidden it in the stable ... because it held things I didn't want my parents to see.

I opened the sack.

I had several bottles of water, a loaf of bread, huge chunks of cheese—the kind Mom hated and wouldn't notice missing from the pantry—and a mess of ham. None of the food was spoiled. Then I remembered I replenished this bag once a week in the event I ever escaped. "I'm a genius."

I unearthed the bag. It covered a hole. No, it covered the tunnel I'd been burrowing all year. I remembered finding my way to a vent, which was both triumphant and tragic.

I wedged my arms through the tiny straps of the bag.

"Snowflake," I whispered. She came on command. "I have to check this out. This could lead to the sun tomorrow." I kissed her nose. "I'll come back, but stay right here until I do." I used pillows to make lumps under my blanket. I slid through the hole and she capped it off with her body, like she knew the drill.

I crawled into the metal vent. Reluctantly, I listened to the part of me that knew where I was. I could navigate this path with my eyes closed.

I needed to be extremely silent because I would crawl over the living room. Twice when I'd done this, Mom and Dad were in there watching their favorite movie. I never understood why they wanted to watch that creepy lady in *Misery* torture that guy over and over again. Sort of like how they could watch me suffer over the years.

Quietly lurking in the vents, I heard Dad laughing below me.

"It was a green shirt. Lime green," he said.

"No, it was blue. I'm sure of it. It was our second date, you don't remember that," Mom said, laughing just as hard. Pushing on inches more, I could see them on the sofa through the vent opening.

"I was so in love with you already that I memorized what you wore that day. And it was a green shirt, honey. I can even tell you the last time you wore it. When you left it in San Juan, on the beach."

They made awkward eye contact that made me want to vomit on them from up here. "Oh … yeah," she said, giggling and kissing him. Nothing upset me more than my parents when they were like this. I used to love watching them together. It was like watching characters in a movie. True love, perfect love. Until *my* love for them spoiled, fermenting into something hateful enough that I wanted to escape and leave them here to rot. Because as much as I loved them and knew they loved me, I knew they wouldn't hesitate to chain me in a room if it came to it.

They'd be destroyed over it, cry and scream and fall into more pieces than Mom's sedatives could fix, but they'd do it. She was weak and he was weaker, and they'd allowed an enemy she used to have to keep us locked in this hellhole.

I rolled my eyes and crawled away as quickly as I could without making a sound. With me safely tucked away in the stable, nothing would stop them from—in their words—engaging in Mom and Dad time in the living room. I shivered, still not close to getting over walking in on them when I was nine, or the sex talk that followed, or that I never got the brother or sister they promised me. I guessed they didn't want to torture another child.

I crawled over the kitchen, suddenly aware that this was the farthest I'd gone through the vents. I usually turned around now, but I couldn't today. I wanted to get outside ... because I'd always wanted to.

The air smelled different, fresher. The sound of water and wind—rain—hummed in the vent. I'd never seen real rain before.

Wait ... I had. I'd sat in it. Ate in it. At school in my real life. I clutched that Christine with wet and shaky hands, threatened with being forgotten forever.

I took a deep breath to gather myself, to gather her, but chuckled instead. Rain smelled ... wet. Just like I imagined it would. Slowly, I poked my fingers through the metal shutters. The rain dropped on my hand, like someone was crying on me.

And now *I* was crying, because I'd done it. Found a way out of this house. Years of longing led me to pull on the vent that looked to be just wide enough for me. It didn't budge, screwed to the wall. I tried my fingers, then nails, then I searched myself for anything small and hard enough to fit into the screws.

A small voice, that sounded calm and rational, told me to crawl back to the stable and use the time between now and noon to plan my next move. But ... why wait when freedom was so close?

I wanted out. I needed out. So much so that my throat closed and I couldn't breathe. I brought my hand up to soothe it, and felt something odd there. Something silver. Where had I gotten this necklace? That didn't matter now. It couldn't matter.

The pendant on this unfamiliar piece of jewelry was shaped like something else I'd never seen in person. The sun. I remembered Dad's songs about it. He always taught Science because it was too boring for Mom to do alone and she couldn't sing about the planets and stars like he could.

I stuck one of the rays into the straight line cut into the screw. I almost screamed when it twisted. I removed them all and pulled the vent from the wall. The air gushed in, smelling of real life. Sounding of it, too. I looked back to the long path I'd crawled through.

Something tugged on me to stop. To remember what I was doing. To remember that I needed to wait for the sun.

A branch scraped the side of the vent. A branch. Like from a tree. Leaves dangled from it. I touched one, shaking.

Dad had brought a bag of them in for me once. Just so I could see what outside life looked like. He'd said he had to travel far to get them. He'd lied. They were right outside.

My leaves all died in that bag; the green faded slowly to orange and then to a brittle brown. After, they let me grow my own plant because I'd taken it so hard. I'd named him Sprout. He didn't last long.

I bet I'd see a whole lot of Sprouts out there.

I blew a kiss to my parents and Snowflake and extended my feet out of the vent. I didn't find anything to land on. Holding on to the slick bottom of the vent, I dangled from my home. I'd seen houses on movies, and mine looked nothing like them. It was made of ... rock, but it didn't look like this from the inside. A raw, untouched, massive rock.

Rain poured from the beautiful sky. I looked up, holding my eyes open against the natural urge to flinch, and smiled.

"Wow," I said, admiring the water cascading from the air and through the trees. I wept over the sounds of things moving, things other than Snow and my parents. Things were alive here. I was alive here.

My fingers slipped from the vent, and I plummeted through the wet air, and the stack of stones that was my house flew past my eyes. I crashed to the ground. Every inch of me hurt until I numbed all over. I couldn't move. I lay there for an eternity as I floated in and out of conscious thought.

I saw Snowflake running through the green. I saw my parents cooing over me. I saw an older woman pulling a necklace over my head.

Snowflake ran closer, her hooves splashing in puddles of water.

I'd always dreamed of riding her outside. My lips formed to cheer her on, but I couldn't manage the sound. She flew through the rain, a beautiful dream, and I felt my sluggish body lift from the ground. Something yanked me and held me in the air.

"Look at this," a voice said. The hands whirled me around. I was staring into the deepest brown eyes I'd ever seen. A man. A dirty one. "How much do you think we'd get for it?" he asked.

It? Get for it? Did he mean me?

"Leave it for him. We owe him, remember?" the woman said.

"This could mean dinner next week. We don't owe him this much," the man said.

He threw me over his shoulder. I tried to get down, but I wasn't moving nearly as much as I thought. The man wasn't bothered. He held me loosely, and my head scraped against the low-hanging branches.

"Snow!" I said, seeing a splash of white against the murky brown and green of the new outside world. I wondered how she'd managed to get out of the house. She wouldn't fit through the vent. Did Mom and Dad let her out? Were they searching for me already? The world was going dark. I saw her again, closer this time. "Snowflake," I said.

Her grunt sounded different. Through my squinted eyes, I could see that Snow looked smaller and not like a horse at all. She barked, and we came to a stop.

"We're sorry. We found her first," the woman said. Snow barked again and sniffed me. I forced my eyes open. If I were dying, she was the last thing I wanted to see.

Her huge brown eyes were replaced with green ones. Beautiful and familiar. They made me feel safe and happy and deeply in love.

"Nate," I whispered, before my body gave in to sleep.

CHAPTER SEVENTEEN

I was cold. So cold. And wet.

I opened my eyes. I saw a blurry toilet, a blurry sink, and a blurry me in a tub with no water.

A tiny finger reached to my cheek and poked me. The little boy giggled and poked me again. He flicked his tongue in his mouth through missing teeth. He didn't seem to notice he was doing it. I remembered that undeniable urge to rub your tongue where teeth once were and would eventually be again. I remembered it well. From two different lives—one with Mom and Dad watching. In the other one, I was alone.

"Corey, stop," the woman from the forest said. She was by far the largest woman I had ever seen in my life. She was well over seven feet tall and broad, but not overweight by any means. Her cheeks were sunken in like she needed to eat. Her hair was dark and horribly matted to her head, covered by a useless red bandana. She kneeled and scrubbed my face with a towel. I screamed and tried to scramble out of the tub. "Sit," the woman ordered. Like I was an animal. Since she looked like a hungry giant, I obeyed her.

I patted under my shirt for my necklace. Still there, still invisible, I guessed.

"Where's my bag?" I asked.

"Your things are mine because you are mine. Until I trade you in the morning."

"Let me go!" She laughed and turned the water on in the tub.

"Dead bodies still sell for parts, little girl."

The part of me that remembered fighting Kamon and the triplets pushed me to grab her neck. She snapped and my arms fell lifeless to my side.

A witch.

A bark shot through the silence.

I craned my neck to see the floor from the tub.

"Nate!" I screamed. He barked again and bumped his nose against the woman's leg.

"She's not yours, Nathan," she said. She was wrong. I was completely his. "I can't afford to trade you. It's been a slow week." Nathan jumped into the tub and stood on top of me. He growled at her, and she rolled her eyes. "Go get your father," she said to the boy.

Corey returned with an equally as large man. He was wearing overalls with no shirt underneath it. "Oh, dear," he said. "It looks like we have a situation in here. Fine, Nathan. What are you willing to trade?" He yanked a white robe from the back of the door. Nate jumped from the tub and trapped the ends of it in his mouth. He trotted out of the room with it and came back as the boy I was in love with.

Oh, God. It was really him. My love. My heart. My everything that I traded for nothing.

"I'll watch Corey for a week free of charge," Nate said. "You can take extra shifts." The man smirked like that wasn't a bad deal.

"Fine. And we're square from you giving us clearance through the forest earlier?"

"Deal," Nate said. He pulled me out of the tub and threw me over his shoulder. I wished he would've kissed me, but at least I was on my way out of here.

"Now, get out before I change my mind," the man said. "Shannon's right, you're weird about that forest. It doesn't belong to you and the things in it don't either."

Nate grunted and carried me to the door. Corey ran and hugged his legs. He gave him my bag and Nate ruffled his hair before we left.

"Nate," I said, when the decrepit door closed behind us.

"My name is Nathan. Not Nate," he said, lugging me down a dark street, only lit by torches in handles. Not streetlights. And he was in a thin bathrobe and didn't seem to be freaked out by that.

Something with wings blew past us and circled around. It ... she ... maybe he ... glittered and flew into my face. It flicked my nose with its tiny fingers, and I flinched.

"Nathan, what's this?"

"My business, Olivia. Goodnight."

She fluttered around to his face. I tried to lift myself up to see, but he pushed me back over his shoulder. "I hope you get something good for it. I heard you haven't eaten. You know who was talking about it with *you know who*."

"I'm not in the mood. Goodnight, Olivia," he moaned.

He grumbled about Olivia and her gossiping as he hauled me down the street. The magical street, apparently. In this life, they weren't in hiding. That made sense; there was no Lydia Shaw to make them follow a treaty.

He opened another rickety door to an apartment lit by candles with barely any furniture. He laid me on the floor and stepped over me.

"Nate."

"Look, lady, don't worry. I'm not that kind of guy. I'm not going to hurt you. I need to get a raincoat, and I'll bring you home. What part of town do you stay in?"

"The forest, I guess."

He laughed. "Come on, you don't have to lie. Kiya would've traded you to anyone for food or gold. I won't do that. I'm going to trade you to your parents. Do they live around here or on the upper side?"

"I don't know what you're talking about," I said, and stood from the dusty floor.

"Witch, right?" he asked.

"No."

"Then what are you?"

"Human." He stumbled over a rocking chair and ran over to me, raincoat in hand, still in the robe. Then he slung me over his shoulder again without saying another word.

The rain that had captivated me through the vents started up again, and he maneuvered me around while he slipped on his raincoat. "Nate, what's going on?"

"It's Nathan, and you're on the wrong side. You're probably worth a good bit. The decent thing to do would be to take you to your border and trade you there. Luckily, I'm a decent guy."

Border? And what the hell was all of this trading? And why was he carrying me everywhere?

"Put me down, please," I said.

"I can't. I don't trust you not to run away, and I'm not in the mood to chase you." It seemed as though I'd traded one prison for another. A mansion for dirty streets on the way to whatever this border was. At least this sentence involved Nathan.

People in the strangest clothes, velvet jackets and dresses with ruffles and too many buttons, passed us on the street. They either spoke or waved to Nate on the way, not mentioning the girl on his shoulder or that he was in a white robe covered by a yellow raincoat.

"Where are we?" I asked.

"You're out of it, aren't you?"

"What?" He responded with a laugh. "Please tell me."

I scraped my wet hair out of my face only to have it fall and stick to my skin again. I was close to fainting from the blood rushing to my head.

"On the lower side. Magical jurisdiction. West. Obviously," he said.

"And ... you're taking me where exactly?"

"The pigeons I usually trade talk a lot less than you."

A bundle of blankets in the middle of the sidewalk shifted as we passed it. It took me a moment to see the man huddled inside. "Are you ... some sort of salesmen?"

"No."

"Then why ..."

He sniffed loudly and grunted, cutting me off. "You have got to be kidding me," he said. He adjusted me on his shoulder and turned down a thin alley, walking towards music and laughter. It wasn't radio music. It was live, mostly violins and drums. It sounded folky and medieval, like it should be danced to with bells dangling from your wrists, barefoot under the moon. Nate sniffed again and made a quick right, down an even thinner alley. "Let it go, Nathan," he told himself. "No. I'm *not* letting it go. Not tonight." He pushed the swinging door open and carried me into a smoky bar. The violins and drums shrieked in my ears.

He sat me on a stool, right across from the bartender—a dwarf with blue hair. I blinked hard several times to make sure he was really there. "Don't move," Nate said. "Hey, Vern."

Vern eyed me like I was the weird one. "Hey, kid," Vern said to Nate. "I like you, but no scenes tonight."

"Not planning on it," Nate said, pushing past a crowd of people dancing to folk music like it was hip-hop. Vern poured frothy beer into a mug. He climbed to my eye level and pushed it to me.

"No, thanks."

"Nothing to trade?" Vern asked.

I grunted. "What's with the trading? Is that ... like a magic thing?"

He laughed and drank the beer himself. "Oh ... you're *that* kind of girl. Look, we don't sell that stuff here. You'll have to go down the street a ways."

"What?" He stared at me with eyes that matched his hair and grinned with his rotting smile.

"You look ridiculous," a girl said, pushing Nate back to the front of the bar. She had on purple velvet pants and a black corset. Her red hair fell in waves on her bare shoulders. Compared to everyone else, she was stylish. At least she saw that Nate looked crazy in his robe and raincoat ensemble. "I'm not doing anything wrong. He's here with his friends. It's a total coincidence. You look jealous and nuts."

Jealous? Of?

"Whatever, Shannon," Nate said. "Tell him I said hello." He turned away from her, and she caught his arm. She pulled him closer and pressed her disgusting red lips against his.

This was what it looked like for the world to end—Nate's lips on another girl's. It felt like buildings were crumbling and the whole sky was falling, pressing in on me, as I watched their lips part.

I wished the fall had taken me out. No, I wished I wouldn't have climbed out of the vent. I'd rather die a slow death in the house with my parents than see my soul mate kissing someone else. There was nothing worse. Not even seeing my father sedate my mother.

"I'm sorry I didn't tell you I was going out. Forgive me, baby?" she asked, lips still on his.

"Yeah," he whispered.

I slid off the stool as they went at it again, heading for the door. I'd find a corner to hide in until the sun came up. Or I'd die any moment and it wouldn't matter anyway. My parents were happy. Nate was happy. All without me. More evidence that I was a mistake my parents shouldn't have let happen. They should've been more careful. I didn't belong in this world or any.

"Hey, get back here," Nate said.

He picked me up and threw me over his shoulder yet again.

"Who's that?" Shannon asked.

"I'm about to trade her. She's human. On drugs. I should be done in a few hours."

She came around to his back and pinched my cheeks. It took everything I had not to spit in her man-stealing face. "Get something good for her."

"Okay. See you later on?" he asked, turning me away from her. She took longer to answer than I thought it should have.

"Uh … maybe. I have plans," she said.

He sighed. I smiled because it was his annoyed sigh, and I really wanted him to be annoyed with her. "Whatever, Shannon."

"They're just plans, Nathan. You wouldn't know anything about that. It's something fun people do. We don't sit and twiddle our thumbs in the forest."

He walked away and took a deep breath. He stopped suddenly and spun around.

"You know what, Shannon? Do what you want. Have fun with your plans, if that's what you're calling him now. Don't come over. Maybe I have plans, too. And tomorrow either. Don't come over then. Don't come over ever. I'm done."

Done? With her? Perfect. If he weren't about to trade me, I would say things were looking up.

"Did you just break up with me?" she asked. God, I hoped so. "What's wrong with you? Why are you acting weird?"

"Maybe I'm just tired of finding you in bars with your ex. Have a nice life."

Dangling over his shoulder, I watched the redhead as we stormed out of the bar. She rolled her eyes like she hadn't taken him seriously. Maybe they broke up in bars often and she wasn't worried. She snapped, and a drink appeared in her hand. Stupid witch.

"That was nuts," he said to himself as the doors slammed behind us. "Just what everyone needs, another reason to think she's turned me into a lunatic. Wonderful."

"Nate…"

"Shhh. Don't talk to me." He paced in an alley, making me dizzy on his shoulder. "Today was not supposed to go like this. It was a normal day. Then I met a human and broke up with my girlfriend."

"That's good. I think I would've died if you kissed her again," I said.

He grunted. "What? Never mind. Let me get you to your border so I can get to bed. I'm tired. And cranky, obviously. I can't believe I just did that."

He walked out of the alley and into a noisy market. He waved to a couple arguing over bread. They paused the quarrel for a moment to speak, then went back at it.

"Nathan, how much?" a man at the next booth asked.

"She's not for sale, Jack. Sorry," he said.

"You're no fun," Jack huffed. He winked at me and sped my heart. I couldn't speak until we'd walked far away from him and the distance had turned him into a speck in my eye.

"How do you sell a person?" I asked.

"It's simple, crazy lady who won't stop talking. Let's say I'm hungry. I have you. I give you to someone with food, and they, in turn, give me said food. Understand?"

"Why would they want me?" I asked, ignoring his sarcasm.

He didn't answer. Maybe he was too much of a gentleman to state the obvious reason why a man would buy a woman.

We left the market and walked to a quieter part of the neighborhood with bigger houses with more than a few inches between them. The roads turned from dirt to broken concrete.

A woman leaned out of her window. She was much cleaner than Kiya and her husband. "No trading on our street, Nathan," she said.

"Yes, ma'am. I'm just taking the shortcut to the forest. Have a good night."

"You, too," she said, skeptically, watching me as I dangled and cried on his back. But she made no moves to help me.

Nate pulled me down from his shoulder and draped me over his arm. He stood in front of a gate lined with barbed wire. He rubbed his fingers across a jagged edge and winced. Drops of blood sizzled on the wire, then streamed to a keyhole. The gate opened, approving of his blood, and he licked his finger to heal it.

The door slammed behind us, closing off the rest of this new world. The seclusion crumbled me. "I missed you," I whispered.

"Excuse me?"

"I missed you," I repeated.

"You're nuts." Hanging over his freakishly strong arm, I cried for a minute. A long, quiet minute of crazy. "I'm going to let you walk. Don't run away." He lowered me to the ground. "If I had shoes, I'd offer them to you, but I don't. You'll just have to deal with it." I shrugged my shoulders. I had on shoes he couldn't see, so the ground didn't bother me. "What happened to your tags? I don't even know what section to bring you to."

"What?"

"Your tags. Your IDs."

I treaded through the high grass at his side. "I don't know what you're talking about. I just came from my house, and I need to just sit somewhere until tomorrow. Then I'm going to fix everything."

He sighed and looked over his shoulder to me. "Look, I know things are hard. We're all having trouble, but it's no reason to turn to drugs. You're an attractive girl. You can do a lot better than getting high in the forest. Do you know how hard it would be for your parents to get you back if someone would've sold you to the wrong person? Especially without tags. Do they know you're on drugs?"

"I'm not on drugs. I'm in a parallel universe where my parents are nuts and my boyfriend dates redheads. You, by the way, are *my* boyfriend. And you just kissed a girl right in front of me. I'm being punished." He laughed, and I glared at him. "Laugh away, Nate. I'm not kidding."

"I'm sure you believe that. Are you going to tell me that your name is Shannon next? And that I just broke up with *you*, and not the

272

other way around for the first time?"

We came to a stream cutting through the forest floor. He hopped it and held out his hands to help me over it.

"She breaks up with you a lot?" I asked, when we reached the other side.

"You're my girlfriend, aren't you? You should know." He laughed. "Man, you must be on some pretty strong stuff. Is it human grown or magic? Either way, you need to lay off for a while." The branches hung lower on the trees. He held the dangling ones back like a curtain so I could step through.

"I don't. I need to fix my mistake, Nate."

He chuckled. "Why do you keep calling me that? Do you always make up names for people when you're trashed?"

"No. Just my boyfriend." He seemed to know his way around the forest well, ducking under branches and leading me through flowery caves. It felt like a date, a weird one that was about to end in him trading me for food. "The border thingy you're bringing me to ... is it far?"

"Uh ... yeah. But we're taking a shortcut."

"Could we ... not go at all? Could you just let me stay here?"

"Against the law," he said, absently tugging flowers that didn't budge.

The flowers didn't budge!

I paused as I remembered something from my real life, talking with Mom in the sacred forest.

"Are we in the Congo?" I asked.

He laughed. "No one has called this place the Congo in years. I've never met someone as strung out as you. It's funny, in the saddest way possible."

The rain slacked up, and he removed his hood. He tousled his hair, and I pouted. God, I missed him. "You're American. You sound American. Why do you live here?"

Why did *I* live here?

"America?" He shook his head and started walking again. "You can't be older than eighteen, so you've lived here most of your life. I came on the first trip after the war. You're probably richer so you came later when things didn't work out in the wealthier countries."

We trekked through a patch of beautiful flowers, a rainbow of colors around me. My head pounded as I started to realize the magnitude of what I'd done.

"What do you mean?" I asked, cautiously.

"We have a bit of a walk, so I'll humor you. After the war, many of us migrated to the empty parts of the world, the poor parts where the humans didn't last long during the first war. Rich people stayed in the better parts of the world until they went to hell too from fighting and all the other things rich people do to destroy things. Now we share the last continent. What's left of the world, remember?"

Tears stung my eyes and spilled over. I fell to my knees in the field of flowers. "What's left of the world?" I asked. He nodded and guilt crushed me. "Your side, does Dreco run it?"

"Yep."

"And the human side?" I asked, shaking from the answer I already knew.

"Julian Polk."

I'd changed more than my life. I'd made the world end like it would have without Mom. How many people had I killed? Millions probably.

My stomach heaved, and I lurched up on all fours as I vomited.

I'd fought murderous urges for years at St. Catalina, trying to prove to God and myself that I wasn't a bad person. Killing someone was always my worst fear. I'd done more than take the lives of horrible bullies. Much more. Another wave of vomit twisted my chest on its way out.

I'd killed millions of innocent people by forcing Mom *not* to be Lydia Shaw. How did I not see this happening when I'd jumped in the portal like an idiot? How did I let selfishness blind me and make me forget about what she did after she had me? The thing that landed her in the history books?

I couldn't bear asking if he knew of Sophia or Paul or Emma. Something told me he wouldn't. And I would die, right here in the puke-covered flowers, if I knew I'd killed the people who loved me.

"I guess the drugs are coming out of your system," Nate said. He kneeled next to me and held my hair as my shame found more food in my stomach to dredge up.

When it finally stopped, Nate pulled my collar over my mouth to clean it. I smiled. He was taking care of me, like he always did. My instincts made me wrap my arms around him.

I all but died when he jerked out of my way.

I tried to stand, but I couldn't. I was heavy with the weight of them, all of the people I'd killed. He grabbed my arm and tugged me up from my knees.

"We have to keep moving," he said.

I closed my eyes and cried as we walked. It couldn't get worse than this. I just wanted to lie in the flowers, sleep away this nightmare. It was a strange feeling not having anyone to blame for my problems. Sienna, Julian, Kamon, Mom. None of them had ever done anything as horrible, as damaging, as I had.

Kamon's words rushed into my head. *Oh the people you will kill, the blood you will spill*. Like he'd said, he wasn't as dumb as I thought he was.

I rubbed my fingers across the links around my neck, my only chance at redemption.

"What's the rest of the world like? What happened?" I cried.

"Duh ... disease, violence. It's terrible," he said, like he was tired of talking to me. "I wish you could sober up and help us skip this walk. Even with the shortcut, it's going to take us forever at this rate."

"I don't have powers."

He stopped abruptly, and I bumped into his back. I probably could have stopped myself, but I wanted to touch him.

"Are you saying that you are—" He huffed and backed away from me. "Not possible. Those sort of humans don't exist anymore." I covered my mouth, trapping a scream inside. I'd killed *all* normal humans? I was nauseous again. "I can't imagine what you're worth, dead or alive."

Just great. I needed to escape from Nate so I could fix the world. I needed to find a place to hide and make a wish under the sun like Sophia knew I would need to do.

"Must be the drugs talking," I said, faking a smile. "I have powers. Of course. Just can't use them when I'm high. Can I have my bag back? I just want to hold it. I like to ... do that when I'm high. Hold things."

He chuckled and threw it to me, looking relieved that I wasn't a human without powers.

I let him walk ahead of me, slowing my steps as the seconds passed. When we had a few feet between us, I took off running in the opposite direction. Whether it was to or away from my house, I had no idea.

I hobbled and stumbled, jumping over roots, tripping over them too. I didn't hear him until he passed me, whooshing wind and rain around us.

"Where are you going?" he asked.

"I need to just stay here. Thank you for your help. Goodbye," I said, stepping around him and running off again. He grabbed my shoulders. My feet roamed in the air for a few seconds like a cartoon character that hadn't realized they'd stopped running. "Nate, let me go. Please."

He threw me over his shoulder and groaned. His strong arm braced against my legs. I had to make him believe me, or else the world would be stuck this way.

"You have scars on your back. Four slash marks."

"So you're psychic. Whoop-de-do. Like every other person in your territory."

"Powers don't work on you. People can't read you. I never could in our old life."

He stopped in his tracks and pulled me down from his shoulder. The rain picked up again, drenching us both. "I've never told anyone that."

"You told me!" He studied me, gazing from my feet to my head then down again. "My name is Christine Gavin. You know me as Christine Grant. You are a shifter. Canine. Your parents are John and Theresa Reece. You don't like them very much. You think you were born with those marks on your back, but I don't believe it." I wiped my face of tears and rain. It was soaked again in another moment. "You are my boyfriend, and the world is not like this. If you just let me go, I can fix it."

He circled me in the rain; the girl who was awed by it tugged at me still. To keep her weak, I stared into his eyes, remembering the moment I saw them first. In New Orleans with Sophia—the woman I couldn't forget.

"I think you're crazy," he whispered, rain cascading from the lips I'd kissed a million times. For hours. Many times until the sun had come up.

"I sort of am," I said. I was more than sort of crazy. It wasn't my history with depression. It wasn't possibly inheriting another dose of it and a pinch of psychosis from my mother. It was the fact that I was deluded enough to think changing the past would give me everything I wanted.

"I never take my shirt off in front of anyone. Ever. How do you know about the scars?"

"I've seen them. Countless times." I smiled. "You hate wearing shirts. You feel better out of one."

He smiled slightly then it melted away, faded as the rain trickled down his face. "I could get a lot of food for you. Days worth."

"Close your eyes and let me walk away. I'll just disappear. Please." I held out my bag. "I have food. You can take it. Just let me walk away."

I threw the bag at his chest, and he caught it.

I took off running again. I didn't get far before he caught me. His beautiful eyes locked with mine. He squinted for a moment then shook his head.

"I can't just leave you. You won't last a minute out here by yourself. You're high. You might fall or something again. I'll just watch you for the night. But after that ..."

"I just need tonight. Tomorrow, everything will be okay again." He took off his raincoat and threw it over my shoulders. He was still staring into my eyes, like he was searching for my soul, as he pulled the hood over my head. "Thanks, Nate."

"No one calls me that," he said.

"Not even *Shannon*?" I asked, whining her name like a five-year-old.

He chuckled and helped me over the stream again, or it could have been a different one. I had no sense of direction, completely lost and at the mercy of my soul mate.

CHAPTER EIGHTEEN

He seemed to relax more and more as we walked around the enchanted forest.

"So what is it that you're on again?" he asked. I glared at him, and he laughed. "Just saying … you might know some stuff about me, but you're obviously high. You don't even seem to know where you are."

"I *don't* know where I am. Well, other than that we're in the Congo."

He laughed. "Please, stop calling it that. You sound ridiculous. You know what? I'm going to show you where you are. I bet that would sober you right up."

He made a sharp left turn, looking up at the stars as if they were guiding him. The ground grew steeper and harder under my feet. Soon we were full out climbing up a hill. My foot caught on a vine, and he grabbed my arm before I fell. He pulled me up to his back and carried me the rest of the way.

I closed my eyes, resting my nose against his back. Tears streamed slowly. I had to fix this. This could not be the last time I held him.

He had to pull me away at the top of the hill.

"Okay. That way," he said, pointing to our right. "That's Julian's territory that he won from Dreco. That's where you live when you're not getting high."

I chuckled. "You honestly think I'm a drug addict?"

"You honestly don't remember just confessing that?"

I hunched my shoulders, and he pointed to our right again. In the distance, lights flickered, the signs of a vibrant city. "His territory stretches to the ocean. I've been. It's incredible. Not nearly as crowded as our side. Only five million people live there, the last I heard. They did well with their land. You know … it reminds me of old pictures of … what was that place called?"

"New York?" I suggested.

"That's it."

From here, the buildings looked like they were made of glass, reflecting glowing lights. But it was silent. Impossibly silent to say we were so close. It sounded like there were no cars or buses honking or rumbling. I shook my head, realizing they wouldn't need those things. They moved around with their minds.

"I hear it's not as fun as that place was since Julian has a major stick up his butt."

As fun as that place *was*? I willed my heart to keep beating and my legs to not give out. This battle to stay upright and not fold under the crushing guilt was the hardest thing I'd ever done.

"How'd he win it?" I asked.

"WW Four," he said, looking up and letting the rain wash over his face. "The inevitable clash between the human freaks and magical kind. No offense."

"None taken," I said. "Do you mean WW as in World War?" He nodded. "And Julian won?"

"It was a draw so they split the part of the world they hadn't bombed to death. The two men fighting over world domination were only left with a piece of that world to rule. Isn't that funny?"

It wasn't funny. He wasn't laughing either.

He pointed to our left to the city lit by fire. "We just came from the edge of Dreco's territory. Lower side. We have more land than you, but it's not as nice as yours. Dreco is stricter than Julian on what we can build and create." Like my Nate, he made me laugh in a serious moment, sticking out his tongue farther than necessary to taste the rain. "You laugh a lot. The drugs?"

"Maybe it's the bathrobe you're wearing," I said.

"A jokester. Okay. I like that." I copied him and tasted the rain too. "Are you sobering up?"

"Yep."

"Good. Do you remember if you stay in one of those shiny buildings? Do you have electricity?" I didn't answer because I couldn't. To keep myself from crying, I kept collecting water in my mouth. "You must. Look at you." I glanced over at him. He was staring at me, and when I let myself look at him, I couldn't stop. "I'm not *too* jealous. I suppose we live similar lives minus the hot water and television." He sighed and whispered, "And food."

"You don't have food?" I asked.

"Not every day." So that was the problem his girlfriend—*ouch*—had mentioned. And the little fairy-thingy, Olivia. "Sometimes Shannon's magic is on the fritz, or she stays out late. Or I'm watching Corey and he takes it all. It's just something about kids, even if they've eaten already that day, you still want to feed them. I have friends I could eat by but …"

"You hate mooching," I finished. He looked down at me with narrowed eyes. He took a deep breath and let it out in a sigh. "You don't have money or anything to trade?" I asked.

"I do okay. The taxes are outrageous, though. You know, we pay Dreco because we live here, then a portion to Julian to keep the peace. What's left over is just enough for court fees."

"Court fees?"

"Yeah. Shannon and I were caught trying to use a spell to create shelter a few years ago. It was really her, but I was there. So ... we owe the court a few tons of gold." He laughed and shook his head like he was ashamed of that. I was the one who needed to be ashamed. I'd done this to him. To everyone. "I could be eating like a king if I'd turned you in, you know?"

"There's meat in there."

"I'd feel like a jerk if I took your food. You're like a stray cat you just want to help. A really high, stray cat."

I laughed. Because he was so *him* right now, I risked it and asked, "How about we share it?"

He smiled and bent down in front of me, telling me to hop onto his back. He held my legs tight around his waist and jumped down from the hill. I leaned my head back as we sped to the ground, and the imprisoned girl smiled. She felt so free with this stranger—*no,* Nate. I was with *my* Nate.

The boy I loved. The boy Sophia introduced me to. I held the memory of her close to my heart, hoping it would guard it.

He ran, turning the beautiful forest into a blur of colors, and stopped in front of a shed.

"My house," he said. "Welcome, uh ..."

"You remember my name."

"Christine," he said, letting me down and flashing his sneaky smile.

He stepped in first and struck a match. Soon, the shack glowed from the flames of countless candles. Multicolored wax covered the surfaces of his home from years of burning them for light. It was easy to be in love in a place like this. It was the perfect night. Rescued by a stranger, not turned in, and now we stood in a cozy cabin with light dancing around us.

Not a stranger. I cringed. My memories were fading faster, flickering on and off like a dying light bulb.

We dripped on the floor that had gaps between each wooden board. I could see the soil underneath us and the little plants growing up to fill the openings. I sat down and rubbed the leaves of a plant that looked a lot like Sprout. To test where I thought I was, I yanked at the leaf. It didn't snap.

How my parents managed to build a house inside of a rock in the Congo, I couldn't even begin to understand.

"So tell me about this parallel universe your drugs bring you to," he said, rummaging through a cabinet in the kitchen. He pulled out a towel and pitched it to me.

"How many times do I need to tell you that I'm not on drugs?"

"Actually you told me you weren't, then that you were. Look, I'm not judging you. Everyone does it. Not me. Not yet, anyway. My friends say it's easier looking at this world when it spins around you. I've given myself a year and a half before I become an addict. Twenty is a personal goal of mine."

Twenty?

"Right, your real birthday wasn't a few weeks ago," I mumbled. "When was it? When did you make eighteen?"

He hummed. "Shouldn't you know your boyfriend's birthday?"

"John and Theresa told you the wrong day." He arched one eyebrow. "In our life you don't know when it is."

"January 24th," he said.

"I'll tell you tomorrow." He laughed and jumped up on the rickety countertop surrounding a rusty sink.

"Are we speaking of my parallel self?" he asked. I nodded and dried my hair. "Tell me about this Nate who doesn't know his birthday."

"*You* are kind. Goofy. Like very goofy. Sweeter than anyone I've ever met. Even Sophia. You have her beat. You are as beautiful on the inside as you are on the outside." I buried my face in the towel, losing it. "You love me. Before anyone showed me they loved me, you did. And you snore." I jerked my head up and pointed a finger at him. "You swear you don't but you do. Every single night."

He laughed, and I wanted to die at the sound.

I swallowed the brick out of my throat and continued. "And you're always in time, like in perfect timing and step with me and the whole world. *Always*, and it's magic to see. You smile at the right time, observe silence when it's needed. You always laugh at the perfect moment. Either from something our friend Paul says or if you fart or something."

He laughed again and of course it was perfectly placed.

"Nate sounds great. Maybe I should take those drugs with you." He chuckled and hopped down from the counter. He touched his stomach, his probably empty stomach, and I opened the bag. I spread the food on the floor. He sat across from me, and I built him a sandwich with my dirty hands. He didn't seem to mind. He sunk his teeth in without giving it a second look. "So how did you get here from your alien universe," he said, as I stacked my own sandwich.

"A portal. I changed my mother's memories and changed the whole world without meaning to."

"But ... if Nate loved you so much, why would you do that?" he asked, skeptically, like he'd found a flaw in my story. He'd really found a flaw in me. Like Dad said, I only saw the bad.

I looked up at him, crumbling to tears again. "I'm sorry, baby. I was just trying to fix things, and I thought you'd always be there."

"Call me Nathan." I rolled my eyes. "Seriously, Christine. I don't want to hurt your feelings. This guy, whoever he is, seems important to you, but I'm not him. You'll see when you sober up."

He lay back on the floor. I watched as his face showed what was going on inside of his head. Nate was guilty for having me here. Maybe it was too soon after his breakup or the fact that I was human.

"Why do you live in the forest?" I asked to change the subject and lighten the mood.

"I work here. It's protected land. I make sure no one is trying to live here without authorization. I've been doing that for about four years now." He wasn't very good at his job. My parents and I lived here without authorization. He sighed and turned over on his side, propping himself up on his elbow. "And I live here because it's peaceful. I used to run away to this place when I was a kid at least once a week. Finally, Dreco's guards offered me a job. They told me I was perfect for it. They didn't have to pay me much, I can live in any climate, and they didn't have to fix this place up. It doesn't bother me because it's mine." He smiled, eyes fixed on the floor, like these were happy memories from his life in this awful world.

"Is that why the guy said you were weird about this forest?"

"Ellis? Corey's dad?" I nodded. "Yeah. He's not the only one I know who thinks that. Everyone does. They're wrong though. I don't feel like I own it. I feel drawn to it. Like there's no other place for me to be. I belong here."

I wanted to crawl on top of him, kiss him and show him why he couldn't stay away from the forest. "It's me," I whispered instead. "I live here. You're drawn to me." He sat up and packed the food in my bag. It felt like I was losing him. "I smell good to you, don't I?" He packed slower and looked at me for a moment, then back at the floor. "Like cake batter and spice."

I lost him then.

He jumped to his feet and disappeared into the small hallway without answering. In the five minutes that he was gone, I finished packing my getaway bag and tried to dry the rest of the water out of my hair.

I kissed the necklace and tucked it back into my shirt. It was my only hope.

At the door, ready to disappear into the night to stop badgering my soul mate, I looked around his little home. It was charming in a way. Like him—impoverished and severely uncared for, but sturdy and beautiful despite it all.

"I'm leaving the food," I said, dropping the bag when I thought to do that. "Have a good night."

"Wait. That's dangerous," he said, from wherever he was. "Someone will capture you and God only knows where you'll end up this time." He leaned halfway in the room with me, half in the hall. "I have some dry clothes if you want them."

I nodded, and he disappeared again. I walked back there slowly. He was in a little bedroom only big enough for his worn, full-size bed.

He fished through a pile of clothes and gave me a red and blue button-down shirt and a pair of large gray sweats.

"You have normal clothes, but the people we saw … they didn't. Why?"

"Normal?" I nodded. "These are just old. Donated. They were free because they probably came from the raids. Human ones. Sorry."

I hunched my shoulders. It wasn't his fault that normal humans were extinct. It was mine.

"Bathroom," he said, pointing to a curtain behind me. I pulled it back slowly. By bathroom he'd meant a hole in the wall that happened to have a stand up shower and a toilet.

I pulled off my wet clothes and stepped into his shower, ignoring the different towels hanging on the rack and stopping myself from wondering which were Shannon's. The water never warmed, so I jumped out when it felt like the grossness of the day was on its way— rather sluggishly—down the drain.

There was one messily folded towel on the back of the toilet. It was dry, so I used it.

His shirt came to my thighs. If we were in California in our old life, I'd consider going out there like this. But I'd traded that life, so I put on his pants.

He was just pulling up a dry pair of jeans as I stepped out. He scrambled for a shirt, awkwardly throwing his arm across his back before turning it away from me. I chuckled. "You don't have to hide your scars. I told you I've seen them. I'm surprised you're self-conscious about them."

We walked out of his bedroom, wonderfully close together in the narrow hall. "Why are you surprised?" he asked.

"Because the scars don't bother you in our old life. You like when I touch them."

He cleared his throat, and I gave him the space his expression said he needed from me. Avoiding the leaks in the roof, I toured his little home. It looked like a child had built it two hundred years ago. The wood used to be a few colors, most recently a greenish-blue. It reminded me of the pool house in a way—the way he kept things, in an order only he saw in his mind. I knew he'd meant for the tattered armchair to be slightly crooked.

Testing him, I nudged it with my knee as I passed it. Slowly, he walked behind me and nudged it back to its crooked place.

I laughed. He was *so* my Nate. Time and this awful world hadn't changed him a bit.

"What's funny?" he asked.

"Oh ... nothing. Um ... why don't you two have pictures? Don't happy couples have pictures?"

"I don't know how happy we are. *Were.* But even if things were perfect, we wouldn't have pictures. Do you have any idea how much a camera costs on Julian's side? I saw one at the Common Market once. Ten whole old world dollars."

I laughed and spun around with my eyes closed, enjoying the light moment in the midst of pure death. "Ten dollars is a lot of money to you in our old life, too. Even though no one else would think that, you would."

"And that amuses you? My poverty?"

"No. It's just funny today. Not so much before I jumped through the portal. Money, or the lack of it, was sort of an issue in our relationship. I bought you a car."

"A what?" I rolled my head dramatically around my neck. "Like ... a vehicle thing? A human thing?"

"Yes, Nate." I chuckled. "A human thing. Oh, dear God, I need the sun!"

I plopped down on a worn little sofa that looked like someone had left it outside in the trash. The green and white flowers gave me vibes from the '70s. So did the mildew smell coming from it. To keep warm, I pulled my arms inside Nate's shirt and huddled my knees under it, too.

"It gets pretty cold some nights. This forest has a mind of its own. I could make you a fire," he said.

He threw a few logs into a little fireplace that looked way too small to contain real flames. But I wasn't afraid. Even though this Nathan was a stranger, I felt completely safe with him.

I remembered my wet clothes and undies in this bathroom. I hoped Shannon wasn't planning to come over. I didn't think I'd win that fight. And there would definitely be a fight because Nate was still shirtless and unbearably sexy, leaning over the little fireplace to make me warm. He didn't need the fire. I wanted out of these clothes as I stared at him.

"There was water in your bag. Do you want one?" he asked.

"Sure."

He threw his bundled shirt over his shoulder, like he'd decided not to wear it, and brought me a bottle of water.

"This plastic looks so clean. Did you boil it or something?"

I shook my head. I didn't even know what that meant. I took one sip and lay down on the smelly sofa, soaking in the warmth of the flames and following Nate around the room with my eyes.

He leaned his head back, tilting water into his mouth, making his body curve in a way that twisted my stomach in painful knots. He moaned. "That's … *really* clean water," he said, like it was pure gold. He inhaled the rest of his bottle as I stared at the lines on him. I needed to touch him. Stupid Shannon. How could she want to dance to folk music more than being in this charming house with this sexy boy?

When he'd emptied his bottle, he stared at it almost in regret. Maybe for drinking it so quickly.

"Want mine?" I asked.

"No, it's fine. Drink up."

"Come on. You know you want it. Just take it," I said, holding out the bottle to him. He just stared, at me, not the water. He shook his head fast and crossed the invisible line that marked the beginning of the kitchen.

He returned with more water in his bottle, browner water.

"You're nervous," I said, because I knew him better than anyone. He didn't pace when he was nervous. He was always overly normal, doing things that wouldn't be out of the ordinary for no reason at all. Like looking out of the window and drinking water just a little too intently. "Relax."

"How? I brought a human to my house. I'm worried that someone will come barging in at any moment and ... take you. " He sighed. "Which is stupid, since I just met you."

"Are you saying that you care about me?" I asked.

"No." Clearly a lie. I chuckled, and he glanced over his shoulder to me. It took him a moment, but he smiled. It took every ounce of restraint I possessed to stay seated. "What would Nate think about you caring if I cared about you?"

His tone was blatantly flirtatious. It made me giggle like an idiot. "What would Shannon say about you sounding jealous?" I asked. "Of yourself, might I add?"

"She wouldn't be surprised. I'm jealous of everything and everyone, according to her."

He sat on the floor in front of the fire and rolled over to his stomach, his head on his arms. He closed his eyes and breathed in deep, pressing his nose against his skin. "I like talking to you, " he whispered. It sounded like a confession, a guiltless, honest confession.

"Me too. "

"I was never going to turn you in. It takes about three days to walk to the human border. I thought … maybe you just needed some time to sober up and someone to talk to."

"Wow. I didn't get that at all. You seemed sort of annoyed with me at first."

"You *are* annoying. In a really adorable way." I laughed, and he peeked his incredibly cute eyes over his arm. "In the way that bunnies are adorable. I didn't mean anything by that. "

"Whatever, Nate. "

We sat in peaceful silence until my teeth started hammering.

"I'll bring you a blanket," he said, as he pushed himself up from the floor, uselessly and wonderfully flexing his muscles in the process. He slammed doors and ruffled things in his room for a while.

He eased into the living room with an odd look on his face. Apprehension, maybe. He cradled a fur blanket in his arms, being careful like it was precious to him, and stared into my eyes as he covered me with it. We'd had a lot of intense moments together, sliding down the slippery slope, but the seconds it took for him to cover me topped them all.

"It's the only family heirloom I have," he said, his voice shaky and breathless. He cracked a smile and forced a chuckle. "So don't mess it up."

I was too far gone to laugh with him. I was surprised the fire raging inside of me hadn't caught on to the blanket and mildewed sofa. But it caught on to him.

He fell to his knees and pressed his forehead into my stomach. "This isn't fair," he whispered.

"What isn't?" I asked.

"I've been hearing about this from other shifters for years. What the right girl will smell like, that her scent can hook you for life. It's complete bullshit that you ... smell like you do. You're human! You're on drugs. I don't understand what I've done to be so unlucky."

He ran his fingers lazily through my hair without moving his head. I didn't know if I should smile or cry or kiss him. He wasn't the real Nathan, and he seemed very distraught over how my scent made him feel, all of him but the hand in my hair.

"What do you mean?" I asked. "Why are you unlucky?"

"What else would you call smelling something heavenly fall from a rock and trading her for something I really can't afford, then breaking up with my girlfriend because she smelled sad when we kissed?" He paused and I smiled, elated that he'd broken up with Shannon for me. "And now I can't move. I shouldn't have gotten this close to your scent. I literally can't move."

I twisted my fingers in his hair, and he groaned.

The girl who had always lived in this world tugged at me. She wanted to claim this stranger as hers and stay with him forever. The world was nothing like she thought it would be, not happy and free, but there were more wonderful things in it than Snowflake. There were handsome boys who turned into dogs when they wanted to.

No. I pushed her away again. I had to hang on to my real self until twelve tomorrow or the necklace wouldn't work.

"You don't have powers, do you?" he asked. He looked up at me, and I shook my head. "You're going to get me killed. This is *so* bad. I need to go apologize to Shannon, turn you in, and get back to my life. I can't … feel this way about you. Not this fast."

"How do you feel?" I asked, wanting to hear him admit it.

"Like you're mine."

I became very aware of my lip between my teeth and that his eyes hadn't moved from it. He stretched his hand over my cheek. I leaned into it and closed my eyes. I puckered for the kiss that my lips felt coming, buzzing in anticipation.

When the moment fluttered away without it happening, I opened my eyes.

"You are a stranger," he said. "And I am a sensible person. I'm going to bed." He pulled my hands from his hair and moved away from me. He blew out the candles, one by one, slowly casting us into darkness. "Please leave in the morning. I patrol the forest at nine." He pointed to the decrepit clock on the wall in his kitchen. "Make sure you're gone before then."

He lifted his hand and waved slightly, only lit by the dying glow of the fire.

The storm picked up again when he left, rocking the little shed. Thunder rattled the walls, and a new leak seeped through the roof, right above my head. I flipped to the other end and hid under the blanket.

The rain masked the sound of his shower, but I heard the knobs squeak off and the curtain open. Wiping my drool, I tried to think of anything other than my sexy boyfriend's body double in that room wearing nothing.

The rain eventually made the sofa inhospitable. I took the blanket and huddled next to the fire.

The necklace was cold against my skin. I closed my eyes and thought about Sophia, begging myself to remember her—her hair, her laugh, how many times she'd barged in on me in the bathroom and held a conversation like we were in the park.

"Sophia Ewing," I said. "I remember you."

I clutched the necklace and watched the fire crackle. Something moved in the corner of my eye, red hair blowing past the window. I blinked and it was gone.

I stared out of the dirty window for minutes and saw nothing. Heard nothing. Surely if a girl had seen another girl in the house with her ex-boyfriend of a few hours, she would have done more than pass by the window.

"I'm being paranoid," I whispered, and went back to the fire.

I sighed. There was no fire. Not anymore. I stretched out on the floor as the last of the flames died out. And now I was freezing.

After ten minutes of shivering, Nate tiptoed into the living room and picked me up from the floor. I couldn't look at him. I would have kissed him if I had.

"I can't let you freeze out here. Do you trust me not to try anything?" he whispered. I nodded against his chest. He was still shirtless.

He laid me on the bed, wrapped in my own blanket, and pushed in close behind me. "Tell me when you're warm."

"Okay," I said, knowing I wouldn't. I wanted him to hold me all night.

I closed my eyes. Everything in me wanted to turn around. All of my heart. My brain. Every inch of my skin.

As the longing for him grew, I felt myself slipping away.

Years of wanting something like this bombarded me and crushed me into his thin mattress. I'd talked to Snowflake countless times about the person I'd fall in love with. I couldn't have dreamed a better guy. Gorgeous and caring and newly single.

Mom had told me once that she loved Dad from the moment she first saw him. Fast, intense, and forever. That was love, and I felt it for the guy holding me in his bed.

"How does Nate sleep with you every night with you this close to his nose?" he asked.

Nate. God, I'd almost let him slip away. "Maybe he's used to it."

"That doesn't seem possible," he said. He worked his feet under my blanket and enclosed mine between his at the exact moment I needed him to, when I thought they'd freeze and snap from the bone. I knew I had no hope of hiding how the foot rub made me feel, so I didn't. I curled my toes against his skin, shuddering and feeling him do the same behind me. "He's lucky to have you. Is he a drug addict, too?"

"Shut up! He's not. I'm not either."

We laughed. The motion somehow brought us closer in bed, and he slipped one of his legs under the blanket with me.

To keep the real Christine from slipping away, melting into him, I told him about my plan to fix things and Sophia's instructions involving the necklace and knife he couldn't see.

For what felt like hours, we talked about his world and mine. It became increasingly difficult to decipher which was real or not. He felt so real next to me.

To help with my memory, I told him about every date, which led to every kiss, then to exactly how far down the slippery slope we'd gotten. With every plummet, he inched closer until he was completely under the blanket with me, pressed against my back. His arm slowly wrapped around my waist, and I had no choice but to turn to him.

My lips brushed his and he pulled away. "I'm not him. I'm not the guy you love."

"You are." He rolled over, and I followed him. "Turn around."

"I can't. I can't look at you. " I scooted closer and pressed my face against his back. "Christine, please move. I'm really confused right now, and I need to be alone."

"Do you want me to leave?" I asked, unable to keep my hands still on his sides.

"No. Yes. No." I tightened my arms around him. "Just go to that side of the bed. I can't do this. You're not mine. You're crazy and high, and when you sober up, I'm going to go back to being with a girl who only wants to be with me sometimes. Please. Stop touching me. I'm sorry."

"Fine," I said, giving up, dizzy from his mixed signals. "For the record, Nate, I *am* yours."

I kissed his scars softly before rolling away, just to torture him. He rolled to the other side of the bed with me, and I laughed. I wanted to see what our dance looked like, pulling closer, then repelling, only to find each other again.

"You don't think the scars make me look crazy and damaged?" he asked. I shook my head. "Shannon thinks so."

"I hate her!"

He moaned. "I think Nate might fight with you on purpose. You smell even better angry."

I turned around in his arms, and he didn't try to get away. "If I really didn't know you … why would I be in your bed with you like this?" I whispered, close enough that the words brushed against his lips. "You have to believe me."

For a moment, it looked like he was going to say something smart, but his eyes lingered too long on my lips, and we both forgot that we were talking at all.

The kiss started slowly—so slowly that we could've pulled away, continued the dance, and pretended nothing had happened. But then he rolled on top of me and kissed me harder.

The world, both of them, paused as both versions of me got exactly what they needed. His lips on mine, a joy I'd both never felt and thought I'd lost forever. Nothing compared to it. No memory of us. No lonely desire for this. Nate and Nathan, my soul mate and the kind stranger, all melded into one as he clutched me in bed.

As I both memorized and remembered the taste of his lips, I rubbed my fingers up and down his back.

He chuckled. "I *do* like that." I was having a hard time understanding what that meant. Whatever it was tugged at me, begged me to hold on. But I didn't want to be nagged, so I let every thought blow out of my mind and crushed myself closer to him.

"The rock you fell from," he said, breaking our kiss and panting. "I sit there all the time. I've been sitting there for years. Sometimes I sleep there. I stay there all night, waiting for something. For you."

I twisted my fingers in his hair, and pulled his lips back to mine. "I'm glad you were there tonight. You saved me."

My heart warmed, thinking of this perfect guy waiting outside of my prison. Waiting to rescue me.

"Stay with me," he said. "It feels like I've wanted to be with you, exactly you, for my entire life. Please don't leave." We kissed for a while as I tried to formulate a response. I was trying to remember why I couldn't stay. "I know I'm asking a lot, but you're my mate. That's why you smell like this to me. I'm begging you to give up everything, the drugs, your boyfriend, everything, and stay."

"I'm not on drugs," I said. "And you're my boyfriend, Nathan. Isn't this what couples do?"

He kissed me again and smiled against my lips. "I am? This me? The real me?" I nodded. "So you're staying?"

I couldn't think of one reason to leave him. Where else would I go? Who else could I ever want to be with?

"Forever," I said, breathless and falling into another kiss.

CHAPTER NINETEEN

"Just give me a minute," Nathan said.

He kneeled in the corner of his kitchen, digging under a loose board. I dodged the water streaming into the room with us. It was a stormy morning. Stormy, but beautiful. Apparently, Nathan kept his eggs in the soil. He'd been digging for a few minutes, the longest we'd been apart since last night.

"I thought you said you had to go to work," I said.

"I did, but that was before a certain someone completed my life." He turned around and made a silly face, reaching his tongue out of his mouth and crossing his eyes. I laughed. He reminded me of a cartoon character, zany and wonderful and capable of getting hit with an anvil or worse without being seriously injured. Hilarious and indestructible. Maybe that was why he wasn't afraid to harbor a human. Forever, as he'd promised last night. "Found them!"

He unearthed two tiny eggs, way smaller than the ones Mom and Dad used for breakfast.

"I bet they'll be wonderful," I said.

He picked me up and spun me around the kitchen, kissing again like we'd done all night. That somehow led us to the floor. We forgot about the eggs for a while as our kiss went from soft to rough to soft again.

We stopped when we heard shells cracking.

"Oh no!" he said. I laughed. "It was all I had, babe. I'll have to go into town to trade something. I need to get my things from Shannon's place anyway."

"Can I come?"

He winced and bit his lip. "That's probably not a good idea." My heart sank, and he sniffed. He frowned and kissed my cheek. "What's wrong?"

"Don't hide me," I whispered. "Please. My parents hid me. Last night was my first time out of the house. Please … don't do the same thing."

He narrowed his eyes. He looked like he was about to ask for more information, but he sniffed the air around my face and kissed me yet again. "Don't be sad. I can't take what you smell like when you're sad. What would make you happy?"

I had two options—going back to bed or going to explore the new, outside world with him. We must've kissed for longer than I'd thought because it wasn't raining anymore. Since we'd thoroughly explored the bed last night, only stopping when he'd said he didn't want our first time to be on the night we met, I pointed to the door.

"I want to play outside."

I felt five-years old. I was sure I had said that very sentence when I was younger, and my parents had scared me with gruesome stories about monsters. If only they'd let me go a few feet out of our home, I would've found my love way sooner.

"Then play outside, we shall." He led me through the door. He tapped my shoulder and ran. "Tag!" he yelled, darting through the trees.

I knew I couldn't catch him. He moved so fast that his body blurred. I took my time to find him, touching every living thing in my path and watching the birds fly over my head.

They were so beautiful. I had to stop. I was crying too hard to keep playing. Spending your entire life locked in a house with your parents will do that to you, I guessed, make mundane things the most beautiful sight in the world.

I almost didn't feel the arms wrapping around me, too entranced by the sky and the black dots fluttering in it.

"Honey!" Dad screamed. His voice jerked me out of the sky. I screamed and scratched at his hands, trying to free myself. "I've been looking for you all night."

"Nathan! Nathan!"

"Come on, sweetie," Dad said. "Don't fight me. There are guards in the forest. I saw them. You're not safe here."

I didn't care about guards or anything other than getting away from him so I didn't have to go back to that house. Nathan ran to me and yanked me away from Dad. His human strength was no match for my new boyfriend.

"I can explain," Nate said. "Are you a guard?"

"No, I'm her father. Let her go!"

I clung to Nathan and Dad wrapped an arm around my stomach and tried to pry me away from my knight in shining armor. "Run, Nathan. He's going to bring me home and lock me inside the rock again. Please. I'll never see you again. He's crazy. My mom is, too."

I looked around for her. I knew she couldn't be too far behind, waiting to scream at me and act like a maniac.

"Please, Dad. I don't want to go back. Tell Mom where I am and that I found someone. Please."

"Mom is gone." His voice broke and he stumbled back. "Last night we were watching a movie and all of a sudden ..." He shook his head to suffice for the rest of his sentence. "That's how I knew something had happened to you. And I ran out, left her there, because I knew she'd want me to find you." Dad covered his face, crying fiercely, unraveling quickly. "She told me she took it back. After your tub incident, she promised. She lied to me."

I climbed out of Nathan's arms and met my father on the ground. I wiped his cheeks with my thumbs.

I remembered the tub incident he spoke of. Mom had locked the doors to the pool because I'd been too upset that day. So I'd locked my bedroom door and tried to drown myself in the tub. That was why I didn't have running water in my bathroom. I'd held myself under for minutes and minutes, breathing normally, not dying like I wanted to. Then Dad had kicked my door in and yanked me out. It had taken Mom almost an hour to stop coughing.

"What are you saying?" I asked.

"Your mother ... *my wife* ... is dead. It happened last night when you ... escaped."

Neither of my parents had explained why I didn't die in that tub. I vaguely remembered a connection between my mother's life and my own. The fall should've killed me, but it had killed her instead. But how?

It felt like I'd forgotten something, something important.

"We need to go home," Dad whispered, without moving from the ground. His eyes were detached like he was no longer himself, like he'd only said that because it was what he thought he should say.

"What's going on?" Nathan asked.

I turned around slowly. "I think I killed my mother."

Dad stretched out on the leaves, clutching his chest like it was about to explode. He screamed her name to the top of his lungs, louder and louder, as if calling her would bring her back. I wanted to shatter on the ground with him, I loved her and I was responsible for her death, but the sound of footsteps racing our way stopped me.

"Shannon," Nathan said, his nose in the air like he'd caught her scent. "And guards. She must've called them. Maybe she saw us together."

"Dad, get up. We have to run."

He didn't move. I wondered if he'd heard me at all. He was still screaming his wife's name as he bawled.

"You promised me," he cried. "Lyd, you promised me you would take your soul back."

Her soul.

I had my mother's soul.

The sun peeked through the trees above us. I vaguely remembered wanting it to come. The footsteps grew louder and Nathan picked me up. "We can't leave my dad," I said.

"Let whoever it is take me," he cried. "Run, baby. Go."

"No! Dad!"

He stood with his head hanging low and walked towards the sound of racing feet, resigning. Giving up on life. I tried to run after him, but Nathan braced me against his chest and ran. Dad howled in the distance, and I screamed for my father.

I didn't stop screaming until Nathan put me down in his kitchen. He hooked the flimsy lock on the door and raced to his room.

"We'll pack. We'll go on the run. It'll be fine, baby." I couldn't do this to him, the same thing I'd done to my parents—disrupt his life and make him live in hiding. "It's nearly noon. If we get past these guards, it'll be hours until we see another. We could get really far."

Nearly noon.

Something beat against my chest, begging me to see, begging me to notice it. I brought my hand to my heart and felt the cold necklace there.

"What is this?" I asked. Nathan didn't answer. He was busy stuffing clothes in a plastic bag.

I blinked and the necklace disappeared. For some reason, that made me panic. I patted my chest until I found it again. I held on tight this time. I didn't want to lose it.

I … I needed it.

I needed it to fix things.

To get my old life back.

"It's noon!" I screamed. I scrambled to find the boots I'd taken off and nearly forgotten. I found the knife and raced to the door.

Dreco's guards were dressed in purple cloaks. One of them had blood on his hands, likely my father's.

The redhead stood in the middle of them and pointed to me.

"There," she said. "That's the human Nathan Reece is harboring. I watched them through his window."

The cloaked figures pressed in and Nate barged through the doors.

The sun gleaned over our heads, and I slid the knife over my palm. Nate tried to grab it, but it was too late. My blood pooled in the center of my hand and I let it drip over the pendant.

There was something else. Something I needed to remember.

My heart crashed in my chest as the guards grabbed us. One of them snapped, and Nate growled.

Snapped.

Magic.

Sophia Ewing.

The yellow jewel glowed, and the necklace shook in my hand.

"I wish I hadn't used the portal," I screamed.

I closed my eyes, begging the magic to work.

The hands around my neck squeezed and squeezed until I could no longer stand.

CHAPTER TWENTY

And then there was nothing. No me. No them. No him. The past and the present crashed into one, deleting all of our futures.

CHAPTER TWENTY-ONE

"Don't do this, honey," Mom said. "We can make this life work."

I opened my eyes in the pool, clutching my mother.

My life. My old life!

"You don't have to do this," she said. "We'll make it work. I swear." I was having trouble forming coherent thoughts, let alone speaking actual words.

The first thing I was able to say was, "Okay."

"Okay?"

"You're right. I should stop. It won't work." She nodded and slipped out of my arms. I grabbed her shoulders and pulled her up again. "The life we have is enough. You made the right choice. I'm sorry. I plead temporary insanity."

She inhaled loudly, like she could suddenly breathe again now that we weren't in danger of me ending the world.

"Then let's go home," she said.

I smiled, and for the quickest moment, I thought I saw a shadow against the white bricks of my home. Fireworks exploded above us and stole my attention. After they fizzled out, I brought my eyes back to the bricks and saw nothing.

I transported us out of the water and back to Sophia's house.

She was there in Emma's old room, waiting for us. I laid Mom on the bed and ran to her.

"Thank you," I said, clutching her in a tight hug.

In my ear, she whispered, "Let's wait to tell your mother about this. We'll discuss your punishment later."

She swatted my butt. I didn't pout. Whatever she would do, spank me, ground me, I would deserve it.

I smiled and stretched out on the bed next to Mom, dripping and exhausted from the last few days that never happened.

"While you two were out taking a swim, you got a call, Lydia. You're needed at the office in an hour."

"Yippie," Mom said with no enthusiasm at all.

She lay on her back with her eyes fixed on the ceiling, muscles still lax from Kamon's drugs. It was quiet except for her breaths for a while. Slowly, she kicked her legs, then wiggled her arms, coming back to life.

"Thanks for disobeying me, angel. They would've opened the portal or I would've drowned if you hadn't been there."

"Don't thank me," I whispered.

"No. You're my little hero."

"Baby!" Dad yelled, bursting through the doors. "I have been going out of my mind. Why did you run off like that?"

He kneeled on my side of the bed. I crawled into his arms, appreciating this dad, the stronger dad, more than I had before.

"She ran off to save my life," Mom said.

"I distinctly remember asking you not to talk to me," he spat.

His words sliced through me, and I ignored the pain. Their relationship couldn't be salvaged, and from what I'd just lived through, I'd say we were all better off with them not speaking.

I cringed. I still had the memories from the life that didn't happen, the countless times I'd seen them make out and *more*. I still wasn't over it.

"Hero," Mom said to me. "We need to discuss something." I turned around in Dad's arms to face her. "I'm disappointed in you. The fighting. The fire. You nearly gave me a heart attack. Do not ever do that again. You could've killed someone tonight. Just because they are copies, doesn't make it okay. They are people, and I never want you to know what taking a life feels like. Do you understand me?"

I nodded silently, remembering how it felt to be a monster. Leah's pain had nothing on what it actually felt like to know I'd killed so many people.

Sophia handed me a vial of my kryptonite, and I tossed it back without complaining. I'd used my powers to fight Kamon and three copies and had won and ended the world. I was too strong for my own good.

But that was over now. So was the threat of July 4th. I prayed that I would get to keep Mom for many days and nights to come.

"So, how about we talk about my classes for Trenton tomorrow, Mom?"

She smiled and slowly stood to her feet. "I'd like that. Have fun tonight."

"Where?" I asked.

"Wherever the guy who doesn't want me to talk to him wanted to bring you tonight."

I screamed and dad clutched me like we'd won the lottery. Really, I'd won more than the lottery. Redemption felt sweet. The relief of escaping that world was almost too amazing, like I didn't fully deserve it after being so stupid.

Sophia put an arm around her waist, helping her stand. Neither of them looked me in the eye as Mom staggered, clearly not in good shape. And she had to return to her life as the famous woman in an hour.

But that was better than her life as a psycho, knife-wielding, prison warden.

I hugged Mom goodbye, and Sophia took Dad and me to our perspective homes. From now on, it would have to be okay that we didn't live together.

I called Nate several times, only to get his voicemail. I hoped he was still on his way. I wanted to explain the misunderstanding in person and also tell him the truth about my parents.

In the shower, I seriously considered asking Mom and Sophia if mental powers could be removed so that I could finally be normal and never kill the human race again.

As I pulled on a patriotic outfit, denim jeans and a red tank top, I heard a sudden commotion in the hall.

"Nathan, calm down," Paul said. "We're here. Just relax."

"You relax! If some dude answered Em's phone and yelled at you, you'd be pissed, too!"

I ran into the hall and jumped in his arms. It seemed to diffuse him completely. With a little less anger and a little more hurt, he said, "Where is he?"

"We need to talk," I said.

He groaned. "Don't break up with me. Give me a chance, Chris. Is it the job? Devin let me take off to come see you. I can do that more.

Are you mad—" I kissed him so he would stop being ridiculous. I would never leave him for another guy, except for his body double in the portal world. "The job isn't more important than you. Nothing is. Whoever this guy is, Chris, there's no way he loves you more than I do. It's not possible."

I chuckled. It was very possible, just a different kind of love than he thought.

"I missed you," I whispered against his lips. I took a deep breath so I could say everything at once. "Devin and Kamon opened a portal to the past, and I used it to change something my mother did. It was awful. I ruined the whole world. You had a girlfriend named Shannon, but we still fell in love. I love you. I want to be with you forever. In any time. In any life."

He chuckled. "Chris, be serious."

"I *am* serious. January 24th." He narrowed his eyes. "That's your real birthday."

"That's ... the day of my first shift. How did you..."

"You told me!"

The weirdest expression formed on his face, hints of shock and confusion with a splash of anger.

"So ... Devin. He's not who I think he is?" I shook my head and pecked his lips. He seemed crushed, like I'd crumbled his idol.

Emma squealed and pulled me out of Nathan's arms.

"I have so much to tell you," she said. "So much to show you. So much! I can't even breathe!"

"What is there to tell?" I asked. She hiked her eyebrows twice, suggesting something racy, and yanked her head to Paul. She mouthed, *Oh my God*, and I squealed. "Details. Please!" Paul cleared his throat. "Okay. Later. When *you know who* is not around. What is there to show?"

She lifted her leg to show me the butterfly now inked into her foot and its flight pattern whirling around her ankle.

"Ouch!" I said.

"It wasn't so bad. Paul got my initials, but my parents would kill me."

"Wow, Paul," I said. "Let me see."

He yanked his collar down to show me the *E. A.* inside of swirling lines on his chest. It was huge and a bit dramatic but romantic, I guessed.

"Christine, if you don't mind, I'd sort of like to talk about ... the guy you're seeing."

I laughed and motioned them to follow me to the sofa in my room.

"Tonight, we're going to Chicago," I said, mostly because I didn't want to disappoint Dad and not show up now that my friends were here. "There's a 4th of July barbecue this band is throwing. I know someone in it." Nate went deadly still and looked at the floor. "He's my father. His name is Christopher. He's not dead."

Their jaws dropped, and I nodded, trying to help them through the shock. Nate spoke first. "You mean to tell me I threatened to kill your father on the phone?" I winced and mouthed an apology. "Oh, my God."

Paul laughed and ruffled Nate's hair. "I was sitting right there, Chris. He lost his shit. He was crying. Cursing. You should've seen it."

I walked over to Nate and sat in his lap. I kissed his cheek for putting him through that. "There's more," I said. "I haven't gotten to the biggest part of the announcement. My mother is alive, too. You guys already know her. She's famous."

A silence that only Lydia Shaw could create fell over the room. Slowly, Nate's eyes widened and his jaw dropped even lower.

"Not possible," he said.

"Very possible. It's why Sophia saved me and why Lydia, my mother, has to approve my every move."

While they stared at me like an alien, I told them my family's story—from my parents' first date to our lives on the other side of the portal.

I swore them to secrecy and endured Paul calling me Mini Your Honor until Emma brought us to Chicago.

We landed in a thick of trees, close enough to hear the music and smell the food, and walked through the park towards the crowd gathered by the tables.

When I saw my dad, my face curled into a smile. I ran to him and tapped his shoulder.

He grabbed me and attacked me with kisses, and I ignored the part of me that wished Mom could be here with us.

My friends caught up to us and I introduced them, starting with Paul, then Em, saving Nate for last.

"So this is the guy who's going to kill me, right?" Dad said. I elbowed him in the side. Nate bowed his head and apologized to the sand underneath us. "Nice to meet you, Nathan."

"You, too, Christopher."

Dad gasped. "Where are your manners? It's Mr. Gavin, to you."

I elbowed Dad again.

"Sorry, Mr. Gavin."

He introduced me to Ken and Meg and their kids who called him

Uncle Gav. He hogged me from my friends until we ran out of things to do. We'd eaten, lost the three-legged race, and lit sparklers and ran around with them.

Finally he said, "Okay, go play with your pup—I mean—your boyfriend."

I kissed his cheek and met Nate by the food table. He looked like a third wheel with Paul and Em kissing under the stars.

I wrapped my arms around him, looking up at the multicolored sky.

The hairs on my arms rose, alerting me that I was being watched. I shrugged it off as Mom, refusing to let anything taint my night. I'd fought too hard to come back to this life to worry about anything.

"Let's do the race," Nate said. "Couple against couple."

"You're going down!" Paul said.

I smiled and hopped on his back, refusing to look at the hairs on my arms that were still standing on end.

EPILOGUE

NATHAN

I plopped a stack of job applications on my bed. Chris rolled on top of them. She'd made no secret of her objection to me finding a new job. Maybe because the one I had quit a week ago turned out to be a cover for a world domination plot. I was still upset with myself for ignoring the signs—that Devin smelled like garbage and blamed it on poor hygiene, and how angry he smelled if someone mentioned Lydia Shaw.

I cringed and tried not to show it on my face. I still couldn't believe that I, Nathan Thomas Nobody Reece, was dating *her* daughter. Even though it finally explained why Sophia fawned over her and why the famous woman cared to keep her hidden, I still hadn't wrapped my head around it.

"You're supposed to be getting dressed to go bowling, not filling out applications," she said.

"I *am* dressed." She pointed to my bare chest. "I will put that leash on when it's time to leave. Shirts are for humans. They're bad for my kind. Actually … shirts are bad for everyone. They are dangerous. Let me save you from yours."

I jumped on her and playfully tugged at her shirt. I tickled her, and she screamed in my ear. I loved tickling her, but not for the reason she thought. I wasn't a goofball. I was a slave to anything that made her scent burst into the air. Laughing, sweet kisses, and anything sweet kisses led to. The freshly baked spice that floated up from her skin and clung to everything she touched was my favorite thing about life. About her. It was only a bonus that she was beautiful, and hot, and everything else that made her Christine Cecilia Gavin.

My fingers scurried up her back and she kicked her legs and flailed her thin arms, trying to escape. Without her powers, since she was always mildly sedated by the potion now, she was a doll in my arms. A precious one, like if I didn't like to play with her so much, she'd be in a box at the top of a shelf so she wouldn't get hurt.

If I were lame and played with dolls, that is. Now … action figures, those were cool.

My phone rang on my dresser. I'd given my number out so many times in the past few days for jobs, that I had no choice but to peel myself away from her to answer it. I rolled my eyes at the screen.

"What?" I said.

"Hello to you too, sunshine," Paul said. "I haven't seen you for hours, and this is how you greet me?"

I walked to the door because I heard his real voice. He was standing in the kitchen doorway on the other side of the pool.

"Your hat looks stupid," I said.

"Hater."

He turned around to the door and adjusted it dramatically, looking too proud of that monstrosity on his head. I would never understand why he couldn't just wear normal clothes.

"Why are you bothering me? We have an hour until we leave."

He smacked his lips. "Don't act like you were busy, Sparky. I doubt today was *special* enough for you. I'm sure you two were just in there knitting."

I flipped him off. He saw me and laughed.

I looked over my shoulder to make sure Chris hadn't seen. I tried my best to have manners around her, even before I knew she was modern-day royalty. Her back was to me and she was curled up in the fetal position, shading a horse she'd been working on all day.

His voice turned serious, a rare moment for Paul. "Dev called." I let out a quiet sigh. "He said he's been calling you all week and you haven't answered."

"I don't have anything to say to him."

That caught Christine's attention. I heard her shift in bed and her heart thud harder in her chest, and very slightly, a guilty scent misted into the air.

"He made a mistake, man. The same one your girlfriend, *my* friend, made. They both had something to change and they went for it."

"Don't compare them. They're nothing alike. Chris wasn't trying to hurt anyone."

"He said Kamon murdered those people on his own. They planned to kill animals like the fish in Florida. Kamon had other plans. Nate, you know Dev. He's not like that. He said his father died in the fire that killed Dreco, but he wasn't with them. He was there working, trying to support his family. Dev just wanted to get his dad back, man. I'd do that for *my* dad."

I hadn't adjusted well to being the only person in the house without parents. Chris was my family, but now she had her own. They stopped by whenever they wanted to, just to kiss her or sing her a song. I'd thought Lydia, who let me call her by her first name, and *Mr. Gavin* were going overboard, maybe to make sure she was happy and not trying to use her powers to change the world again.

"He just wants us to come by to get our money," Paul said. "Em wants to go shopping, we both want to pay Chris, and you worked harder than anyone on that trip, Nate. You deserve your money. Going to this meeting is the only way to get it."

I smelled her behind me before she hugged me and rested her head on my back. Dev had promised me over twenty-thousand dollars to go through with the trip, hiking up the price after I'd left my injured girlfriend. I needed every one of those dollars, but I didn't want to see him again. I'd trusted him, looked up to him, believed who he told me he was over the word of my own girlfriend. My psychic girlfriend.

"When is it?" I asked.

"Now. Em and I are going. Dev just called again, begging us to make sure you're there. He wants to talk to you, man. Maybe apologize. You don't have to hear him out, but at least get your cash. I know you have big plans for it."

I did. I had a huge plan. A two-carat, perfect cut, color, and clarity kind of plan. The surprise engagement that would kick off our special night couldn't happen without that money, and it was more important now than ever with her parents in the picture, setting the bar for true love astronomically high—give you a soul, high. The dinner and candles and roses I had planned before wouldn't be enough for her, not *her*. I needed something bigger. And shiny.

All of my job applications were for retail stores and libraries. I'd never make enough to propose to her, or make her parents believe I was good enough to do that in the first place.

"Okay. I'm coming," I said.

I hung up and turned around to Chris. I was having a hard time looking into her eyes.

"Sounds like bowling is cancelled," she said.

Nothing tore me up more than how Christine smelled when she was sad. Her mood could sink so easily. I was always on duty to cheer her up when someone hurt her feelings or to clean up my own messes when *I* did.

"No. I have to go get my money. That's it. I'll grab it and go. Even if Paul and Em aren't done, I'll …" I sighed and paused. I'd have to sit there and wait until they finished. I didn't have the power to bring myself home, not in time to make it to the bowling alley before it closed.

"It's okay. We'll just go another time," she said.

I didn't know why Christine bothered lying to me. It wasn't okay. She smelled sad, delicious, but sad. It was how the New Orleans house had smelled when Sophia brought me there. Like someone wonderful but depressed had walked around it.

I'd sniffed around until that scent led me to the third floor. I remember pressing my hands against her door, completely entranced. I heard her sleeping in there. She sounded adorable. I hadn't even seen her face, and I was hooked.

I wished she'd come out of her room then, instead of hours later when she saw me shifting and naked in the living room.

"How much of the potion have you had today?" I asked.

"Sophia gave me one dose with my breakfast."

"If you went with me, could you get us home?"

She held her hands out in front of her, watching for tremors, it seemed. "Yeah. Pretty sure I could."

I fished around in my drawer for a shirt, and she pulled on her sandals. "I'll run in, get the money, and come out to you. Then bowling, here we come, okay?" I lifted her chin to kiss her. She smelled fine, I just wanted to kiss.

"If we go bowling by ourselves, it will be our first real date alone," she said. "Outside of the house."

I smiled. Her heart always thudded faster when I did that. "If you don't include the fun night we had in Kamon's prison or our hospital date."

"Except those," she said.

She jumped up on my back, and I carried her into the house where Em and Paul were waiting.

"Hey, that's *my* shirt," Em said.

Chris poked out her tongue at her.

"Let's get this over with," I said. Paul and Em shifted their eyes to the girl on my back. "She's going to wait for me and bring us home. I'm not staying long. We have plans." I'd decided that I didn't want Em and Paul to come bowling anymore. I wanted to go on our first real date. I would have money, so Chris could leave the credit card with her fake name on it at home *and* the crap load of cash her dad had dropped off— his idea of child support.

Support her to do what? Buy a jet? I was hoping Mr. Gavin would be poor, or at least middle class. No such luck. He had music money, stock money, enough money to make me even more uncomfortable.

All the more reason to get my money from Devin.

Em whispered a spell and snapped. We landed in the open field I once believed to be the future home of the shelter we were building. I led Chris behind a tree.

"Stay here. I'll be right back." She nodded and pulled out her phone. "What are you doing?"

"Playing a game so I won't be bored."

I chuckled. "It will literally be two minutes, babe."

She kept it out, ignoring me.

Em and Paul were halfway to the crowd when I left Chris. When I moved far enough from her scent, a wave of smells bombarded me.

Devin's garbage, Shane's must, and the natural smells of the forest and the animals that lived here.

I took another breath and shuddered. It smelled like blood. Fresh blood, still warm. And fear. And wilting flowers.

Devin stood in the middle of the crowd, thrusting his torch into the air triumphantly.

"This is our time. Our day! No longer will we sit back and watch our kind fall," he yelled. Emma looked back at me, fear in her eyes. I coughed as another whiff of wilting flowers hit my nose. It was a smell I knew too well and had tried to forget.

"My brothers. My sisters. My friends," Devin continued. Em's heart was exploding in her chest. Paul turned and grabbed her. "I have failed you. I trusted our enemy and ruined our chance. I shoulder the blame for this. Tonight, I will compensate for our loss."

Faintly, Paul said, "Dude, we should go."

But the closer I walked to the crowd, the stronger the wilted flowers became.

"Nathan, my friend," Devin said. "So nice of you to join us." He smiled. What happened to his cool, surfer voice? It was formal now and menacing. "Most of you know Nathan Reece, don't you?" The crowd answered with grunts and cheers, some raising the torches in their hands.

Something was off. The world smelled wrong and scary and … like my mother.

"If you know Nathan, you know he is a wonderful worker. I am going to miss him dearly. We became great friends. Many nights, he confided in Shane and I. Once about the terrible humans he calls parents."

The crowd surrounding Devin made a space for me. Paul touched my shoulder, then wrapped his arms around them as I shook.

In the middle of that circle that smelled of blood and fear, lay my parents.

"Nathan," Mom said. "Help."

Shane put his foot over her mouth. His bulky boot pressed into my mother's lips.

I'd shifted a million times. I could slip in and out of my fur faster than I could change my clothes. This time, I begged my skin to stay, my legs to hold me up, my back to stay upright. But my bones protested, grinding and twisting until I was no longer myself.

"Nathan has lost his words temporarily," Devin mused. The crowd chuckled. "However, I can speak for him. On those long nights on the road, Nathan told us all about John and Theresa Reece. How they bought him. How they wronged him. What kind of boss would I be if I didn't avenge this?" He paused to laugh. "John and Theresa Reece, for the kidnapping of one of our children, for treating him like nothing, for making his life hell, I sentence you to death."

I didn't want to run, but I couldn't help it. My instincts moved me, forced my paws to race away from Devin and the crowd. Past Paul, past Em, looking for Christine. I needed to get her out of here. The other side of me, the boy with legs and hands, would die if she were hurt. And he couldn't bear to think about what was happening in that circle. He rejoiced in the fact that my animal ears could hear what they wanted to and tune out what they didn't.

My ears found her heartbeat and tuned out the screams. My nose found her scent and ignored the blood. She'd moved from where the other me had left her.

She was crying and screaming into her phone.

I wanted to ask her if she was okay, but my voice came out in a whine. She kneeled in front of me, and I nuzzled my nose into her stomach. The frightening woman I now knew to call her mother appeared next to her.

"I'm fine," Chris said. "You have to help his parents."

"Take him home," Lydia said.

Chris buried her fingers into my fur. Psychic powers were so much faster than magic, there was no lapse in time as we moved. In a blink, she'd rescued me from the tormenting odors of the forest.

"Calm down, Nate," she said. "Everything is going to be fine."

Calm down? I felt calm. I felt tired, actually. Exhausted enough to close my eyes and sleep. So I did. I slept away the memory of those odors. I made myself believe that the smell I had wished wouldn't pass my door without coming in, the smell that was eventually masked by her husband's rot, had not been in that forest, in that circle, with her fragile face under a shifter's boot.

I slept until I almost believed it was a dream.

I woke up in a tub of frigid water. There was blood smeared all over the ledge and on Christine's shirt. She was bawling and panting when she pleaded, "Please, Nate. Say something."

"What's wrong?" She nearly jumped in the water with me, throwing half of herself onto my naked body. "What happened?"

"You don't remember?" I shook my head. I looked around the bathroom to assess the situation. My arms were scratched, gashed really, in several places, and I hurt all over. "I put you in so you would shift back. You—you were hurting yourself." She motioned to my arms. "Scratching yourself, biting, too. And growling like crazy. I put you in cold water because you told me that made you shift once. You wouldn't calm down any other way."

Because her heart was the loudest thing in the room, because there was blood smeared on her face, because her beautiful eyes were red with thick tears cascading from them, I braced myself for the death her answer to my next question could cause.

"Did I hurt you?"

She shook her head, and I let myself breathe.

"I'm fine. I'm worried about you. Nate ..." Her breath snagged in her chest as she tried to stop her sob. "Your parents. They're dead. My mom called. She got there too late. I'm sorry."

It burned for a moment. A quick, merciless moment. My canine side didn't like the way it felt. My bones twisted to change me to a state were I felt less, understood less. But her tears made me stay Nathan.

I grabbed a towel and wrapped it around my waist. I cradled her in my lap on the cold floor.

A few things happened on that floor—I continued to pretend that my mom didn't matter to me, I told Chris for the millionth time that I didn't want to discuss my past, and our lives shifted for the worse. Devin had murdered two humans, Lydia Shaw may or may not have caught him, and he had followers who I knew wanted nothing more than to be the dominant species again.

And I'd just run away like a coward and let my mother die.

The silence in the room seemed to scream: *things will never be the same.*

ABOUT THE AUTHOR

M. Lathan lives in San Antonio with her husband and mini-schnauzer. She enjoys writing and has a B.S. in Psych and a Masters in Counseling. Her passion is a blend of her two interests – creating new worlds and stocking them with crazy people. She enjoys reading anything with interesting characters and writing in front of a window while asking rhetorical questions … like her idol Carrie Bradshaw.

MORE FROM M. LATHAN

LOST – HIDDEN SERIES BOOK TWO
SHATTERED – HIDDEN SERIES BOOK THREE
AWAKENED- HIDDEN SERIES BOOK FOUR

VISIT MLATHAN.COM FOR MORE INFORMATION.

Made in the USA
Lexington, KY
16 December 2015